HOLY
SHIT

INTER-FEAR BOOKS

HOLY SHIT
Danish Locker Room Talk

WRITER: ALx S
ISSUE: 1 Scroll. Paperback version
ISBN: 978 874 301 34 33
PUBLISHER: Books on Demand – Copenhagen, Denmark
MANUFACTURING: Books on Demand – Norderstedt, Germany
          The book is made on-Demand process
TRANSLATION: Achmed Esra
TIME: 2020 Cold Winter
FIKTION

EARLY NOVELS OF THE SAME AUTHOR: The King of Denmark, New Year's Eve Speech! Volume I (2017) The Newest Testament, A Cry from the Desert. Volume II Holy Shit. Volume II + Volume III (2020) Prince of Pride. Volume IV (2019) No Excuse. Volume V (2020)

INTER-FEAR BOOKS

The memory has always played ALx S tricks. A writer with a professional background in architecture, specialization in science and for over a decade has been a leading architect based in Aarhus.

He was rewarded for proposing a relocation of the old main library to DOKK1. And later became designer of i.a. Cerespark's local plan, where he hasn't been, since he turned the first strokes into a master plan. ALx is a resident of the area. The same goes for Salling and Music House expansions, Symphonic and Rhythmic halls, as well as many other houses and areas, which he has also not seen with great pride; since it was just a drawing. *"All that rain forest!"* Not all drawings became evenly handsome, though they "prevailed". There are countless examples of this in the whole country, but especially in the hometown of "City of Smiles". With the exception of the winner in among 140 nations as best new construction in 2016, AU-Botanical Greenhouse, which he also designed for only 30 dollars per hour for the "largest" and "oldest" architectural firm in Denmark. Here he illustrated with the "pencil" in his right hand. The remaining approx. forty large houses and urban areas, which have ALx S's signature in its architecture, stand only as a faint reminder of an artist, who could not keep up with the development. Due to an arm injury using a mouse, he has been drawing with his left hand in recent years. It activated the right hemisphere, which is less visual, and more sound and words interested!

And often you had your hands tied on your back, so you had to draw with your mouth, or your feet in 3D! "A drawing can't always describe everything - You know two thousand words, say more than one picture!!"

ALx has then chosen to stay in a "silence retreat" for extended periods of time without human contact in the hidden. *"With the Co2 consumption that may be due to some strokes, that I have drawn with my French curves and got started, I have learned to be quiet. Otherwise, it could have a big impact on some surroundings, I don't know off. It would require at least 20 earths with those thoughts!!"*

He stays in the Sahara Desert to develop new crystals, but opens up as "evangelists" for leaps and bounds in history - The days of the monarchy are spoken in Denmark. The "Times Up" wave has long since entered, and someone got pregnant before Margrethe number two was in any cast - of the purest Gold.

By the same author: The King of Denmark, the Newest Testament, The Prince of Pride and No Excuse.

TABLE OF CONTENTS:
Scrolls of Silence found in the Desert of SAHARA

Yes, the table of contents appears short of headline - so there is just room for a little extra here on this page. For those who do look at the content, before the story begins?! If the content doesn't end here anyway! Now it begins. After all, some scrolls of paper were found buried in a stone settlement in the desert. Some nomads, who crossed the Sahara encountered them, as they spotted some special black tulips growing on the rocks!? But they could not interpret the scrolls. They didn't understand the language, in which they were written!

"What does it say"?? They screamed standing with the scrolls in their hands.

NOMADE: *"Strange flowers!".*

"Scrolls look important. Does is say anything about Allah? "

THE MORONNICAN: *"No. It's not about you. It's about the Danes. "*

NOMADE: *"What are they not suppose to know, since it has been buried here ?? "*

THE MORONNICAN: *"Ssshh, quiet. It is a retreat, don't you see!! Can't you see everyone sitting quietly on pillows, meditating and doing exercises around the sand hills?? Then put the scrolls back, where you found them. Immediately!! Afterwards, you can tie the camels' legs together, so they don't bounce too far again ..! Then watch out for spiders, snakes and insects and keep them away from people's tents in the evening.*

That's your job !! ".

***

When Denmark is considered to be one of the happiest countries with the least stress year after year, and the envy of many for its high welfare with education and nursing, it is nevertheless not what stands as the greatest parameter for this "happiness". What lies in it, is the generation of trusting relationships built to:

1. They choose not to carry weapons !!
2. They have a common understanding of ethics and good morals!
3. They can do more, because they help each other for good and evil.

After all, it is this understanding, that makes them happy.

I don't think, we would be unhappy about having to spend 15 dollars to a doctors appointment! Or that it would cost 100 dollars to be taught in some subject?!

Identity and function are my preferred choices.
But I do ever so often feel lost of identity and featureless for the most part! Once upon a time when words made sense.

I accidentally activated my brain in the right hemisphere, about seven years ago! But seven years passed, before it became aware of me! My awareness of the right hemisphere is about the same age as my daughter then!? You probably ask: *How on earth did you activate it??*

Well, I was going for a trip to the hot tropics – I do enjoy the sun and warmer climate – Like Greta! You can make a living from it! - Physically! Not eating for weeks – just being in the sunlight! But when traveling to such destinations like the tropics, you must use caution like vaccines!! So I got vaccinated! I went to the tropical doctor and explained, that I was going to Africa, and was going to stay for three months and in various developing countries! *What should I be vaccinated against?*

You must have one for typhoid, cholera, ticks, toxoplasma, e-bola and pills for malaria! Are you right or left-handed? "Right" answered the architect! Then the tropical doctor grabbed my right arm, and stuck the whole-ly shit- right where all the muscles are attached to the shoulder!?

Outsh. I think, he was right-left blind!? And upon my arrival to Africa I was then bitten by a tick, who had decided to mix saliva and blood from my right thigh just below the ball!! Where I don't even look myself! Or being able to make others believe my ass, or just having a look see?? If there might be a reddish circular marking around the bite mark - three months after!? I even discovered, that I was getting more and more lazy on the right side of my body! If I had to grab the pencil besides me, my left arm had a greater eagerness to pick it up, and bring itself into play than the right one, where the pencil lay two inches next to it!! Yes? It made no sense! But one day Mary said:

"Joseph - You have a red mark on your thigh! You have been infected with Lyme Disease!!" Shit! So I went to the doctor – again. And he stabbed me with the syringe, this time in the left arm! Now I can't use any of my arms anymore!!? Everything you are reading, sitting down, or maybe you are standing uprights, when you are reading, or whatever you are doing right now – Picking your nose!? Yes – I have written this with my tongue!! I've glued a piece of lead to my tongue! It makes it easier, to tough the keys on the keyboard! And that is why my dear heavyweight reader, I now operate in both parts of my brain, because I was pacified in the right body part to begin with! It might also be the aftermath of using a famous mouse. It is still not recognized as a valid injury!? But I have always been very one-sided using my right hand. Probably because, I was told in school, that I and most people only use the one

hand, and it is - Drum Swirl! The right hand!! Well okay! Unless you insist being a lefty. But the are some clearly advantages, when writing with a pencil in western parts of the world! So you don't smudge while writing. But a keyboard doesn't smudge! And the mouse is not made for humans! It is unfamiliar for the body and arm to handle with such limited exercises fixed for handling of a mouse! And it would be hard for most people in general to switch hands, using the left one, after having been neglected for so many years!! But I moved the same mouse to my left, and asked "it" to learn, what the right hand has taken for granted, that it was its work! Now try to draw in 3D with your left hand! But then it happened !! What??

The right brain that controls the left hand, is not as visual with silent images!! But full of sound and words! I became paralyzed!! I stopped wanting to draw, although the left hand easily could do the job, and easily after a few weeks of practice!! In fact, it soon became unfamiliar to use the right hand! Unnatural even! But I was a little pacified and lost the urge to speak! Scchhh - Silence is the language of God! I learned how to put my actions, opinions and attitudes - everything that made me a man and ego - to the side! I became a woman! Paralyzed!! But more beautiful - Than a man! No, I became more like a feminine thug, who wants to express "herself" with sound and words! So now I want to make audio books!! But I dislike my voice, so I have to use others.

Keeping my own doctor can easily alleviate the problem with the arm! He, and soon more often a female doctor, may take a syringe and inject a vaccine right there, where the tropical doctor's vaccine may have caused the problem! Now with adrenal bark hormone! It Helps - *You may have a little sore arm tomorrow, but then you won't notice anything anymore! You can use it right away again - full time! Thanks! Are you sure though? Adrenal cortex hormone really?* Facts: Adrenal cortex hormones are also called steroids (corticosteroids)! My own doctor wants to give me steroids!? So I can become a man again!! Help me here! Should I eat the blue pill, and become a man again? Silent Night -

Let us forget all of this female nonsense, that you're becoming a woman - in balance with both halves?! Sitting on a pillow in the desert sand, and writing, whining and working with sound and silence!? Or do you want to enjoy the serenity of your right hemisphere, and just keep using the left arm for the mouse??", "Mouse?? Why a mouse?? What are you talking about?? You do not use mice today!!? No, you use lamb! Action Slam!*

Holy Shit!!

Joe Christmas aka "King of Denmark"

Ext – Sahara desert , Morocco – Morning / Confession

"The King of Denmark" sits in the shade and writes:

IN THE GREAT LOVE THERE IS

WHY DO YOU ASK SUCH LONG
QUESTIONS YOU ASK
THERE IS A LOT OF
TEARS CAN BE STORED IN A HEART
WHAT YOU REGRET AND BITTERNESS
MEMORIES OF JOY AND PAIN
THE VISIONS OF MEANINGLESS
GIVE ME
GIVE ME YOUR BODY
A PLACE I CAN LIVE
NEVER GIVE UP ON ME
LOVE ME, LOVE ME TOTALLY
PREVENT ME IN DESTROYING EVERYTHING
WHAT IS IT IN YOUR GREAT LOVE?
WHO IS THE MAN YOU SLEEP WITH?
WHEN HE SAYS: "I LOVE YOU"
IS IT YOU HE LOVES?
AND WHEN YOU LOVE
DO YOU REALLY LOVE?
BEHIND THE FACADE
ARE YOU SINCERE?
GIVE HIM, GIVE HIM YOUR BODY
A PLACE HE CAN LIVE
NEVER GIVE HIM UP, LOVE HIM,
LOVE HIM TOTALLY
PREVENT HIM IN DESTROYING EVERYTHING
HE WILL FEEL YOU IN HIS ARMS
HE WOULD HEAR YOU SOUND AND CALL YOUR PAGES AND
YOUR CHARM, YOUR KISS, HE WANTS THEM ALL

VANISHED INTO THIN AIR
Ext Sahara Desert Day

THE KING OF DK:
Is it today?

ACHMED:
Cum again?

KING OF DK: Is it today, that you have a birthday?

ACHMED: No, no, no! It's tomorrow!

KING OF DK: Is it?

ACHMED: Yeah, but I got an early birthday present!

KING OF DK: No, relax!

ACHMED: I had a visit on Sunday evening already!

KING OF DK: Well, I could see, there was light yesterday at 12am!

ACHMED: Yeah?

KING OF DK: Did you get to bed early?

ACHMED: 'Amen, we didn't get to sleep at all!!

THE **KING OF DK:** Well!?

ACHMED: Well, we slept from about 5:30, and got up at 8 - 8.30! And then we continued fucking!! Shut up! I'm totally wasted!

THE **KING OF DK:** Yes, yes it can be! So am I! I fucked with three yesterday in one bed!

ACHMED: I can't stand this!? She was totally unruly!

KING OF DK: That's because, you're not exercising! That's why, I go to "bodypump"! You can make your body fit, and such a 28 year old will be taken care of every day!

ACHMED: And she wants to! I don't think, that I will be able to continue for that long!?

THE **KING OF DK:** Yes, I don't know?? No, you can not! The longer life becomes, the less you can keep it! That's also why, I said "no" to my husband....

ACHMED: You where the one, who said no??

KING OF DK: Yes, that's why, I said "no" to him four years ago!! He couldn't perform anymore! I could hear, the last time we did it, it was so close, that he had a cardiac arrest! American men die of a cardiac arrest during sex!

ACHMED: So it's actually for his sake?

THE **KING OF DK:** It's actually for his sake, yes, exactly! I've made it clear to him, that if he launches some form of training, so he can breathe again...!? Then we can consider it! But I said to him one night: *This is not good husband! You must feel that too??* It is actually for his sake! It would have been cooler, if we could have sex at home! Then I wouldn't have to run around in different forests, and alleys and basements and... ?? But yesterday I got so much cock - three big dicks - three guys in their forties, that finally I could barely stand on my knees!! I think, it lasted for 50 minutes!!

Are you nuts!? And then I was back home last night!

ACHMED: Yes, you must be in good shape? Because I am totally devastated!!

THE **KING OF DK:** I'm in good shape! And how many have you "sprayed" your semen to? And how fast can you cum? And can you squirt inside her? And can you cum on command? Nowadays we call it latex free!

ACHMED: Yes, we did that fucking thing too !!

THE **KING OF DK:** Did you??

ACHMED: Yeah fucking hell!!

THE **KING OF DK:** Then you risk her getting pregnant??

ACHMED: No! She is taking pills! But otherwise it is just as much! She's damn lovely man! Then we would have a beautiful baby!

KING OF DK: She takes birth control pills or what?

ACHMED: Yeah, she said that, when I asked about it!! But shut up - she was a bit too flippant! She was a little crazy! She loved, that the harder it was, the better...!? I almost had to rape her, before she got into the "red"!

THE **KING OF DK:** Well, well, I have to admit, that I am not! But I like to meet three guys a year, who want to do it! But I will say, that it gets very tiring very quickly! For what is central to me, and makes it a little luxurious, is to be with a guy repeatedly, when it is not necessary! What took on the idea? After all, is this an idea, that she has gotten somewhere??

ACHMED: Yes, she has been with a guy from the west blocks! Which only fucked her in the ass from the second date, took strangulation, and almost spit her in the mouth! And she could feel along the way, that it turned her on! Although he treated her like a helpless sow! So it's pretty peculiar! But it also turned me on a bit - being a pig!

THE **KING OF DK:** Then you can make such scenes like the gray one! Fifty shades of gray! I think you need to arrange it longer. Place a chess game, then have her in a sect, and place her under the table! Then she can start sucking, and sucking, and sucking, while you get two turns of chess!!

ACHMED: Yes, I could suggest her at a swingers club, while she would get fucked, we are playing a game of chess!

KING OF DK: Will the "miss" like it?

ACHMED: What are you saying?

KING OF DK: Would she like it?

ACHMED: Yes, I think, she would be game!

KING OF DK: Last week I agreed to meet with someone out at Joys, not on Monday, but the following Monday! He was from Varde - Haderslev! So it's a long trip! But he's been there before! And I met him, but he drove home at 10. Then I met him last night in Skanderborg! And there he had not been with any women!! Nice tall guy with full beard! Huge hair! His hair was powerful! It was the power stuff like a steel wool brush! There had been some women last night, that he couldn't do it with! There was a fat woman of 35 years, who got the cock of all the men! And he couldn't attend!

ACHMED: No, of course not! But I have two tinder profiles! And she had written to me, on the one created with facebook id where, I have declared them, I am 35! So she pictured me at 35! And she was 28! So it was along the way, that I went to confession and admitted, that I was actually not 35, but turning 45!

THE KING OF DK: Well! What did she say to that?

ACHMED: She stayed fourteen hours, after I told her! And I lit a spark and some fire in her! And she writes, that she thinks of me and misses me! But she also went on to say: *No, it's a pity! Too bad! I can't have a relationship with you, when you're that old!!*

THE KING OF DK: I should say, that I think, it is too much - ten years! Couldn't you settle for five? It depends on, how much you want to date?? But I am going with 42 at the moment, and there have been no problems at all! But it is only special, when you meet 46 year olds!! They can see, that I am older than them! And in my optics guys get more and more picky, the closer they get to the age of fifty!

ACHMED: Okay – sounds like me!

THE KING OF DK: Yes, you are also in a period, where you feel, you deserve such a skin tight 28 year old!!?

ACHMED: Yes, the most funny thing was, that she then started to convince me, that she was actually only seventeen!! And I started to believe her, with the reaction she had at first, when I revealed my age! But she wasn't! She also said at one point: *That I'm actually more turned on you now, that you're saying, you're 45!*

THE KING OF DK: Yes - I also think, you will get some real women! After all, it's not worth grabbing a 28 year old, who doesn't want you at 45!!

ACHMED: No, no! But she has not experienced anything like this for the past 24 hours - It may be, that she and I are currently. I agree. It may not be girlfriend potential, but fuck we enjoyed the company!!

THE KING OF DK: Don't you go and be lovers, with all the women you meet up with?! What would Isa think, if she found out?

JOSEPH: No, I have to admit, it's an emotional ride too!

KING OF DK: But try to see, if you can turn it off a bit, because! In reality it should have been a lovely sex experience! So in Niles and Frasier, we actually saw that section yesterday, where Niles was knocking around with a twenty-two-year-old waitress downstairs from the café, they meet at every day! And there is also a section, where Niles walks around with an escort girl, but he has given her his account number! So Frasier had to tell him quickly: *"Get off with her!"* She is an escort girl! Then Niles says: *You are envious!* Then he said: *Did she nod to your African doll collection? "Yes,"* he answered! Then he can figure out, that she thinks, everything he does, is great!! You know what? We'll just have to try, Achmed! I just have to walk from the front door up to the car, and the last time I did it....?

ACHMED: We lost the connection? No, I had a dream! I actually dreamed this weekend of a crazy Salvador Dali-like house! So when I woke up, I hurried up and went down and drew, what I remembered!

THE KING OF DK: Well, a house in a dream, it's yourself! It's one's space! And when you discover new spaces, it's because, you have some new pages! If two people suddenly come with a stroller, the dream interpreter asks: *Is there both a man and a woman present? Or is there only one party?* Most people, either there are both a father and a mother.... Or?

ACHMED: Well, yes, but they have become very fine white your new basins?

KING OF DK: Yes, or the balcony I was just about to say! Do you want a cup of coffee?

ACHMED: Yes, in a minute!

KING OF DK: I've been really tired, since I woke up at 4am! I took an early day. I was up very early!

ACHMED: You haven't slept a nap then??

THE KING OF DK: I don't know?? Two to three hours! I woke up.. I thought, I had slept longer! Now I am awake! But I didn't make the tonight's walk with the dogs at all!

ACHMED: When are they walking?

THE KING OF DK: They leave at 4pm! And my husband suddenly says as, he sits down, and I wake up: *"It's ten minutes to five!?"* But that's because, I've been banging this morning on the freeways resting points. With big truck drivers. I usually do not admit to anyone! Mina when she asks: *What are you doing?* I can't answer that question!? I will never tell anyone, what I'm doing! I am just driving around in the car! Errands!

ACHMED: You ride with the bloke !! Ha-ha!

KING OF DK: You have to make sure as little information goes from you to Mary as possible! So she doesn't have to know, if you've got new girlfriends or been on dates!!

JOSEPH: Well, I said nothing either! I couldn't reveal that at all! Ha ha ..

KING OF DK: But did she say, you looked tired??

JOSEPH: *You probably look tired! Yes I am too! I'm totally smashed.*
Every cell in my body has been raped !! Ha ha!

THE **KING OF DK:** That's great!

JOSEPH: Yes, I tell you! It's the best I've had in ten years!

THE **KING OF DK:** It seems every time!

JOSEPH: No .. I haven't gotten anything in ten years !!!

THE **KING OF DK:** That's unusual, too!? I know guys, who have a new lady every day! Well, but I'm just trying to see, if I can cheat it and reel in it! It can do that!

ACHMED: And then they showed the "Child Abusers" program!

KING OF DK: Well? I haven't seen that either. We shall see that afterwards! Although I would like to ask the host Henrik Kvortrup, why he is using gunpowder on it??

ACHMED: Because he's doing spin! He's a former spin doctor! He tries to make a spin, then everything that he himself has done in the past, and has been convicted of at the Ekstra Bladet! He tries to cover it up with something else!

KING OF DK: Yes, yes! No, I do not know, if I will buy that explanation?? He can only do this, because he has people behind him, who applies: *Now you get free reins to run around with a camera team!* And the police must also be cooperative in the civil arrests, more or less! And I have to admit, there is more to it than that! Something more! It's thin! For me, there's something more behind. Okay. Henrik Kvortrup has got the fat in the ass of someone like four-year-old!? That's why, he does it! Because he turns completely green in the head!? After all, he has no understanding of the people, he meets!? I am much better at giving the characteristics of them! I've seen them! I'll met them! I've chatted with them! I have started to say*: You have to watch out, for that Henrik Kvortrup doesn't come after you!*

ACHMED: Ha-ha. Amusing!

KING OF DK: And there I was being blocked by the management! Inside the superchat! Henrik Kvortrup, it is a name, that must not be spelled correctly; then you will be blocked! Then you can't enter again for six hours!?

ACHMED: Henrik Q?

KING OF DK: No with K! Because it's with Kvor. It's not Q!! A friend of mine, Jon Baker, changed his name to Qvortrup, because he got married! But he married someone named Kirsten Qvortrup, when he left high school! And then he took her name, even though his name was Jon Baker! I do not understand?? It's such a nice name!

ACHMED: I know several people called Baker! And it has nothing to do with a bakery !!

THE KING OF DK: Well! So in French there everyone is named "Ger"! Like Michel Berger! Frances Gall's husband! Fleur! Fisherman!

Then there is cream! On the occasion of your birthday, you get cream!

ACHMED: Well, that was great!

CHURCH BELLS RING

ACHMED: Is anyone getting married now?? On a Tuesday !?

KING OF DK: Well, how did it go with Isa this weekend?

JOSEPH: I have no idea?? Yes, I called on Sunday, but Isa didn't really want to talk. And that was actually the only time, I've have called, and it was today. She doesn't really bother talking on the phone! So that's why, I didn't make the big fuss out of calling either. After all, it is not for the sake of the child, that we call every night!

KING OF DK: No, hell! The reality, it's so trivial! So the calling I can recognize with Mireille! It takes one out of living! And I look at people sitting, talking and texts while driving around with headsets in traffic! *No, you're not driving! You sit and talk!* I've seen more today!? And young men, god damn it?! Is it a law, that they must have it upside down, and they drive from hell to ...?? They drive too slow! They run into overpass lanes, and when they turn right, they stop the whole range of traffic behind them, because they can't turn!? What to say??: *"Yes, you don't have to blink 400 meters before you turn! You drive quickly to your lane and turn - Finished! "*

But you know what? Now I thought this Christmas, that I was just about to get well and something like that, and then I asked at the table: *Is it just me, or is the world running out of good manuscripts??* Then Felix scornfully said: *No, it's just because, you've been sick –*

But no, it's true! The world has run out of good manuscripts!

I just saw an advertisement on TV the other day - All the movies that come to the cinemas from Los Angeles, it's effect movies! These are not good stories!? Isn't it crazy, that the world has run out of good stories? Isn't it crazy??

Yes. So what? Have you been smoking weed or something?

JOSEPH: No, I haven't smoked in a month!! But in return I ate a sponge yesterday! I found an old narcotic fungi. Mary is packing her stuff in moving boxes!

KING OF DK: Has she found anything to live in?

JOSEPH: Yes, but she didn't tell me!? I've read it in her calendar! *Apartment lease,* and then she has drawn a heart??

KING OF DK: Well, aren't you talking together?

JOSEPH: Yes, I talk! But she says nothing !?

KING OF DK: Is that right?

JOSEPH: She doesn't say a word! Shuts the door and go into another room, or ask me to go somewhere else! But from June 15 she will move out! In any case, she has a place to live! Near him her new Greenlander boyfriend!?

KING OF DK: Greenlander ?!

JOSEPH: Two years younger than me! He is the same height as me and stands on skateboard 365 days of the year!? All his facebook pictures are only of him standing on skateboard!? But he has some cute kids, because they go to kindergarten with Isa. Yes, it's fun so she gets some siblings now. That's nice! How are you feeling?

KING OF DK: I'm fine! Bit tired!

LE RAT DES VILLES ET LE RAT DES CHAMPS
EXT SAHARA DESERT EVENING

THE KING OF DK:
Then I've also seen another one, that is edible fun - Do you know it?

ACHMED: Yes, yes - It is in Danish too!

KING OF DK: Is it?

ACHMED: Yes, it's called: "The City Mouse and the Land Mouse!"

THE **KING OF DK:** "Le Rat des Villes et le Rat des Champs". It goes fast! Some what fifties entertainment! No, the sixties! It's a seventeen / eighteen year old Mireille Mathieu! They are good! Then listen to her new song!

ACHMED: Which is recorded this year?

KING OF DK: No '84! You know it well?

ACHMED: Yeah ha!

THE **KING OF DK:** Then it ends with "Für Elise!" You could say that in '84, her voice was at its peak! It is very well written! And then the text is good! The fact that she expresses her anger, her grievance, makes it possible to hear it forever. And you can!

ACHMED: They just took off six beats - Do-do-doo-dou-do-doo, and then they didn't take the last note, because then they had been busted! I think, the limit is up to seven nodes?

THE **KING OF DK:** Yes, it is so beautifully written! And Elisha is there! It's like a fatal organ! When morning comes, she is gone! They play "Toujours" - Forever! Then you get to know it! As a child!

 JOSEPH: Yes, I listen to Alizee, then there is something for the daughter, as well as the father!! Ha, ha! She wants to listen, and see that too! And she likes that video, and I don't know, if it's the "Lolita" song? Where a girl is having a quarrel with her mother at home, and then she flees across a field and away from her boyfriend?!

KING OF DK: It's the first!

ACHMED: That video she likes!

KING OF DK: Funny! Well! Yes, but you said, she liked Mireille Mathieu? And it has actually been investigated in France! Mireille is the one, that all kids think is "fun"! Have you seen them there: "The College Fame School"? Children really think, she is attractive! And now throughout her career, she has sung with a children's choir, which Piaf sang with too. And that school has existed, and has been associated with Edith Piaf and Mireille Mathieu, and they have to use a boy choir, and in 1976 Mireille that was going to be her biggest hit! And I've always been able to look at the ten-year-old boys. They are absolutely crazy with her, the forty-year-old lady - Right? Fun! Her voice has exactly the same frequency!

ACHMED: Like Sound of Music?

THE **KING OF DK:** Yes, I think Julia Andrews,
she is something more of an adult girl!

ACHMED: So was Mireille Mathieu,
if she was forty to those kids ??

THE **KING OF DK:** Yes, but it's strange ??
But in fact it was almost not? She was a little age loose!

ACHMED: Should we quit smoking?

THE **KING OF DK:** Yes! Yes, because. Then everyone would hear Bach! Just the tune before she starts singing. Then you can put it on in the morning! Then you can say that, before the song is done - get up!

JOSEPH: Yes, I wake her up sometimes with music in the morning!

THE **KING OF DK:** And the one who is especially nice to wake up to,
that's Bach's prelude! 1820!

JOSEPH: I have to try that!

THE **KING OF DK:** Jack Jackson played it on the piano in the big chapel across the West, when Sten was stoned! Shut up - It sounded great! It sounded really good! And this is something, that has been added in 1996! Many has got the same idea! This is not the first time, that Bach's Prelude has been used for a popular tune! Amanda Lear in 1976 had *"Alphabet"*. *"A - stands for Anything - B - is for Bach!"*. One has to rewind to hear Amanda Lear say: *"Sexy!* We thought, that was one of the wildest things in 1976!

ACHMED: Yes, that's the equivalent of "Youporn" today !! Ha-ha.
No, Mireille Mathieu can hardly sing anymore! And is a pity, that she did not stop at the top!

THE **KING OF DK:** Shut up. She performed five evenings in Moscow here last week, when Putin held elections! Fortunately, there were in Ukraine. I'm going to do a Fakenews article about him! I know, that Putin is a fan of her. I've never met any heterosexual men, who are fans of Mireille Mathieu!? He is a fagot after all!! And I think, the world must know about it! I've been angry at him over it lately. What about Syria?

ACHMED: Putin is a fagot!?

THE **KING OF DK:** Yes and Boris Yeltsin!! He got forty records with Dolly Parton, when he was visiting the White House!? I think, that's fun! She has barely released in Russia, and he was absolutely crazy about Dolly. Then you have to ask yourself on behalf of Boris Yeltsin:

Does it have anything to do with her tits, or do you like the way, she sings??

ACHMED: He was fucking drunk! Those scenes where he takes the conductor and pats the girls!?

THE **KING OF DK:** The White House staff, they asked him and his wife, if there was anything, they could get? And then he asked them, to get a Dolly Parton collection - Complete! And they actually got it for him!

I was excited about my path for homosexuality! My dad must have looked with wonder at, who I was, when I suddenly ... !? Focused on Mireille Mathieu and traveled to France as a ten/eleven year old. But "us," who has it more difficult, get a more enjoyable life. It has been proven in the US! There is nothing like accomplishment, that can ruin a life! And make it monotonous. All "overachievers" have something to prove! But you can have fun as parents, you can't protect your children from adversity. It's one of the only things, you can't. You want to... But: *"If I could, I will protect you from the sorrows in your eyes!"* That's Garfunkel. No, it's Paul Simon. Fucking fagots! This song I have loved! Always!

ACHMED: Yes, but if I have to write a debate post, what do you think the main theme is, that we talk about?

THE **KING OF DK:** If anything, then it must be "Times up"!

ACHMED: "Times up"!? Yes, I write that the days of the Royal House are numbered. The "Times up" movement has long since entered. Someone got pregnant, before Margrethe the second was in the mold! It's funny, that I'm not writing Queen Margrethe at any point! I only write Margrethe, and Margrethe's father, Crown Prince Frederik IX.

It is there, that the "chain" jumped off!! Ha ha!

KING OF DK: Ha ha. "The Passionate Prince" he was called! They called him that - Frederik IX. "The Passionate Prince" while living in Aarhus! He lived on the top floor of the Hotel Royal. It was the royal suite. It was before, they were given Marselisborg Castle! And he was a bachelor here in Aarhus for many, many years before he met Ingrid and got Margrethe.

ACHMED: Surely his cousin??! That family is pure inbreeding !?

KING OF DK: It is during that period, that my great-grandmother Paula got my grandmother with him!

ACHMED: I saw a Danish Radio program, called "Our fantastic planet". It was about the only mammal, that has managed on all continents, and then it told about "Man"! On three continents, someone had to go for three days to find a well of water, here in the Sahara desert. And it was very much about the Sahara. Which again just... ??

THE **KING OF DK:** Sahara has only been around for 3,000 years! It was green 3,000 years ago!

JOSEPH: And the rivers are still under the sand! And so they dug down to grab the wells, and try to dig sewers, that can direct the water to their cities.

KING OF DK: It's the heat, that has created the Sahara. And that has created a worse demographic spread. Because 3,500 years ago, when there was peace down here, and because they coexisted. Then it happens, that a sandy area occurs after their fields, and it runs like rings in the water. So there have been wars around the countries on the borders. One has fought - huh? After all, it has been incredibly fruitful. In Egypt's heyday, 3,500 years ago, it was green! The Nile was green!

And then I don't know, if you can say, that it is the Muslims, who destroy everything?? But they do in every case, too! They do! Fuck, they have destroyed Bethlehem, twice!! I remember Bethlehem looking something like old Brabrand, and then I came there last time, it was a big fucking ruin!!? It was so bombastic!? And so it is the Palestinians, who bomb themselves! It's not Israelis sending bombs in there! It is to convince the world, that they are rebelling!

You can also make a conversation in a chapter eventually, as a form of reconnaissance of two old men sitting and talking, where the one old man says: *"Are you saying, there was grass here on the globe??"*.

"And you say that the sea, it was blue??". "Do you have evidence of that??". "Are you honestly telling me, that there were flowers!?". And then they are completely crazy about something, that today we just take for granted!

Now I've also told my husband for twenty years, that he should write a book about, what it's like to be: "American in Denmark", like the one "American in Paris!" And there is one, that has been on the bestseller list last year. There was a Danish/American woman, who has moved with her husband over here, and has experienced Denmark! And it sold 1.4 million copies in New York !?

ACHMED: So who did she, send it to??

KING OF DK: Probably KNOPF? America's largest publisher! Toni Morrison uses them too. KNOPF in New York. It was also those, who published H. C. Andersen and Karen Blixen!

ACHMED: I joined a Facebook screenwriting group, and there was someone, who wrote, that he had written a book in English, even though he was Danish. So he wanted to publish it internationally, and asked which publishers, would the group recommend? But they answered him:

Listen, the English and American publishers, they drown in manuscripts! If they receive any material from a native in their own language, then they understand it. But do they receive something from someone, who does not have it as their mother tongue?? Then it should pass by a proficient reviewer or an English expert ...!

THE **KING OF DK:** Well, in principle, they are right. But now I can't comment on his English! But I am trained for it, so I can see if ...?

ACHMED: It's something, you would throw up upon??

THE **KING OF DK:** But then there is someone ... Karen Blixen wrote: "Seven Gothic Tales" in English. And the following year she stood in every fourth American home. So she became well known, although the Danes had not published "Seven Gothic Stories" in Danish! It was translated from English. So there is someone, who breaks it there. But in principle, and that was our English professor at the university saying:

"You will never write a book in English!! You must not believe that!! ".

The Dean!

ACHMED: Did he say that, the one who taught you English?!

THE **KING OF DK:** Yes! But "Netherland," a relatively new American success, was written by a Dutchman. And the book about Denmark last year, that has been on the bestseller list. Because everything is Danish, it interests the Americans. They have been brainwashed with Denmark for the last fifteen to twenty years. In particular, they started brainwashing during the "Muhammad crisis". Support campaigns were made for Danes on the east coast. My mother-in-law told about it. But so were many places. It just benefited the whole thing! So that's why, she could sell 1.4 million just by writing "My life in Denmark!". So simple it is called! My husband could have written that many years ago!! And you almost know, what some stereotypical issues need to be brought up, right? It's: *Ecology, it's green, it's cycling, the Little Mermaid and maybe highlighting Blixen more than Andersen, to make it a little more equitable!*

If H.C Andersen had been alive, he would have been hit by "Times Up", and then he would have killed all women!! And bound the men and fucked them. And used his power! Andersen was Europe's most influential person in his own lifetime!

ACHMED: Yeah, I don't understand that??

THE KING OF DK: The Italian emperor and the Germans rolled out the red carpet, when he came by train! It's crazy! And Helena, he always wrote fake love letters about, the Swedish ballerina! She humiliated him and mocked him, when finally stepping up after a ballet in Stockholm once. It's been a tough blow for him.

ACHMED: *"H.C. Andersen was a very, very ugly man!"* Ha ha. It is a little strange, Hans' first short story, that he sent to the theater, was about a baby thrown into a horse-drawn carriage, so the blood sprayed on the "ghosts". My first short story was a burglar, who threw a baby around the nursery. But where you only heard bump sounds, and then you see the thief, come out on the porch with the baby holding in his leg with one hand!! The father standing and tearing his garden, went to the thief, handed him his tear, and went into the house! Sick! It was from a dream, that I had!! H.C. was just as sick of his deadly ingenuity, as I am!? *To travel is to live!?* I pour more to Karen Blixen after Times Up!!

KING OF DK: Unsympathetic in all respects.

ACHMED: Yeah. "The Little Mermaid" can be read as a transgender fantasy, in which Andersen dreams of getting rid of his "tail", and thus getting his prince of dreams. But the Chinese do not know about a *chiang stick*!? So China could also be a market? That is what, I tell my parents! That my target audience may not be in Denmark!?

THE **KING OF DK:** Intellectuals will try to find head and tail in this one!! They will!

ACHMED: But you should just read the book for proof. And then I think, it should try to have a life ??

THE **KING OF DK:** Yes, so the question is, whether the world has come to it, that they should have a book, where there are misspellings?? After all, it will be tremendously honest by the narrator, right? In fact, there are some of these black writers, who have written essays, and Mel Johnson, who has written a Nobel nominated novel in the 60s about racism. There, the publisher simply chose to publish exactly, as she had written it! With the spelling mistakes because it is a black uneducated girl. Then it suddenly has a meaning! That the reader can see, what she is capable of, and slang and then leave it at that. Already in Faulkner's time, he used words like nigger in the book, that you have in hand. And that was it .. Faulkner! My sister-in-law, who was just here, she was furious at Faulkner. She has learned in school, that Faulkner was a racist. But we learned afterwards, that Faulkner didn't write nigger, because he didn't like blacks! But he wrote it, because he wanted whites to understand, that this was, what blackness was!

ACHMED: But blacks use even more racist words among other, than whites do?? So if a white says to a black: *Nigger, come here!* Then it's racist!

THE **KING OF DK:** Yes, yes

ACHMED: When a black says to a black: "Now we go nigger". Then it's fun or friendly!

THE **KING OF DK:** There's a whole lot there! And there is something called internal racism. That's what, Toni Morrison's last novel was about. There she tried ...? It is a child, who is simply a grade blacker than all the other children, the couple has had. So the baby is that black, they can't love it!

JOSEPH: One of the educators at Waldorf education asked our kids - She'd probably asked them all: *What does your father or mother do?* And there she also asked Isa: *What is your father doing? "He makes books,"* she replied then! Because I have shown her my scrolls, and have told her, that I have written them!! *Yes, Dad makes books !!*

THE **KING OF DK:** That's fine.

It doesn't have the same meaning at all today, as it did forty years ago! When someone asks someone: *What are you doing?* And just today as your nephew, who has established the identity of the British high class, the world is a big identity snobbery today: *"This week my dad makes books! Next week he bakes cakes and ..?".*

You think, the grass is greener on the other side! And it is not!!

JOSEPH: Now I'm going to find a new partner, that doesn't have a "body of pain!"

THE **KING OF DK:** The absence of being together and being friends when the three years have passed, where the love and fascination lasts, it's so great! And you can't just do that to anyone! I usually say to my mates:

Oh, I'm so happy, when I'm in love because. Then I know my heart is still alive!! And it has happened three/four times, that I have fallen in love with guys after my husband! So I am someone, who has an easy fall in love. And I'm really happy to have that property. It is so wonderful to be saved in a whole spring by someone, who just says the wildest things to you .. !!

JOSEPH: Or just have one look in the eye! No, that is.

THE **KING OF DK:** Shut up - Jorgen and I just drove by the resting place at Fuglsang yesterday, then some cars parked. Four out of five sat watching porn on their cell phones!? Inside the car ?! Imagine driving to Fuglsang to watch porn!? Why not get out of the car, and fuck with someone, who comes along??

ACHMED: To cheer themselves up?

THE **KING OF DK:** Yes, that's right! After all, I'm coming to yawn. I'm ready to strip! This morning I wanted to have a beautiful one, as I got out of the car! I had just fucked with three guys in a row! I just got rid of one, before the next entered! Yes, I just heard Simon Kvamm, I think it was, say that: *People love music*! A lot of people listen to music!

ACHMED: But not his !!!

THE **KING OF DK:** Tove also expressed that this morning! She can't take him either!!

ACHMED: They were on the Danish Television the band Nephew! I don't know, why a woman has joined the boy band!? They have to add Niece to the name!! But then they all sang a cappella, and he, Simon played the piano! And it just sounded terrible!!

"We are in the new Danish hymn book !!".

THE **KING OF DK:** Did he sing it in the lyrics ??

ACHMED: No! He said that in the interview! He was glad, that one of his songs entered the hymn books!

KING OF DK: Do you know, what it is?? His entire career, it does not stop!! His wife has fucked with one of the most powerful at Danish Radio Broadcasting network!! That's the connection to Simon Kvamm's success!! It is the wife and her pussy, that have kept him up to five million paid a year in KODA charges at Danish Radio!! Then I understand his appearance in "Clemmens" the other day, and him defending Danish Radio! Ridiculous guy!! Shut up, it was ridiculous! Did you see that? No! There were four in the panel! And then they discussed the cuts with Clemmens! And the other three were twenty years older... ?? He was styled, and he had so much blush, that he looked like... ??

ACHMED: A fagot?

THE **KING OF DK:** Yes! Wildest! When I prepare myself a little extra gayish...

ACHMED: You just use a little extra mascara ??

THE **KING OF DK:** No, I don't now! That's not, what makes me extra gay! It's my clothes! Tight pants with holes in them! But there are some of the guys, who say no to.... Holes in the pants - So! The most fussy forty-year-olds, if you have holes in your pants, they can't get an erection! But twenty-year-olds, twenty-five-year-olds and fifties - they don't care!!

ACHMED: Twenty-year-old girls buy a pair of expensive pants, and then they immediately start cutting holes in them?!

THE **KING OF DK:** Do they ?? Do they think, it's trendy ??

ACHMED: The more holes - the better!! Right where it almost reveals skin under the ass!

THE **KING OF DK:** That's inviting! I regretted, that I bought my 2000 kroner Diesel with holes because, only later did I find out, that they also exist totally the same....?

ACHMED: Halfway?

THE **KING OF DK:** No! No Diesel business is closed! There just wasn't a market for it in Denmark! No one wanted to go down and give $300 for the "newest pair" !!

ACHMED: No!

KING OF DK: I did that with these. I paid 300! And just because I had to have them, and because they would cost $350 in Bangkok! In Bangkok, they were small in the Dieselstore. And when she just discovered, that I didn't have $350 in my wallet, she wouldn't spend more time on me!?

ACHMED: No, that's logic!! I was in a Diesel in Mexico, which was selling winter clothes! Perfect in any Danish weather. And It was cheaper!

THE **KING OF DK:** But, it's expensive! It is also hand-made in Italy - Some of it! Well, now we have come so far! Now we need to relax!!

ACHMED: Yes. It's stressful!

KING OF DK: I haven't seen it there either!? It has to be something about?

ACHMED: Arhh, my stomach muscles!!

KING OF DK: What about them? Well they got....?

ACHMED: They got raped yesterday! Shut up, man! And she wanted to suffocate!? And have it in the ass!!

KING OF DK: Was she clean?

ACHMED: I didn't bump her in the ass !!

THE **KING OF DK:** Did you say "No" to something?

ACHMED: No! I didn't say "No" to anything! But I didn't put it in her ass!! On the first date!! Or second date!

KING OF DK: Although she would??

ACHMED: No, she didn't say, she wanted it! She said, her previous acquaintance had, and he only fucked her ass, since he persuaded her on date number two! Yes, and then he took a stranglehold on her and, incidentally, treated her like a sow, saying that she should leave, if she came unannounced. And it had turned her on for four months!!?

THE **KING OF DK:** Then he's probably gay... !?

ACHMED: Yes! I should have said that! Ha ha. Yeah, I posted a note for a medical student, who was about to get dressed, and she put on her socks, like the first thing?! - Slowly right in front of me, so I could get a good look at her great pussy for a long time and everything else! But I never got to ask her name!? Then I called her inside the facebook group!

"Dear medical students, who tried to convince me that as a vegan, I should eat pork, do you want to meet up and elaborate your comment, as I fear for my health ;-) ??"

It was terminated within ten minutes!! They wouldn't allow it on the wall of the group!

THE **KING OF DK:** No!?

Do you also have such a few working days at Waldorf?

JOSEPH: Yeah, we had one on Saturday! I was at the winter bathing club opening night - party! So I couldn't come - unfortunately! Too bad someone would say! I have a rule, that the educator told me about:
We have a rule, that parents should not be in class for too long, because it easily becomes a parent cafe! But I was the only one sitting there, and Isa had asked me to wait for a minute, and she would finish playing!

Then I said to her: *There are no danger!! And it sounds like a weird rule to establish! But I can tell you about my new rule, when it comes to the forthcoming workday on Saturday! I will not show up, since there is no need for a parental cafe!* Ha ha!

KING OF DK: Ha ha. Now we have to evaluate, if "Clown" is fun today!

I liked it, when Else and Knud-Erik gave each other some cuddle!

ACHMED: Yes, that is loving!

THE **KING OF DK:** Now Casper Christensen begins, and he has a red nose!? Have you seen those press stunts that "Anden"-"The Duck" made in connection with his 25th anniversary? Yesterday morning they advised at 7am: Yes, "Anden" arrives at 9am! And today - There I saw him! I don't bother him at all!? I don't even want to be exposed to photos of him, because he is max ugly! And then I am angry, that my husband likes him!! And you can imagine that, the anger can hardly find anything... ..?!

ACHMED: The man probably doesn't use toilet paper?! He just wears his pants again!

KING OF DK: Yes, but nobody does from all Middle Eastern cultures!! But that's the itch! Do you remember it from childhood? Yes, if you did not dry properly, it could start itching? It has done, how to say it? That I've been clean, since I was four! I can not understand that Arab men, they live with it running around and being so distraught!? Shut up, those gays must have a lot!! I have come out of the world, where there are gays, lesbians and heteros.

ACHMED: For me, everybody are ... ..?

KING OF DK: People?

ACHMED: Yes! To you, they're all what ...?

KING OF DK: Horny! And the men who say, they are the most heterosexual, those are the least heterosexual!! And all the guys who log in the super chat and in the "Man-man like bi-guys"! These are men, who in any case do not seek women! I say that to them a couple of times a week: *The eight bi guys in here, they just have to know, that there are no women here!!* I'm damn tired of guys having to ..!? I was taking it in the ass by a 25 year old - nice, nice guy. I had just got his guy in my mouth, then he ejaculated! Then he said, when we were done: *You go the other way!* He didn't want us to leave together from that tree at all!?

ACHMED: No - of course!

THE **KING OF DK:** And there was none! The time was...??

ACHMED: And I had bought rubber, but I didn't get to use it!

KING OF DK: Latex-free sex? Ha ha!

ACHMED: Yeah, that was nice!

THE **KING OF DK:** It's the power slaves! I really like rubber, but it requires a guy to fill out all the rubber!

ACHMED: It's getting chilly! Oh. I will not bother this cold any more anytime soon! There is Mars!!

THE **KING OF DK:** Ah. I am totally crooked man! No. That's damn good! They have a hard time selling houses or apartments down in Aarhus Island. Our apartments are rising in buyers' consciousness! Because there is peace and quiet here. It's not down there! I talked to one last day living in "The Iceberg", 35 years old! He was tired of it! Tired! Tired of city events during the summer, tired of it all!

ACHMED: Yes, and the cruise ships whizzing in the horn on the way in and out of the harbor! Seven o'clock in the morning! *BUUUUU*! It's really noisy down there! *BUUUUU*! I can hear it from miles away!

THE **KING OF DK:** Yes!

ACHMED: Have you seen Mars?

KING OF DK: Is it Mars?

ACHMED: Yes!

KING OF DK: A yellow star? But I was in contact with the moon! Fuck - What did it say? *"I'm full - I'm full!!"*.

ACHMED: I watched Netflix, a "documentary" about UFOs! They have satellites orbiting all the celestial bodies, Mars and its moon Phobos! And suddenly they lost touch with the satellite! But seconds before they lost the signal, it had taken a picture and sent to Earth! Of a cigar-shaped object at least twelve kilometers orbiting the satellite !?
"I don't believe in it !!!". *"There are no UFOs !!"*

KING OF DK: *"I was walking up the Hill, I was looking at the Sky, and I saw a strange looking object, caught my eye!! Then a man comes out with five arms!"*. *"And you saw us walking hand in hand, in hand, in hand, in haaaand!"* - Finished! Ha ha.

Americans have a different form, fairy tale story than ours. Thus, "Tina's Magic Wand" is an arch-example of American adventure and "Mary Poppins" and "The Wizard of Oz". It is just brilliant for kids to learn: "The Wizard of Oz"! Empathy is especially the key word, when it comes to "The Wizard of Oz".

ACHMED: But "The Wizard" has a different humor?

KING OF DK: Yes, it's cool. It's different. It's less romantic! I end up believing so!

ACHMED: In any case, I figured, when I was in Mexico, and met some American tourists, that I were more closely related to the Mexicans humor than to the Americans! They don't have sarcasm to the same extent as Mexicans or Danes!?

THE **KING OF DK:** I don't know, if H. C. Andersen had?? But he had "Womanism"! Women were terrible to him! They were small! They were stupid! They could do nothing! They kicked ducklings! They looked like witches! And that is also the narrative, that we see through! And how interesting is it that girls, and boys are so different sexually! It would have been crazy, if it were the same things, that they wanted!! But it is not!!

ACHMED: But sometimes it's close – to magic!

KING OF DK: Yes, but how do I put it? You have just had such an experience, where it seems like that! But I can already imagine, that you can not ...? You couldn't be together for three months!?

ACHMED: Why not ?!

THE **KING OF DK:** Well, because you would become..? You wouldn't be..?

ACHMED: Man enough?

THE **KING OF DK:** Yes!! You will not find satisfaction, in all that you have to do for a 28year old! To maintain it you might not even be able to endure!? But right now! You can see, how long you will last!

Niles and Frasier have a program that is exactly about this! And since he's been with her for one week Niles ...?

ACHMED: He's used !?

KING OF DK: Then he realizes that.... *What the hell is that??* In any case, he ends up saying it to her! He asks, if he should just talk to her! She is a waitress down at Café Nervousa, where they usually gather! "Nervosa" - Nervous! And today Roz ordered a table for Frasier and Niles at "Chez Shrimp". "At Shrimp"! The French people laugh, because there is no restaurant in France called "Chez Shrimp"?! There also have a restaurant called: "The Willing Cigar" - "Le Cigare Volonte"!

"There are tables! I booked a table at "Le Cigare Volonte"!" And he says to her down at the cafe: *"Can I just talk to you for a second?". "What?? Are you breaking up with me?! Am I just a little whore from the café??".* And then she yells, so everyone hears it! He can't even tell her?! Because! But....??

Do it! So have sex business with such someone! Find out what kind of fun stuff it is! Basically, you have to wait for the moment, that you do not want the other to leave!

ACHMED: Yes, but at least she taught me more about the vagina, than I've experienced in the last fifteen years! I can tell you that!!

THE **KING OF DK:** What??

ACHMED: Really!

KING OF DK: Yes ??

ACHMED: Information where my knowledge was limited:
"Well - I had no idea!?".

KING OF DK: Well? Which? That there is no virginity or .. ??

ACHMED: No, how to stimulate a woman, and "ease of her pain" on the clitoris!

KING OF DK: It's not on the clitoris itself, it's in the surrounding area!!

ACHMED: With her it was right on the spot!! And it should be such monotonous movements. And if I made a break in my monotonous movements, then I had to start all over again!?

KING OF DK: Yes, yes! But it is the same with a dick!!

ACHMED: Yaa?

THE **KING OF DK:** After all, you have to work with the one, who owns the cock!! If you want him to cum! I promise you, that there are men also fucking different!! A guy I had today, in my mouth, was not too big, thin truck driver, really thin, with a proper iron! He is coming within two minutes!? It is strange that such a man of fifty years of age, can keep it coming so easily?? When I was just with a 35-year-old, I where was almost complete in the arm at last, to make him.... ??

ACHMED: Yes, but it is all in the mind!!

THE **KING OF DK:** Well?? Yeah, I don't know! But I can see for myself, that there are some licks, that can make me squirt. It is rare! But when some synergy is right?? There are a couple of guys down at Fuglsang, that they succeeded in! Who has something!? I don't know, if it's the mouth, or what the hell it is ?!

ACHMED: A piercing??

KING OF DK: So you can't count on being able to handle all guys?! After all, I can't count on swinging with all the guys! I've noticed some guys, when they've got the dick in, from behind or something, they don't really know, what to do next!? It's not just useless to poop!? You have to have contact with the person, you are doing it with, and build something up! There are many guys like Jorgen, for example, who turn on the groaning loudly! That the one you are fucking moans!!

I think, it can be just as naughty, if it's the one, who fucks that moan!! There are a lot of guys, who are getting a lot...? And my second swinger, he yells!!

"SO I'M CUMING NOW - I CUM ON YOU BITCH - FUCK I'M CUMING - OH YOU LIKE DICK??" Ha ha! He goes completely crazy! Well, but I didn't intentionally take all the strawberries??!

ACHMED: Be my guest!!

KING OF DK: No, it looks delightful! I love whipped cream! And I have never figured out, how the baker does? Getting the whipped cream to be like that ??

ACHMED: He uses spray cans !!

KING OF DK: No !! No!

ACHMED: Well! Shall we see "Survivor" soon?

KING OF DK: You haven't seen any of the programs, which is called "Married at first sight"?

ACHMED: Married at first like?? No!

KING OF DK: I saw the first program the other day! And it was really interesting. There were three couples, who were happy with each other, and then there was a mismatch of carats! A woman of 45 and a man of 45! He was such a childish type of man, a little sex in that! A little fat, but not too fat! And she was an anorexia! Pretty from the front, but looked like a witch from the side! Small! Ate nothing! He thinks, it was a mismatch, because they couldn't share food joy for example!

He was right! It was a damn fucking match! And then she suddenly told him, that she had some deadly disease!

ACHMED: No!

THE **KING OF DK:** Yes! And he got really upset!
"Then I can't love you", he said !!

ACHMED: No, terrible!

THE **KING OF DK:** I can understand his points!
This is a damn good match too! Uhmm!

THE **KING OF DK:** There is a shift, in what the young people want to see today! They want to see men cry nowadays!

ACHMED: They want to see what??

KING OF DK: Men cry! All the people in "Survivor", every time they get letters from home! Jesus wept! It saturates!

ACHMED: Yes, no it is good, that we have to eat it all!

KING OF DK: Yes, we had an Othello cake! We had our wedding day last Sunday! Kvickly put offers on their cream cakes after 7.30pm!

ACHMED: And REMA offers their bread at the same time! I bought a whole bag of Bavinchi rolls for two kroner!

THE **KING OF DK:** Well then it's paid too! But I do eat cream cakes! So I sometimes buy them! But many times they have nothing! Then they are sold out!

ACHMED: Yes, but there wasn't much to choose from either!
No, she is horrible woman!

THE **KING OF DK:** Yes! She's a real witch!

ACHMED: Yes!

THE **KING OF DK:** She has to control things! It doesn't bother men to listen either!! Who is Benedicte? Is it her?

ACHMED: It's her sitting there!

KING OF DK: Her - there?

ACHMED: Yes! Then he should have picked some muscle men on his team, instead of taking a magician and a little girl!?

THE **KING OF DK:** No, we have never seen a Survivor, which was settled on physical strength!!

ACHMED: No, but it has a lot to say anyway!

KING OF DK: Shut up - I couldn't stand to believe him! I am tired of him! He is Paki! You get really tired of him!!

ACHMED: I think, Jamil is sympathetic!

KING OF DK: It's him, that I'm saying, I'm tired of !?

ACHMED: Well, why then??

THE **KING OF DK:** It's just, that his hair is teased there and those Tarzan...!? And he's guaranteed, to be a little girl sitting with loops in his hair at night, when no one sees him!? Then he sits and nails the long hair! I can't take it! No, look how terrible, he is! His eyes are also completely out of balance! She has a masculine side, and a feminine side! She looks a little like the American actor, who everyone is so excited about...? Who got an Oscar this year? Yes, such a sick man! Isn't it strenuous?? And that is also strenuous?! So where are they in her life?? It's not strenuous!

That is nice! You see he has a completely different calm over his person?

ACHMED: Sure, but his tattooed seventh on the shoulder is also strenuous!!

THE **KING OF DK:** He's guaranteed single!
There is no woman, who wants such a ??

ACHMED: He's sitting with the cards - him the magician !?

THE **KING OF DK:** But I don't really know, what to think about Henrik Kvortrup!? Putting traps out for pedophiles ??

ACHMED: He scares all the kids away !?

KING OF DK: How do you mean ??

ACHMED: Then there are no children, who dare to join any chat!?

THE **KING OF DK:** Yes, it's a storm in a glass of water,
or what do you mean?

ACHMED: Yes!

KING OF DK: He has dyed hair?! Him the nice Dane there!? Uh, I thought there would be commercials!? Arabs, they are in any case hiding everyone in the back!? Then they are laughing like that! They are girls all three! They cannot be loyal - Arabs! No - a terrible woman?! This is also the hallmark of all Arab culture - Achmed! They ask:

Who are you voting for? And then they say the name of the one, they can get away with to vote, so they don't get their heads chopped off!? And then they go down, and vote for someone else! They can't do election surveys! Every one knows in the Arab countries! They tell one thing, and then they do the other !?

ACHMED: *"I vote for Erdogan !! He is very nice!*
He is a good representative for Türkey! ".

KING OF DK: Fish shellfish?? Did you hear "Cover Wives" last week? Jannie Ree, she woke up with a hangover in Mallorca. All the Coverwomen had been to Mallorca! *"Oh, I can't stand that alcohol!"* A fifty year old lady! And Amalie, the younger one! *"My sister says that the clothes, I design, make me look like Christian the fourth!! I'm not quite strong in geography!! "?!*

ACHMED: Ha ha !!

THE **KING OF DK:** It is the best fucking program! It's "Cover Wives"!

ACHMED: Yes !? No, I can't watch it!!

KING OF DK: I'm not doing too long either! So I just have a period at the moment, where I get to know something like that! Otherwise, I have no appetite for it for a long time! Shirley Maclaines daughter has just published a book about her mother! And it's really burnt in the minds of some in the US! She talks about how, she was put on a plane – Alone! Like biennial!? To Tokyo!? And how she did... !? When she was eighteen, she had not been with her mother for one week !!

ACHMED: That's tragic too!

THE **KING OF DK:** She has a mega need to be with her today! And now she has three boys in five years! And Shirley Maclaine hasn't seen them! How bad their relationship has become! And then there is just ... A lot has happened in the diva world this week! Liza Minelli's sister has said some things about their mother Judy Garland! And Barbra Streisand's sister was at him. The journalist with the long hair, who insults everyone! What the hell is he called ?? Joey ...?

He sat there, the journalist, who I come to think of in a little while:

So does your sister give you free tickets for her Concerts? And then she said, Rushland, Barbara's little sister: *Oh, I just say, I'll be there! But does she give you free tickets?? I think, I know about you and your sister! You hate your sister!* He said to her!! Ha ha! *Because she is so successful, and you are not!* They are both two singers! Both Liza has Lorna as her little sister, and Barbra has Rushland! And already in the 60's Lorna and Rushland had RSA! They released with that record label: "The Dog"! They released four LPs with Liza's sister in '69, '70, '71, '72! But no one bought them!? And the same with Rushland! They both pretty much sing like that. But not good enough, that I wanted to buy some of them! But why should they also sing the same style of art?? Why don't they go into Rock & Roll, one of them?

ACHMED: I also bought a record with Eddie Murphy !! Ha ha!

KING OF DK: Yes, he also made only one! No - two!

ACHMED: That was some shit though!

KING OF DK: Was it music?

ACHMED: Yes - he sang!! Really bad!

KING OF DK: Yes, I remember! But he could do almost anything! So he has also composed the music himself, I remember! He knew everything! And he tried everything! The guy who Vanessa Paradise - Johnny Depp - He has tried too! But he did not succeed!

ACHMED: He's still trying! He is no longer an actor according to him - He considers himself as a rock star !!

THE **KING OF DK:** It's a trick, that's not quite successful! And who else has made a recording? Di Caprio!

ACHMED: Depp is completely bankrupt with a high consumption!

THE **KING OF DK:** He's gone bankrupt!! By just trying to launch the Rock & Roll concept! Vanessa Paradis, she has been to "Una Parque Che"! Some Saturday interview program, where she has explained, why she does not support him! He is a mother after all?? He is the father of her daughter, Emily Rose. And she's nineteen years today! And she is the star now in France! She made a record! No! She's made a movie! Vanessa's daughter! Emily Rose is her name! And it's Johnny Depps! And just now when Johnny Depp was declared bankrupt ..?

ACHMED: Yes, he had not paid wages to his crew!

KING OF DK: It was Christmas last year! There, his company representative in Los Angeles had stopped all his accounts! He drank wine for $2,500 per bottle! And at the same time he called the agent, angry saying: *I need more money!!* They wouldn't! They stopped it! He was address less! They've sold his house! It was all declared bankrupt in December! And there she went on TV and said that:

"I don't want to support him anymore! I've spent so much money on him for the last five years!". After all they are divorced!! When a star in France

gives her American husband a wife's allowance, it's because, she is a big star; that she cannot have the ex-husband homeless on the street!

Once money, always money! And he is a fool!! And it shows, that he has failed completely because, if it has not failed?? Then he would have been able to keep codagrammar revenue from Rock music, that he sells! He has tried several times!? Goldie Hawn! I have a record with Goldie Hawn! Who else? Carrie Bonet made a record, that didn't sell. And Meryl Streep has done a lot, to become a singer, but she clearly doesn't have a tone in life!? But she has however, been able to use some voice in the two "Mamma Mia" movies! Because she has always dreamed, just like her friends, Barbra and Liza, just to sing! The audience will determine that! She has sung in three movies - Meryl Streep. Real, really good, well-chosen songs for her! Because you can't just sing anything! And who else has composed a record? Shirley Maclaine! But she actually has a hit! It's Shirley Maclaine, the very first time hearing the song that Shirley Basset pretty quickly made a hit already in the 60's! '65! Bob Fosse directed a ballet film with Shirley Maclaine called: *All that Jazz!* There Shirley Maclaine has a number called: *Big Spender!* It is her work! But she doesn't have a very good voice. So Shirley Basset sang it much better! And she has another one also from another musical: *If my friends could see me now!* These are not some radio singles! It is probably from the time, when people went to the theater! If you wanted to hear something new! Don't know: *If my friends could see me now?* If my friends could see me now! *I'm lying in bed, and I am fucking!!* Ha ha! Now we have arrived? How old do you have to be, to get a cell phone today?

ACHMED: I don't know!? There are some kids, who have an Iphone!

KING OF DK: Is that right ??

JOSEPH: Yes, Isa noticed it a couple of years ago! *"Hey dad! She has a phone!". "Yes? That's not good honey. She is exposed to dangerous radiation"!*

KING OF DK: I don't know, if you saw that commercial? Well, you did three or four weeks ago! Where Jorgen and ..?? What is the host called? Thomas?

HOST: *I'm not making advertising for you!!*

THE **KING OF DK:** It's also the negative! That is, what is changing at the moment!! And in less than two years you will see commercials on TV, where Crown Princess Mary sits in her royal toilet, and shows the shit

38

on toilet paper?! We are really moving in a new direction instead of romance and efficiency! Now we have to pay attention to us in some new ways, because everything else is passé! And of course the comedians will join the beat! The one who has been so successful: *Should you pollute my freshwater? With batteries*! You wouldn't think of it to be an advertisement – Two people, a married couple getting into a quarrel!? But that's not the focus here! But I think, that is the truth today. It is difficult to use that kind of commercials on American TV! American TV has shown such crackling advertising clips in any case, like the one with the batteries. It was terrible!

ACHMED: But that's because of the sarcasm! They don't use it!!

KING OF DK: No - exactly! They haven't!

ACHMED: And some Danes don't have it either!

THE **KING OF DK:** They spent a whole year Casper Christensen, Frank Hvam and Tina Bilsbo writing the manuscripts into English. And was in Los Angeles for a month and a half, where they were in every television company, one after another to show them! And it takes an hour like that to meet with five executives! And then they have to explain, or maybe they had some subtitled versions of the Danish "Clown"? But no one was interested! No one dared! They curved their toes! We do too, but we want to curl our toes! But they won't! Because all sections of the Clown in the United States, such a thing will pull a tail of lawsuits. The association for...?

ACHMED: Gay and lesbian?

THE **KING OF DK:** What is it called? Ostomy! They will oppose to the scene, where Frank accidentally pushes a girl with the ostomy bag in the pool! It had to be replaced with a million dollar claim!?

ACHMED: That is the good thing about Sasca Baron Cohen. All those he involves signs a contract, and he owns all rights.

KING OF DK: But what about Paula Abdul? The time when he used her to sit on Mexicans ?? After all, she got angry and left! It wasn't acting!

ACHMED: No, and there are quite a few, that are not! But they have all signed up to be part of it!

THE **KING OF DK:** And Paula Abdul is a one-hit wonder after all! But she still earned a...?

ACHMED: Checkout! Have you seen the latest of his movies? Where he pretends to be an Israeli military agent, who wants to promote, that three-four-year-olds should be allowed to carry weapons?! Because then they would have a change to defend themselves in school shootings!? And many in the Senate, serious senators think, it's a fabulous idea !?

THE **KING OF DK:** They do!

ACHMED: And they would love to see it happen! Because how do you stop a bad man with a weapon? *Well, a good boy with a weapon can make that happen!!* So they wanted to be interviewed! And it is on youtube. There was a clip on how to stop a naked terrorist! By biting him in the dick! And then he had a strap-on, and got the senators to try biting the thing! He is in makeup, and difficult to recognize, but you can hear it a little in his voice, through the thick accent. He's just good at making dialects, so he sounds a little different, than the other characters he usually does!

KING OF DK: Yes, it will be fun in the future to create such scenes, that are completely perfidious! And if it looks like, people are surprised! A kind of hidden camera! The Americans need to see it! I think, it's brilliant with the shit and the vacuum cleaner! That such a shit can pull a tail off track ?? Well, now they're bored with it all !?

THE **KING OF DK:** Listen to their language: *"I want to vomit - It's insane as good as it tastes!".* They are making the negative adjectives the positive ones!? And it has actually happened before!! Well It really means the opposite of shit!?

ACHMED: Yeah, it tastes terribly good!!

THE **KING OF DK:** Yes! It will be difficult to learn Danish for foreigners someday!? *"The shit is maximum good!! Depressingly good!!"* It's a whole symphony! Yes, it was not very good! Well, he's also dyslexic, and he can't count and ... !? *Well, you're so ..? It's the best! That's the wildest thing, it's the mayonnaise I just got !! "??*

ACHMED: *Yes, it was better than sex!!*

THE **KING OF DK:** No, the wildest thing I've ever experienced, that's when Olivia Newton John entered the Radio Studio up in the north of Aarhus - That was my unique moment! And I had forgotten my camera!! But it was fun! I recorded it all!

ACHMED: Now he wants to go back to the hospital to have a drop, because he's hungry!?

KING OF DK: He's a fool!

ACHMED: He's been cultivating too much bodybuilding. That's what has smashed his back !!

KING OF DK: Yes, he has been eating steroids! It has smashed his system! Is he going to leave ??

ACHMED: Yes, he was going to the hospital again, because he is still hurting with kidney stones!

THE KING OF DK: Oh poor! It does hurt!

ACHMED: Yes, I got that in Kenya as well. We where on a long trip in the back seat of a jeep! I just felt, that it wasn't good for the kidneys!?

THE KING OF DK: They shake loose or what ??

ACHMED: Yes, when you sit sideways on a shaky ride in a bad jeep without suspension?? It smashes everything! I was sitting in the back of the car - On some wooden boards on top of the wheels - Sideways!?!

KING OF DK: No, sideways?! It's terrible! I've tried it in Thailand! Turdland, where they mistreat their women, and shit all over the place!?

I saw one the other day with such thick hair, and he was no more than seventeen!?

ACHMED: What?? Danish?

THE KING OF DK: Yes!

ACHMED: What !?

KING OF DK: It was some high school students on TV yesterday! In an interview! Two girls and one boy! The ones who had gotten free tickets to Obama! There were three students from a high school, who had been given free tickets! And the were High school students! And he was sitting with a mat of hair from another world!? The guy?! He is very similar to - Yasser! He is very similar to our vegetable trader at Vesterbro place! It could be their third brother?? Because there were two brothers down at Vesterbro place!! One is hired, the other is the boss !!

ACHMED: And the third is the money launderer !? Ha-ha!

THE **KING OF DK:** Well, they alternate between being Paki and Danes!! Isn't there ..? And a Paki? When they become Danish, do they become Danish like Casper Christensen, Lars Hjortshoj and so on are?

Or do they become Danish like....?

ACHMED: Nasser Khader??

THE **KING OF DK:** No, eh Helle Thorning Schmidt and the chairman of the Social Democrats? Like the ladies?? Is it the voices of ladies, that set an example for a whole generation of immigrants? Or is it the men?

ACHMED: It's the men!

THE **KING OF DK:** No, I don't think so!! I think, it's the ladies!! I can hear, when they have disagreements, it's because, the kanakes behave like bitches!!

ACHMED: But they don't like Pia Kjærsgaard, and she must be their diva, if that were the case!?

KING OF DK: Well, hate and love, it's so close! They don't actually hear, what the men are saying! Because there is also confusion in the picture in the form of Pia Kjærsgaard! Because my students were very attracted to Pia Kjærsgaard, even though it was totally negative! She had hero status in the classroom at Langkær highschool! There was a team of Danes, who would defend her, when they were with kanakes, who were very angry! And they have no idea?? Kanakes doesn't know why, they should be angry at Pia Kjærsgaard!? They are just influenced to be angry, but they can't...?? None of them can cite an example! *Give an example! "Yes, she said that, all Muslims should be beheaded in Copenhagen! "No, she didn't say that! Stop saying such nonsense!! –*

Now you spend ten minutes google on the computer, and find examples of, what she has said! ". And then no one could find anything!! Well - then we know!

ACHMED: No, she's ugly!

THE **KING OF DK:** She's a witch!

ACHMED: *"I really like you!!".* No.

THE **KING OF DK:** What the hell is she called, the one who received an Oscar this year?? How to investigate that..?? Best ....?

ACHMED: Academy Awards?

THE **KING OF DK:** Francis McDormand! You know her well!!

ACHMED: Yes, yes, yes!

KING OF DK: Can't you see, that I think, she looks like Benedikte !!

ACHMED: Yes, that's right! I see it! But I didn't see it at first!

KING OF DK: I don't know, if I'm mad at Benedikte either? I just like to see the game, that she controls! And I would probably do that myself!! *"You are so greedy Ulrik!!". "Well what do you mean??". "Well then you must look in the dictionary "greed"!!".*

ACHMED: Yeah ha!! *"If you don't know, what that means!!!" "Well, you have to elaborate a bit!". "We know very well what greed means, but why do you say that about me ?? What the hell is the relevance!? ".*

THE **KING OF DK:** No!? Well, the only thing we consider, is that it is too unhealthy to be thick!?? Because it gives all the psychological inferiority complexes!?

ACHMED: Yes yes - The "wild cat", that I was fooling around with, was fat, just three years earlier!! But she is not anymore!! Ha ha! And she has almost as many tattoos as the ones from the villain's team!!

THE **KING OF DK:** No !! It is so strenuous !! And then it costs !!

ACHMED: Unless you fuck with the tattoo artist !! Ha ha!

THE **KING OF DK:** No, it's not! You just know, that life with such a person is expensive!! They've decided to cut out all kinds of sex?! Is it really the truth, that those people aren't sexual during the day as well !?

ACHMED: Well, they aren't!! They get a pill!!

KING OF DK: Yes?? I think, it is a lot about the mood that affects them, but.... ?? Well, but it is because of his age! They are so naive men, until they are 25!

ACHMED: Oh my god!

THE MAGIC ARTIST: *I signed up with Survior to take home $70,000!!*

THE **KING OF DK:** *And then you just signed up for a death fight!?*

ACHMED: Yes, he is terminated!

KING OF DK: *I want to fuck you, before you go!!* He becomes a good teacher! What do you think about Iran demanding Danes extradited ??

ACHMED: Iran??

THE **KING OF DK:** Iran!!

ACHMED: Does Iran demand extradition of a Dane?

THE **KING OF DK:** Demands many Danes handed out!! All those who are members of a particular organization in Denmark, who predicted 25 dead in a parade in Iran! Haven't you heard about it?? Lars Lokkes foreign ministry, they received a claim on Sunday evening! And there are some wogs, who now admits on TV, there support of them! Iran now demands them extradited! And we demand criminals handed out as well! When someone has offended us, we have to hand them over! Fucking kanakes planning such an event of terror in Copenhagen!

ACHMED: Because they commented on it, or because they participated?

KING OF DK: Because they have planned a bomb blast at a parade on Sunday!

ACHMED: Well, I heard that! But I haven't heard of extradition ??

KING OF DK: Well, but it just came! Ekstra Bladet has not written about it! So I assume, it must be very secret ?! Or? But it has been in the press! Iran demands Danes extradited!

And why did Türker take the death toll!? He just wanted to go all the way! *"Shut up supreme"?!* He just forgot that little one!! It's also hard then! Fucking limits! I am sorry to hear! So did my pusher to me!

Turker can't say that!? No, it will be exciting! No, he can't count or write! He is a pizza worker! Türker has guaranteed no weight eh...! Well!

ACHMED: The magician also surpasses himself all the time –

"I have a good ball eye!". And then he throws the balls to the east and west!? Well? Shall we see commercials !?

She doesn't bother to write !? Sweet bitch :-)

KING OF DK: The older I get, the fewer people I think exist around me!? After all, I think, somewhere it is true, that there are only eight types of people on earth!

ACHMED: Eight? What are they?

THE **KING OF DK:** Someone's here to forgive themselves! For mistakes they made in the childhood! It may have labeled them for the rest of their lives! And then there is someone here, to learn how to love other than themselves! And then there are eight different purposes!

And that's about the types, that we distribute!

ACHMED: There is some one, who would like me to email her !?

KING OF DK: A tinder? What is she writing?

ACHMED: *Hi, what are you looking for here? Sorry I am not often here! It's not good to speak here! I have an idea, I send you my mail!*

And then she sent a g-mail. Her name is Siamisha!

THE **KING OF DK:** You can't hear, it's fake !?

ACHMED: *Maybe I won't use it here anymore, but I use my mail everyday!* Is it fake?

THE **KING OF DK:** Totally!! It's someone trying to scam you for something!? Any intellectual woman in Denmark doesn't start writing: *You can't write me here, because I'm not here - Sorry!* What a mess! And you should also not meet a person, who doesn't know, how to contact a man!! It is completely like Somalia land!

ACHMED: *Where are you from? Somalia?*

KING OF DK: I'm afraid of such someone?? Is it Messenger?

ACHMED: No, it's on Tinder, that she wrote it!

KING OF DK: That she should terrorize you with mails!? *No, you can write to me here*!! Bitch! Write it! *Write me here you fucking cunt!* If she can write to you in tinder, then she can even answer again tomorrow?! What is that?! *I need your account number! In order to answer you!?*

ACHMED: *I check my bank account everyday! When I see, you have posted 500 kroner, I will send you my e-mail!*

THE **KING OF DK:** I don't know, if you saw a program on TV, that dealt with? It was something like Kontant – Cash?? They found the office, where young Polish men work from 8 am to 4 pm, and fit ten accounts for ten different "women"! And have long lasting affair, writing every day to old men all over Europe! *Hey Honey!* And they must remember a little suggestion from time to time, and day to day! But they substitute for each other's accounts, because they can just go back in scroll! It is a bit more extensive, but they can reach more, if they are present! And some are good at it, and others less good at it!

There are so few, the program ended with finding; *there are so few of the messages sent from women!* No, he looks nice!

ACHMED: Turks? But he also reminds a little about the "Moroncan"! Please just shut up!

THE **KING OF DK:** That won't work, because Türker can't do it!

ACHMED: He can't hit it !? No, how embarrassing!

KING OF DK: Türker, he is brain damaged! He can't read, he can't write, but he can balance, after all! Try to imagine how enchanted he, the magician, becomes for a woman!? He will give lectures to her for the rest of her life! It's like my brother-in-law, with a similar name! He was giving a lecture to my sister, from the time she got up from bed! She had to say to him: *Now you must shut up!*

ACHMED: *I've heard it before!*

KING OF DK: No, because she doesn't care at all about, what he talked about! Guitar positions and ..?! And she asked him to stop playing the guitar! That's how he sat with friends all the time!! And she wouldn't here of it, when she got home from work!

ACHMED: I'm appalled, that it lasted that long !?

THE **KING OF DK:** Yes, after all, they were together what? Twenty years!

ACHMED: Yes, it has not been for the sake of the children!

THE **KING OF DK:** Yes, it has just been for the sake of the children!

ACHMED: Sure, but the kids didn't enjoy it!

KING OF DK: No, my nieces have a very special relationship with their father and men in general! But they are good mothers! But every time one of them opens their mouths to their boyfriends, some of it are bad language.

How can someone be so stupid and love seeking?! And try to hear the sentences: *I'm so sorry, I've won over my opponents!* They are so fake - Arabs! Arabs are so sensitive! Danish men would not care!

Well, it was me, who knocked you out of Survivor!

ACHMED: It's committed! Then you shouldn't have signed for a death fight!

KING OF DK: Say if you need more coffee!

ACHMED: No. Then I won't fall asleep!

KING OF DK: My sister's got a boyfriend!

ACHMED: Has she?

THE KING OF DK: Yes!

ACHMED: Well, then he came!

THE KING OF DK: And with someone that we have known since childhood! Magda, down from School of Engdal! Henriette - we called her Magda! She had the biggest tits down in Brabrand! When we were fourteen, both Magda and I went to San Francisco! And when there Magda came and visited me, out by Jack and Joyce. And in the afternoon we went down to a communal swimming pool! The rich had a communal tennis courts and a swimming pool! And there were thirty women with their forty children! And splashed in the afternoon! Then came Henriette, fourteen years from Denmark. There was me, Joyce and Jack! And then she took off her top!?

ACHMED: Had they never seen that before?

KING OF DK: And then all of a sudden you could hear the theme from "Jaws"! *Do, do, do, do, do, doo!!* Then came white sharks swimming! And the women, they screamed! Fuck, it was ugly! Didn't she know, she didn't have to take off the bra!? Well, but when we finished school, Magda went with a guy named Henrik! We called him Henny! He was such a nice guy! A bit like Brad Pitt! And they were married for a twelve / fourteen years, and had a child together! Henny's little brother Per is my sisters new girlfriend! Such a skinny guy!

ACHMED: She's into skinny guys?

THE KING OF DK: She likes those, who are into French music! And then I said to her, *"When Henrik is called Henny, what should be Per's nickname?" "Yes, we call him Pernille!"* But he is a lot of fun, and a party animal! I met him the day, you were here too! The day when you left the chairs here??

ACHMED: Stella!

THE KING OF DK: The day there was Stella, she came with him, and asked, if I would drive them home!

ACHMED: Well? They were there too?

THE **KING OF DK:** Yes, what happened? I drove them home, and then I went over to you! They left half an hour before you! But he's cute!

He had been looking forward to meeting me! After all, we know each other from childhood! He, like me, has had the thyroid removed! Not quite! He had his bi-thyroid removed! So I also think, he gets Eltroxin just like me! And he has been suffering from illness for over two years! I have just had my illness extended!

        ACHMED: Did you!? At the sickness benefit office?

KING OF DK: Yes, she kept terrorizing me the last week! And then I told my doctor last Monday: *They are pushing me to get a quick report.* I wrote to my doctor. *But I don't feel ready!* Then I went down to him a week later, and had blood tests. And then he said that from the blood tests, he would not report me quickly! *Now, you have to talk to the sickness benefit office.* And so he did, and then he got laid on them! So now I've got at least one more month!

        ACHMED: One month !!?

        THE **KING OF DK:** To have sex in !!

ACHMED: I'll have a cigarette! Ohh my stomach! Fuck, it is worked out! You use a lot of abdominal muscles, when lying on a bed and doing sheet gymnastics! Only the ones here are in play, and I haven't used them in ten years!!

THE **KING OF DK:** When it's physical, you can feel it all the way down! Instructors sometimes tell new students, to those who workout: After all, many people do not have...?? What to say ..? Used their abdominal muscles for twenty years, thirty years!? I have a habit, when I'm behind the wheel! Then my entire torso is excited! I don't sit like that and relax!! I'm sitting like this! Just try to tag me! Just try to get right to me, notice how tense my cylinder is all around? It's muscle! Also there!

ACHMED: Yes, and this is the fucking muscle! Just try to feel how excited it is !!? Ha ha!

THE **KING OF DK:** Yes, of course! And some have not excited it like this for thirty years. Then it's just completely soft! And they have not been able to get in touch at all by tightening! And it is especially women, who have giving birth and lose the feeling with this. But those who have quickly returned after giving birth, and have recovered this. That is also the case with the singers, when they do not suddenly have that cylinder here anymore! Then they don't have the big singing volume either! After all, you can be both thick and thin to walk around with tight cylinders! The magician who disappeared! Sometimes I can convince myself that some men... ??

ACHMED: Can only do this? - (Making moves of fucking!!)

But the reason why we haven't been to the moon since the eighties, is because we were met by aliens, who told us, *"This is ours!" And you have to keep away"!* That's what "Lance Armstrong" said - Almost?!

THE **KING OF DK:** Shirley once said to Bassey, when she was fourteen! *Your father is actually not from here on earth! He is genetic from Mars!* Then the reporter knew, she was "out there!" There was a lot of talk about that in Maclaines books! I know her books really well! I think Bassey is going a bit demanding! Joan Crawford's daughter wrote "Mama Dearest" in the 60's. It doesn't fit at all to go behind her mother's back, who mistreated her! Bizarre stories! But that's a good story!

You feel like shit after eating an Othello!

ACHMED: No, you don't!

THE **KING OF DK:** Well that's the muscles! I think, something really fun is happening this year - in Copenhagen, Zealand! The people there live in such a no man's land! And they don't know, how to embarrass each other in the best way possible! Uffe Ellemann is in legal action against his neighbor – in Klampenborg, big huge villas! Where they depend on them to use the same style! Uffe Ellemann suddenly conflicts with one of the richest men in Denmark! Who has decided, he wants to paint his carport green! Something! And Casper Christensen is totally knocked out for Clown! Something has happened in Denmark?? There must be some big disasters ??

ACHMED: Joakim and Frederik will both *cum* out as gay??

KING OF DK: Yes, I don't think, Joakim can hold his mask for much longer either! He's really mad! He hasn't spoken on any level for the past five / ten years! And he drinks! There comes a time, when he meets a reporter, who is in disguise... !!

ACHMED: Yes, and then he still smokes his own brand! He should probably remain unpopular! And stop smoking, won't do it alone..

KING OF DK: All the success he has - Frederik, he was just on TV-news again last night, city opening! He is acting like a rock idol!?

Throwing himself on stage down at "Beautiful party – festival", Simon Kvamms concert - Nephew!? They workout together in the same fitness.

They have a small fitness team for only six people!? And it's Simon Kvamm and Henning inside number 3's brother, Crown Prince and three others! The six have done a fitness together! In Frederik VIII's mansion! And they are all something about the music!

ACHMED: Gays?

THE **KING OF DK:** Kurt is gay!! Simon Kvamm talks a lot about his wife. I don't think, he has come so far mentally yet, that he has explored it?? From the age of seventeen, he was popular as a comedian! He hasn't tried to get loose! He was with her already the year after! They have such a small exclusivity club – There.

Mina said to me one day, *"Why do you have such a resistance to the Royal family?".* "Well, in the Royal family among many explanations, the monarchy is the biggest obstacle to equality for example! Because the monarchy still uses the system, where they hand out orders and prices. And even though we don't see that much in Denmark, you shouldn't be mistaken for its existence!? If you read Berlinger, and Borsen and so on, the journalists also make a little bit out of telling when Albani Brewery gets organized! And what they give to become a supplier at the Danish Royal Court! For example, it was said, that Frederik where offered two Ferrari's available all last summer 2017!? And it had offended Henrik, that he hadn't got same offer?! Because why give Frederik two?? And not one for Henrik, and another for... ??*

ACHMED: Joakim - the old racing bull?!

KING OF DK: I don't know!!? Etc! *But why should companies be rewarded?? Why arrange orders and dinners at Amalienborg for those ass lickers, who come in their finest clothes?? Why?? After all, this is the aristocracy that the population, since Christian 4th, has demanded to cease!! We still have it?? Yes, but if we want something, and if we want democracy in its true form, then we have to come forward in truth! Exclude it! Because I can see all the women in my life, being influenced by what Mary does, and what Mary says!? And if they are not influenced by the organization's speeches, then they are influenced by her manner, formation or... ?? And now they think Frederik is cool, because he behaves like a slut!!? That fucking gay!? I'm so mad at him, with that discus collapse! He is the force of Denmark's discus prolapse!?!*

And I think, it is extraordinarily silly of him, that he has to make Denmark's Royal Run!! And then hurry off!?

ACHMED: He even landed in my backyard! With two helicopters?! Schizophrenic?!

THE **KING OF DK:** *And then rushed in!! And had an operation in the back!! Should we also pretend, that we should throw ourselves, into something we couldn't bear!? And are we treated just as well as you in the operation? Stupid prince!? And then, after all, they have no human rights!*

And it was a language, she could understand Mina!

ACHMED: Okay, did she insinuate that?

THE **KING OF DK:** She had been to a party last Saturday with a friend of hers, and she had been misspeaking - twice. She was tired of it though! The one time there was a guy, a rich man talking about his ladies in Thailand! And then she had come to say: *"Do you also think, it would be great, if it was your daughter used that way!?"*. But the man couldn't see that, it was the abduction of the woman into prostitution, even though it is in the guise of such a Thai adventure!? And then there was a woman present, she said: *"Who suddenly picked up a wallet - in python skin!?"*

Then Mina tells her:

"You are well aware, that the New Mexico Convention states, that it is prohibited to import?! And you know, you've got it smuggled into the country!?" She knows something like that, Mina, because she writes articles about it! And maybe she shouldn't have....!? But she does! She says things!

ACHMED: That's cool!

THE **KING OF DK:** And when she speaks, everyone becomes completely silent! They should all be allowed to try once, to have a feeling!

ACHMED: Then use a basketball technique!

KING OF DK: Why can't he have a hair elastic in ??

ACHMED: Doesn't he?

THE **KING OF DK:** Yes! Can they lift him? What is he weighing? No, how hard is it to be a HR consultant, at the false level and speak of her sick aunt!! There was one, who threw himself into the air! Well? Are there dogs or what? So it's a shame to interview her! Because she doesn't say anything anyway! Why do they show it then?? They must have so much else!? That was damn good for her!

ACHMED: Oh, he was the one, who hit his head the last time!

KING OF DK: Yes, he was also drowning just before, as he smiles!? Yasser! Nasser Khader, are also ugly names! What did she say about yesterday? She hasn't responded yet?

ACHMED: Well, she just wrote now! Shit, I'm also really tired! I wrote, she buzzes in me! *You are buzzing in me too, Achmed! I'm with a friend and have fun. I'm free tomorrow! I also hope you are well?*

KING OF DK: Melis? Who is it?? Is it a girl? Yes it is!

ACHMED: Yes, Ulrik should have chosen muscle men, instead of having those magicians and clowns!!?

KING OF DK: What did she say?!

ACHMED: No, she's going to be voted out next!

THE **KING OF DK:** Yes! Why does she do it!? So Benedikte decides! She has annoying attitude! What do you think of her receiving an Oscar? There she did the trick, where she had to say, thank you! She followed a little on that campaign with "Times Up!" And then she said like a real grandmother: *I want everybody here to get on there feet - Yaa! Come on get up! All actors and actresses, come on your feet!* It took four minutes, before she got everyone in the theater to stand up!? And then it wasn't crazy either!? What the hell was she going to say!? Surely no one wants to abuse her !? Ha ha!

ACHMED: The funniest thank-you speech is held by Roberto Benigni, when he stood on the back of the chairs, and tilted the audience up to the stage! *It's amazing! I luve you!*

KING OF DK: When was this?

ACHMED: It was for the war movie, where he got a tattoo number on his arm, and then they had entered the competition for a ride in a tanker at a concentration camp!

KING OF DK: When was it?

ACHMED: Yeah, when was it!? Yes, it's about to be a few years ago! It's probably fifteen years ago!!

THE **KING OF DK:** I know all my movies on the publishing year!! No, it actually doesn't fit !! The other day I played some youtube videos called: *The Hits of 71!* And then all of a sudden it jumped to *The Hits of 78!* And back to 73 !? Where I listen without looking! And there I could hear:

Yes, OK. Fuck, I'm wrong for some years !? I can't control, what songs that are from 78 or from 80!? In between there is a lot, that is blank?! And when they play Bonnie Tyler, "It's a heartache", I really thought, it was 76! Then it's 78!

ACHMED: Yes, it's two years difference!

KING OF DK: Yes, at least I know that Grease is in 1972! And that "Saturnight Fever" is 1977! And *Sanadoo* with Electric Light Orchestra it's 1980! And Barbra Streisand is from 1980! Barbras songs from 77-78-79 do not apply initially! It may also be, that if it is a French production? Then again, it may have been a hit, some years later than in France! After all, I go for it! But I do forget more and more! This time!

Are they making alliance plans now?? Isn't Benedikte's group set to loss?

ACHMED: Yes!

THE KING OF DK: That's why, she looks like ...?

ACHMED: Shit ?!

KING OF DK: Well, there are messages in the air for her the third one there!? Are there any creeps?

ACHMED: "I vote for the magician!". "I'm still a lonely dog!"

THE KING OF DK: Pedophile!

ACHMED: Why does he give himself a sacrificial role !?

KING OF DK: Because he's a pedophile! He has something, he wants to say! You can look at him! What a jerk! They never give a little of themselves - kanakes! *"I'm just a winner!". "I just can't lose!".* Where are his qualitative arguments for such statements?! Fucking pizza boy!

 ACHMED: No, it was the Danish magician, who worked in a pizza shop!

THE **KING OF DK:** Well, but then it's him selling the weed! Stop it! Then it slips out!! He is soft!!

ACHMED: It's you who needs to be inclusive man!

THE **KING OF DK:** Well, he invites her to a dance! He must shut! The rest of us can see it!? Why does he need to say that!? Stupid boy! He knows, he is losing ground by saying something like that! After all, it's not wise! It is pointless for Jamil and the others, to become friends with her!?

ACHMED: That's because, he knows, she's leaving! No, she is a horrible person! She is the epitome of a scary woman!

THE **KING OF DK:** These were some, who got angry in the old days! Women who advanced with masculine strength! *Oh, she a witch!*

ACHMED: Last in, first out!

KING OF DK: It looks like such a Christmas decoration, that they are in!? Are there snow in the Philippines!? Yes, it is also tactical, if the three foes vote one out?? Well!

ACHMED: *Benedikte, Benedikte, Benedikte goodbye, then it's out you cow! Benedikte! My team!?*

THE **KING OF DK:** *"She shall not be here a minute longer!"*! No, I think, I'm enslaved in this show on TV3, not being able to understand, why Yasser isn't the one leaving!?

ACHMED: He wasn't the worst back then. Benedikte was more of a witch!!

KING OF DK: Sure, but it's not a surprise, it's the dull show! A thrill would have been, if it had been Yasser terminated! And then they should have feature a movie, which showed, what an idiot he was !!

ACHMED: But they did such a stunt a little while ago, having raised "Sonny" to being the big idiot! Or the villain, who laughed at everything and everyone. And he was unpopular in the beginning. Then he turned the mill, and became a more popular character! When he was threatened and shockingly close to be voted out, they changed the rules!? And then all of a sudden the voting wasn't about, who was leaving the show! But who deserved to win! Then he wasn't naturally at the bottom of the rank anymore!

KING OF DK: *No, you're not at work now! You're in Survivor! "Greed - Look it up!" You're not a nurse or doctor?!* Well - She gets misunderstood?!? It was like that huh? Lame! And if you have some ...? She's cross after all!

ACHMED: *"I may possibly be, much wiser than you! I said "Possibly!". "It is you, who misunderstand!! ". "I might be wiser than you!".* Yes, you may be crass!

THE **KING OF DK:** Then she finally got a hug, that girl Louise! No, she was guilty of taking on that mother role! Because educators can't help it! Like Nancy, my sister's neighbor, she would have done too, if she had joined! And in my sister's job, it is her main function, to put herself at the forefront! Such sex-crazy sixteen year old girls! She has to be the leader there! And then release it, when she's in other situations!

ACHMED: This is how you practice sex ??

KING OF DK: It's a little difficult, if people just behave a little bit ...? And that is what empowers all men! You can just see the Arab:

"I have children myself, you can't teach me anything!". "I am now king!"

ACHMED: It was then, I turned on the TV!

KING OF DK: Well, that was late!

ACHMED: Yes, he said: *If you want to talk to the one, who was voted out - Benedikte -* I heard that!

THE **KING OF DK:** That was guaranteed, a lot of lubber who would! Don't you think? Dikes, they watch incredible much television! Gays, they barely watch any television!! Ha ha! No, we're not typical gays! Very far from! We do not have the party every weekend culture like....?

ACHMED: Hairdresser Mogens ??

THE **KING OF DK:** No, neither does Mogens! No, Mogens has been very atypical! But there are a lot of them of my peers hanging down at the G bar on Friday, Saturday and Sunday!

Husband, do we have that tape, or Frazier and Niles are dating a 22 year old?

HUSBAND: I think, I erased it!

ACHMED: He spends almost $10,000 on cigarettes a year !!? Ha ha - It's just sad! Just look at him!? *"I just want two packets of smokes a day. I just need my smokes"!* And then they film him smoking, sitting on his garden chair!!

THE **KING OF DK:** *"If you will not stop smoking! Then I'll start crying, and I won't stop, until you've stopped!".*

It's not interesting enough like Kardashian! They are interesting, because they are so sublime rich, that everything they piss on...?!? Did you see her oldest daughter - Kim - She has mega psoriasis outbreaks during a photo shoot?! Red spots everywhere on the legs! But it was easy for the makeup artist to straighten out! But the whole program was about psoriasis that day!

ACHMED: So were you happy?

THE **KING OF DK:** I don't know, what my thoughts were on the subject?? I thought it was interesting, that so many people got involved in a discussion about psoriasis! I have not..? I've never been one, who has ..?? I have seen many posts on TV, where psoriasis patients have complained and many posts on facebook in my psoriasis groups, dealing with reactions from strangers, who do not know about psoriasis!! I have never felt, that my surroundings have had a hard time coping with my psoriasis!

ACHMED: When did it break out?

THE **KING OF DK:** On me? Well, but it has only been done periodically, since I was fourteen! The ugliest scenes of psoriasis I can remember, have actually been with Arabs! Who sees something, and they dare not to look!?

ACHMED: I remember being in a water park, where a fat guy was sitting in a small hot tub, that I was about to enter! And he was just ruddy, dotted and all kinds of things, I just thought: *"Fuck!! I don't want to be cooked in the same water with that pig right now!!"* And it wasn't because, I was afraid, it would infected me!

I just wouldn't have any of his skin cells on me !!

THE **KING OF DK:** I've always accepted ..! The kind of fight that they initiate such fat guys, and showed their psoriasis, they break down with pity and everything! And in the pictures on Facebook, they have an undertone of: *We fight for psoriasis to become widespread in Denmark, and knowledge must be widespread and accepted!* Because then you wouldn't behave like that in a situation at a swimming pool! But I always think, that psoriasis has an ugliness to it! I want to.. ??

I've noticed some of the guys, that I always cruise with, I don't want to live with them, when I'm in Israel!! I stayed with a really nice racing driver. I actually regretted not wanting anything with him! But I didn't want to in the thirty days, that we shared a hotel room in Israel!

And he even touched me one night, when we turned off the light! But I thought, he had such a flat ass! And then he just had so much psoriasis, that I didn't get turn on, even though I suffer from it myself!

ACHMED: *"Uhh - what's that!!? No, adddrr! What is it then? Is it infectious?? ".*

THE **KING OF DK:** He was a racing driver! And during the World Cup in Sweden, he had fallen off the motorbike. And where he had scrape marks over his body, and in those places it developed psoriasis!!

ACHMED: No!? And before that he didn't suffer from it??

THE **KING OF DK:** Or did he not have psoriasis before?? - No! It was so stressful for his body - that experience! And he was really straight! I remember, he had a fun fascination of me! After fourteen days living with me, and seeing how, I did things! How I washed, smoked! He didn't smoke, but I smoked on the balcony in the evening of course! We did not smoke in the rooms! But then he got interested in me!! And then he suddenly says to me in the evening: *"Just tell me a little sex adventure with women!"* Then I told him about my experience with Ali in Cairo, who took me to a Turkish brothel, but then he couldn't even get a hard on!? *Now I'm tired! No!* Just like that! *Stop!* So in that way I fired him!

ACHMED: I regret, that I did not have the courage, to ask the medical student for her name!?

THE **KING OF DK:** Yes, there are some regrets, that are swirling!!

ACHMED: I told the "wildcat" about the incident with the medical student, who had made such an anticipation in front of me, and took her socks on first. Then she said, *"No, it's because, she is interested in you!"*

THE **KING OF DK:** Yes, it is!

ACHMED: Where my thoughts just went: *No!?!*

KING OF DK: But you didn't get anything activated then either!? You didn't go over to her and said: *Well, should I just notice??*

ACHMED: No, but I started talking to her then! While we were dressing! Slowly!

THE **KING OF DK:** Yes, but you will have to skip to some degree of obscurity!

"When you put your clothes on in such a manner in front of me, should I interpret something into it?? Would you like me to touch you?"

After all, there are some, who will appreciate the openness!

ACHMED: I don't remember, if it was the same on?? But there was one, standing closer, than you do now! She was standing at this height, and I was sitting on a bench, and had a direct look straight forward into her..!?

KING OF DK: Surely there are some, who get into trouble there? There have been some complaint cases?

ACHMED: Yes, there was someone, who felt offended by a big hand gesture on the ass in a sauna! Last year. But that's the only thing!

KING OF DK: And who was the "clerk"?

ACHMED: It didn't say!! But everyone said, they knew the circumstances! And they were also inside the sauna, when it happened. So in context!

THE **KING OF DK:** *"We heard it clearly! - It cut into the air! "*

ACHMED: *My ear still hurts after that whack!!*

KING OF DK: Yes, that's interesting! So you did find a girl describing an incident? But if girls are not horny, then who is?? The normal woman would like something in the *"Can"* once a day !!

ACHMED: Yes, that is the case with the "wild cat"! Fuck man, and several times a day! After all, this is how girls do turn on the joy volume on "older men"!

KING OF DK: You haven't seen the program, what the hell do they call it..?? I don't even know, who features that program..??

"You are allowed to, I am allowed to! "

ACHMED: *You are allowed to, I never succeed??*

KING OF DK: Filmed in the park at the University. She could get a lot, and he couldn't get anything! Is it Odin, that I have talked to about this??

ACHMED: I've seen it with half an eye, it hasn't caught me! She's not that interesting!

KING OF DK: Well? But she does have a lot of sex obviously! But that's how it is for a girl!

ACHMED: It's clear! Yes, I would like the picture, where Donald Trump and North Korea's leader standing arm in arm!

KING OF DK: Would you send me the picture of Donald Trump?

HUSBAND: Yaa!

KING OF DK: Yes, I'll send it to Achmed!

ACHMED: That was a hilarious picture! We haven't talked much about Trump, but he is probably very much in the tumble! Do you ever see Colbért? Bryan Colbért? He probably mentions Donald Trump eighty-four times each time in his show! Fuck, he doesn't like Donald Trump!

KING OF DK: No, I think, it's so strenuous! It is a good example, of how it is the very left wing of self-righteousness! How they all of a sudden could become fiery dragons showing another side of themselves! I've seen Barbra Streisand say the wildest, ugliest things and risk her career! No, Trump is showing teeth! When it wasn't Mireille Mathieu, who was the most beautiful woman in the world to me, it was Barbra Bach!

ACHMED: Yes, I saw her. I goggled her, and saw that, she was married to a Beatles boy!

THE **KING OF DK:** Ringo Star!! Do you think, she was beautiful? Yes, she was damn nice! And she was grounded! Here she is, Major Amasova! There's her husband - *l kill you after this mission!* In fact, I think, this is the coolest soundtrack of them all!! And that's John Berry!

ACHMED: In any case I would say, it's not Roger Moore performing that stunt!!

THE **KING OF DK:** No! There he is with a parachute! Is that Roger?

ACHMED: No!! He has to imagine it, but he doesn't have the cat's movement! Not compared to Daniel Craigh, he is a James Bond spider machine, who knows, how to move!!

THE **KING OF DK:** Well! I think he (Roger) is a James Bond! Much more! And my husband is also most into Roger Moore!

ACHMED: I think, he's so fiddly! But he is the one, with whom I grew up!

THE **KING OF DK:** Yes, I am too, because I was at the cinema to see "The Man with the Golden Gun"! That's the one, that comes before "View to a kill"! And by 1977 we went to see it!

ACHMED: The man with the steel teeth had only been cast, because he was tall! And good at biting into all things!

THE KING OF DK: Yes, he has only featured in two movies! And then he had shown a third, which was not a James Bond movie!? But we were pretty intrigued by the intro there! We were! Real movie art at a high level!! I wanted such an aquarium, when I was young! *I want to!!* A saltwater aquarium is not easy to keep! So yes, I was very intrigued by James Bond!

ACHMED: Yes, but "The Man with the Steel Teeth" is a handsome tall man! He was shown in Guinness's record book, as the world's tallest man, or actor!?

THE KING OF DK: *Nobody loves me!* No, of course, all people must have a love need and a sex need! So how to solve that?? There are really many marriages, and more divorces among the elderly today! Just watch Mina and her husband! Their kids are 30, 28 and 24! They just suddenly woke up to realization, that their parents are no longer together! Where he'd rather have an affair with a secretary!

JOSEPH: That's why, I struggle about getting the "residence" of my daughter! Mary has asked, if she could have it, so she could get some aid for housing! *"And we can easily fix that by the Register of People!".* I did not reply to her mail!

THE **KING OF DK:** For Mary it's only about...?

JOSEPH: It's all about....!? I sat in the sauna, trying to figure out, how much money she has received, tax free in the past years. She has received child allowance and until the last date! And it is close to 100,000 kroner!! For buying clothes and shoes and so on! And yes she has bought jump suits!

THE KING OF DK: I understand why, you're not answering it! There is no logic in that?! It should not be spent on cafe visits and French lingerie!? It is healthy! She has to get into the situation, that she needs, to find a way, to make some money!

JOSEPH: Yes, now she will work again at the Ignatius Healing Center !!

THE **KING OF DK:** Yes, if it can give her some money!

JOSEPH: It makes no money! It's free labor! No, that joint smells good!

KING OF DK: No, it doesn't! I am proud of you Joseph, that you have not smoked weed!!

JOSEPH: Yeah, it's been a month since yesterday!

THE **KING OF DK:** And that is, that there is no chance, your urine test can show ..? So you're really going to get her trump card out of hand!

JOSEPH: I don't know with psilocybin mushrooms, how fast they disappear out of the body? She has more THC in her blood, because she takes CBD drops every day?! But what I said with the Social Legal Aid, and the reason I talked to them, was to hear, what rights you have as a man today! And when the child is six! And that baby is a girl! Then the lawyer looked at me: *"Do you have common parents authority?" "Yes we have!". "Then it's fifty percent. It's 7/7 ".*

KING OF DK: And what do you want?

JOSEPH: Fifty percent!

KING OF DK: Do you want fifty percent? After all, my dad wanted us both, at the time my parents got divorced! He went to the Supreme Court to get us! And it tore my mother down! She wasn't ready to take that fight! My dad, he was crazy! It was before, she decided, she wanted to move! Then he thought, he could keep the kids!

JOSEPH: But he wasn't allowed to do that ??

KING OF DK: Yes, yes.

JOSEPH: Weren't you divided?

THE **KING OF DK:** No! I lived out there for shorter periods!

JOSEPH: But if Mary gets Isa more days than me, if it is 8/6 or 9/5?

KING OF DK: That's not it! Then it will be every two weeks!

JOSEPH: Yes, but there are some, who have 9/5 or something like that! But if there is the skewed distribution, then I also have to pay Mary's parental contribution! But if it's 7/7, then it's all right!

THE **KING OF DK:** Well, did she explain it?

JOSEPH: Then it's equal. Then I will not pay Mary a penny, because I have our Jesus child just as much!

KING OF DK: There's no need to aim less! There's no need to play nice now! It is she, who breaks up. So don't go out and play nice school Joseph!

JOSEPH: So I have to go after the kid's money too?

THE **KING OF DK:** Yes, you must go for at least half that! Otherwise, his Greenlander kids could spend Isa's children's money ??! You should also avoid such a thing! What to say? Also, avoid letting go of some stupid decisions or some greedy decisions now! You might as well just lay the cards on the table right away, and say: *That this is a partial matter here! We must have fifty percent of custody each for a new home!* You can also go even harder like my dad and say: *You want 100 percent custody of her! You can have her every other weekend! - After all, you are her mother! "!*

JOSEPH: Ha ha - *Yeah, you can see her every other weekend!*

THE **KING OF DK:** Well, but I'm glad Joseph then, that you're so strong!

JOSEPH: Yes, I have to admit, that I prefer it this way, than if it was me, who put my foot down! Because then I would have been sad, if Mary would break down! And that it would then go beyond Isa!

THE **KING OF DK:** Yes, if it was you, who put it in position, then she would have done something crazy!? Which definitely... ?? You have to look at it as the best!

DONG

THE **KING OF DK:** Is it Mary, who sends you messages??

JOSEPH: No!! I think, it was an app, that said that sound !? I actually do not know?! I sometimes have my doubts!

KING OF DK: She stopped that?

JOSEPH: But she just sent one, where she writes: *Sleep well Joseph, when you get there!* My usual phrase!

KING OF DK: What do you say - June 15?

JOSEPH: Yes!

THE **KING OF DK:** Shit!!

JOSEPH: Yes! It's coming soon!

THE **KING OF DK:** Yes! How did you find out, that she has been given an apartment?

JOSEPH: I've read it in her calendar, that she has an apartment! I have no idea where?? And I have no idea which? I have no idea how??

Or anything! But in each case she will have more expenses than a thousand DKK a month, which she now pays including internet, consumption, car! No! She pays for the nursery! That's a few thousand DKK! So all in all, she has expenses for three thousand including a child in kindergarten and for the rent! But she won't find that else where, now when she has to pay for half the Waldorf expenses! And then she has to pay for a rental apartment plus consumption! Then it might be, that she wants to receive something ..? - What's it called?

KING OF DK: Support!

JOSEPH: Housing Support! But it will still be more expensive, no matter how you turn it! But she does have a set of parents, who support her, when it comes!

THE **KING OF DK:** That's good enough! This is also why, you should go after you share the child allowance, if you have to share the parental authority! Because then they can support, whatever they want! It can only benefit Isa! And if they want to take her on trips to Borneo, Australia, South Africa and modern safaris in Krüger Park?? Then it's just okay! After all, it's only in your interest! That is it! My sister's ex-husband has been delighted, that my father has so much traveled grandchildren! Because he didn't, do it himself?! One day he paid the bus down town!! There he showed, how to buy three heavy metal gramophone records!!?

ACHMED: Ha ha! *This one - it's a damn good record!! Classic!!*

KING OF DK: That's what, he said to my dad, when he met my parents in '92! It was that, he dreamed, that Sis and their children would take a year off and live in South America! And it hit home by my dad! For he has always dreamed of South America!

ACHMED: That's fucking the most dangerous place to be!

THE **KING OF DK:** Yes!

ACHMED: Next to India!

KING OF DK: But it didn't matter! Yes, India is brutal too!

ACHMED: Shut up the girl, who got her head cut off and raped and everything!?

THE **KING OF DK:** Yes! Crazy man! They are insane!

ACHMED: No, you know what?

THE **KING OF DK:** That's religious fanaticism! They do things and things on every behalf! But so now I don't know the specific case there, but eh ...? Some of the articles that I told some of my students to read about India! And we had India course! It wasn't hard to find the wildest articles, about brothers-in-law and grandparents lying in ambush when their village youth, who had made naughty times, came back so... .. ??

ACHMED: Did they get acid on them!?

THE **KING OF DK:** They popped them up with sabers!! And showcased their heads and so on!! And then they have such a secular existence next to the residual system!?

ACHMED: Here a "another new book!" About equality and everything else. Fun! Everything we have been talking about!

THE **KING OF DK:** It's funny! Well, that's right! We're limping backwards! No, in fact it is because, we are not lagging behind! That's because, we're limping ahead! The Netherlands has done it one way, and Denmark has done it the other way, and now we see different results from it! In Denmark, you see a completely unauthorized group of men, who have difficulty adapting to the equal society! In the Netherlands you see a group of men, who have embraced and thrown themselves into the new world, and have eaten so much sugar, that they all now have teats - Size C! And goes with palettes makeup, and will suck dick! In other words, the Dutch have simply become a little nimble. You must see one my father knows, a Dutch man who has been married to a girl from Risskov, and they have had two sons. He has probably retained his passion for women somewhere, but he is also just such a "nice cousin" at this time with his makeup company ... !!? Shut up!! Yes, he sells makeup - him and the wife. When we met them in Thailand at a hotel, that they just had to work for an hour and a half, to fix some things, they came out to "play!". *We just have to work a little",* she said all the time! He had to sit and arrange orders in his company. There was only him and Kristine, and they sell beauty products. They have them stored at home in the garage.

ACHMED: But it's hard to send, when you're in Thailand ?!

THE **KING OF DK:** It's on mail order. It's on the Internet. He can then just open the account, and see, how many people have ordered since yesterday!

ACHMED: And then does he have anyone in the garage to send out?

KING OF DK: He sure does!? One to pack or something. Then he will probably have to approve all trades himself, or check that the money has gone in. It's probably prepay, just like when I buy "jog straps" - right? There I also get a small message in the evening, that now the order has been shipped! I barely press "Send" before it is on the way!!

ACHMED: And how long does it take from Australia then?

THE KING OF DK: "Aussiebum?" It didn't take long! And when I traded "Aussiebum", the second or third time, they had already set up a delivery center in Switzerland! Well! Yes, but it was a really good birthday. I bought a completely impossible Eurojack lottery ticket. It starts with number 34!?

ACHMED: As the lowest number ??

THE KING OF DK: 37–42-46-49 and so on. So it will be interesting! It's purchased on my birthday!

One gives importance to things. This is also why, the structuralists began to read novels more freely in the 70s! Because the great writers discovered, that it doesn't matter, what you write. If some one wants to read something into something, then you can't prevent them from doing so!!

ACHMED: I was out swimming in the sea twice yesterday. First thing in the morning. Nudists! Then a dwarf came, and laid down right in front of me, and she was black! I didn't mind her being black. I didn't mind, that she was a dwarf, and I didn't mind, that she was right in front of me, and looked straight at my naked crotch with sunglasses on! But she smelled like crazy! And the wind came down from the sea, over her and up to my nostrils!!

KING OF DK: Did she have menstruation or?

ACHMED: I can't say...?! I do not know!? Terrible! Ugly. I simply could not breathe. I had to think: *"Well, that was my beach trip! And then I must be on my way!".*

KING OF DK: Shit!

ACHMED: When you sit with those Tinder profiles, I get so many ideas for a thriller! Where you run into some problems, where you should just have swiped the other way!! Ha.

KING OF DK: It's damn dangerous too - love! It's dangerous for Odin!

And that he finds them the same way every time.

ACHMED: Where does he find them?

THE **KING OF DK:** At Galten Inn!

ACHMED: Yeah? What is it called? "Limelight?"? My uncle started that!

THE **KING OF DK:** It's all someone, who's divorced, living with violent husbands, and being an alcoholic. Odin has not pinched a woman, who has not been an alcoholic for the past fifteen years!

ACHMED: Well, then he knows, where he has them!

KING OF DK: Odin has gotten really tired of him the ayahuasca guy. He's the worst idiot ayahuasca guy. Odin has shown me his website one day! Not two words are spelled correctly!? And then he gives courses in self-awareness-raising drugs !? Take a break!

ACHMED: Next time you go to Flensburg, may I come with you?

KING OF DK: You don't bother! Don't have anyone under forty at all! It is direct death. And you need to pair up with some needs, and needs and needs!

ACHMED: Well, well, there's no one over forty, which is still neat!?

THE **KING OF DK:** Nooo !!

ACHMED: Well, I haven't seen many ?! I have to admit that !?

THE **KING OF DK:** You must be like John Travolta, his first was fifty-four. You can get someone with money - now!

ACHMED: Yes, it is! Well, I also say "yes" to those, who are doctors, even though they are "ugly!" I go after those, who have money and access to drugs! Ha ha. Those who can print prescriptions!

KING OF DK: It's exciting!

JOSEPH: We were to a parents get together. There was one of Isa's best friends, her parents who are both doctor and the other is a nurse! Then I said, *"Well, then, you can write some prescriptions? - Can't you? ". "No, yes, yes. Not too many!"*

THE **KING OF DK:** And the younger you take them, the less they can relate to Isa! So it can be outright evil, to bring a young woman into her life!

JOSEPH: Yes, I agree! But I also don't have to bring everything in !?

THE **KING OF DK:** Yes, you will!

ACHMED: It can also just be sleep, fun and "play!" New word to the Americans! "Play!" Read "Make it naughty!"

THE **KING OF DK:** You can go out and get some experience, but then in any case, do not go out and burn the needles again! Larry did! After a year and a half Anette ripped him for 200.000 dollars! And that means, he has no money today!

ACHMED: And that was wife number two??

KING OF DK: Last Sunday he took one of my husband's "pecan pies", and while no one was looking at the buffet!? There he just shoved half a pecan pie into a net, and then he went!

ACHMED: Were you eating at a restaurant?

KING OF DK: No, we were out with a couple of friends in Auning. One turned fifty and had fifty people.

ACHMED: And there he went and stole the food??

THE **KING OF DK:** There he went... ?? He arrived late and was there for twenty minutes, and then he filled a whole bag of food, and then he left! I was the only one, who saw it!

ACHMED: It was a bit rude then !!

THE **KING OF DK:** Yes, yes. He is original, and has no cultural formation! He is a factory worker, who has been poor, and could not even afford the US! So they have had a whole army of social problems! This is also why, Canada has become democratic according to a Danish model! And they have no formation up there! It's the same with knife and fork, and they fuck their kids!

ACHMED: Well !? I thought they were more civilized since ...?

THE **KING OF DK:** The French will not know of them! The culture! The French have always been that, whatever came from Canada, they do not deal with! That is why, Diana Dufresne and almost Celine Dion did not make it in France! It was because, there was something, that they couldn't afford, to get used to!

ACHMED: Why don't you adopt a child from Somalia?

HUSBAND: No!!

ACHMED: You can get them for seven dollars a month, they write in the advertisement!

THE **KING OF DK:** No. I am totally immune to those there. But I can't stand it with animals!

ACHMED: No you. They just need some nerve poison!

THE **KING OF DK:** It's awful, that they neglect, they multiply like that to a degree. And their wars and their...!? But they did not have any information time. So it will be long before...!

ACHMED: But now they have cell phones, so it might be a little faster !?

KING OF DK: Yes, that might help. It may help!

ACHMED: No, there was a newspaper article here last week, listing the ten most dangerous places to be a woman!

KING OF DK: Yes, I saw it well. USA, Pakistan, Afghanistan.

ACHMED: All these nations frightened and looked at tenth place – USA??

THE **KING OF DK:** USA. That's right. But me, who is so educated in the US, and I think right away: *"Yes. Okay, that's what, it's about to be a melting pot!"*. It is simply, what is embracing all the cultures. The ones that are most dangerous for, the women for whom they are most dangerous, are still the Mexican, Pakistani and Afghan women living in the United States. After all, it's their men, who commit the same crimes over there. And then black. So because they have been slaves for 300 years, they have a psychological baggage, that makes... ??

But the world has entered a stable period! Don't you think, we will have world peace over the next few days?

ACHMED: It depends on, whether we get more drought!

KING OF DK: Yes for sure. But if the rich, instead of spending their money on speedboats, invest in any way to supply the world with water! Then the problem will not be so big!

ACHMED: That's what Saudi Arabia does!

THE **KING OF DK:** Well, it's no more complicated, than having to force more cooperation and less autonomy. And the masses will demand it! They will tear each other apart! It will be so ugly to be rich within the next twenty years! Greed has become more sinful. I can already see it for me! I can already see that from the young people. Those who are 16 years old today, do not think, that being Bill Gates rich is great!

ACHMED: But that's why, they're there anyway, and they're barricading themselves more and more! And build walls and fences around their big modern houses!

KING OF DK: But that's because, the reality is something other than those, who distribute gingerbread!

ACHMED: We are becoming more and more Americanized, and the differences get bigger and bigger.

KING OF DK: Well, I don't know, what you mean by Americanized?? Yes! So Americanized, is it because our people want the whole truth? About the policies? Is that, what you mean Americanized or how?

ACHMED: No, I mean inequality is getting bigger, just like it is in the US.

THE **KING OF DK:** No, I don't think so! Nor do I think, there is any reason to say so!?

ACHMED: You don't mean that inequality gets bigger ??

THE **KING OF DK:** No - not in Denmark. I do not think so!

In my eyes, there are people on transfer income, who can't make the money. And that's because, they have overconsumption! All those cash beneficiaries who are willing to come on TV!! They are revealed one by one with being down in the shopping malls all the time, buying designer clothes in sports stores and this and that; as they think we, who have the money are buying!? But I haven't been in such a business since Christmas!! And there it was something completely different, that I bought! They get plenty of money. Now you just see, that you can handle it, okay?

ACHMED: I can afford to buy a Chinese motorcycle!!

KING OF DK: And now you get a bonus more by getting rid of your…?

JOSEPH: Yes, it was the state administration, that informed me about it:

"Remember that you can also apply for child support! - But you should have done that three days ago, because it is quarterly, so you can't get it until October!" ? " Well, but thanks for the information anyway! ".

THE **KING OF DK:** Did they say that?

JOSEPH: Yes. But it is your duty to investigate yourself! I didn't know a fuck about it!? And that is until, you get a girlfriend or a new partner. Then they peel that supplement off again! So getting a girlfriend is expensive. It costs a thousand a month!

KING OF DK: Yes. This is also why, there is so much scam with it! That it can pay well for customs and tax, to have cars driving around! For them, the Arabs are probably not late to exploit! But one has to hope, that someone is not!? But they probably have a hard time finding anyone - the press! Surely they could show any of those decent Arab immigrants, that they talk about there being?? They never found anyone!? They are beset with social destruction. They pull a tail behind them. Everybody. There is only him the newsreader, who has jumped out like a fagot!

Does Mary still live at the women's shelter?

JOSEPH: Yes yes - There she can stay until August 1st! But then she moves back out into the Marialystpark, where she lived, when I met her.

THE KING OF DK: That's good enough - Because it is a case to live in a crisis center??

JOSEPH: Well, Isa thinks, it's nice enough, because there is someone, to play with at that shelter!

THE KING OF DK: Yes yes - But it is also good enough to have someone, so she does not think, it is rude! But that is it - And you should not be mistaken, that when the parents are separated, the child suddenly learns a lot about life. And that's what Isa is about. A lot of tragedy. It will make her sensitive. It will develop the empathy, that you have called for.

ACHMED: Yes, now she has met people from Syria, and places where there has been war!

KING OF DK: She may be the educator of the future!

ACHMED: Yes. About her father who committed "psychological violence" on her mother!

THE KING OF DK: Surely nothing is being talked about ??

JOSEPH: No, I never did anything !!

KING OF DK: But Isa knows that. You must also prepare a defense on the 7/7? Because Mary will try to go after it all or what?

JOSEPH: No, I don't know??

No, I think, she will go for having the residence!

KING OF DK: But that in itself, will also be rubbish!

JOSEPH: But that in itself will also only be a financial incentive! Why else go so high up in the residence?? We have 7/7, and she can write her name on the mailbox!

THE KING OF DK: It gets messy, when all the divorcing couple's children live in two places!? But of course there is not so many post offices, and you do not receive letters from the public anymore! So it might not be a problem?? That is a problem for the police and the personal register?! Does that mean, you get a letter calling for what ??

JOSEPH: To the District Court!

THE KING OF DK: To the District Court??

JOSEPH: Yes, I think so!

THE KING OF DK: Will you then stand in the District Court and present your arguments each ?? With lawyers ??

JOSEPH: Yes.

THE KING OF DK: And then must the District Court decide?

JOSEPH: And the State Administration gives the District Court their recommendations, which they had also given to the Appeals Board!

KING OF DK: Well?

ACHMED: And that's the temporary solution!

KING OF DK: But you already know, that they recommend 7/7! So, after all, it's going to be a court case, that's going to be about, there's something, that needs to be changed about it!

JOSEPH: Yes and residence!

THE KING OF DK: And that the mother demands the residence?

JOSEPH: Yes, if she has her place of residence, she might as well start saying it must be 10/4. Where it is now I, who have the residence, so I can get no less!

THE KING OF DK: So you can start saying, that it should be 10/4 too??

JOSEPH: Well I could. But you might not win anything by that ?!

THE **KING OF DK:** No.

ACHMED: And that Isa is six and a half years, it has weighted on the weight bowl anyway! And there is also something about girls, maybe "getting better at tension" with the father, and sons "connecting" better with the mother??

KING OF DK: Well?

ACHMED: But it is only for a certain age.

KING OF DK: This is legal. There is no scientific evidence for that, so they probably can't sit down, to say anything about the argument! Or what? I do not know!?

JOSEPH: But Isa has been given the psychologist hours through the crisis center, which Isa can use to talk to a child expert!! And that's fine enough too! She'll probably need it, when we go to court! Especially if she has to stand up, and talk in front of a judge. I just told Mary that too!

"No, she shouldn't !!".

THE **KING OF DK:** It's probably an immortal woman!

JOSEPH: Yeah, but I got a big hug then...?

KING OF DK: Yes, you shouldn't... !! Well that's all her tactics, that's how, she was to you in the beginning too! You know, she uses it systematically to accomplish things! That there is nothing deeper in it!

ACHMED: So there is something deeper in it, if you use it as a tactic !?

THE **KING OF DK:** It doesn't reflect positive feelings this !!

JOSEPH: No?

THE **KING OF DK:** It reflects: *"Okay, I'll just check, if I can actually use my female charm to haul him around a bit now! Here's where, we're split! ".* Because that's how many women manage! She wants to go to the limits! She wants to use Isa, to achieve everything, she can! It's a big hit for Mary, that she's got Isa. After all, that's the only thing, she's getting away from you!

JOSEPH: But it was also the only thing, she wanted!

THE **KING OF DK:** And then her life can break so easily, because now she has to both be an alcoholic just like her mother. She has to follow in her mother's footsteps! She has decided that! That she wants to do everything! She thinks, her own mother is the greatest success, life has shown her. So she wants to do everything just like her mother! And it is a fantastic pity for Isa, in fact, that it becomes so weak a mother image! She could also have had Barbra Streisand as a mother, which all men are afraid of !! But then you should have fucked the old Jew !!

JOSEPH: Yes, that is not good enough!

KING OF DK: You called back then, that we had gangbang, didn't you?

ACHMED: I don't know ?!

KING OF DK: Didn't I tell you, that I was on Meth last week? Two days? No, it was Odin, that I said it to! I had put some pink sheets over the furniture, so it is not disgusting. I have cleaned! But it was sunrise, and I didn't go out with the dogs! And my husband called in the middle of it all!

ACHMED: No!!

KING OF DK: Then I lay with my legs spread! We had put a mattress on the table there, because we have no swings! Then we could lie two with spread legs next to each other, and then two could stand to fuck!

ACHMED: So what did you do ??

KING OF DK: What are you saying?

ACHMED: Did you then go outside or what?

THE **KING OF DK:** No, I asked everyone to be quiet!

ACHMED: And could they manage that??

KING OF DK: Yes. Yes because it was 11 o'clock in the morning!

ACHMED: *"I just lay asleep. Hey darling!!".*

KING OF DK: I could barely concentrate, about talking to him!

There is hardly any "ware and tare" at this home, when my husband is not here!! I hardly need to clean!! For in no way do I make it messy myself. And maybe I think about the toilet more than anything else! So my husband is also dragging...?? When I have just cleaned the bathroom, my husband wants to brush his teeth. Then he just takes the whole tap down to his mouth, and it is filled with toothpaste!? If I say that to him?? Then it will also be filled with toothpaste on the back just suddenly!? So it can't help saying something!? He should get the idea himself ...!

So, if that's the price I have to pay, then I'll pay! But it is still fun, that he is so happy for me!!

JOSEPH: But it's the same with Isa, when she's home! Then it also looks like Jerusalem's devastation after just one day!

KING OF DK: Well? It's a nice little challenge, to get her taught some order! But I know my great sense of order, it probably originates from losing my mother! So..?? It might also be nice to let the child be a child!

And the other day I had lunch with Lotte Heise.

ACHMED: Were you?

KING OF DK: Yes.

ACHMED: No !!

THE **KING OF DK:** Yes! Then I asked: *"Lotte - What did you really earn from the Vanish commercial?"*

ACHMED: Vanish?

THE **KING OF DK:** Don't you remember, that there was an advertisement with Vanish on TV ??

ACHMED: Yes! Has she been part of it?

KING OF DK: First year of Vanish!

ACHMED: Five million!!?

THE **KING OF DK:** Almost three years salary!! So that was her main salary for three years! It was shown back in the '00s!

ACHMED: So that money is spent!

KING OF DK: Yes, yes! She then has a huge consumption! It was because, I came over to Mina with a fat spot! I had just been roasting, roasting pork, then I said: *"That you have to accept this fat spot on my clean pants. But I simply do not want to wash them again. And I've been trying to get it off! ". "Then you should use Vanish,"* Lotte said. Ha!

ACHMED: *"Do you really believe in pigeons yourself ?!".*

THE **KING OF DK:** *"Then I would really like to ask you, because it is one of the country's biggest advertisements - at that time. You must have made a lot of money from it!". "Yes, but it wasn't bad,"* she said! But she has not been used in commercials since!

No, but she likes me, because I know opera!

ACHMED: You know opera ??

THE **KING OF DK:** I can do some opera!

ACHMED: And so does the hysteria suffer ??

KING OF DK: Well, she is...? That's what, she lives of now!!

She has *Lotte's Opera Theme* on P2! Week by week by week. And it has become the biggest program on P2. She has had that for four/ five years!

ACHMED: Well! I had no idea!

THE **KING OF DK:** And then she was on TV, the day the students graduated. There she was in the evening show, as a representative of parents, who have had such an "agricultural machine" on a visit filled with students! She's on the TV, and the evening show talking about anything! *"But have you been examined for dementia?"* I asked her! Ha-ha. No! I had just read, Mina has written a book with Lotte. Did I show you it?

ACHMED: *"Have you been examined for dementia?!".*

KING OF DK: Well, Lotte was on TV the other day, and in crossfire with three men. So, they were a panel of four. And what did I tell her?

"Lotte, you aren't in the room with the three guys!? So you sit down and make your own! You sit and gesture, and when they say something, you sit and twist your face!? And it looks like, you have a whole world to yourself!?"

ACHMED: Did you say that to her ??

THE **KING OF DK:** I told her then!

ACHMED: Is she performing on Go'morning Denmark?

THE **KING OF DK:** No, it wasn't Go'morning Denmark! It was a panel, that was invited by TV2 News in the afternoon! Who should discuss something for ten minutes! And it was shown three times during the afternoon! So it's probably been busy in the morning! There I said to her, *"Have you been examined for dementia!?".* Because I think, she's diffuse! Either she is Lotte, or she is Lotte Heise! And she's not quite sure, when she's what?! So I said that! And that, I think, was to do her a favor!? For I actually think, she has such a searing dementia!! So, it is too crazy to see a Lotte Heise together with three specialists in one or the other political, that they should discuss! In any case, it wasn't the burka ban! And then she sits there in her underwear, just like me now. And she just sits, while they talk and fixes her!? And she's looking at her bracelets!? I think these are signs of dementia! And then she also closes her eyes, when talking: *"Well, I think so ... -"* And then only brief eye contact, and then they're gone again! And she talks loose!! And so Lotte suffers from things, that I don't like about my father either. A lot of what comes out, these are clichés!! I can hear her saying this - ten times before! What the hell was it, that I got to say ?? Well yes. I came to say:

"That they are some fucking Catholics!". "What do you have against Catholics??". "Well, they are just double moral, and then they have no charm, and then they fuck kids!". No, I couldn't say! But she is progressive after all and has many modern opinions! So I'm probably just modern enough for her! I've also tried my main points! Odin always quotes me for saying this, and I said that: *"Well, are you so in love that everything should taste good? Do you have a love affair with your taste buds?? Is there nothing, that must be healthy?? ".* I said that one day! And she's a vegetarian so! But she's in a hurry, when marshmallow arrive! She can eat that. To sit and eat sugar! And Mina and her are drinking rosé wine! No, the other one! Wasn't that the one with the rose wine and the sugar?? The other thing that provoked...? Yes!

My favorite clamor sentence for students in cultural understanding:

"No, I don't give a fuck about your cultures!! I've been there, and seen how you discriminate against women, and you can't get proper education and everything. And I don't give a fuck about your older generation in national costumes with feathers in their hat! We must have created a global personality as soon as possible, so that we can all live in peace! And then you must bring your Gods into the bedroom!".

And then the class rebelled! And she should just swallow it, too. Because Lotte is still in that phase: *"No, where is it nice to come to Majorca!". And: "They are some nice clogs, that they sell - Well I simply need a pair!!".* Because I'm tired of something like that! I like Denmark. But I don't like much else!!? I will not travel to Thailand and their shit country !! Ha-ha Shut up what a shitty country Thailand is !!

JOSEPH: Her half-Thai with whom I was dating, could tell something about her mother's family and their children and upbringing! And is it that children are allowed, to eat their own vomit?! Eat their own stools!? To teach them to behave properly!? And do right, and do what is said! And yet they have so much decency, that as adults they want to care for their parents, who have treated them so miserably !!?

THE **KING OF DK:** They are being threatened! After all, they are forced to do so, because they do not have a cultural settlement. Nor do they have an equality account. So in Thailand, they are stupid like cods!! Thais are mega unintelligent!! They still stand in Hua Hin today in high school, and cite Kings back and forth!!? There are no subjects, that are scientific in high schools over there?! There is no math!? There's no biology?! There is no physics?! There are the Kingdoms, Buddhist teachings and so on!! And if they knew, how bad it was, they stopped coming there too! It is a pity for Thai children to live in such royal ignorance! That they have to live like a prostitute all over the world !? It's a pity!

ACHMED: But that's good for us others! Ha-ha

THE **KING OF DK:** Ih yes! There have always been slave people.

ACHMED: What I can see is, that it's an error in my upbringing, that I haven't been to Thailand!

THE **KING OF DK:** You can say: *"I have class, I don't go to places like that!".*

"We must not be affected by anything! You should not be sad, you should not be happy - you must be in yourself!! ".

Two of my friends have called and said to me: *"Joe, I'm in no man's land, I don't know, what I'm bothering!".* And then I said to one: *"Then try to be in that room, and see what opportunities emerge!".*

ACHMED: *And then go hang yourself!!*

THE **KING OF DK:** And to the other one I've said: *"It's a whole trend in society. Not all men in your age group, have a clue, what the fuck they want !? But I can tell you, they all want it in the ass! ".*

ACHMED: *"And if you don't want to?? Then you can grab a rope and hang yourself! ".*

THE **KING OF DK:** But it really is my impression Achmed, that something has happened to our society over the past two years, which I only discover now - Men have been so far out on a sideline, that a quite ordinary role is so undefined in 2018, not least in relation to gender equality and the role of women. They just mentioned in the press today for the first time, that on the further education ...?

ACHMED: There are only women ??

THE **KING OF DK:** That on those who require over B in average, there is only one man for every tenth woman! That is, doctors!! It will be the first thing, the people can feel. *"In seven years you can no longer be allowed, to prefer a man!"* That's how, I think, he said on the radio! The one novel I would like to write about the women's community, where a man is banned. I should have finished it by now too !!

ACHMED: You can still do that!

I was on a date with a 27-year-old nurse, who is graduating, and just takes all the overtime hours and guards, she can pull!

THE **KING OF DK:** Why ?? Does she have kids?

ACHMED: No! No children! And she was so attracted to me! But again, I'm being cheated, the pictures are from here and up!

THE **KING OF DK:** And then she was much bigger ??

ACHMED: So she was great!

KING OF DK: You know the girls, that are just a bunch of slim ones, they show it! Those who are not... ?? I never fumbled around in that! I've been able, to see that - Always! And I can see on the cheeks of a boy, if he has fat between the buttocks!

ACHMED: Yes, but it's harder on the girls !!

THE **KING OF DK:** Yes, I would like to believe that!

ACHMED: At least I couldn't see it there !?

THE **KING OF DK:** You can see him the magician, who is so skinny. If you only saw him from above ?? So there are such 25-year-olds, such as 95-98 kilos, he can in principle be relatively slim. But I must say, that I am such, that I do not even begin to explain anything!! I'm just pressing "No!" No, nothing to notify! I press, so I disappear out of his ...? And you could say, that I actually have the feeling, that two or three guys in Aarhus are a little mad at me! At least I can't log in as "Glory8000C" without a few negative comments!

ACHMED: About you as a person !?

THE **KING OF DK:** I don't know, who that is?? Someone wrote: *"Watch out for your gloryhole!"* There he was angry. And it was one, I had rejected the first day! And that's also, what he says: *"41-year-olds looking* *for young!"* But then he just suddenly wrote to me! Because there are no youngsters for a 41 year old at 120 kilos!! It's a fat man sitting around, looking for young men. It's hard for him. I feel like writing something to him someday. Jorgen writes to people like this: *"Get a grip!".* Or something!! But I don't bother, when I don't know, who people are!! So it may not be my problem to solve their problems. But there are probably many, who are in trouble!

ACHMED: But it can't be that fucking big an environment?!

THE **KING OF DK:** But it is! Because?? But I don't know, if I told you? But they said that in the press! It has been three weeks since Ekstra Bladet had an entire page, which was the abbreviation of a PhD, who had come from Sociology in Copenhagen. It said, and the girls discussed it in P3:

"Every third Dane dreams of having sex with others!". There are numbers on them!

ACHMED: That's quite a lot!

THE **KING OF DK:** That's a lot!

ACHMED: Every third? That's 33 percent!

THE **KING OF DK:** Every third person dreams of having sex with others! There were three girls on the radio in the afternoon: *"And which one of our men,"* they said, *"dreams of having sex with others!!?".* And they weren't for it. The three girls were not into the idea, that their husbands were for sex with others!

ACHMED: But Danes?? After all, it's both sexes !?

THE **KING OF DK:** The second most startling thing was: *"Every third Danish man has sex with other men, without identifying as a bi or gay!".* It is new. That's a high number!

ACHMED: The first statistic applies to both genders .. ??

THE **KING OF DK:** Yes, it applies to both genders! There were such twenty different considerations!

ACHMED: So it's every third woman, and every third man who dreams of having sex with others?

KING OF DK: Yes. And then there was actually one in the press that evening, I saw it quite briefly. It was before my husband traveled to the United States. I just heard, that he said, that it was not gender, it was not love or anything. It was the dick, that he went after. You can't get that from a woman! Then he didn't think, he was bi !!

ACHMED: It just doesn't make any sense !?

KING OF DK: Ha ha. Yes, but it makes sense to me, and what I've always said that Achmed: *"The categories don't exist at all! Everyone knows everything! It's just a matter of, what fucking idea, they have up their ass! And it's your grandmother, who helps shape it! She helps validate for you!".* That's why, I also don't like, when Oliver and Vera tell us, what's right, and what's wrong! *"You don't know, what life she is going to live!!?".* You can see, my dad did everything to teach me, that being gay was something terrible!

ACHMED: And you didn't listen !!?

KING OF DK: I did. I had a hard time coming out of the closet! Well, that was tough! Where today, they burst out with joy!

ACHMED: *"Cheers dad !! Aren't you happy now ?? ".*

KING OF DK: Funny! We were at Benny's birthday on Sunday - Saturday! Mayas and Bennys boy's birthday - One year! Then they sit and tell, Maja and Benny. Benny's dad, he can't actually be with their little son without sitting around crying!? Every time he looked at his grandson, where he started to come fourteen days ago! And he cried so much. He's a grandfather! And he's a bald man with tattoos! A real criminal who has been in the damper - Guaranteed?! They are not talking about that?? He has been divorced from his mother, since Benny and his twin brother were...? I said to Benny: *"Well, with a dad howling like that?? - Did he really take care of you?? ". "No, we haven't seen our father very much",* he said! Then that's why, he cries like that!

ACHMED: Because now he can see, what he's missed !?

KING OF DK: Then he has built up all that grief, and now it must be imagined, that every time he looks at the grandson, it is joy!? No, it's sadness! *Don't worry about not having been with you! And if I were you, I would say to my dad: "You should stop crying like a slut your fucking tail!".* I said that to Benny! I can't take it, when they cry! Fuck, I can not stand, those who cry. The Crown Prince!? And all those lady men, who are at home on the couch watching love movies with their wives!? And all of a sudden, it is kisses and hugs!!? Well, you don't! The world not that modern yet! Don't you agree?

ACHMED: Yes. Snort.

KING OF DK: I fell out of a third floor bed, when I was on scout camp! There at the age of seven! Two and a half meters down on a stone floor !!

ACHMED: Did you fall down?

KING OF DK: Yes. I still have this bulge in my forehead !!

ACHMED: Yes, yes. Is it from that time?? Is it from, when you were little?

THE **KING OF DK:** Yes!

ACHMED: It's the same with the Thai boxer. He had fallen out of a bunk bed from the third upper bunk, and landed with his head on the lower bunk! And knocked all his teeth out!! So they pointed forward!! And the pedagogues who discovered, that he was lying on the floor, just lifted him up in the bunk bed again, and went in and continue their party!?

KING OF DK: How old was he?

ACHMED: He can't remember it! It was in the nursery!

THE **KING OF DK:** Well clearly, you cannot make an omelet without breaking some eggs.

ACHMED: Well, that's still awful!

THE **KING OF DK:** Today you know such a concussion, as I once got, it has consequences!

ACHMED: It has had that too !!

KING OF DK: It has it!! That is why, I am completely empty-headed today!

ACHMED: Of course, I can't even remember it !? But I was told by my older siblings, that I had fallen from our attic, and landed on a stone floor head first!! And there I haven't been many years old either!

THE **KING OF DK:** No? But you know today, that those who strike ...? I just said to Maja and Benny, because their boy had a huge bruise on his cheek, then Benny says: *"Yes, that was the door, he walked in! But it goes away fast!".* But then I turned around and said, "Well, you just have to remember, that all the bruises you have, that the skin is thin, when you turn forty/fifty years!! There is nothing free, even though one is only a year old! For example, a blue eye or a stained eyebrow that is much more porous to the skin, than where it is not beaten! If he gets psoriasis, then* *you can be sure, he gets psoriasis in those places!".*

ACHMED: Did you say that?

KING OF DK: Yes. Because Benny was talking like, it was free!! *"Well, he gets bruises all the time!".* There I just thought, *"Just try to protect him from it!"* After all, he just got his willy popped up and sewn back together!

ACHMED: Benny?

THE **KING OF DK:** No, his boy!

ACHMED: The child? Was it a foreskin narrowing?

KING OF DK: No, he was born with three pee holes !! When he was peeing, it came out in three places!

ACHMED: Well !? That's smart!

KING OF DK: No, nonsense! Sorry! It's one of their friends kids! No, their boy had a pee hole - right here over the penis! The penis hangs here, and then he poked out of a hole just above it! That's how, he was born, and there are many children, who are born like this today! And boys who get through it, they get the penis opened! Cut up and then insert a tube. And he has been able to do this week, and has it sewn back together! And then in a year, they do a cosmetic operation, so there is no more to see!

ACHMED: And then they make it longer !!?

THE **KING OF DK:** No!

ACHMED: *"Could you please make it a little longer? It's my son! ".*

THE **KING OF DK:** No, I don't think, they know much about, whether it will stop or inhibit growth, that has been opened and closed!? I do not know??

ACHMED: I think, before I started memorizing, I have been cut up for foreskin narrowing !?

THE **KING OF DK:** Well. It is common!

ACHMED: Yes. But I discovered it myself, when I could see, that mine looked a little different than the others!

THE **KING OF DK:** You can't do that on the operation, that Maja and Bennys boy have had! It's circumcised now!

ACHMED: Circumcised? Why?

THE **KING OF DK:** Well, he will be, when it's all over! Because one retains the foreskin, that is to be modeled with and so on. The last thing he gets, is being circumcised! And then they can't see it at all! So it's nice, that you can make it. There are a lot of grown men peeing around, and peeing over the penis!! Because you haven't been able to make it until now! But you can't look at your friends, unless you stand right next to them and pee!! And you can be sure, that those who have such a circumstances, are the ones, who will not pee with others!! So!

They have been hospitalized for three days with him at Skejby. Both Maja and Benny. No, I don't think, he should embarrass her every time, they are together! And then their boy!! My sister had called her daughter's father-in-law, the grandfather one day, to deliver the boy up at Stjernepladsen by sisters place. Which would suit him for the rest of the day for Maja and Benny. There he had come one hour late! Because he had been sitting, staring at the boy playing!? Well, he had thought, he was so nice, and then he was sitting and crying, when he had to leave him!? And then he had stood, and said a lot of stupid things like:

"That no one else should care for him - Only you and me, who must !?"!

Why take such a hyper interest in his grandson!? *"Why not have been with your own children anymore?".* So we the others must hardly look at him!? And he has no one to turn his attention to! He only has... ?? And they moved home to ...?

JOSEPH: It's kind of the same thing, I've noticed on Mary's dad! In connection with the State Administration! He is also stepping into something! To have a chance to have some time with our child! Because he himself just missed the chance to be with his own daughter then! And that's why, I also asked him out in the hallway, when he came and helped fetch Mary's stuff from the barn: *Do this remind you of anything??* And then he started thinking about the birthdays, he attended!? *"No, I meant you 33 years ago!!". "Well, yes, yes!".* No, I deleted him on facebook and all the places, that I was connected with him! But I think, he was more sweet than Mary's mother! But I thought the first time, I saw him: *"What a weak man!"* I came to help with a move of Mary's stuff, when I had just met her, and she had to move from a three bedroom apartment to a one bedroom. But it was me, who had to manage it all with moving, packing of car and trailer ..!

THE **KING OF DK:** And he could do nothing !?

ACHMED: No, nothing! Nothing!

KING OF DK: It's typical too! But now they are probably pearl friends! As long as Mary can maintain the courtesy ??

JOSEPH: I asked Mary over facetime, if they had a good trip to the medieval festival in Horsens: *"Yes, it was excellent!"*. *"Well did you taste some of the good food?"*. *"I had packed a lunchbox! - I have nothing!"*

KING OF DK: Well, you were supposed to know !?

JOSEPH: Yes, yes - *"I have nothing!"*

THE **KING OF DK:** *"Then go out and find yourself some sugar daddies!"*. Didn't you say that? Why?

JOSEPH: Because I was on facetime with my daughter !!

THE **KING OF DK:** Well - yes, okay!

JOSEPH: But she wants to know, if we can share the children's money? I was actually going to write: *"Then you should drop that lawsuit!"*

THE **KING OF DK:** Yes, I think, that is the least! And my aunt just asked, how it went with you! And then I turned around, and then I said:

"It's me, who runs that show! And I told him, not to share the child allowance with her!". And then she shook her head! Then she said:

"Now remember that it is best for Isa, if they have a relaxed relationship with each other!" I said: *"You can't have that, after what she has done!"*. You can have a tolerable relationship with each other! There can be no exchange of sympathy! She's going to do this to others! Just wait!

JOSEPH: She's not going to meet anyone! She becomes like her mother, and stays single all the years to come!

KING OF DK: Do you think? Is she done with him "the Chinese" or what?

JOSEPH: Yes, I think so! He is a Greenlander. After all, I meet him every morning, as I deliver Isa on the way to school!

KING OF DK: Can you notice something on him?

JOSEPH: No, I hardly greet him!

THE **KING OF DK:** *"What are you still fucking my ex-wife !?"*

JOSEPH: Do you think, I should ask that ?!

KING OF DK: Yes. *"Don't you think, she gives too little anal sex ??"*. Ha ha.

I don't mean that! It may also be, that it's too rough! It could also be, that he turns around, and gives you one upside down! No, but I know, how good you are, so I said to my aunt: *"So it wasn't really a matter of Joseph getting mad! Just a little bit more evil!"* Otherwise you would have given horse and stable to her and everything possible at this time!

ACHMED: Has your husband had a good ride?

KING OF DK: Yes. He is totally ecstatic!

And I can tell you, I was worried!! Because not only was I afraid, he would have to defect and meet a seventeen-year-old in the four days, he had in Santa Cruz for himself. And I don't bother asking, what the hell he's done?? He booked himself ...? He says, he has booked himself at the Holiday Inn! But I think, he has rented himself at such a motel!? One of these with a swimming pool in the middle, where they leave the room doors open in the evening and something like that. And then I was a little nervous too. Okay, when he's in such bad shape at home, and we can't have sex?? So he's not in better shape over there, if he's with strangers!? So that way, I was a little nervous about misunderstanding his own condition! And then be much more healthy than he really is!? And then lie dying from a cardiac arrest in front of some seventeen-year-olds, who think, he is exciting for one day! And then I also think a little about life giving, and life sometimes takes. But I hope the hell, he comes home tomorrow! Then I will be the happiest man in the world! I would probably be blank, if he didn't come home. Fuck, I'd be blank!

I've always liked being number two! Because my whole childhood I was number one - right?

ACHMED: And you like being number two??

KING OF DK: Yes, so my whole childhood I was used to being the first born boy in the family!! And it had an impact, when the whole family was together, and my cousins were younger than me. I was used to getting the biggest piece of meat, if there were five meatballs in front of me. Then I got the biggest one. And then I met my husband, and he was used to being number two, because his big brother was used to getting the bigger piece. And between my husband and I, he just took the lead in a way. So I've gotten used to the fact, that now my husband has to get the biggest piece of meat! And now I am reduced to my sister's place. I get the second biggest. Ha ha. And I have used that figuratively.

Three weeks ago I started introducing a new food culture!

And I've developed an amazing salad of iceberg, and avocado, raw onions, oil, vinegar and freshly steamed clams! Which has not been submerged, but steamed, because then they get delicious like pubic lips! And there I noticed that after three weeks of salad every other night, I am no longer in as good control in anal sex, as it is necessary to have in anal sex contexts! After all, I have anal sex four times a day!

ACHMED: Salad ruins !?

KING OF DK: Last week, as I told Odin and not to you. Last week there was a lady at Bird Song, last Saturday, nice and with her husband. And the man fucked her, she was completely naked, 35 years and light hair, totally slim. He was damn good looking. He could be waded right into a Hollywood production! Huge limb and he came, so sperm sailed down her leg!

ACHMED: How could you see that ??

THE KING OF DK: I actually came a little late. I had seen, that they had arrived! I didn't know, they had come to fuck!! When I came there, I could see three guys standing with the dick in her mouth around her! They stood together the three guys, as they can, so she could reach all three of them! And then her husband was behind, and he just squirted, when I arrived! And then he took her, and then they slipped! And then the three guys stood with the thumping limbs!! She was sucking on them! And she also looked very disappointed, that he took her in the arm!

ACHMED: *"I'm done. Now we go! "Ha ha.*

KING OF DK: Yes, she looked over at me and smiled! And then I could see: *Fuck, now we're going to have women today?!* Him with the largest limb. Fucking big and stiff. Are you crazy?? He was two feet tall.

Then I got gangbanged with the three guys for 45 minutes and a fourth came. Shut up man! Him, the big one there, he was taller than me. He hung me up on the limb, and then he just had… .in forty minutes !? There I just hung! No, that was good! I thought, *"Fuck man, where do you have the leg muscles to stand?"!* It was just so good! All because of a woman disappearing from under their noses! But shut up there were a lot of people at Bird Song today! Down across the field, down in front of Bird Song. There were four or five other guys walking around with their pants down! - They were just so horny! There was such a fat guy of 24 years.

Yes. I have chased away those Italian campers, who have been staying at Poplar Circle, who had camped up there?! I think, it's the ones, who are sneaking around and in to the apartments of the older couple up there!? She got up and reached for her purse! And as he took her hands off her, and spoke to her in broken Danish!? These are the Roma, who resided over here at Poplar Circle!!

ACHMED: It's Roma? Not Italians?

KING OF DK: No, there are Roma, who would like to appear as families, and there are many ways, that they try to do so!

ACHMED: I always thought Roma were from Romania?? But maybe it's from Rome?

KING OF DK: Many of them do too! But I don't see, what else to do there?! For that is the few Italians, who drive to the Botanical Garden and live for a month!? I had to explain that to the police! But they were good at coming at the site. They drove out. I talked to them nine days in a row! And after those twenty days, we started calling 112! And told them: *"They're here now!"* And the police apparently drove out six times, before the left! So that in itself was provocative too!

ACHMED: *"She says, she wants a caravan!"*

THE **KING OF DK:** They had the system, that they kept up there two, every three days or every other day about. Then two came from outside! They had been up in North Jutland to steal, and came back with the goods and so on. So it was very organized! But it was typically not tourists!

ACHMED: But the police did not make searches ??

KING OF DK: No, there was no reason to suspect anything! Besides they had broken the parking laws !!

ACHMED: Mysterious !?

KING OF DK: And then things started happening! Else and I stood down under the bush once with some dogs, as a man was walking down the path and all the way down there! Then he left! And I saw, that he took the inside of the wall on the grass, and not in our lane. And when he then discovered us... ?? He hadn't seen us, because we were standing under the bush. It was raining a little. Then he got annoyed !? He didn't want to be seen. We could look at him. And Else said "Hi" - ha ha!

And then he couldn't help, but shudder a little! They got out of the cars in the evening, when it was getting dark or in the afternoon! And then they had to go around and rob! And that "we" stopped! But it took nine days!

ACHMED: And they had been here for twenty days?

KING OF DK: Yes. And the police had standing orders to get all Roma out of the country at the moment! It was something, they read in the TV newspaper, that there were 387, that you do not know, where is !?

And then I was over the border one day too! Last week! Didn't you call that day too?

ACHMED: Well, I guess, you said, you would!

KING OF DK: Well, now Mille has become a doctor, did you see that?

ACHMED: No, Doctor in what ??

THE **KING OF DK:** Culture! Moscow University gave her a doctorate! She received 500,000 or one million! Last week! Then shut up what a mess on the web! Inside Youtube! *"The stupid cow! They can keep her"*, someone wrote.

ACHMED: In French?

THE **KING OF DK:** Yes, yes. And then there is someone, who writes ..? And that's probably, what has caused the most anger! There is a girl of 22 years, who has written: *"Yes, Russia is also just the country in the world, which appoints, what is "tacky!"*

Amusing! Did I get a message?

ACHMED: That was probably my phone!

KING OF DK: No, mine is in slumber! Then something happened this afternoon, while I was gone!? Are you sitting on your "Grinder" - "Tinder"?

ACHMED: Yes.

THE **KING OF DK:** You get *"high"* on that! Don't you??

ACHMED: No, I have to admit that as time goes on, these are some kind of sad topics! And none of them write! And those who write there, I think, it doesn't matter! Or they are a hundred miles away! I simply don't want to commute a hundred miles away to get on a date ?!

THE **KING OF DK:** No!

ACHMED: Well, if it is the right one?? Good night!

KING OF DK: Here, just try to see her entrance at St. Peter's Square! Just try to see! They drive her into a horse pail, just like the queen! And she sang. She actually sang pretty well! She just had a great evening! Then the next day she had said: "Yes" to receiving such a doctorate there, but everyone in France is furious!

ACHMED: Gerald Depardieu has also got something?? Or was it just citizenship?

KING OF DK: Barbra Streisand received a culture doctorate from Harvard last year! That's fucking great!

ACHMED: Then Mireille got a doctorate, even though she never went to school ?!

THE **KING OF DK:** Mille has never gone to school! She's went out of seventh grade! Has anyone written anything to me? Because I just ...? I went in and wrote. What did I write down below ?? She sent me a whole script! *"Take that French!"* Ha ha. Then she wrote the model here:

La Russie est aussi le pays au monde qui desés ce qu'il est recard! Recard can almost be translated as" tacky! And there was one, that got furious! Shut up, he went nuts! George, he wants to defend Mireille as?

ACHMED: Like what?

THE **KING OF DK:** 72 years? My dad turned 75!

ACHMED: Your father?

THE **KING OF DK:** Yes!

ACHMED: So is he younger than my dad ??

THE **KING OF DK:** Shut up, he went crazy! *"The country that has Tolstoy, Kharkowski and so on, has nominated her for her contribution to Russian culture over five generations!"* She is the most popular singer in Russia! Over Elvis! There are two songs definitely! There are two specific songs! And the French press has not got it at all!? There are two specific songs. That one! When she had been a singer for five years, she made it here. It's a girl, who wrote it! *"Excuse me - my childish behavior!"* Sis and I made a circus inside the room, when we heard it. It had a sound like in a circus! The Russians absolutely love it! Even if they don't understand a meter!? There she goes to Starck's cottage in southern France. In Cannes he had a cottage! The Russians are very horny, and then one called "Ciao bambino, sorry!" It's the one, where she sings: *"Vas fumer ta marijuana!"* *Go out and smoke your marijuana!* "A la frontière de Nevada", in the Nevada desert! And then she sings: *"Redford, Newman, ça n'existe pas!".* *"Redford, Newman, they no longer exist!!".*

ACHMED: Well, but you can try to hear, if they can't put the basins outside next time, so you get a few extra square meters of terrace!

THE **KING OF DK:** It's like those wogs, who are neighbors of my dad and Else, who have been in TV right? Didn't you see the program, that was about "Hejredals street" two or three years ago? "One street - Two worlds?" My father's neighbors back there, they are one of the couples there. The convert, he's converted and she's .. ?? Well, but they came over a month ago and asked, if my dad and Else would help make a new hedge that separates their houses! It is my father's backyard, and because it is on a slope, they want it to be one meter inside his plot !! And Else has called them to say: *That it will not happen!! So there will be nothing, that you plant a hedge on our ground!!".* "Plant it on the division!" How naive can one be ??

ACHMED: *"We would like more land !!"*

THE **KING OF DK:** I was smoking a blunt in their garden the other day, and there I could hear them sitting, talking on the terrace! The scarf wife and her friend, and then there were three or four children running around! *"He's good for you! He wants your best! It's not because ...! No, you have to...? He must...?".* So that's what, it was all about! It was that the friend, who apparently did not like her husband, to whom she imported! And then she had to convince her, that he was good for her!? Stupid bitch!! Fuck, what an ugly burka fat girl, that I had to drive afterwards on the highway. So she just got the finger too!! Then a fat woman turns around in burka! She drove five miles on the highway, with a tail of cars behind her !? I overtook then!

ACHMED: And you couldn't overtake inside?

THE **KING OF DK:** Ehh ?? There were so many trucks !! I really wanted to, but I couldn't !! What is she driving in the overpass for ??

Have you eaten? Then your sister-in-law has come down to Aarhus... ??
Now they are lovers again?

ACHMED: Yes, they are totally in love!

THE **KING OF DK:** Yes, it's because, that's not, what they share!! But it is not with couples. When you get old, it becomes passion! There is nothing that can charm a girl like, if you can be there in the situation, where you need someone! Then you can have a girl, who actually didn't want you! If they are suddenly in a financial situation. So give her $ 200! Then she is sold!

ACHMED: The four minute test !! Just look them in the eyes for four minutes!

THE **KING OF DK:** Ha. Why do you think men, who have money, they easily score?? Just give them a hundred bucks!! Two hundred dollars!! When they have done it twice, she is hooked!

It's damn edgy, then this is being teased! But it was slavish. I've been hospitalized from Friday to Saturday! It was only 24 hours! I could barely keep calm! And the nurse that I got attached to, she was so boring! And then she started pissing me off! Then she started calling!! Instead of going down to the isolation room !? Cool bitch !!

ACHMED: Well, she called you??

KING OF DK: Yes, to my cell phone!? Because the cancer department is on the second floor, that the nurses belong to! And I was in the isolation room downstairs in the living room at the other end! There are 250 meters! Then she calls: *"What do you want to eat?"*. *"What can I get?"*. *"Look at the menu,"* she said! Then I looked at the menu! *"I'll take that fish fillet with shrimp!"*. *"You can't have that!!"*. *"Then give me, what I can get!"*. Then she came with two buns in curry !!? On a bloody rice !!? And then, I didn't see her anymore!!? Yes! Then she came at 8 with coffee !! And a piece of cake! 8. 8 o'clock! So, didn't I see her, until I saw the morning watch at eight in the morning!? Then I called her! There I could smell, that there was coffee out in the hallway! *"But that is coffee for the living room, so you can't have that!! It must be picked up on the second!"*. And then I couldn't have three eggs !?

ACHMED: That many!

THE **KING OF DK:** Many ??!

ACHMED: I can't eat three eggs!!

KING OF DK: After all, I'm so embarrassed, when I came back from the hospital! But I almost manage to explain it. Almost! Then I met an Olympic sports athlete. Something so nice! He had participated in a hundred yards of running in '84 and '88. He had fucking thin legs! He was in Seoul! But he manages to win - The Color of Gold! Then I had seen him three times. Then I thought: *"I'd rather ask, who he is?"* Such a man, he painted his eyebrows! 190 high! He ran ten miles every day, he told me, when I started talking to him! Then I said: *"I can't run !!"*.

ACHMED: No, that's boring!

What's going on ??

THE **KING OF DK:** I saw a sociologist, who said the other day on TV2 News, that if you want to be a star in today's Denmark, not least on Youtube, then you have to be willing to give in to your tragedies and tears! It's not at all like before, where you had to sing well, and go up on stage and look good! I also saw a young man on TV one evening, who said: *"I'm trying to forget, that I have a diagnosis!!"*. Try to think of all the moms, who diagnose themselves with their children, because it is an advantage for her! After all, they get money!! Most mothers end up getting 2/3,000 kroner, + Reduced working hours!

ACHMED: Because their child has a diagnosis ??

THE **KING OF DK:** And then there is nothing wrong with the kid!! Other than that he is cuddly!! I'm in the process of my second piece !!

So have you heard anything new from the case to come?

JOSEPH: No!

THE **KING OF DK:** No, but is she still thinking about it? Or is it ongoing? Or...?

JOSEPH: Yeah, I don't think, that mill can stop !!

KING OF DK: What are you saying?

JOSEPH: No, I don't think, it can just stop!

THE **KING OF DK:** No! It's just a matter of the number of cases, that they have, before you get a letter or ..?

JOSEPH: Yes! In each case, they have found out - the National Register, that is, what is the very big body! They are the ones, who have assessed me to be a resident parent! And it was a break-up period that Isa was "kidnapped" for three weeks, so it doesn't count! And after that it has been stable for seven days one place and seven days the other place!

But the residence is with me!

THE KING OF DK: Yes! Now, make sure you don't make it this far, that I'm losing the point !? They have established that ??

JOSEPH: I received a letter from the municipality saying, that they have finally found out, that I am a resident parent! They do not care about the decision of the State Administration! They have looked at the National Register!

KING OF DK: What was the mistake they made ??

JOSEPH: They have considered ...? After all, Mary has received the bill from the Waldorf Kindergarten! And after Isa has "lived" with me since May, even though she was kidnapped all month, I have to pay for the Kindergarten, and is not Mary, who has to pay! Then they will return the grant from the Kindergarten back to Mary, and then I have to pay the Kindergarten fee! I then have to apply for "free space supplement" and all that! So it is repay the money to Mary, and then Mary can give the money to me, and then I can give the money back to the municipality !!?

KING OF DK: Didn't you start by telling me, that they have found out, that you are a resident parent ??

JOSEPH: Yes! The municipality has just found out through the Population Register, not through the State Administration!

THE KING OF DK: Then it's you, who has to pay the bills for the Kindergarten back then?

JOSEPH: Yes, for kindergarten! It is me, who pays the bills for her school in the future! So now I also have to pay for the Kindergarten from the month of June, even though I paid Mary! And then Mary called the municipality and said: *It doesn't matter - I got the money from the resident father! So why are we going to change that?!*

THE KING OF DK: I have become good friends with Torben in number five. He has a wife named Annie, and they have a son of thirty-seven in Copenhagen, Finn. And Finn has become twenty-five pounds too fat, and he has psoriasis all over his body! And that's why, he's depressed. He is unemployed. He has been unemployed for fifteen years in Copenhagen. And he's with Torben and Annie, his parents, all the time!? Now they are in Rome again! Four times, five times a year they travel with Finn! He is thirty-seven years!?

ACHMED: "Find Finn sausage skins" on cash beneficial??

THE KING OF DK: On Cash beneficial! But Torben and Annie pay for his expenses. But why doesn't he move home, I ask myself?? What is he doing in Copenhagen? *"You sit and are depressed over at Norrebro or what?".* Because he is not a stranger to anyone!? He looks too .. ?? I was just on his facebook page. Fuck, he looks disoriented!! And he is fagot! I can look at him and see that! He can't come out of the closet?! To his father apparently!? And then he doesn't have sex, because he has psoriasis! And then he comes to live a sex-free life. Fortunately, I have no psoriasis. Cause one of the guys yesterday: *"Shut up, you got a nice ass!"!*

He said that completely unmotivated. Of course I was glad to hear it, but I also want to see for myself, what it is, that he thinks??

ACHMED: If only you could see, what I have seen, with your eyes!

THE KING OF DK: There was a Ph.D. student from Kiel, who a few years ago said, he had a very special ass! Well, I thought. We lay and banged. We rented a boat down the river Gudenaa. Then we sailed out, and then we simply lay in the canoe. Several sailors came by, and we were discovered in many places. Naughty!

ACHMED: I just asked, when I showed some young people this book, and then they read on the back. I asked if it was something, they would possibly read?

KING OF DK: It's postmodernist literature. It fits incredibly well with time! I have no doubt somewhere, that the little book has the right luck! Then it can be an extension of Paul Auster, and Stephen King !!

ACHMED: I don't know, if you can picture it ..? But I imagine, we are sitting in the desert talking together around a campfire! And have a small social debate/concession about everything that is in Denmark!

KING OF DK: But you do not control it with hard hand, what works!! So the one who doesn't know you, would ...? How would a reader perceive the book, that did not know us and our history? You don't even know?? Because as far as I see it, then is it postmodernism! There isn't someone, who controls the environment and the scene pretty hard ??

ACHMED: No?

KING OF DK: After all, it's not like H.C. Andersen: *"Denmark is a lovely country. There are lakes everywhere, and the ducks squeaking"*! And before he starts to tell, he gets the whole environment established!?

After all, there is freedom for the individual to decide for himself, what is going on!

ACHMED: But I still write over every chapter, that we're here in the Sahara desert, and what time of day it is ... But, uh ...?

KING OF DK: It could be a great fun idea. It could be that eh ..? Do you have an extra? So at some point it could be, that we could drop it over to Mina?? Then I will try to ask Mina: *"What do you think about this?"* Or I could include it in this literature group, I am in, in Silkeborg and ask them, without saying anything??

"When you get a book like this in your hand or show it, what do you think?" Cause I am going to meet with them here during the month, and there we will come up with suggestions for things to read. I simply can't read anything on command, when writing myself!!?

Where I write myself: *"Albert had always been a great opponent of immigrants, regardless of the country of origin. Denmark was for Danes, and here they spoke Danish!"* I have to have somewhere in the book, where I just like to say such a few things here. So now I've let it be said through a character. And then I sat the other day, and had to choose in levels now with care, how to describe a true Danish racist.

"Most people here were blue-eyed in the most positive sense of the word, and many had blond hair. The dark hair that the obvious immigrants and refugees wore stood out. And when a series of morning articles held a movement, he foresaw a cultural clash of disastrous consequences for Danish, and from then on completely avoided hiring than in socializing with foreigners!" Wasn't that a good sentence?

ALBERT: Yes.

THE KING OF DK: *"He forbade his buyers to shop in Bazar West on Edwin Rahrsvej".* There I deleted "in Brabrand!". *"Even though the goods you could buy there, were somewhat cheaper, always VAT-free and only rarely in unsatisfactory condition. Vegetables, in particular, were suspicious and could end up decaying before reaching home! But the prices were also accordingly! The price of meat was, of course, well below the market price, and it was halal slaughtered, which it could hardly be tasted. Women dressed in burqas and scarves, he called hooded gulls indiscriminately! And he called all Arab men either great criminals or thieves. "They don't know the Ten Commandments at all," he said, because he thought, they had no reason not to act!".*

No, I can see, that I must have changed the time a bit!!

"Over time he became a little more radical, but he did not change his attitudes. He quietly continued to remove things and to hide them from any vengeful thugs or Arab thieves, he imagined would come one day! ".

ACHMED: That sounds great! What do you call it: *"The murder in the City of Smiles?"*

KING OF DK: Yes. Now I'm five chapters in, and I'm still in the process of describing Axel and Albert, the two brothers whom Ali got a job in the house with and their prehistory! And I haven't actually come to that yet. I haven't told the whole story of the two yet. So things are going slow. But while I am describing them, I then get some such remarks about the immigrants in Denmark. For while in this description of Albert - While I read, Albert is sitting, rubbing some lotion into his fat fingers. Ha ha.

Am I excited when it comes out one day, whether people will like it? I have no doubt, that I can deal with any other writer. And I have more control over my grammar. No, I must stop now!

ACHMED: Now this is a movie script in a book form!

KING OF DK: Yes?

ACHMED: I've been in doubt, whether I should elaborate more features:

"He said, taking the cup with water and pouring over his head, because that was the only way, he could wash off the sand from this harsh environment!" ?

KING OF DK: That's another discussion, you're having there?? Then you tell me that: *Joe, I doubt, I should make it more reader friendly?? Do I need to help the reader a little more, so that he gets a better understanding?*

ACHMED: As I see it, it's just unnecessary filling!! And that's what Dan Brown uses, and which I quickly read past?!

THE KING OF DK: That's what, he does. And he already knows from the start, what he wants to go through, which is historical.

ACHMED: And the street as he describes it: *How many of the Corinthian-designed lamps, that were offset, and how many of them were lit!!*

THE KING OF DK: Yes, it makes me want to puke!

ACHMED: *And a dog that was barking in the background!* There are so many details, that one just thinks: *Shut up, you just fill up on indifferent* *information?! What is it about?? Why is it there? What does this have to do with the case?? Why? Is he schizophrenic??*

KING OF DK: Well, he just writes for movie screenplays. He is just trying to "paint" the picture itself. The director gets nothing left to himself! Because Dan Brown will decide it all!

"What is your novel about?". Fuck, it mentions several "crimes" and several "crimes" are resolved, so it's not just one mystery, it's three in one. But basically, it's all about immigration and the Gellerup planning. And I also write in the new things, that stay in it. The comic. I must have mentioned that at some point too! The Muhammad cartoons. Yes, it should be mentioned!

ACHMED: The drawings of Muhammad ??

KING OF DK: Yes. When we are that good at drawing from Aarhus! Then it should be mentioned.

ALBERT: Yes, that's right!

KING OF DK: You haven't been down to see the Queen's dresses? Ha.

ACHMED: No, at ARoS? No on ..?

KING OF DK: In the Old Town!

ACHMED: In the Old Town. No!

THE KING OF DK: Our parking lot was fucking completely filled up! It's just before, they drive up to our plenary on Saturday ?!

ACHMED: To come to see those dresses ??

THE KING OF DK: Yes, yes. It's sick!! It doesn't matter, what gets evicted from the royal address ??

ACHMED: Yes. Oh, I wrote a fun dialogue, which I also included in the new one. I don't think, it's included in this one? That they have found some scrolls, where one says that: *"We have to go to Denmark, there is one family, they get one billion kroner a year! And they get houses and cars and everything else for free. But okay, they are thirteen in their family too! But we are 48 Machmud after all, so we get a lot of money! Should we pack the camel and get going? "*. I think, that was how, I wrote it? Shut up man!

KING OF DK: *Pack the dromedaries, and let's go!*

ACHMED: No, I just think, it's really fun! And I have to admit, that while I wrote it, I thought: *Fuck, it's almost stuff for standup comedy on stage!* I just still haven't... ??

"I KNEW, YOU WHERE A MAN EATER!"

EXT-SAHARA Desert Evening

THE KING OF DK:

I haven't seen that movie with Stillman - but it is very much about AIDS?

ACHMED: Well? I heard my nephew talk about a movie, where a guy had a horse, which he was really pleased about. One day when he was out horseback riding, a stallion came by, who really wanted to fuck his horse! While him sitting on it!! He sank completely between the two horses in that intercourse. The stallion had its forelegs over his shoulders, and it moaned into his head!! It had been such a traumatic experience for him, that he had to shoot his horse, when he got back! Cause it had been too embarrassing! The whole village had seen the incident, and he was helpless. Just picture it. Hilarious!

THE **KING OF DK:** Was it a movie?

ACHMED: Yeah, it was a movie!

KING OF DK: Yes it sounds fun! The next movie that I look forward to seeing, I will watch it with my husband, is named "These Old Broads". It is a movie made in the years, that we traveled from Hollywood to Denmark in 1991-92. So it had its premiere in the US, right after we moved! And it has never been shown over here. I totally missed that both Elisabeth Taylor and Debbie Reynolds has parts. There are plenty of stars in it, Shirley Maclaine. They all have roles in it. There are also some smaller ones. Carrie Fisher is in it! She wrote it!

ACHMED: Princess Lea ??

KING OF DK: And because Carrie Fisher has written it, it makes it more or less autobiographical material! In any case, there is a scene with Elisabeth Taylor and Debbie Reynolds, in which they have to talk about something, they have become unkind to - a man! And the man, his name is Eddy Hunter. But in the real world in the 60s - in the 50s, Eddy Fisher was not a Hunter, but a Fisher. He was married to Debbie Reynolds and they got Carrie Fisher as their daughter.

ACHMED: But Carrie Fisher died before her mother ...

KING OF DK: Yes, it was last year! But Elisabeth Taylor, she took Eddy Fisher from Debbie Reynolds. Debbie Reynolds sent Eddy Fisher over to Elizabeth Taylor's house. They lived opposite each other, to comfort her! Elizabeth's husband had fallen and died! *"Why don't you go over there, and consult here for an hour?"* And then he never came home!? It's been the great drama of the late 50's! Or in the early '60s? I don't know, when it's ...? In any case, it is incorporated into that movie! There Debbie Reynolds says: *"Oh no, I forgive you years ago!"*. *"I knew, you where a man eater!"* She says that to Elisabeth Taylor. And Elisabeth Taylor answers with total lack of acting. So, she was really a lousy actress: *"Yoou Thiink everybody, who has a normal sex life, is a man eater!!"*. She speaks in a bad English, and I can't understand why, it hasn't been re-recorded or "Another take!"?? Let's see that movie! It's probably fun!

But the Hollywood era is falsehood and lies, and it's over!

In reality, we should produce a movie, about a man who gets beaten, until he dies!! And then get a really well-known actor to take on the part. One that gets prober beaten!

ACHMED: By his wife?

THE **KING OF DK:** Yes, it will be extra juicy by his daughter!

ACHMED: By his daughter??

KING OF DK: Of his daughter and son knocking him out, one with a bucket and the other with a baseball bat!

ACHMED: But that's what Angora Boys did long ago!

"Here father" - "Aw" - "Here father" - "Aww!"

THE **KING OF DK:** Yes, that's right, there was something! But if they had built on it! They didn't, they totally, let it go! It was not proven, what they meant by that!? It was just hovering in the air! If they had built a character? If they had the opportunity to make Angora films, then? But it ended! Nobody wanted to record movies!?

ACHMED: My mom has a birthday today, so when I was out there. Then I said: *"Aw. I've been raped"*!

THE **KING OF DK:** Group Rape??

ACHMED: No, the "wild cat" that I was with! Then my mother said:

"Did you have sex with her?? We didn't have sex with each other, until a year had passed !!"

THE **KING OF DK:** *No! What decade do you live in Lilly??*

ACHMED: *Yes, I can't wait another year!*

THE **KING OF DK:** *"Lilly - You are becoming like grandma!"*

ACHMED: *"I was only seventeen. You didn't do something like that at that time!!".*

THE **KING OF DK:** *"In '69 there you ran around with tits and headbands! And smoked marijuana mom - Did you forget that?? ".* No, your mother didn't!

ACHMED: No, I don't think so!?

THE **KING OF DK:** No, mothers, they are perfect for lying! After all, there were someone, who has been grouping for Jimi Hendrix and Elvis Presley?? No one will officially admit it!! Only in France! There the women queue to enter the TV studio, to tell, who they have fucked with! It's just so crazy! I can see, the older I get, that he has some eligibility. But as a kid, I couldn't see why, Chevy Chase was so popular!?

ACHMED: Well, I could see it back then! But today I have a hard time coping with him! Yeah, I think he was funny! Back then!

THE **KING OF DK:** It was fun, too - "National Lampoon's Vacation"!

ACHMED: Yes, it was a bestseller! Everyone has seen it!

KING OF DK: Because when I don't bother to watch any movie at all, because I think movies are a musty thing! Then I think that "National Lampoon's Vacation" at Christmas, when we have eaten, and I do not bother to see "The Sound of Music", then "National Lampoon's Vacation"! There is such a commotion in it! Also the ugly kid moving in and the ugly brother-in-law. And it all goes wrong for his light show !!

ACHMED: I saw Griswalt, as the family is called, I saw his son take the same trip, as his father had given him on vacation to an outdoor water park. Then they end up bathing in sewer water!! They took a shortcut to the water park, and did not reach the right basins. But jumped into something, that they thought looked like a fountain! And their car was smashed in the meantime. And they end up driving home to their parents, where Chevy Chase is the father! He's in for five minutes! Yes, it was a lot of fun too!

THE **KING OF DK:** You haven't heard anything from him! But you heard one of his colleagues? What the hell was his name? Also from Saturday

Night Live? They have all become stars that way! What the hell was his name?? He made as many films as Chevy Chase, but him and his wife have become homeless!!

ACHMED: Yes and Bill Cosby is getting ten years in prison!

THE **KING OF DK:** Ten? Did he get it?

ACHMED: No, but he's going to court, and he's going to be sentenced to ten years!

KING OF DK: He has behaved badly all his life too! And sometimes he treats them, and then she comes with such a charge!

JOSEPH: No, I should have written a consent statement too!

"I have the right to tie you to the radiator!". "Bite your lips!" "Rip your hair!". "Lick, and twist your ...?".

KING OF DK: Then it reveals in the case, that you should have known, that she was a victim of a sex offender, and you took her for a very vulnerable period! Women can really focus on such things. If you look at Mary, and Mary is in a fierce bombardment, because you are her closest and "her father" and so on, to become the solution to the financial problem, that she just suddenly pushed herself into! There will come more of them Joseph! And you must pair against them, and you should not give her personal information in connection with all the offenses there! Even though you will be glad, she just suddenly shows you that confidence, nothing lies deep in it! It is just her language. And at some point the attention will come away from you towards some other guys, with whom she can play something like that! And you can do that with guys. Odin meets several, who has such a story in their past! And then he has to step in and be the prime mover for such some half-alcoholic girls, who want nothing even!!? Other than being a good mother! And I don't know, if they really are!?

JOSEPH: But I really wanted to. And I'm glad, she's suggesting, that we should share the children's support. Because I can figure, that she has received around 100,000 kroner, and let's just share them!!

THE **KING OF DK:** How has she been able to get 100,000??

JOSEPH: Well, Mary's got $700 a quarter for Isa for the first three years, and then it drops a little year by year by a few bucks.

THE **KING OF DK:** That's the money, she's missing now!

ACHMED: She has received close to DKK 100,000 !!

THE KING OF DK: A year ??

JOSEPH: No! In six years!

THE KING OF DK: Well. Well, that's the money, she's missing now! And those are the ones, she's fighting to get back!

JOSEPH: That's it! Now she must try to live without! *"But now we have her for seven days each, is it not fair, that we share the money !?".* I think, I will let the lawyer consult me here!

KING OF DK: But now we have January, then you can share them anyway!!

JOSEPH: No, it's not in January, it's not until April! But there is no date. The Parliament has unanimously decided, that divorcing couples must share residence and child allowance!

THE KING OF DK: But are you divorcing couples??

JOSEPH: After all, we're a parent couple with shared custody, and now we don't live together anymore, after 11 years!! So I think so !!

THE KING OF DK: That they interpret it this way?

ACHMED: Yes, that is how, it is interpreted in each case, if you need to receive cash assistance !!

THE KING OF DK: Then I think, there's even less reason for you, to join this case! And she has? She comes with....? Well, the least you can say to her is: *Well, you are bringing a lawsuit against me now!! Well then don't! Then you have to withdraw that case !?* - Crazy bitch !!

JOSEPH: Yes, she said, she would like to withdraw, if she is allowed to reside. She had to use the residence, so she could get some more economy support! She can get that, if she has the residence!

"And you do not receive housing subsidy !!".

THE KING OF DK: Aren't you !?

JOSEPH: No, but I get the child allowance and child support now! I receive approx. DKK 6,000 a quarter for the first time ever!

KING OF DK: Yes. Well! But then you lose them, if you lose your residence !?

JOSEPH: I'll lose them, if I give her the residence!

KING OF DK: Then you lose more, than she wants to get ?!

ACHMED: No, because then she will also be able to receive different child allowance and housing allowance!

THE KING OF DK: Something completely different on a slightly more idealistic level, that is! Don't you also think, it is a little ridiculous to give your daughter residence to a girl, who is so ...? What should we call it?! Who has a loose agenda with Isa's basis of existence, that can so quickly, tear her up and out and at the asylum center and everything possible !?

ACHMED: Yes, right!

THE KING OF DK: So what if she goes to the moon next time, if you give her the residence?? Then you have NOTHING to say!??

ACHMED: No!! She can do, whatever she wants!

THE KING OF DK: Yes! No, she is crazy then!! I think, that if my dad had given my residence "away" to my mother, I would be shocked today!? I'm damn glad, he was strong in all, that he was through! Or else?? So all the violent things, that happened around me, they were weighed down by the fact, that he was hard as granite!! He could handle everything! Lions!! He made us believe that! And we were scared, if we saw him weak! It was the way, that we rested within ourselves, my sister and I. It was because, we had a strong and rich father!

JOSEPH: And you know what? That's how Isa rests!

KING OF DK: Knowing that you are stable!

JOSEPH: I called Mary on Saturday, but she didn't even pick up the phone. But they called right back two minutes later, where Mary then said:

"Yes, we just had a controversy! She only wants to wear rubber boots, but she has to wear sneakers!! It is no good! Can't you help explaining it properly to Isa??".

Isa is not making any controversy at home with me!? At All!! And she never has!! Never! I've always had to repeat Mary's words to emphasize:

"Isa now you listen exactly, what Mom says!".

KING OF DK: Well, you knew that a year and a half ago! That it is so!

ACHMED: And there will be much more to come! Isa becomes contending with her mother!

THE KING OF DK: You can say to Mary: *"What I offer my daughter at this time, is to be the stable of us two parents! And that means, among other things, that she has her residence with me - Mary! Under no circumstances I could think of giving you the residence! You could live on the moon by next year! I have no idea?! It is not longer!".*

It isn't fun to be a kid, where you just fly between parents!? And she was born and raised there, so there is no reason! Mary should have reflected on this in advance!? So I'm excited, if your lawyer will advise you any differently?? Then you shouldn't give him a damn salary!

JOSEPH: She! We have our girl 50/50, so I can help her sharing half the quarter! To show some goodwill too! But not to move the residence!

THE KING OF DK: But that will be the case in the future anyway! From April or when ..?

JOSEPH: Yes, at least in the next year!

THE KING OF DK: I don't see you speeding up either way!? Possibly as a "punishment" for all that she has done, so don't rush it!

"So no! In fact, I do not think, that you have been very sympathetic in this process, where you abducted our daughter and so on. So no can't do bitch!!".

She has shown all signs on how not to behave with sympathy!? And it is doubly unsympathetic to run the tone, that she is running now! Because she does not stay on the other side of the upcoming case or below! It will be the same Mary again!

JOSEPH: But she actually wasn't! She was cute as an angel! Heart warm and easy to tears! Talked about how hard, she had it! And went to the park, gathered apples, so that she could make applesauce, and put it on oatmeal!

"Well then, shouldn't we suggest that all the child allowances go to Mary??" asked the female judge! *"Ahh, Joseph has the same basis of existence! Your Honor, he is just accountable with a bank!"*

But I like to share! Equality! So if I write anything, and now I have not answered it yet! Because I would have discussed it with the family over the weekend, but I didn't actually! Just good to hear some other arguments!

KING OF DK: It's a desperate attempt to get some money! These are the opportunities, she has!

JOSEPH: She's started to do some black cleaning work!

THE KING OF DK: Then we must hope, that she doesn't get caught!? Because then she has nothing! It's such a thing, that they want to stop! And we are so far inside the surveillance community! Just that the municipality, they get the news, that she spent more money in a month, than she earned, then the hammer falls! In other words, cash beneficiaries, they have to take care of having a consumption - on paper! In any case, it must be black money, that they spend for the rest of the money! We are in a monitoring community, where such things need to fit together! It was, also what my grandmother was called for, when she had a perfume shop down in Bruunsgade sometime in the 70s. In 75 there she was fined 50,000 kroner. That was a lot, a lot of money back then! It was basically about having her under observation – the Tax office! And they had seen her consumption, the purchase of cars and that it far exceeded, what she had from the income in the perfumery! So it was black, that she ..? Everything she sold was black! Surely in such a business inside Bruuns!? But one had a much more solvable attitude towards black money. And today they well know that 75%, they have black cleaning! Kenneth and Brian have a "black" nanny for their twins! We saw them just the other day, coming with the twin van!

ACHMED: A black and white baby?

THE KING OF DK: A man of 55! And a man of 50! Two twins!

JOSEPH: Isa's best friend's father is living the life of grand fraud. Where he has set up with a Latvian bank account, a Gibraltar company, and an online business in Spain! At the same time, lives in Hojbjerg in a newly built house, with B&O in all rooms. A big SUV Audi, automatic transmission, leather seats, and of course a Cooper S for the wife. Now he has been in a Spanish prison from summer to December! His friends deceived him! They took drugs! Cocaine! Copied his business plan, and shut it down, and he ended up in prison! The kids don't know anything!

"No, dad is at work honey - in another country!". He has not seen his children, or attended children's first day of school, all semester in fact!?

THE KING OF DK: Then he gets out of the picture at some point?! Then you hear ..? Then you go in these years thinking....?? All those who in my school class in Brabrand, we went to class with Leo Sorensen, the

105

haulage company, and so was Kjeld Tolstrup's father. He was editor-in-chief of Jutland Post. And then there was Lars Moller's father, he was the architect, who invented the cube for recycling! And then there was Marianne Justensen, her father had invented the auger. We were in competition with everyone! And Anette, an adoptive child, her father owned a shipping company down at the harbor! A huge shipping company with 50 employees! They went bankrupt one by one ... ?! Kurt Tholstrup was fired as editor-in-chief. So he was probably the one, what to say?? The most creative of them all - my dad!! Although it took a long time, and it did not appear like that !!

ACHMED: The hypnosis guy, Jan Hillingso, has a dating program, with people who can't sell themselves or date others. And here he is helping a guy, who is only 21 years old, who says to his date:

I grew up in Sweden, started a company as an eighteen-year-old, and as a nineteen-year-old I got the first employee, and as a twenty-year-old I had 30 employees. Now I've had three companies, and I just sold it all and retired!

With his latest girlfriend, he had just sold the companies and earned the cash, but then she broke up !!

THE KING OF DK: Well, he can't be very delicious ?!

ACHMED: He was a nice guy!

THE KING OF DK: Well? Was he?? Then he has a small dick!! So there is some secret here because, if women really don't want a guy, who is rich...??

ACHMED: He wants a girl, who won't take him just for the money! But it made no sense, that he then opens his conversation with that statement!?

THE KING OF DK: It is also peppery to turn, when you are first rich. Then the power issues are hard !!

ACHMED: Then you have to play Beggar Boy!! Like me! The Wild Cat took off, when I said, I'm on "cash benefits"! No, it didn't turn her on! She did not pass the "test" - The Prince and the Beggar Boy !!

KING OF DK: Here I think specifically about some of that Judy Garland complaining in the CD releases, that have come in the last twelve hours, where she speaks in a Dictaphone. Some of what has gone really wrong in her life is, that she doesn't like men!! From the age of fourteen, after she was in the "Wizard of Oz", all the men take her with the object of being Judy Garland! It was damn hard! Yes. Thanks for the cake! Want the rest home?

ACHMED: Yes! Then I have to offer a guest, if I should be surprised, and get a visit from someone special! I just need to relax on my birthday tomorrow. Although my parents were quick to say:

"We'll pass by!". "I need nothing. My door phone is switched off and the doors are locked! And I just have to sleep for a long time, and look for some jobs! ". And play with my bright "Cat"! "

THE KING OF DK: Yes, it's great to have free time!

ACHMED: It was nice!

KING OF DK: Yes, it was definitely nice! Do you have your bag out there?

JOSEPH: Well, yes, thank you for the CD and the honey! I was just in a recycling shop finding some children's books!

THE KING OF DK: Well to Isa?

JOSEPH: Yes! I found one with all the princess adventures with Cinderella, Snow White and so on! I've been told, that you have to read for your children!

THE KING OF DK: Yes, you should too! Because as I remember it: *Fuck my world opened to my inner gaze!* It's so great to read! It gives a rest!

ACHMED: Yeah? I have to admit, that my parents didn't read to me! But my biology teacher / geography teacher / history teacher read in all his classes for all of us students! And he used it as a means of pressure, if we didn't behave properly in the classroom. Then there was no five minute reading! He was also the librarian!

THE KING OF DK: Was it just five minutes of reading??

ACHMED: He spent five or ten minutes reading, while we were drawing. And if we were nice, he read for a little longer. But if we weren't nice, then there just wasn't storytelling! It also meant that, if there was any trouble in the class, and there was no reading! Then it wasn't the teacher, who was unpopular! It was all of them, who were guilty of making trouble!! It was a little ugly! It smells a little ugly here !?

KING OF DK: Yes, I just turned on a menthol!

ACHMED: But the wild cat is a smoker! And she smokes joints, and she likes to take drugs. She started by saying: *That if you are going to be with me, then you must respect, that I use drugs!* But you know what? My brother said the same thing to his girlfriend, when he met her! I've been on six / seven dates so far. But here she is, she is almost certainly my dream woman!

KING OF DK: But you must discover something !?

ACHMED: Well, after I met her, I had considered deleting my tinder profile! Not to say that, I'll hold on to her! But more to express: *I actually think, I'm well stocked !! And I don't feel like exposing myself to multiple rapes any longer !!* Yes, that was good! God damn, it was good !!

KING OF DK: Ha ha! Yes, that's how, I feel every day! I fell asleep here today, with the idea that fuck life is good! I could hardly wake up again !!

JOSEPH: Marie, and not Mary, would have sex almost every day, in several places and in every room! And I was ready! But I have to admit, that I think, I was filled up then too !!

THE KING OF DK: You've also just played a family father for a long time!

JOSEPH: For ten years now, I have totally cast sexual energy and urges! But now it woke up! Now comes the force, who just says:

Should we continue, where "we" went off ?? Where you left the idea??

THE KING OF DK: Well, there are ladies, who are at least as naughty as men! So just look at those, who wear the dress! Why do some women insist on going in a dress?? That's because, it's easy! And most people go with rings!?

ACHMED: I told her, that my samurai sword was to flake her clothes off!! And she was turned on!! The more naughty, dirty and more vulgar !!

KING OF DK: Yes, you just have to find another energy! You have to be able to play on the entire register, and not just that!

ACHMED: So do I!

KING OF DK: Because you get tired of it! Because I am tired of meeting such guys, who want it a little hard! So it's fun once!

ACHMED: Yes you do. And it was also only that one time. But it was 24 hours in a row!!!

KING OF DK: You have to be able, to keep on turning on each other! Always!

ACHMED: Yes - always!

THE KING OF DK: That's good! Men also get absolutely crazy at the thought! Danish women put up with Danish men for three years on average! It's hard to keep it running for 25 years. My husband and I had 23 years, before we "stopped"!! So there you can see, it is another starting point! Instead of being upset: *Well, now we don't do it anymore! Should we then go apart?? No! We don't have to!* And in the meantime, between all the fun and the good, and the stable, I think, it was cool, that he wanted me! And I was so coveted for so long! Then it started to fill less! But today we are just such good friends! The other day I said:

Are you sorry, we didn't celebrate our silver wedding? No, we'll celebrate 50, he said! Then I was totally touched! Then I was just about to start whining! But I didn't do it !! No!! Well, but happy birthday tomorrow!

ACHMED: Yes! And make a good day my friend! Hey.

THE KING OF DK: Hello!

ACHMED'S BIRTHDAY
EXT Sahara Desert - Morning WILD CAT

I met a girl at the winter swimming club a few years ago, pretty, blonde, naked. I walked over to her, and stood right in front of her with a casual towel! I had overheard her talk about an injury, she had sustained. She had a neural damage. We stood with approx. three feet's distance, so there was a good view both ways. My brother is trained in cranio sacral therapy, so of course I suggested to her this method for *"bad nerve pathways"! "Really? Does it work? I do not know of that! I have to try that, please!".* It's some years back! I have often seen her since, because she cleans the place!? Scrub the toilets, showers, wood benches, floor, fixtures, everything! She arranges trips to other swimming facilities for the club and...!? And then she is trained as a CRANIOSACRAL therapist, and provides on site treatments!!? It's funny! No, you have to monitor your words with care, even just the short sentences that can have a landmark meaning in the other! Exchanges matter! But emotions apply both ways. Especially when you meet, and get to know the other over a few days, how much we as "anonymous people" are exposed to words, actions and courage! You can quickly push each other!

I'm good at finding them on Tinder! The girls! It is especially the girls, who in their daily subjects either as educators, life coach, occupational therapist, nurse and so on have to deal with severely disabled and brain damaged patients in their work!! And they say that I *"remind a little of their "citizens"!!?"*. Thanks!! She was my first blonde, the Wildcat on my *"half ninety"* birthday! I probably haven't been a gentleman! She had brought no gift! I had written to her that: *I was a Jehovah's Witness, and did not celebrate my birthday, but just come! It will be nice, and I will be happy, "Joy Girl" at 28!* Social-health worker at a place of residence for the severely brain-damaged patients, heavy lift, diaper change, personal care, washing their penises. *"Loves her job"*, and her sour matron executives. She likes to post before and after pictures on her instagram about the glorious morning guards, night guards. But she gets angry and leaves, if they get too close and wants sex. She dreams of sex, all the time!! Nymphomaniac! With slow orgasms that last forever, and she like repetitions, because it's better the second time! And amazing the third time! Then she lies completely unconscious, staring blankly into the air, with red cheeks! Because she had accidently smelled the sweat of some young teenage boys, who had been in the public bus!? And they were boys, who were on their way home from a soccer practice!? Sex, sex, sex! So I had bought a gift for her on my birthday! Where she arrived small, petite, slim, fit, tight! A dildo! Black! Monotone! Yes. I know, that not everyone would be happy about such a gift. But she was! She even used it within 30 minutes, after she received it, while I was collecting takeaway!! And I was glad, she got it! Because then mine could also be relieved! Her first three sentences were:

"I use drugs, and I love it! I will not stop! I owe a lot of money away! And have to appear in court - But I'll just stay away! I've done credit card scams with someone else! I'm kleptomaniac! I steal from people's pockets, so they sponsor my trips, when I'm at a disco! I have been caught shoplifting with three pair of pants, where I just bought the one!

I smoke a blunt every night! I'm not running until after dark! I love electronic music! Unterwelt goes straight in the panties! I throw all my clothes and dance on the tables, when I'm at "Hats" in Randers, and I just chill too wild! It is awesome! I get the wildest kick, as I walk down the strip and show off my tattoos in thigh short dress! Especially when the older men turn to me, and the wives say, "Did you see, how she was tattooed?". Huhh that makes a rush! My New Year's resolution was that: I should be "tattooed all over my body in under a year!" Some of them I paid with sex!

And the tattoo artist has a big dick! And I just scored him! But he is not as good at tattooing as my new friend! I love my friend! My girlfriends are almost all diagnosed borderline, and I think, I am too?? My parents got divorced, when I was 16! My father is stationed at the Thule base, and has got a new Greenlandic girlfriend! So I'll see him again in three months for Christmas!! Long distance relationships do not last! Since I was 16, I have lived in communities around the country, and had sex with a lot of men, but have only had three boyfriends! The last relationship lasted for 7 years! I've never been my boyfriend unfaithful! But he had been unfaithful for five of the years, I found out! I'm good at spotting something like this and other girls' hair! Don't be unfaithful to me!

I like to watch porn, and double penetration turn me on! My latest Tinder boyfriend was a guy from Aarhus V, Bispehaven, who from the second day would only fuck me in the ass, while he was choking me, so I was fainting! And I loved it! I cleaned his entire apartment, when he had visits of his son, but he wouldn't let me meet him! He borrowed money, so he could go on trips with his son without me! We were together for four months! I often drove down to him, didn't I! From Randers! And he could swear at me, and call me a sow, if I just came by unannounced! I still write to him, because he owes me 2,000 kroner!

I've been fat once, but I'll never be fat again! So I eat lots of lactic acid bacteria, and sometimes I take from the strong medicine cabinet of the residence for my own consumption!! I once infected my rich ex-boyfriend with Chlamydia, on purpose! So he was to infect his new girlfriend! If you do not know, you are infected, and if she doesn't get a treatment, then she may risk being sterile! I flashed to her down in Brugsen, as I passed her - Here's how! They are both two of rich families, horses! So it was great to get back at them! I have strength minus 6 on one eye, and am almost blind! Wears with disposable lenses, but I also have some great glasses!

I love sex, and it has to be monotonous always! With variations you break the rhythm, and then you have to start over!".

I have two cats. "Peanut" and "Samba" and they have to sleep in the bedroom in the bed, except when we are having sex. Then they interfere with my concentration! So you decide, how much you want to see the cats?? ". "Yes, you haven't said a wrong word yet !!". I mumbled!

And then she stood in my living room, dancing to electronic music with all her close off! And I danced closely! And there was only her, wild cat! Klit Kat!

She had three hundred dollars in her account, when we wrote the tenth of the month!? And she had just spent DKR 1,500 on a new tattoo with "whip shading" of flowers!? Floral decorations? But she had become godly, and looked like a young beautified version of Marilyn Monroe! She wasn't just a fat peasant girl anymore! Her first sexual debut was with the utility merchant. He was 21 years old! She was 16! It was at a Christmas lunch in the shop! And they fucked out in the parking lot, where she rode on top of him!

It went well, as long as we met at my place! We never left the apartment, only once for an electronic event! And she was a little sad because of the leadership in the job! I had brought three small vodka bottles and some soda! But those bottles were empty within 15 minutes!? Her social anxiety should be thrown away, instantly! She consumed it without soda! And the stockings were to be thrown, so you could see her tattoos on her legs! In the dark rhythmic theater! A theater that I have designed in the expansion of the Music House! *"Where are the toilets?"* She asked! Yeah, where the hell was it, that we ended up squeezing them in!? It's been almost 15 years, since I designed the scheme! *They are just outside! But just throw it here! Yet it is so dark, that no one sees it!* But I saw it! She was a masterpiece!

I did not look at the theater, the DJ Bjorn Svin (He is not pig!!), who danced in his strange way, but only at her! It went on for so long, it lasted! Condensed with hours, and days! She said, she was best to come visit! And after visiting her for four days, it became too much for her! I gave her an Eckhart Tolle book about The Power of the Now! There might be some tools to relieve some trauma!? Especially if it could last for long! I read the book aloud to her, while we were sitting in the bathroom! She thought I had a good reading voice! She didn't know him! But she had all of Jim Carrey's good advice posted on her facebook, quotes by Eckhart Tolle!? She was happy, free and alive! The fridge was empty! The mattresses lay flat on the floor! The bed creaked too much, when having sex! So it was removed. There was listening in the old half-timbered house at Slotsgaarden! But she could break up a loaf! And make soup! And she had the most beautiful blue eyes, almost only surpassed by Terence Hill! Oh but....

RANDERSVEJEN BLIND ROAD?
EXT - SAHARA DESERT EVENING

THE KING OF DK:
Hey, hey - Come in, come in! Lock the door!

ACHMED: Vie - Yes!

KING OF DK: Hello!

ACHMED: Hello!

KING OF DK: So you got to drive to Randers? It's slave to drive that way huh?

ACHMED: No, I don't know? - I'm taking Randers road!

THE KING OF DK: Well! Ha ha!

ACHMED: Yeah, I don't mind driving on the highway, headwind! Then I can squeeze it up a hundred!! You are watching Frasier - for a change ?!

THE KING OF DK: Yes we do, always! I just said to my husband:

Don't we have one of the sections, where Frasier dates more women?? And so they are part of it! There are some, that are fun! Where he is about to touch a woman at his piano, and then the phone rings. And the answering machine is: *"Oh Frasier, about our date tomorrow night ..?!"* They are funny!! All is well?

ACHMED: Yes, I think so!

THE KING OF DK: Are you balding Achmed, or have you been shaved?

ACHMED: No, I've shaved myself! But yeah, I'm bald!

KING OF DK: Can't we get hair done at Mogens? Such a long Brigitte Bardot hair? Or Bob Marley?

ACHMED: Yeah, and I also thought, you could just get a wig and then glue it on, and that's the concept too! But these are disposable wigs!? That is, they last for four weeks, and then it starts to lose hair! And you have to have a new one! And it costs at least 1,800 kroner !?

KING OF DK: What kind of hair is that? Are they real hair?

ACHMED: Well, yes, unless they put gray hair in!

KING OF DK: I want Chinese hair! It's probably cheap!

ACHMED: Cheap and Hairstyle! That's between DKR 1200 and DKR 1,700 in a fixed subscription in fixed costs for such a hair craze! Per month! So it is not a very cheap pleasure! You can smoke that much!

THE KING OF DK: Yes! It's more expensive, than having a wig anyway!

ACHMED: Have you got a new pusher?

THE KING OF DK: No!! Sure, I've gone back to an old pusher! As I know, buy something cheap! And I can stay away from smoking! When I buy for a thousand kroner, I get ten grams! Skunk! And it is powerful! If I smoke a joint! Bing, then I'm crooked! The way I smoke now, it's just to soothe the medicine, that I should have from the doctor! I save the community a lot of money!

ACHMED: Yes, you self-medicate! But the wild cat smokes too!

THE KING OF DK: Well, Randers the girl! It is great to have someone, who has a relaxed attitude to it!

ACHMED: Yes, then she brings a small chunk home from work!

KING OF DK: Is she getting it at her job??

ACHMED: Yes, by her colleagues!

KING OF DK: Yes ok! Should we just go in, and get something to eat? Well, but that's nice! It's in a section with Niles, where he dates younger! Her unbearable! We need to hurry, we have a lot, that we need to see! I also just saw "Clown". It was fucking mega fun!

ACHMED: It was?

THE KING OF DK: Yes!

ACHMED: It wasn't yesterday?

THE KING OF DK: Yes, I saw it this afternoon! There was at least some fun! Now, of course, I won't say too much!

ACHMED: Did you get curved toes?

THE KING OF DK: Yes, I must say that! The way that they got to do, what they were supposed to do, it was not in my spirit at all! Frank and Mia going on threesome sex?

ACHMED: Threesome sex? Oh boy!

THE KING OF DK: Mia was dressed up, and Frank was going to talk to the gentleman, whom she had chosen! That's not my way! I think, that's too brutal! Never expose your wife to that! Cause had he said no? Then it could have killed their sex life - Forever!! Because women cannot bear to be rejected! Rejections! You must never reject your partner! Then you have to find another way, if you want to hurt your partner! But when you find out, which points you can reject, don't do it! Because then the partner will not stay with you!! That's what many people are mistaken for! So if she just rejected him twenty-five times a day. Today, like Odin! When Odin has been with a girl for just three days, and the crush on him goes over, he continues to bring flowers, even though he has a bad conscience!! And there is a time, when they start rejecting the flowers, and then he becomes totally unhappy!!

ACHMED: But could he be turning on rejections?

THE KING OF DK: No! Unfortunately! He grabs so many ladies, then he quickly jumps on the one, who is a little more friendly than her, who is not friendly! So that way he has no stability either! Than a Charles Aznavour, who has been fifty years with Ulla! His third wife! Because Ulla could give him the quality of life, that he lacked as a famous star in France! She could give him stability! She could get him down to earth! They had three children! There, of course, she has demanded, that he join social events with the children! And he has come to love it so much, that he could reject all the ladies on the world tour and so on. Because there are many other artists, who can't at all!! I couldn't either! Ha ha! Even for the party I was at, there was something so fun! And there were transvestites! One of them was trans from Brazil, with a proper horse cock! He fucked me so much, he could barely walk in the end! Him the Brazilian trans, he had one thing in his head! He wanted to see people coming!! All those with whom he was engaged, I could hear him speak:

Have you come ?? Have you come? Have you come? Why is Brazil sending a trans?? Catholicism is tough on anyone! For Marcus, as I knew, he could do everything possible in bed, as not many others could!

ACHMED: I should say, that the Randers girl knew nothing about boundaries either!! She was hoping, I would jump on her anytime soon - again! Even as we sat by her sister and brother-in-law, who had just had a newborn baby !!

THE KING OF DK: That's great! That's great! If you have an appetite for it? But then you run into the problem, if that situation should arise, that you do not want to!! But you have??

ACHMED: Yes, yes, but probably not as much desire as she has! I also like to smoke tobacco, but I take it out of my mouth once in a while! But then she doesn't say anything! I'll just hear her thoughts later!

WILD CAT: *Yeah, it was a shame, you didn't just jump me yesterday!!? I felt really horny!!*

ACHMED: *Really!? When you fell asleep on the couch for Netflix?? And I had to drag you to bed?? And I lay playing with your newly tattooed hand?? Who did you want?? I thought you were sleeping !?*

THE KING OF DK: Then Achmed must move to Randers!! Randers??

ACHMED: No, I'm not moving up there!!

THE KING OF DK: They have such a big metal horse !!

ACHMED: Yeah, she just lives three steps and a spit from there!!

KING OF DK: Well? In the city? That's great! I cut some thin strips of meat! It has simmered a little since 12 o'clock!

ACHMED: Okay? Then it is tender too!

KING OF DK: That's it! I've just been up at Grethe with food!

ACHMED: Is she still hurt?

KING OF DK: Nah, but I just thought, there was so much! And then I had the roast for only seventy kroner! Then I thought, when I have so much, I have to hand out! She's happy about that! Then she'll probably die soon! So everything with the elderly, they come to such an age, where food becomes a diffuse subject for them!

ACHMED: Yes, it's because of the teeth! Any taste becomes irrelevant!

THE KING OF DK: Yes! And from there, things like that go really strong!

ACHMED: When you say your grandmother is fat, and her doctor says, she shouldn't lose weight because; then it was a sign, that you were heading down! *You should keep the weight up !!*

KING OF DK: And my dad has just been out there! I said it before, and I told him. He suddenly said to me one day:

No, I don't want to eat anymore!

Then it is clear, that when you have four teeth, that you cannot use! It is good, that you say that dad, then you can start preparing for us! Because then there is only one way, I told him. And I saw that with both my grandmothers! From they said, what you say there, to the grave that took one year! And that is right! Both my grandmothers dyed of old age. They were 94 and 93! But we could keep them alive, just like any of them who come on TV, if they wanted to eat! They couldn't bear the little illnesses, that came in the 90s. They had become too exhausted!

Well! We must have my world famous mashed potatoes!

ACHMED: It looks so good!

KING OF DK: And I've served it both for a guy in Australia, one in England, and with my husband in the US! It was actually the mashed potatoes, that made him propose to me!!

ACHMED: Well, *"the famed mashed potatoes"!*

KING OF DK: Then we will see, if it is so good, because I can't taste mashed potatoes!

ACHMED: But there's carrot in it, I can see?

THE KING OF DK: There's just one carrot in! I always think so! That's because, the kids get it in baby potatoes! I think that gives a good taste! It must look a little gourmet! And then I made a sauce! And then I made carrots! And then we have to have lovely mango mousse cake!

ACHMED: Yeah, where is it from?

THE KING OF DK: They were cheap in Fotex, where they had reduced them to 35 from 80 kroner!

ACHMED: A sale at the baker before 1 p.m. 6.30 ?? After 7.30pm?

THE KING OF DK: No, 12 o'clock today!

ACHMED: 12 o'clock ?! It was early to sell them cheaper!?

THE KING OF DK: It was so, she could see it! But I had to go shopping! And then, I saw the mango cake mousse! And we have to see Survivor, so we have to eat orange!

ACHMED: Funny because I bought a blueberry and a cheesecake for my birthday! And I asked the pastry chef*: "Should I choose the blueberry mousse or mango?", "Well, I can't stand mango"*, she says then! *"Well, let me get a blueberry!".*

KING OF DK: Who said that to Mango ??

ACHMED: Yes, so did the pastry chef! Every time I look at a mango, I think of, all the kids in the Caribbean walking around naked with mangoes in a basket on their heads, eating them !!

KING OF DK: And in Thailand they make mango drinks! A mango drink! We have got two new puppies here in the complex. So the happy new owners have been in the Czech Republic to pick up!

ACHMED: In the Czech Republic !?

KING OF DK: Yes, two Scots! Two shots in fifteen weeks! We just met them for the first time now! They are cute! They are called "Hexi" and the other should be called something special!?

ACHMED: Why did they go all the way to the Czech Republic??

THE KING OF DK: There was nowhere else! When they bought the first one, they flew to Scotland! They are so rare to grab them! Or is it the time? I do not know!? Yes, it may be, that it needs salt?? I'm trying to get the right amount of salt! Try eating the mashed potatoes without gravy!

ACHMED: Yeah, it tastes good! How are you?

THE KING OF DK: Yes! Quietly! I just talked to the endocrinology department about my last blood test, and he said: *That it is, as I want it to be! So you just keep on your medication!* So now I have to get hold of my own doctor! After all, it is him, who is going to continue my illness! And then I hope, that we can negotiate until after Christmas, or something like that !!

ACHMED: Yes, or before summer !! Ha ha! Yes, I also saw in the newspaper about someone, who had tapped her child for blood! So it looked like, it was constantly in anemia! Clean von Münchhausen!

KING OF DK: It wasn't long ago !?

ACHMED: The newspaper headline was renewable here! Yesterday or the day before yesterday!

THE KING OF DK: I remember such a case, where a woman used her child ... Woman wanted for massive scams!? I hope that it's not my aunt!?

ACHMED: There: *Woman drops blood from her son!*

KING OF DK: How old is he?

ACHMED: 1 year!

THE KING OF DK: No, no, no !!

ACHMED: That is sick man! Every second week!

KING OF DK: Has she done this to him every other week ??

ACHMED: Yes!

THE KING OF DK: There are some women, who suffer from a mental condition in which they inflict harm on the children, to attract attention!

ACHMED: Yes, it's Münchhausen by proxy!

KING OF DK: Yes, when I was living in Los Angeles, before I met my husband! There, there was one of my girlfriends, who was dating a bodybuilder guy. He was so beautiful. We ran together at Santa Monica, and Venice Beach, them and me! When he was a kid, then his mother had, from the age of one, she put him on the kitchen table and threw boiling water at him with teaspoons! When he's been naughty! Then he was put on the kitchen table and .. *Splash, splash ?!* Such?! He had scars all over his body! It was his girlfriend, who told me that, because she sometimes had to explain it! He was very special!

ACHMED: You would be fine, if your mother threw boiling water at you!?

KING OF DK: That's where my aunt works. That's one of her colleagues!

ACHMED: She raised DKR 110 million for her own pension !?

KING OF DK: I'm just trying to turn it down! I'll just call my aunt! She must be able to figure it out ??

Hi Auntie, I was just reading on TEXT TV about some social scams!? Can you figure out, who it is? Well, ok, ok? Well, it's in Copenhagen! Well, ok, ok no. Ha, ha. Well, well, yes, it says it may have taken many years! But they have registration back for a few years! Nah, it just says ...

ACHMED: 111 million !!

THE KING OF DK: *Well, yes, but it was good! Yes, but it goes well in many ways! Right now I have talked to endocrinologists, and they have said, that they are happy with, how my metabolism is working! But this is the first time, he's not changing it! So that's fine! It all - Yes, I'm ready for life! Well, he's much better! Yes, have you seen him? Recently? No, no, but I think, it will work out! Yes, yes and he gets a lot better too.*

Those are some good things, that they said to him! Everything is something, that we can do something about! Yes yes. It may well be! Yes, yes. And then he continues his training, so it is doomed to go better! Yes, he does! He is good at that! Do you feel good too? Well, ok, ok? Yes, yes. Well! Are you down in Beder? OK? Odder! Well, but that's healthy! Is it team workout or what? Yes, I also started in the gym. It goes well! Yes, I signed up three weeks ago! So I attend a team again! No, but actually with many of the coaches, and some of the others on the team. Fitness down in the bus lane is closed! And those who workout down there, have been allowed to workout in the Prism! In the gym that I am a member of now! Yes, it does. So that's good! I have to greet him! Yes, I have a free guest ticket...? Which I can spend on him! Yes, yes. It's a nice place, that's it. Yes, yes, but it came back soon. I have already been called well trained after three weeks! Yes, but my stomach, it is still tight, although there is some obesity around it! And the less I eat, the more it will appear! Well, but I have to say hey, and you have to say hello too. Yes, no, no. We'll find out one day. Yes, I could understand that! She sits on Cayman Island or something! Yes! Have a good time. Bye, bye!

Unfortunately no. She doesn't know, who it is !?

ACHMED: It is also a crazy amount, that she has ripped !?

KING OF DK: She said: *My intuition was, that it was one in the finance department in Copenhagen! Someone who really has knowledge of IT!*

But they write, that they can't even see, how long they've been doing it !?

ACHMED: It's totally crazy! She is nobody, wants to fuck voluntarily?

THE KING OF DK: It's saturating! Yes, it melts on the tongue! But come eat something more !!

JOSEPH: It tastes lovely my friend

THE KING OF DK: It was good! How was Isa doing?

JOSEPH: Well, now it's been so long, since I can't remember it!? Yes, I was at school with her on Friday. Then I had promised Mary, that I would wash some of Isa's clothes! But our washing machine was booked, and I couldn't get to the laundry. It was also just a few things! But I met them after school with the dirty clothes! Then we were in Dyrhaven, and feeding wild boar with rotten apples. Afterwards, we were a little down by the eternal bridge! The round bridge at Varna! So we were together for a couple of hours, and that was it. Then I drove home! Last Saturday was at my aunt's birthday - for lunch and the whole family was there pretty much! My siblings and their wives. I drove up to the wildcat at seven o'clock in the evening, and have been there until today! So it was pretty long too!

KING OF DK: Meat? Husband a little bite more?

ACHMED: I was grocery shopping, when I was visiting her! There was nothing in her fridge!? Yes, and then I bought a big Chinese box yesterday! And we shared it!

KING OF DK: Yes, I love them too! I think, I can taste, that I've got white pepper in!! I know, you're getting black pepper. But white pepper is one of the secrets of Kentucky Fried Chicken! It's one of the eleven spices! And white pepper can do some things!

ACHMED: Do you still eat from there?

KING OF DK: Yes, we do! Once every two months! It's probably three weeks ago! But then I buy a bucket of twelve! And nothing else! Then I bought coleslaw over in Fotex! And then we're really just eating chickens and coleslaw! I probably bought extra ferrets that day too! I also made it, that I bought a bucket of twelve! Twelve leaflets. And then buy two grapefruit from McDonald's! And then direct home! But such twelve pieces, it's more than a chicken! They cost 220 kroner?! That's damn expensive! But there are almost two chickens in! Twelve pieces, three breasts, and the rest thighs and wings! In Dough with Safe Boilers! You can see on Youtube, how they make the food! You make Kentucky Fried Chicken in exactly the same way, as when he was alive! The only thing that has been replaced, is the cooking oil, the chickens fry in! It is vegetable today, where it was animal fat before! The dough that they dip consists of eleven spices! There have been hundreds of shows on American TV, where people have been trying to get just about close! Even Oprah Winfrey has had Kentucky Fried Chicken in her shows! And I have the two recipes too, but I don't think, it tastes as good as theirs ?? And today, with modern technology, it takes twenty-five minutes to make! And they can't make it in twenty minutes. It takes twenty-five minutes in a safe cooker! To make the chicken tender! My husband and I actually experienced some time, when we came to Marlboro, and wanted to order Kentucky Fried Chicken for my husband's brother and his three boys wife and I - Couldn't that be in Marlboro?! Because they don't just make two extra chickens! There were four or three within proximity! But some of the restaurants may not carry such an extra, extra! *Don't you remember, that we have to wait in line and ... !!?*

When you come down south, there is nothing but KFC, then there is Churches Fried Chicken ..

ACHMED: Dominos was in the tumble too !?

KING OF DK: It's pizza!! Pipey, that's what, I wanted to say! Uhh, it tastes good! That's why, black people get so fat! When my husband was studying in Washington, we lived where, we went to KFC every night! Closest to the US Consulate, close by! We lived pretty close! But that's slum half of Washington! It's black slum! Many are being killed in Washington! It is..? What to say? Rich and poor mixed close together!! There are loads of homeless people in the streets! There were so many securities to enter the parliament buildings!

ACHMED: 64? And she's wanted?! We don't even know, where she is?! But you never get that money back!? After all, she has used them on travels!

THE KING OF DK: Yes, how can that be possible?? Which bank can accept it?? No, that might not be a remarkable amount?

ACHMED: Do we still have questions, about the answers we have? Yes, thanks for the food my friend, I said, as the king groaned to the sofa!

KING OF DK: Did you never have a birthday with your parents?

ACHMED: Yes, yes. It was then, that I had bought a blueberry mousse and a cheesecake!

THE KING OF DK: Were they good?

ACHMED: The consistency is good in both cakes! And the bottom is good in the cheesecake, but it does not taste much of cheese ??

THE KING OF DK: Well! Well, it usually doesn't!

ACHMED: I had the notion, that a cheesecake could taste a bit of cheese!?

THE KING OF DK: No!

ACHMED: Not in the US either ??

THE KING OF DK: No! It's not a cheesy cheesecake in that sense! There is cheese in the cake. It's cream cheese! It's not really cheese !! It tastes like butter! It is a kind of cream, that is turning into cheese.

ACHMED: Shut up! We get 32 degrees on Saturday ??

THE KING OF DK: Do we? My niece is pregnant again. Juhu! And that's a second child! Lea was born in November, and now she's pregnant already !? And she's even in the third month ?? Because otherwise they couldn't say, if it was a boy or a girl ??

ACHMED: No, it's fast too!

THE KING OF DK: Lea writes, that she is looking forward to meeting her little brother! She is adorable Lea, but she is fiery red-haired, and they may risk it being beautiful? And that she becomes mega beautiful! And my nieces are beautiful, are you nuts!!

ACHMED: In "The Perfume" it was also a redhead he captured - Virgins!

KING OF DK: But in the US, they think, it's something special!

ACHMED: But she has two cats up there, and is called Cathrine, and calls herself Cat! The Pussycats Peanut, Samba and Cat! And of course they should go to the bedroom, when we were sleeping! So they didn't smash the whole living room! I tell you, the first night, I slept for a total of one hour! Number two night I could sleep for five hours, and the third night I might have slept through the night!

THE KING OF DK: So just being you?

ACHMED: Yes, be me, and stay overnight - and at the risk of toxoplasma gondii parasites from cats in the bedroom!? And she sleeps on mattresses on the floor, because she thought her bed creaked, when she was having sex !?

KING OF DK: Well, so do you? Then you lie on mattresses on the floor and...?

ACHMED: Yes, but it's not optimal! No.1: You destroy the floor. No. 2nd: You don't lie good on the floor! No suspensions!

JOSEPH: Yeah, I got to meet my lawyer on Friday, and then I'll be in court next week!

KING OF DK: Has it gone so fast ??

JOSEPH: I don't know, if that is fast? From all this controversy and so far? Mary suddenly says, it's nice, that we can talk together now! But we have always been able, to do that!

KING OF DK: But last week you hadn't been told?

JOSEPH: No, our lawyers had talked together on my birthday!

THE KING OF DK: Well, now

ACHMED: Yes, and then we have spoken French and German!

KING OF DK: Her, Cat and you?

ACHMED: Yes, she had French! I haven't, but I always say: *Merci bu'cu, jou vie! Jet t'aime* and what I can just imagine!!

THE KING OF DK: Yes, yes, I also say *"merci beaucoup"* in the shops and I like it, and it comes to me very naturally! And I also go and speak French to myself inside my head!

ACHMED: Yes, I also said *"mercí"* to the cashiers in Randers! It has also become quite natural for me!

KING OF DK: I was sitting today listening to the radio in a 1965 interview, with two people and one French journalist! And I had gotten that over to an mp3 file! There I thought, that if I sat down, and translated this to you, what they say - then you will learn it all in French! Because you can almost figure out, what it means, when you know the context! After all, for French words, those that are used in English, are a lot!

ACHMED: I also understood Margrethe (The Queen?) And Macron's speech, which was not subtitled! At his visit!

KING OF DK: Well, yes - I think, he's a good guy! He is nice!

ACHMED: Yes, he is very, very likable and skilled! But her in Randers, the Wildcat turns on my age, but mean while weighing it! However, she does not want to be with younger guys!

THE KING OF DK: Yes, I think, that is nice too! No, they are also bonded, because they have no idea, what to invite! And they won't either! After all, they haven't learned the concept, how to give yet! That's what the relationship does! It teaches one to give! Instead of taking!

I get more release giving Grethe a meal, than I get satisfaction for receiving something !! Elvis was like that too!

ACHMED: Yes, and Santa Claus gets endorphins released too, but it settles on his stomach !! There is something about it to give! I also gave her a copy of "The King of Denmark"!

THE KING OF DK: Well !? Does she read it?

ACHMED: Yes, she probably does!

KING OF DK: Shit, I got a splint in my finger. Fuck how slave!

ACHMED: Isn't it starting to rain soon?

THE KING OF DK: No, there will be twenty degrees! I do not think, it seemed that because, when the French speak slowly, it is easy to follow! Well, but I would just make one more, if we are to stand here! And we need Mangomouse cake too!

ACHMED: Yes, it will be exciting! But I will say, that the cheesecake is my favorite compared to the blueberry mousse! I even think, I have some leftover from it in my fridge! If I haven't eaten it, before I drove to Randers!?

KING OF DK: I got two cakes in my youth! One in Norway and one in California! A cake that I would give my right arm to taste again! But there is nothing, to do! It was up in the Norwegian mountains, where Soren and Gudrun went on vacation in the Clover Cabin. And I think, they knew, I had a birthday? I think, I turned ten? Then they bought a coffee mocca cream cake from the local baker! And we were on vacation! It was pink, and that coffee cream it just tasted like... ??

ACHMED: Did you like mocca back then ??

KING OF DK: Yes, we were up to sixteen people, and I don't think, I got anything but a tiny piece ?? In any case, that wasn't enough! And when I spent fifteen years in California, buying Joyce a fruit basket, over at a bakery in Santa Fe, in a town thirty miles away in Nevado - twenty minutes from Nevado! Shut up, it was a beauty! It was a white cake with white cake mass inside, but then there was banana, strawberries and some other fruits in it! It was perfect in its consistency, and then there was cream all around. And then there was coconut mold on the outside. It had taste, and then it was tall! I had never seen anything like this !!? They really can do anything with cake in America!

ACHMED: Well, I thought, they were enjoying Danish ??

THE KING OF DK: It's just one particular cake!

ACHMED: Isn't it a whipped cream cake?

KING OF DK: No, it's a Spandau! A Danish! Cremecheese in the middle instead of as we put cream! And I also don't think, that you can taste the difference honestly?? But in America, it's not puff pastry! There's the cookie dough, so it's such a heavy thing!

Well, what happened in Survivor last time? What happened was, he, Türker won over the other wogs!

ACHMED: Yeah, he beat Yasser! And then Yasser came over to the other's team! And he was happy! Because he could see, that he had been on a losing team!

KING OF DK: Yes, it was almost a thorny kiss! It brought the Turk back to life!

ACHMED: In turn, Jamil started to anger Yasser before the scuffle! Like they lost big!

I think, it politically suggests, that there will be elections soon!

KING OF DK: The right wing knows that! Have you seen, that Morten Messersmith has written a hate campaign against the three hundred families, who helped refugees last year?? Because, now I haven't read it! But he probably writes something about the fact, that it would be destabilizing for the entire Danish economy, if all families were to lie down, and help people, who should have had asylum here !? So we can't push that much money off the ground !?

ACHMED: Then you have a storage room !!

THE KING OF DK: Well, that's how, some of you have been cut! After all, it is those, who have children, who have been exposed to cuts! And when such municipal workers take so much under the table, then you can understand, that they can not get the budget together !?

ACHMED: And she's probably not the only one !?

KING OF DK: No no no! It is in every city !! They can make a team that in Copenhagen - a travel team ...?

ACHMED: Who checks up upon those pool rate funds!!

THE KING OF DK: And then she is the target!! She had a forceful moan! Benedikt was the target the last time, but she....?

ACHMED: Doesn't matter?

THE KING OF DK: Now they're blood brothers! Yes, his eyes are evil!

ACHMED: Yes him! Yasser was laughing at that exercise then!

KING OF DK: Yes, damn it!

ACHMED: He sat whining about nothing last time!

KING OF DK: Yes, he's gay! He's a girl! Like him at the Evening Show! Felix! He is so thin! He never eats! He is so anorexia! He vomits every time, he gets something in his mouth! They weren't pretty good at puzzles either !?

ACHMED: She said nothing!? *"It's nothing but colors and strokes!? I would like to sign out here!! "I want to participate, glance and say nothing!" ??*

THE KING OF DK: And Jamil? I don't know, what he looks like !? He looks like a Christmas tree crown!?

ACHMED: But are they going to merge anytime soon? They can't keep being three against ten!? She was so good, the one who was voted out! Unreasonable! Then they just have to win the rest of the gloom! After all, it's only three against three!

KING OF DK: Achmed, Coffee?

ACHMED: Thank you! They seem to be far along, and now Jamil is moaning!

KING OF DK: Again !? You can see, what I'm saying, he dresses up with rat tails at night!

ACHMED: Yes, I can imagine that!

THE KING OF DK: He does! And he mirrors himself, so do all men with that hair! They have to look for periods! If he was here, he would be standing in the hallway, because we have the big mirrors out there!!

ACHMED: What was it, that you called that cake?

KING OF DK: Mangomousse cake!

ACHMED: Mousse - with two o's?

THE KING OF DK: M-o-u-s-s-e! Do they become, like eating beef ??!

ACHMED: I can see, that the bottom of the cake is like the blueberry mousse! It was different from the cheesecake, and it was good!

THE KING OF DK: I'd rather pay for an othello birthday cake, because it's the hardest ones to make! Did you see, that they baked octopus cake in "The baking contest" show? No, you haven't seen that ?? It's hard to make! I also like othello birthday cake, but it does taste very good! Well - are they redistributed? That guy I don't think, I've seen before ?!

ACHMED: Ha ha - Newcomers have joined Survivor just before the finals!?

THE KING OF DK: Him there!!? What happened to Sonny and those, who made the teams !?

ACHMED: They were only in the first section !!

THE KING OF DK: Shouldn't they join !?

ACHMED: No, obviously not! Yes, it tastes good!

THE KING OF DK: Yes, I love to sit eating cake, when there is Survivor!

ACHMED: Yes, it's great, that when they get nothing, there's more for us others to compensate !! *"I am so hungry!!". "Is there more Othello ??"*

THE KING OF DK: Yes, it's such a comforting discourse! No, it's guaranteed to be fun advertising! It is good! I think, it's fun! What the fuck!? No, they didn't show the whole story! Something was missing for it to be extra ordinary fun!? Because otherwise you can just put dicks in the forehead of people then!!

ACHMED: Yes, that's the lowest common denominator!

THE KING OF DK: Shut up they get to show some commercials !!

ACHMED: *"Yes, it's fucked up, now I'm going out to buy some chips, a coke and cigarettes!".*

KING OF DK: It's funny, there are some people, they shop like they had a rocket up in the pussy!! In my family, my sister is a big spender! And if she doesn't have a dress for five thousand to buy!? She has just bought glasses for forty thousand !?

ACHMED: What !? You can't buy glasses, that are so expensive !?

THE KING OF DK: She has bought a new contract with an eyewear company! They have to supply her glasses for the next ten years!

"Amen, does it pay off?", my father said, when he heard of it! *"Well, Dad, when I have to pay between five and seven thousand a year for glasses,*

you can figure out that in ten years, it will be seventy thousand! Now I get it for forty! And then I get new glasses! My eyes are changing so fast, just to be measured!?! When the glasses are made fourteen days later, there is already a small mistake !? - And it's only on one eye, and..... "!

ACHMED: I must admit, that when I was told, that I needed glasses, the seller said, I had an astigmatism, and had to use glasses every day! But I only used them at a computer screen! And now I don't use them much. I almost don't use them in front of that screen! I'll bet my vision hasn't changed, because I've forced my eyes to be used! What about the eyes to rest !?

THE KING OF DK: I have then discovered, that the days when I drink enough water, I do not need reading glasses in bed !!

ACHMED: What!

KING OF DK: My vision reduction it correlates with my lack of water! And there it is precisely, what they say, that coffee is not water! When I drink one and a half liters of clear water a day, I see better!

ACHMED: Loco!?

THE KING OF DK: Loco, is his name! He is also Paki!

ACHMED: But that's right. The guy with the full beard, we have not noticed so far !!?

THE KING OF DK: No! But he must have joined the group! But it is also just our nature, to get to know them slowly! Try to see, that the Turks do not have such an Arab nose, as the others have! He has such a small fin??

HOST: *Now the teams have to be distributed!*

SURVIVOR PARTICIPATES: I think, I'll take Türker!

KING OF DK: I can understand that! What? What did he say "Satan"?

ACHMED: Jamil?

KING OF DK: It's obviously Survivor's premise! It's that, there must be equal numbers on the team! Well, so does it conflict, if he is on her team!!? Well, there is trouble! One left!

SURVIVOR PARTICIPANT: He has also proven to be the team's weakest link!

ACHMED: He doesn't understand!? But he probably shouldn't have figured out, that he had no chemistry with her!? You have to shut up with things like this!

KING OF DK: Well, some guys like him can be unbearable! And they feel, they deserve teenagers and down! I am sure, that what went wrong, is that, he has surely believed, that he could hit on her. But he is too old for that!? She couldn't accept it! There are some women who.... ??

We have just had Sigrids and Knud Erik's granddaughter on a dog walk! They have been to Copenhagen this weekend, and she is almost 90! But she said: *One of my grandchildren will come, and look after the dog! But she has been told, when to join with him!* And she came too - At 8:30 in the morning! At 4 p.m., and 9.30 p.m. 21.30! There we met this granddaughter! There were some of the men in the evening, who were slightly confused, that there is such a twenty-two year old dog owner!? They were just as charming enough!? And I could see, that she was having a hard time responding! She was just staring down at her cell phone all the time! She didn't know what to do, while we were telling all the stories!

ACHMED: The guy Ulrik is their weak point!
You should have taken him with the beard instead !!

KING OF DK: Ulrik, they showed from his domestic the last time, where he stood with his two children. He had asked his children, if they would like to see him in Survivor?? He even thinks, he's the strongest!?

ACHMED: But he is not! Thank you my friend! It goes absolutely wrong!? That's embarrassing! He must paddle like hell, and not just sit still in the canoe - steering!? Then you do not progress as much!? Damn it! *"I can control it!"* ??

KING OF DK: Fuck, how embarrassing for Ulrik!

ACHMED: Well, he's embarrassed! He is so embarrassing! I think, he has cried every time!?

KING OF DK: Yes, there is more cake both of you! I simply just don't want any more !!

ACHMED: No, I sense we need a break! It was delightful!

THE KING OF DK: Yes, it's something like this, that Grethe needs. She's getting strong! Instead of what else she would think of eating! A body of

88, it doesn't need oatmeal for dinner!? It needs some fat and some cream! There was cream in the mashed potatoes! Instead of whole milk! There are some, who just don't feel it!?

ACHMED: Shut up, can't they even get out of the water ??

THE KING OF DK: Yes, and then they are attacked by a shark !!

ACHMED: And what are they fighting for?? To get the guy there?? How hard is it, just to row in a canoe !?

THE KING OF DK: Someone who has no feeling at all - huh?

ACHMED: *Paddle while you control the fuck !?*

THE KING OF DK: That Loco is just a bitch!

ACHMED: Dentist?? No, now you must control yourself!

KING OF DK: Spark steel? Now they need to smoke all that !!

ACHMED: Well, they'll be so crooked!

THE KING OF DK: Well! Have you come across Kim Larsen's death?

ACHMED: No, I still rave about all the marches, that have been there !!

KING OF DK: And him from Ekstra Bladet, he wrote the old material, that Larsen has made, it's just for the funeral - Kirkegaarden!

ACHMED: Yeah, all of them. Nearly *"My woman!"*

THE KING OF DK: *"It's a cold time, that we're living out! Everyone walks around and freezes! "*

ACHMED: I don't miss him! I have to admit, I'm tired of having so many copy bands !! There are at least five, who imitate Kim Larsen at home!?

THE KING OF DK: And then I like that too: *I came to the world on the fifth floor! My dad was crazy, my mom was normal.* It wouldn't work today! That was, when the women's liberation began! Is it very strange to sing?! It's only now, that I realize, how great a man Charles Aznavour was! Take a break! He said no thanks becoming President of Armenia!? He has sold at about the same level as Mathieu! 85 million records sold. He has six songs! I've been sitting, and hearing a lot.

He says in an interview that: *There are six of my songs, that gave way, and went all over the world! She, yesterday, when I was young, the old fashion way, La mama -* These six numbers, they have recovered from

100,000 every year! Then he has three children with the third wife. And the last one he has been married to for over fifty years! They have lived in Switzerland, but have a huge farm at Avignon. It's an entire park like Amalienborg! And then he wrote all the time - He wrote over 100 songs! He has been something more productive than Kim Larsen!

ACHMED: *"No, Kim Larsen is a workaholic, he works all the time"* said Erik Clausen! *"Yes, I work a lot!!"*. *"But I rarely worked more than a minute on a song !!"* ?? Yes, we can hear that!!

KING OF DK: I liked: "Player, player, play for me!". I think, they are good! Well composed! Spot on!

ACHMED: But what the hell was he doing in Odense for over twenty years?!

KING OF DK: Went back and forth to his tavern!! And act first with Bellami, and then it was the Kjukken!

ACHMED: But he was from Copenhagen with a capital C !?

THE KING OF DK: But it was the wife, who raised him out of it, and then he found that on Norrebro, he never had peace! But down there he was allowed to go in peace! And then it's in the middle of the country! You must expect, that these artists are driving to the ends!! Then he lives in the middle. It means a lot! Then there is even distance to Zealand, and Aarhus North! Lis Sorensen lives in Thisted! It is difficult! To the airport and then to North Jutland, in and then fly out of Aalborg all the time!? Sometimes every day, all week! It is transport, that is slavish! They haven't done anything about the transport problem!?

ACHMED: Oh, it'll be good to come home to sleep in my own bed! Love my own bed! I don't like, to go to sleep in someone else's beds!

KING OF DK: Yes, and try to see, how difficult it is for people, not to sleep in their own bed!? There are some things, that people would like: Own bed! Did you know, if anyone wrote to me on this one!? If it doesn't glow blue, then there isn't! It's not there! It is well! Yes, it's been a tough week too, so it's good to relax!

ACHMED: I said at one point, that if she was with me, and that we became lovers, then she also thinks, I will be the first to get together with her at a swingers club!

THE KING OF DK: Yes, it costs 300 kroner for a couple! 200 DKK for single guys, also on Saturdays! And they have been redesigned in almost every room! These are two very different experiences!

ACHMED: She wants to go to Tucan, where she says, it's a little younger audience!

THE KING OF DK: Well, it's all ages coming there! It costs five hundred kroner, no - seven hundred!

ACHMED: It's expensive!

THE KING OF DK: It's two very different experiences! But it may be true that, there is a slightly younger audience down there! But not on Fridays!

ACHMED: She doesn't bother being with old men! I am her age president, that she has ever dated! And she has surely dated a lot!? But you notice that!

KING OF DK: He will be voted out in this program!

ACHMED: That's why, he was presented: *"I'm a seller!"*. We saw images from his private home, as if he were to be voted out!?

THE KING OF DK: So now we have to sit and watch the Arabs eat !!?

Well, she looks cute! What is she doing?

ACHMED: Well, she works in a home for the severely handicapped, which Hammel Neurological believes, needs help for the rest of their lives! She changes diapers, and washes them.

THE KING OF DK: Well! That's nice with a caregiver!

ACHMED: And some of them are struck on the frontal lobes, and want to have sex with the staff!

THE KING OF DK: Well. They go for it! And so it is, if it is a nice body, then it is not to be overseen!! Want coffee again? Or do you want...?

ACHMED: Yes, thank you very much! Türker eats rye bread every single day!?

KING OF DK: Well, that's nice! He also looks very much like a Danish boy!

ACHMED: Well, he is more Danish, than he is a Turkish!

KING OF DK: Yes, but he can't speak Danish!? He can neither count nor spell Turkish! He has said that himself! She really characterizes the girl Zanne!

ACHMED: They've got eel fyke nets, and they can catch some fish!? Why don't they dig that death bracelet in the sand, and pretend they haven't found it!? No, he is nice!

THE KING OF DK: Yes, he is a psychopath! If he doesn't get his will, you must see it into those eyes!

ACHMED: No, he's a nice guy - He's a bartender in London! He is also nice with short hair!

KING OF DK: The nicest feature is, he is thin! There are many guys, who are as him, but they are not as thin!

ACHMED: No, they don't even bother looking at him! No! He cut his own branch, as he expressed his attitude! It's his last meal!

THE KING OF DK: He can't control himself! It's because, he just had food, that he can't forget! But isn't that, because he was chosen by them!

ACHMED: He was chosen, because they can vote him out, and they will still be a full team! He takes all the death battles!?

THE KING OF DK: He then has a damp skin on him - Yasser? Totally scarred of pimples !?

ACHMED: Muslims, who admit they drink !?

THE KING OF DK: Mikael, the tall one, reminds me a lot of my high school colleague, who also hangs at Fuglsang! *Tell me - Do you do anything other than "cruise" buddy ?!*

Then the other team sends Yasser off! Then one of them goes!

ACHMED: No, they only get two votes! Amusements?! It is a death struggle!! He is sated! It is the one, that is most hungry, that has the most drive!

THE KING OF DK: I actually think Lasse wins! He seems somewhat stronger!

ACHMED: He's laughing all the time. He's just in paradise!
You don't have a lot of energy?! You are in the digestion man! No, no, now.
It's about getting off to a good start!

KING OF DK: It was damn close! That's the benefit of being number two! That's it in the turn game! As the kids call it!

ACHMED: Pair. Two zero! Three zero! It's not even a lie!

THE KING OF DK: Death's head! Is it stupid then to turn something, that has just been revealed!? He can do nothing Jamil, if there is no one, to turn it for him!? Now he's done as a football player, and he's doing commercials! How come, he has put his eyebrows so crooked!? And he has had his eyebrows cut off?!! Bizarrely!

ACHMED: What?

THE KING OF DK: Bizarre program !?

ACHMED: Then fuck her - man! *Pull yourself together! Beating of wings??* Is that what, they call him?

THE KING OF DK: No, Jesus! They call him Jesus! Then he just has to picture the others, that he won! Yes! There comes the prince.

ACHMED: Kim Larsen! It's such a win win!

THE KING OF DK: Are they in the dark again !?

ACHMED: Yes! Now they have to compete against each other, now in for the kill! And those who lose, will probably get a vote against them too?!

THE KING OF DK: Well, I think, he speaks in truth! It's the blue eyes, it's all about! When you have such a small stable body, that has not been at war. He has had incredible stability! But it may be that an incredibly stable life, does not prepare a young man well enough for adulthood?? Having a good upbringing is not always a benefit! All American overachievers have had a tough childhood! Madonna was fucked by all the men in the street, when she was growing up! But what the hell!? She's become the biggest star over there, hasn't she? Mind blowing Yaa! What does one gain from winning the contest? Just don't lose! They are fucking 'far out ?? Yes, what if they sail into each other? Can't they just skip a few steps ?? Parkour Lasse !? It is probably a discipline, where the boys are far ahead of the girls!

ACHMED: *So you have to make the solution on the ground! Lasse, what do you have a sun in the middle for? No it is not! Yeah, I'm not voting for you in the next island council, if you just join me as my boyfriend, behind that bush for five minutes!*

THE KING OF DK: When I was with Lars, it was probably 8. There I had told my husband, that it would probably be 11, and he had told his wife, that it would probably be 10. But then he stayed one hour extra time! I was just smoking some point in time, and a few came into this cabinet! A little wide guy with his bitch, blonde with big tits in French lingerie! And she stood with her tits in front of me in the smoking room!

ACHMED: And you were licking them ??

THE KING OF DK: No, I just got really tight! There is a smoking cabin, where ventilates the air. And there are two bartender chairs, and they gave me one, and then they stood with the other ...?

ACHMED: And fucked?

KING OF DK: I don't think, they fucked! He had a towel around him! But she was smiling at me, if I didn't notice! I don't think, boobs are particularly interesting !?

ACHMED: No ?? It's funny, that you don't like it !?

THE KING OF DK: Do you think so ??

ACHMED: Yes, I love breasts !!

THE KING OF DK: Yes, I like tight man's breasts! And other people go crazy on my breasts!

ACHMED: Yes, you look a little like Lasse too!

KING OF DK: No, but you can't see either, that I actually have a stomach!

ACHMED: No, you hide it just like Casper Christensen!

THE KING OF DK: His inferiority complexes, they reach the top here in section number five! There he is swirling into his office, where Frank and him are trying to make a screenplay for a movie with medieval cuts. The camera is completely down to perspective! So he looks great! And then he has a red-nosed nose! And Lene's father from Norway has visited: *I am Norway's richest man!* "He then says," *A great experience to meet me? ".* "So here you get a keychain!!". "Really? Do you make key chains"??* Frank asks him! *Yes! "We are doing another thing too !!".*

And then Frank forgets his key, as he comes home with a stranger on a date, that Mia has chosen to join a triangle! Then the guy and Mia are kissing in front of the door! And Frank just stands! And then Casper

Christensen finally says: *Then you shouldn't have thrown that keychain away!* Lene is so fun in it too. She is ...?

ACHMED: Did you see "Message in a bottle from P"?

THE KING OF DK: No!

ACHMED: It was also a Norwegian, who played the villain!

THE KING OF DK: Was it a Q movie?

ACHMED: Yes, Jussi! He had six million in sales revenue, without writing anything!? Last year!

THE KING OF DK: Is it called? - The new movie?

ACHMED: No, I can't remember, what it was called ??

KING OF DK: Mina invited me to premiere on it!

ACHMED: I have to admit, I didn't bother to see it. I don't bother for Jussi! They are boring!

KING OF DK: But she invites me to something every day! And the other day we should have been tasting together with Bjarne Rise and Anne Dorthe Tanderup in a garage in Aabyhoj!! But then I was just so tired at 6, that I canceled! It's a pity, that I'm getting tired! Because otherwise I would like to see Soren! All day today she, her fashion creator, Isabel...? What the fuck is she called ?? Danish fashion designer in Paris ??

ACHMED: And you could just drop by?

THE KING OF DK: I went and picked up the dog a few times!

ACHMED: Then she had a nice visit! ??

THE KING OF DK: She only bothered knowing, and seeing me! Pernille Rosendahl came over and said one day! It was Saturday at Saint Poul's Church! *"Don't you want to hear them? And hear her sing out loud? ". "No, it shouldn't be right now, that we have our reunion, her and I! I've had a lot to do with her! ".* But Mina has visits from her too!

No, I am not up for all that "star" licking circus! Then I have to say:

"No, you sing very nice!?".

ACHMED: She sang Kim Larsen's "Langebro"! Where she said afterwards, that she has sung it on tour for two years! Her version was very good though!

THE KING OF DK: Yes, Pernille has something! She has a good voice, and she can do something with lyric! Many of the Storm songs, they are good! My colleagues loved them, and I heard them on P3 as well, two three pieces of them in rotation. So I could well.... ? It is not something, that I would buy myself! But they were so recognizable, and so well created the music, I noticed! And we have workout to it at Fitness.dk! They loved it! And I even loved Swan Lee! Pernille's first record - Fuck, it was good!

ACHMED: Didn't they also just make that one ??

THE KING OF DK: Two! And I even recorded one of the songs in French! I think, my voice was ringing in the microphone. A full sound she couldn't deliver herself, because she had this sharp!

"You must make an effort!".

ACHMED: I never heard that before!? You haven't played it for me!

THE KING OF DK: I also have only a small clip of it!

"I went over the Lange bridge!"

ACHMED: Well, that was short!

KING OF DK: Yes, I have it in a long version too! But this was a jingle for the radio! She was deeply fascinated in French! And she heard Nina Simone, Serge Gainsbourg! That was just before Tim Christensen! In that circle they loved Serge Gainsbourg!

ACHMED: Nina Simone was great too!!

THE KING OF DK: They have a clip with her on youtube, where they go crazy on someone - Then they stop the clip, where she is about to quarrel with him! It's simply gold!

ACHMED: No, he is a person, I could never stand !!

THE KING OF DK: No! I couldn't either!

ACHMED: He looks terrible! "The judge" from "Crazy with dancing"!

KING OF DK: Terrible gay! He has two full grown daughters!

ACHMED: I thought, he was a gay!?

KING OF DK: Mega gay!

ACHMED: He's always so feminine!?

KING OF DK: Yes, as you can be!! Every gay man in Zealand is deeply envious because of his female persona! No, he is heterosexual, and there have been interviews with him in the evening show, and where they show their everyday life! The whole family is engaged in dance!

ACHMED: That's fucking hilarious! *Aren't you glad, I lost, so we can get an additional contest!?* She's pretty there too!

THE KING OF DK: Yes, she also has makeup on there - Then it is something completely different! Is she in entertainment? Yes she is!! She has some really ugly features, compared to what's normal! I have that too! Yes, he should shut up! He should have turned it off!

"I think, Lasse is so delicious, that he annoys me! Yes, I think, he has a great body" - I think, he's going home now!

"I can't stand standing here next to him! ".

ACHMED: *I look at him all the time – He makes me feel so sick!*

THE KING OF DK: Now I want to know, if he has a big cock??

ACHMED: It was a long time, it was inclement weather??

KING OF DK: But it shines and rains every day at the same time !!

ACHMED: Everyday ??

THE KING OF DK: Yes !! In each case during the rainy season - But not in the summer! *"I want it more than Lasse ??!"*

ACHMED: *"I've wanted it all my life! It was the first thing, I wanted, when I was born! You have to join Survivor, my mother said! I'm not going to play with my former teammates! I know them inside and out!"??*

THE KING OF DK: That's a hard clip here! They have nothing special today !?

ACHMED: She's annoying to listen to! He looks good!

THE KING OF DK: *"If she has - I have a little idea, if she has"* !! They can't just change Danish grammar?! And this is, what is called a "man bun"? And these are men, who want to be women!? Well, he has a little bit of hair on!?

ACHMED: Who? Lasse?

KING OF DK: Yes, but not on the stomach!

ACHMED: *"Yes - I haven't thought about that!". "I actually had no idea!"*

HOST: Who feels the pressure here?

ACHMED: Ha ha - Lasse doesn't feel pressured! He was the only one, who didn't raise his hand!? And he even has a vote against him in the urn!! Lasse didn't feel threatened!?

THE KING OF DK: Yes, now you have said it !! Now you can't say "right" multiple times! He has said right six times in two sentences !? Such an inferiority complex !!

ACHMED: Then it's great, he is leaving the show! *I was really depressed!?* Then he just turned on a plate!! Then we hear a little of his background, why he is so happy!

THE KING OF DK: Shut up! Then "Cover Wives" is something more exciting! There they easily end up in arguments going out for lunch!

Jannie Ree went crazy the other day, when they came home from a restaurant, where Ribena was in the welcome drink!

ACHMED: What did they use, you said?

THE KING OF DK: There was Ribena! Juice in the welcome drink!

ACHMED: Well, did she complain about that?

THE KING OF DK: Then all the Danish men have been discredited! Then it's the Danish women against the Middle Eastern men!

ACHMED: And now they regret it, because Lasse's mother died of cancer!? Now they lost as a team! Three girls and two boys! Ulrik is gay, and that's why, he keeps up with the girls!

THE KING OF DK: No, Ulrik is with the girls, because he has girls around him! His family, his big sister, his wife! He is most comfortable with women! He doesn't like other men! They are dangerous! I don't know, if he's a gay!? It might as well be! But he doesn't look like that ??

ACHMED: *No, it was good, that you voted him out, who became number three in the contest!* Hell, stupid men! *"But the one who lost the battle, can stay, because she is good for the team !!".*

THE KING OF DK: I will definitely cut it out! Did you see that?

ACHMED: What? - Is he just dead?

THE KING OF DK: Yes! He was on TV all Saturday night you! Live 94 years! Charley nominated him for the greatest cultural life of the 20th century! Higher than Elvis and Bob Dylan! They gave him a star on Hollywood Boulevard last year!

ACHMED: When did he die? Yesterday? Or last Monday that he died?

THE KING OF DK: Last Monday! 80 movies !! Mireille is there! Let's just see, if we can see her for "The Statesman's Funeral!" She had not curled her hair! She has not curled it in! It hung down flat! Here's Madame Macron! The famous people are not here at all!? Well, that's because, they start here! There's Mireille! It was Mireille, who demanded... - She wrote to Macron, and said on the phone right away –

"He must have a national state funeral!"

ACHMED: What a facade they painted on that flat !?

KING OF DK: *You are the one for me, for me, for me!* Lasse and I saw him in '87 inside the Music House! And then, I saw him again the following year in San Francisco! It was so cool! It was Lasse, who wanted to hear him! The one who went to class with your oldest brother in high school! But god damn it, he could also entertain for a whole hour!

ACHMED: Was Lasse a low guy, and then he suddenly got tall!?

THE KING OF DK: No! He was low, he really was!

ACHMED: He didn't get tall?

THE KING OF DK: No! I think, that's something about 1.60! But he has played athletically! In his first movie, he played marathon runs! And then French TV has cleared all their programs for a week! Or every station they have every night - Charles Aznavour! And then people come in and sing his songs! And they sit and discuss and show clips!

ACHMED: I couldn't stand it for two seconds at all! If they did it with Kim Larsen! But they have already spiced it for too long!

THE KING OF DK: Yes, they have given a damn lot of attention! But no one has mentioned Mireille with a word!? They have all agreed, that what they have done together, is not among the most beautiful! They totally agree! It's strange, that I don't even know my playlist, when I'm on the TV!? There he was on television Saturday night! It was last Saturday night, And then he died on Monday! He had just returned from a tour of Japan! You can see the 28th in the ninth!

ACHMED: So what did he die of?

KING OF DK: He slept at night. He was healthy, when he went to bed, and he was dead in the morning! He slept!

ACHMED: And he has not been autopsied, if he has been given any wrong medication ??

THE KING OF DK: He wasn't on any medication!

ACHMED: But he didn't sing until his death?

KING OF DK: Yes, he gave a concert in Japan the day before!! And he was booked for 59 cities! And the reason he was on TV this Saturday, is because, he is starting another tour in Europe! Brussels and ..? And I got a shock, when I went for a walk on Monday, where Mina suddenly says: *That Charles Aznavour is dead!* Now I would have said Sunday morning, that he was going on the world tour! And how good he is!

ACHMED: So should Michael Jackson! On the world tour!

KING OF DK: It took him twenty years to make a break through! The French did not immediately like him!

ACHMED: That is clear! Wasn't he Armenian !?

KING OF DK: Sure, but hey, he was born in Paris! Well, it's his parents, who are Armenians!

ACHMED: Sure, but it's the same in Denmark!

THE KING OF DK: The reason is, that they didn't know his style at all! They should get to know that! He was far too rhythmic. He took in all that jazz music!

ACHMED: No, man, it's been a tough weekend! Strange that they insist, that there should be such a sound, when browsing in youtube !?

KING OF DK: Do I think, I can turn it off too? Do you think?? In settings? He was a slave for seven years! For seven years she banned him from writing music to others! But she only recorded two or three tracks with him and ..?

ACHMED: What was the name of Liza Minelli's mother?

THE KING OF DK: Judy Garland! And with a film director Vincente! I actually saw him in a clip! It should be here?? I just had such a period with Judy! There's Judy and Barbra together! It's fucking edgy fun!

Liza is included in that too! Judy, in her sixties, they gave her, her own show for the first time! She had made theater then! Then she got the "Judy Garland show"! It's the one, who put out the original footage! It is very fun! *We have got Barbra Streisand, and she is nice, and she has such a voice, and she has got such an announcement!* She had a starring role in a movie after all! So all the Americans thought, they owned her! There she is forty years! Liza is seventeen! And it's just about dawning on them, that Liza is just a cannon!

ACHMED: Surely she was nicer too ?! Well, she was, if she was younger!!

KING OF DK: But they did not know at all, that Liza was so good !! It was impossible to know! That mother and daughter, they could…. ?? That it could be inherited! And that's only Barbara's second TV appearance!

ACHMED: It's a tobacco advertisement?! Shut up man. It is many years ago !!

KING OF DK: I've had it on CD for many years! Barbra is only eighteen!!

ACHMED: At this point?? She looks great!

THE KING OF DK: There was just one gay guy, who advised Barbras and Judy's duet the other day! Inside youtube, making footage of himself, stopping the clip every three seconds and saying: *"And here you can hear Judy's vocal damage!! And here Barbra surpasses her! And here it sounds really good!".* Ha ha! So if anyone is being analyzed to the death, it's Barbra! Cause she has just finished her career! Her fans are extra feisty - translated needy !!

ACHMED: But she was sexy, when she was eighteen!

THE KING OF DK: She's still pretty!

ACHMED: No, I'm going to throw up!

THE KING OF DK: An advertisement is shown, and then it just stops everything !!? What the hell ??! Back !! It is very fun!

JOSEPH: We have to go to court twice !! It's new procedure! That was what the attorney secretary wrote to me! Then the lawyer called and said: *"About Ida!". "Ida??". "Yes, isn't it your daughters name??". "Well, then you are well versed in the matter!?! I am more calm now?! ".*

She couldn't investigate her "customers" just a little !?

THE KING OF DK: No, you must not expect that! They can't! Should they then sit and... ?? This is also the problem at the municipality. That reports are written about children, that no one ever reads again!?! So it's a big problem, that it needs to be funded ?! That they should be written?! When the system is now such, that no one bothers to read it again !? Nor do they feel, it is necessary, when a case is in progress!? Can't you see it? It's totally crazy! Of all the things that have to be written down by the municipalities, that have to be registered, because it may have to be used, if it comes for... ..?

ACHMED: A Supreme Court judge?

THE KING OF DK: It's so special!

ACHMED: He's set too!

THE KING OF DK: Yes, it's all French! Cloclo was the one who died in the bathtub! The one who wrote "My Way!"

ACHMED: With a hair dryer?

THE KING OF DK: Yes!

ACHMED: No!

THE KING OF DK: Yes!

ACHMED: No, you should not have a hair dryer !! So close to a bathtub! Use a towel??

THE KING OF DK: That's because, I just hoped, that a single with Charles Aznavour would come! Him Terrylion, who was standing there, singing with her, he imitates Charles Aznavour! No, there is none!? I was annoyed this morning, because no one has celebrated the six songs, he actually made with Mireille and sung with her 30 times!! I think, that's too bad!

ACHMED: Then why not do it yourself?!

KING OF DK: No, I have nothing to upload! And you can see, how delicious they are together! You can see, how much he loved her! Charles! "Slowly" - Mireille Mathieu! There! Their voices match up incredibly well! Then six times in his career, he called her, and he has been with her from the beginning! *I've written a song for you! Slowly!*

ACHMED: It's playback !?

THE KING OF DK: No !! They hold a microphone over them! It is not one of them, that they have recorded! There is only one song, that they have sung! Twice they recorded a song together! And in '76 he recorded it himself. Then he called it "Ciao! Ciao Bambino"! And his version is named "Ciao Bambino, ciao" - It's a small change in...?

ACHMED: But amazingly, the sound is good, when you can't see microphones in any direction!?

KING OF DK: But it just hangs over them! There's one with a tripod! Try to hear her - how strong her voice is! And he was almost fifty, and she was twenty-seven! Ha ha!

ACHMED: Then she gets to dance with old men!

THE KING OF DK: Yes, it's the speaker! Delux - Very famous! Very famous speaker! But they have worked together insanely many times! And some of the coolest thing ever was when, she flew to Finland to sing with him! And there he had written music for a movie about Tehran or something! Tehran Symphony Orchestra and the whole shebang! And then he introduced her to a Finnish audience! It's really incredible!

Why in Finland ?? I don't think, he's ever been to Norway and Sweden !? I've always thought, it's a fantastic number with Mireille. Not many others like it! *A life of love! It's La vie de amour!* He has a good voice! I don't know, if she sounds good?! No, it is not well recorded?? If it is to be recorded well, then there must be microphones in all instruments and voices, but it is not there !? But fuck, he could some other stuff Charles Aznavour! Play acting! He wrote Liza Minelli's first record in '67! What I thought was very interesting! She looks damn good too! It says in the French newspapers, that they had an affair, but they did not !! *"He's just been my mentor,"* she replied. It's Judy Garland's daughter!

ACHMED: No, she's not sexy!

KING OF DK: What do you say ??

ACHMED: She's not sexy!

KING OF DK: Have you seen "Cabaret" ??

ACHMED: No, but I can see there, that I'm about to throw up!!

KING OF DK: In 1991 Liza gave a concert all over the world! But she's still thin! But it's horrible her French! Two years ago he got an award for his lyrics! There she met up and introduced him!

"I need to say it: Charles Assanovouur"!

I just talked to someone from workout, who said, he had a very special relationship with Liza Minnelli! *"I was so in love with her, after Cabaret! That I couldn't watch other movies! For five years! I traveled to concerts with her in the US, and from home!"* It was very funny! She was 72, when she got an Oscar for the role in Cabaret! The world was shocked by her performance! She was damn naughty! Have you never seen her ?? Which one should we choose? Which one is she most naughty in? After all, it's a movie of a novel by Christopher Isherwood, *Welcome to Berlin*, or something! And it was filmed with her starring! Liza Minnelli. Cabaret! So what do we get? Her songs were called: *Money, money, money, money, money, money, money, money,* - There were many songs! There were five! Ten songs written by John Kander and Fred Ebb. *Madams and monsieur's, ladies and gentlemen's - Welcome!* There she is twenty-two!

ACHMED: I remember that movie! I have seen it!

KING OF DK: I've seen it too. I can't remember it! It's a political movie! Decadence! He said, he was obsessed with…. ??

ACHMED: But she is not delicious! She is both cunning and crazy crooked…??

THE KING OF DK: Ha ha - I've always thought, she looked like Judy! But then I came to see Vincente Minnelli one day, and then I could see ..?! That even though he had white hair, he was dark-haired as a young man! And he was gay! Judy found him in bed with someone else! And then she wanted to be divorced immediately! And Liza was thin that year! That's damn good!

ACHMED: But she's not thin there ?! But she has a good voice!

KING OF DK: I've been dancing with her!

ACHMED: You have what?? Danced with Liza Minelli ??

THE KING OF DK: Yes!

ACHMED: How did it come about ??

KING OF DK: Yes, how did it come about? Because we knew someone named Klaus, who worked at the Falcon Concert Theater! And Sis and I had paid DKK 1,000 each! And then we went to Madame Arthur afterwards, and it was win or loose. But she came along with her entourage! They had been told: *That if you were to go into town, it would be no more than half an hour!* She was more interested in coming home! But it was also just thirty years after this one! Strange song!

ACHMED: *The Cabaret, Un Cabaret, the Capareeeet !!*

KING OF DK: Which one is the best? Where is she best? Liza Minnelli - Liberty show! Yes, there !!

ACHMED: She looks almost like a Madame !?

THE KING OF DK: Mireille Mathieu opens that show with Andy Williams and Frank Sinatra! It's the Statue of Liberty's 100th anniversary! Then take a full break. She made a whole stadium go crazy! Liza, her voice was just that big that night! Look we are also getting a skyline - *Aarhus, Aarhus! Skyline!* It's time to turn that "Home to Aarhus" away! *"Aarhus, Aarhus! Skyline ".*

ACHMED: Yes, now I drove from Randers, and past IKEA - And it wasn't pretty!

KING OF DK: No, not from the north and not from the motorway! It's put in a profit place! Because it's nice, when you come from the south! That is damn pretty! But then Hadsten is an ass city! And people who live out there, are going crazy!

ACHMED: All the way to Randers it was nothing more than a peasant robbery! Sporring, Odum, yes Hadsten! Shut up man! It must be cheap!

KING OF DK: Have you been playing "Tina's magic web" for Isa?

JOSEPH: Yes, yes! We heard it once!

KING OF DK: No, how fun!

JOSEPH: And then I asked her the next day! *"Shall we hear it again?".* *"No father!", "Well"!* So I don't exactly think, it caught her, but I have to try again!

KING OF DK: When you hear it next time, think about Mina, my friend, she's a journalist! It is so much fun dialogue at the time, when the spider and animals go with the pig to the market! *Don't you bring me*, the pig asks? *Well, you have to have someone, who can write!* And there are several journalistic comments about Mina at the end of the record!

ACHMED: Personally ??

KING OF DK: No, not personally, it's just fun! Liza Minelli is dying soon! She is lying near death! It's been two years since, she's been seen in

Beverly Hills! She could barely get up over a curb! A journalist was standing right next door! And then she actually gets angry, when she discovers, he is filming her! She is a bit professional, so she does not scold like Barbra! She puts on her best grimace and says something! And then she takes the step there - oh - She can hardly walk !?

ACHMED: *I told at my cousin party, that Kim Larsen was dead! No, he's not dead! Yet! Yes! Soon! Now he is! It was in September!*

THE KING OF DK: Now I've figured out, why Bowie and Larsen have died of prostate cancer! Because when all the men, I see go to workout down there, when they get prostate cancer, they know a lot about dietary change. And many are starting to workout and so on! And neither did David Bowie or Kim Larsen!! Who says straight to David Bowie - *"You have to eat something else!"*. After all, they don't! The need must come from within! After all, no one has guided Bowie in a lifestyle change! Surely no one has dared!? And Kim Larsen has not wanted to exercise, and he has continued to smoke the same smokes !!

ACHMED: Yes, I would not say, that my father is well again. But he is outside the risk zone!

THE KING OF DK: Oh no, that's not his song! He held such a concert in Rome, inviting the wildest names! Montserrat Caballé. Barcelona. You may hear, that it is not the original language! And then all the instruments are included. It's a huge orchestra! She's been singing in the music house!

ACHMED: Liza Minelli?

THE KING OF DK: No! Montserrat Caballé, who died on Tuesday! She's Herge, Tintin's author - He's invented her! It was her, who was the opera diva in his cartoon!

ACHMED: Just dark-haired! Fuck man it is possible to fit three people inside her !!?

THE KING OF DK: Yes, it's naughty, as Freddie Mercury takes her home and plays for twelve hours! He loved her! She was his diva! He wrote twelve numbers for her! And she sings amazing!

ACHMED: So he is not pretty either!

KING OF DK: Yes, damn it! Sure fuck, he's delicious!

ACHMED: He looks like the man with the steel teeth!?

THE KING OF DK: No, he is just way up his ace!

ACHMED: Where is it, you say?

THE KING OF DK: Barcelona! 500th Anniversary! In connection with the Olympics!

JOSEPH: Montserrat? It is a sacred mountain at Barcelona! Where Ignatius caved in!

THE KING OF DK: Then she's probably named after a mountain! Ha ha!

ACHMED: Is she called that?

KING OF DK: Her name is Montserrat!

JOSEPH: Ignatius healing center is going on an annual mountain hike there!

THE KING OF DK: But she sings fantastic!

ACHMED: In hindsight, there are UFO conventions down there, because it has such a big... ??

KING OF DK: Altitude?

ACHMED: Yes, energy, experiences, sightings!

KING OF DK: So he sits and does analysis on it?? The latest thing is that, they sit down, and do their analysis, fucking gays! Well, just try to see, all that Charles can do! They all talk at once on French TV!! Did you hear, that he mentioned Mireille? For seven years he was a singer with a friend - Pierre Roche. But then they couldn't succeed, so they moved to Quebeck! And they liked it! Those who act. They were a couple! He's terribly him there! They have all looked up to Charles Aznavour! It's him sitting down! He wrote "La Mer", the world's hit! This is Georges Brassens, he also had a good record sale in Denmark! Sailor Showing! It's Annie Cockedey! *For me, for me for me!* That's him there with the accident!

ACHMED: What an accident?

KING OF DK: With a razor!

ACHMED: I thought, it was a hairdryer??

KING OF DK: No, the lamp! He reached for a lamp in which, there was a bad socket! Along with an American girl of eighteen years!

ACHMED: Who's also dead?

KING OF DK: No, she's often on talk shows, and talks about how, it was with him!

ACHMED: He then got nicer with age!

THE KING OF DK: Charles? Yes, he did in many ways! He also got his nose operated! Armenia, when they were detached from the Soviet Union, they wanted him as president! His wife said: *No thanks!!* But otherwise he has been an Armenian ambassador to the UN for the last twenty years of his life! *Sur ma vie!* It means On my life! And he recorded it with Johnny Hallyday! But now they are both dead!

ACHMED: He looks like a lion!

KING OF DK: Yes, he has lived in Beverly Hills for the last twenty years of his life! Fucking gays!

ACHMED: No, now I want to go home to see "quilts"! What do you need all week?

THE KING OF DK: I'll just lie down and relax! I heard a song with Mireille, in English! Now you can hear, why it didn't come through! "Realize"! Can't you understand that ??

ACHMED: No, not much of it! It still sounds French !?

KING OF DK: There you can see, that Starck has spent money on expensive translations into English! And then he didn't spend money, to help her get something ...?? *When love has past you buy!* But it is a lot of fun to hear! Well! It was nice friend!

ACHMED: Yes, thank you so much for good treatment and coffee!

THE KING OF DK: I'm not going to fuck! I have no plans!
Here are your headphones!

ACHMED: Fuck I've just been looking for them?? I just got to a position, where I forgot about them somewhere !!

JOSEPH: You say your niece is depressed?

KING OF DK: Yes, my brother says, she feels it is hard to grow up! Where everything should go besides the dog Ella!

JOSEPH: No!

THE KING OF DK: Yes!

JOSEPH: And she's the same age as Isa! And have she started school?

KING OF DK: Yes. And they have asked her, if she didn't want to start something new? Then she should learn, how to play an instrument! I probably think, it was a wind instrument! Then they arrived to school, and she wasn't able to be there!? So she is strenuous!

JOSEPH: Well !? I would say, that my daughter is easier then! After all, she does everything, I ask of her! And she conflicts with her mother! About shoes and rubber boots!!

THE KING OF DK: Well, that's nice!

JOSEPH: But she doesn't mind talking on the phone with either of us! She's in the now! That with being available! Asking her if she has had a good day at school, it is soon to be many hours ago! She can hardly step into that anymore! *What happened then!? What did you do?!* Now shut up: *"I'm doing something, Dad!"*

KING OF DK: But could you teach her the summary? *So what does dad mean, when dad asks, what your day has been like? There you can just say two sentences fast honey! Then you first say something exciting, that you have experienced, and then what mood you have been in! And then no more!* So teach her that way! Because then she knows, that giving you the résumé will make you happy !!

JOSEPH: But I also tend to ask her questions like that? Attempting to lance this boil!

KING OF DK: Yes, well, but that's good! Because I also remember that, it was a thrill for them to know! When I couldn't figure out, what to say to find out! No, I'm not at a level, where I can say that, now I have finished my novel! But it's coming!

ACHMED: Yeah? I have ordered Volume V- "No Excuse!".

KING OF DK: Yes? I should send you to the book club! There our dogs are! *Helloo!*

ACHMED: Is it Beaute? It's gained on a bit!

THE KING OF DK: No, don't say that! She's so cute!

ACHMED: I should say, that Bobo has become slim! He is a Muscle dog!

KING OF DK: *Hello, Sigurd, hello Bella - this is the dog flock, it's Achmed! He has to go out and have a player!*

DOG WALKER: Surely you are not living in Haderslev right??

THE KING OF DK: Noo!

ACHMED: No, I didn't bother!

DOG WALKER: No, I can understand that!

THE KING OF DK: Not on that spot!

DOG WALKER: But to live in Haderslev at all!?

KING OF DK: Yes, damn it!

DOG WALKER: So you might as well live in ..?!

KING OF DK: Sausage of Death!! You might as well live in Germany!

DOG WALKER: Yes, or in Herning! And where the hell is Herning!?

ACHMED: Elvis Presley has folded in Haderslev!

THE KING OF DK: Yes, it's not even a lie, he was live, because he was posted in Friedberg! And he had an affair with a Danish woman! A weekend! At least that was said then!

ACHMED: So that's the only place the "King" has been in Denmark! So not a bad word about Haderslev!

DOG WALKER: No, I would say so! Then I would like to live in Haderslev, when Elvis has been there!

THE KING OF DK: There's nothing in between! It's Vamdrup, and Open Door??

ACHMED: And I have actually drawn the master plan for the harbor in Haderslev! So no more evil words about Haderslev!

***

TIME OF DECISION
Ext Saharan Desert Evening

JOSEPH:
It went well in the courtroom!

KING OF DK: Well, but it's good to hear

JOSEPH: Yes, that's it! I'm not unhappy! I also said, that I do not oppose sharing the child money! But I do not want to get rid of the residence, because I do not want to risk Mary having a fun idea. If she thinks, it is too expensive to live in Hojbjerg, and then suddenly want to move somewhere else! Another municipality or to Greenland!

THE KING OF DK: That's right! And I thought about that before too! And what I would call to say, to you is, that if you would like to say so; that you want to appear as the stable in Isa's life; and then the wife is allowed to get many fun ideas! Then you said it yourself! Yes! Was she satisfied or what, Mary?

JOSEPH: Yes, she was! But she is upset, that she can't get the housing allowance for Isa!

KING OF DK: But didn't she object?

JOSEPH: Well, she tried that. That is why, it also took two hours to write down verbal agreements, on what we agreed upon!

KING OF DK: Won't you meet another time?

JOSEPH: No, it doesn't look like that!

THE KING OF DK: No, that's because, they have to have an *"in mind card"*. That you, and the dissatisfied party, has to go home, and think about things! And then to call the parties back together. That's why, you have to say, that you have to have twice encounters!

JOSEPH: Immediately my impression is, that we have agreed. We have a good cooperation, and we must succeed. And now she gets half the child's money already from the twentieth of this month!

THE KING OF DK: There is not much in Isa's life right now, that is governed by parental idealism! So she is becoming more and more financially oriented!

JOSEPH: No, and at one point the judge said:

"Joseph, do you mind, if Mary then gets all the child money, because she has nothing to do, but pick apples and make apple porridge??". Where my lawyer responded: *Listen they are financially equal - They are both on cash benefits! Why should she be disadvantaged, because she might have a higher rent, and Joseph should be schooled in front of a bank ??*

THE KING OF DK: Yes, yes, so good enough!

JOSEPH: So she made sure, that of course you don't transfer all the money! No! And I also said: *"That Mary had left nothing to Isa, neither shoes, clothes nor pants or toys?! I have had to invest in many things"* - *"Well, you don't have to buy double! I can just bring it with her, when I pack a bag and everything else!". "Oh well?!"* Isa is also thrilled to have to carry a large suitcase every time!?

THE KING OF DK: Yes, yes.

JOSEPH: It's kind of weird for her to be here with me in a way, and have her clothes and toys here. And another way, and have her things there! So yeah, I'd say, it's been a slightly tough fall holiday! Mostly because of her The Wildcat in Randers, which I've had a hard time keeping out of my mind!

THE KING OF DK: Oh stop it. Don't be like that every time! It just has to run professionally on assembly lines! Woman after woman!

ACHMED: Yeah, I've already lined up Friday - Saturday, Sunday, with three different ones!

THE KING OF DK: Now make an extra ordinary naughty party! I will be helping to fuck an incredibly nice Canadian this afternoon, in an apartment outside Aarhus V. I am absolutely delighted!

ACHMED: Yes, I can understand that! How old is he?

KING OF DK: He's twenty-six! Who turn out to be a drug slot, which is totally nice, and he does not give a care at all!? And he has found, that the Danish guys think, he is naughty! And then he goes the extra mile! Because here, nobody knows him! So this is something, that they have been talking about here. I just get a message, when he comes again! It's really funny! We only have the fun, that we make ourselves!

ACHMED: What are you saying?

THE KING OF DK: We only have fun, that we make ourselves!

ACHMED: Yes, it is! And I have to smoke something fun soon! Because it has not been fun! There wouldn't have been an alarm, if I had smoked this whole fucking good summer man! But it was fun enough to try!

THE KING OF DK: Yes, yes. Well, Achmed I have to go! Hi!

ACHMED: Hi!

***

ACHMED:
You must remember this, a kiss is just a kiss!

Even though I want to strangle you, with my cock up your ass!?

It seemed funny, at the time I wrote it! She liked strangulation and anal sex!? No! It was stupidly replied! Blocked! She blocked me! The age parted us anyway! Seventeen years! It didn't bother me! Old pig? No, young pig! Try to tag yourself! I was setup! And I believed it! No. I'm only "Half /Ninety!".

WILDCAT: *Achmed, sweet Achmed. I don't feel the same anymore unfortunately. After getting to know each other better, I have seen, that in certain areas we do not fit together, as well as I previously thought. It takes time to find out, if we fit together, and I have now seen, that we do not. You are a nice man, but not one I want a relationship with, and so age still has a big impact on me too ... sorry it hurt you. :-IN*

***

ACHMED: The King of Denmark called one day, and asked if my good friend the carpenter, Builder Bob was named "Lamp" for surname? Yes - He has become a caretaker at a primary school here in the area! It was the Monk from the failed band "The Broken Beats", who had asked, if anyone knew someone with that last name? Because then he wanted a little talk with this Lamp! When in his position as their new caretaker, he had clashed with the Monk's wife, who also works at the school as a teacher. Yes, it does not surprise me! He loves ladies! And they like him! They want him! What is he supposed to do??! No, *fuckrooms*! That's what the young people want!?

If I have to look soberly at the development of the home, from living close, low - to living far and high; and from many in the same complex to one in each, there has just been an ongoing development, where people join, relax, pull up the dress and then...?? The private spaces and niches sneak into the public areas.

And in the bigger cities in Germany, the dark basement rooms offer an opportunity for the visitors of the café, to get to know each other more intimately!

***

ACHMED: When such a beautiful bird lands in your cage, you should tie the bird to the bed, or keep doors and windows closed! And so to say:

"Now I will pinch you for the next four days from sense and gathering, and you will think back to a time, when time just ended. And although you are sore and barely able to walk, it was actually, annoying to the tangy half psychopathic nice to get fucked in the ass, while getting the stifle! Or gargle in the c... ..! Then I release you, when we have rehearsed repetitively enough for four days!"

No, I am filled up, in front, behind, out for a long time !!

THE KING OF DK: Not a word is free! And there is something wrong with age, when it gets too big between couples! It is a disease and a reason for it to dissolve in a therapy community! But there is no such thing as economics that binds people together! Haven't you seen *Farmer seeking love? Or Married at first sight?* What a mismatch with someone, who had various diagnoses, autistic mentally ill bandit - *"I'm moving slower"* !! No, such as Türker, he's been fucked, since he was four! He can neither read nor count !?

I was just past Mina, who had a visit from Ole Henriksen! But he couldn't be impressed with anything! It was nothing compared to, what he had seen and heard in LA!? His brother lives here in the complex, so he is often over! Someone just gets through it! Charles Aznavour writes his own "The Secrete", as he turns forty! He has acted immediately for twenty years, before the French accepted him! It's kind of funny that some things does not make it in Europe, and something does not hit the billboards in America! We didn't like Liberace, and they don't bother Cliff Richard!

I want to win the lottery! - What rhymes with lotto? That will be my motto! But when I was at the doctors office, to test, if I had Chlamydia in my mouth, then it was a mockery, that in the waiting room was a health magazine with Nikolaj Hybbe on the Cover! It was him, who infected me with Chlamydia in the mouth at our latest Gangbang!? Did he even apologize for writing me!? No, my kids need to learn, how to grow up with two moms!! Boys!

This year, it is probably an Arab, who must win!

I must have eradicated all my phrases, that make me old! Moan when I sit down or get up!

Then they are like stylists, and those with gray hair, the ones who haven't had enough with their father, who keeps the relationship for five to eight years!

ACHMED: Marilyn Monroe - The Wildcats! Why doesn't she have more followers or likes? Because she has to block all her dates, which is headaches for her?? Maybe just some of them? Or is it just me, who can't follow her anymore?? I have to create a secondary profile on instagram, so that I can anonymously view the photos, she chooses to share with everyone and the 400 interested, who are not blocked!? She just got a new job in a kindergarten! It wasn't long before, she posted a note, that she was looking for new job on facebook, and then it just landed! But from the brain damage, that she loved, to the children, she admitted, was not a dream scenario! She doesn't really like kids! Besides her nephew in a few months! But I should never have entered into a good tone dialogue about her interactions with her mother!? Idiot man! Stand by your Man! Equality! Woman! Don't make the same mistakes again! Too bad! The wild cat! RIP wildtobacco, which was my latest post on instagram, with her empty tobacco box on my wall!

The court came, Joseph saw and triumphed! However, it was just at closing time, when the lawyer called, if he was on the steps?? Joseph stood outside the door, with the handle six feet up in the air. So yes! He stepped in, and caught sight of her in the entrance room, and was about to walk across the little band to her! *"No, you have to go right through the airport check here!"*. "BIB" Joseph's riveted belt! The metal rings, the coat! Five minutes later he was ready to discuss Isa's best interests with five women - one man! Joseph Vs. Mary!

The child expert, who spoke most of the time, was amazed, at how smoothly the two hours had gone! The residence will stay with Joseph! And Mary has to endure herself, to "just" be a parent! However, in 50/50 - Fifty fifty as we say! Joseph misses only half of Isa's life! On the other hand, Joseph is helping to shape her life 50 percent!

And of course, they share all revenue and expenses equally! And if they speculated on tax fraud, they transferred DKK 1,500 a month to each other. Then they would get 50% in tax deduction! But it just seems nonsense !?

THE COLOMBIAN ELEPHANT!

EXT Sahara Desert - evening

ACHMED:

So now it's back on the horse! On an even younger horse?! Yes, just cut off three more years, so "we" are now on a 20 year difference in age!! Yes, before it was "only" seventeen! I am older by three / four years to her biological parents in South America, who became parents at an early age after all!! No, it's horrible, that people in the Western world are planning their family life so late! But such a little goodie! Yes, she is ripe for her age, you must say! I thought, we were almost peers! 25 years! Yes, it's not R. Kelly, that's it !!

"The Colombian Elephant!". I don't think there exist elephants in Colombia at all!? But it was her *force animal*, as the only tattooed element on her body! The adoptive child who came to Denmark as a three month old baby! When she moved away from home, at eighteen, almost on the day, her "dad" would like to break ten years of silence. And he announced, that he wanted a divorce! Now that their little youngster had moved from the nest!

"Well, yes, more champagne dad, and thank you for helping with the move, and helping with my first own apartment - YUHU. Cheers dad?! ". No, he lasted a long time! For her sake!

When she was fourteen and growing up as a dark stranger in Hinnerup, one day on her way home from school she was torpedoed by a van! She did not wear a bicycle helmet, when she flew twenty yards off the road, and ended up at the Neurological Center in Hammel, after putting in a coma! Yes, she was good at singing, the young talent! This could be heard on the youtube clips available from before the accident, where her sound thundered out of the speaker like another Whitney Houston or Beyonce! Now the children in the institution with which she works as an educator say: *"You speak strange!" "Yes, she's from Columbia too! But she was born and raised in Hinnerup! So that's probably why, she's talking weird!".* She had to go through years of voice training just to make herself understandable again! After four years she had a big tongue operation, which has helped on the verbal! The skin hunger that she called her urge to throw her clothes, and lie naked on my couch, urged me to do the same! From early on, she had to put her urges on hold and focus on her rehabilitation! She doesn't drink alcohol! Or something that could endanger her blood vessels. Her sugar cravings were hard to hide!

So she did not resist my chocolate cake, which was melted in the middle, candy mix and a bag of chips that I had brought on our first date! But otherwise eating healthy! She does gain some weight, but is quite suspenseful in a slightly erotic, chubby way! She likes, when I call her a *Palestinian boat refugee* waiting for a visa and a Danish citizenship - and still has to suck it on forty men, before it can even be considered!! Or the jungle girl, who was taken from her tribe, and placed with a Danish pedophile in Hinnerup! Who could keep his marriage to the girl turned eighteen!? No, it's not fun!! Well?? I wonder if anyone caused her accident intentionally?? Was it investigated as a attempted murder?! Terrible! But she's still delicious! Yes, she is! She is in my mind! For now!

JOSEPH: She just wanted to spontaneously look past one day, that I had Isa! Thought I wouldn't spoil my daughter, that a friend was passing by!! But I had completely forgotten, that Mary would call to say hello at 6.30pm to her daughter!! *Why are you whispering Isa??* Asked her mother on the phone! *There's a girl here!! A girl?? What girl!?* I received six SMS's afterwards!! Mary felt entitled to know weeks in advance, before that I had to set up some kinds of meetings with new girls, who would meet Isa!! Well OK!! Yes, not two days passed, before Mary had created a profile on Tinder!! And then not a month after she announced on Facebook, that Mary is now in a relationship!!? Yes - I was told one week before my daughter Isa, about mom's new big love?!! Yes - I probably asked for that though!

NEW ENVIRONMENTS
EXT Pacific in a boat Day

ACHMED:

I would like to ask for two half student loaves please! Or if you have just two half pairs? Then you can get half of it in payment!

I've probably never felt, that I was good enough as an architect! But I was! I just always think, that most of what I have drawn looks like shit! The dash itself! It's a little more camouflaged through the computer! It's the same with the handwriting itself!? The same goes for the art! And soon this book series of handwritten scrolls in the desert too!! I don't like very much! But as my former mentor at the School of Architecture said, if I didn't like my drawings - then turn them upside down!! So now you turn upside down!! Soon we "wake up" on a boat in the middle of the Pacific! Instead of sand, it is water as far as the eye can see! But I haven't told "the others" yet! It's a surprise! So. There are six men sitting in a carpentry fleet in the Pacific!? And not in the Sahara desert anymore?? Scene shifts!? Switches! We do what Dirch (Passer - translated) Fits us!! I repeat! The book's protagonists are no longer in the wavy landscape of the desert! But they are now replaced by billowing seawater! Same principles only on smaller square feet! Still a Pacific Retreat - Overnight! They fell asleep to the heat of the glow, and woke up on a wet boat deck! None of the protagonists have been informed of this shift in scenery - with the exception of most. But some are unaware of this move from a tent to a boat! Then you might ask, if you've read more scrolls:

YOU: Tell me, aren't you more than six people just in this volume? Last time I counted names, there were at least twenty !!? Where are they??

ACHMED: Who? Him the weird one? Who kept sitting, talking to himself on the seat behind the bus driver endlessly - Don't count!

WEIRD GUY: Jap, jap, jap, definitely not this way!!?

ACHMED: Although I have just mentioned him, and now he is here too! Do you see, what I mean?? It just keeps going! Said who?? It's hard to limit the stories and people! They can unfold like Bob the Builder?? Maybe he should jump in the boat instead of the Thai boxer, who is in Thailand for next year anyway? Yes, you can control your characters in your head, and who's on the break!

QUIET QUIET! A feminist hair ball!

Service reserved for people with schizophrenia!
EXT Pacific somewhere - EARLY EVENING

THE KING OF DK:
Hello Achwel welcome

ACHMED: Boun Jour

THE KING OF DK: Buon jour!

ACHMED: I have locked the door!

KING OF DK: Can you speak Colombian now?

ACHMED: Yeah almost! It's pure salsa!

THE KING OF DK: She's salsa dancer?

ACHMED: No, she isn't, but she can move!

THE KING OF DK: Yes, but so can all those with salsa! That's what, they were brought up with! And why shouldn't they be?? But I've just met several people here in town, who come here to fuck Danish women! Under the pretext of dancing salsa!!

ACHMED: Yes, but it's not the same pretext, that you use when traveling to the United States and are visiting?

THE KING OF DK: Yes! But I was just too stupid to make porn movies back then! I should have made porn movies! It was stupid, because you can't do it like a fifty year old man! But you can as a twenty year old! They begged me to do porn movies! I considered it an error in a program, if they asked me! Because that's not, what I was looking for!? But there were several who said: *That way you can get a job easier! Then you can easily earn a high salary!*

ACHMED: *Then you can get the big role after, that you got it in the ass !?*

THE KING OF DK: It didn't matter to get it in the ass! That was lady porn! I would not! That lady porn was such a soft porn! Where you shouldn't even have your pants off!

Well, but I've seen the coolest documentary on French television! I have one about schizophrenia! It's a dangerous disease! And then I've seen one about France's four craziest people! Which is at institutions where they protect! Wild programs! That's what they are good at!

Documentary! Here they are visited by some poor young French men - Unemployed. Where they have been taken in Peru!

ACHMED: Unemployed Frenchmen running around Peru ??!

THE KING OF DK: Unemployed as tempted by Peruvian drug dealers' offer to smuggle cocaine! And they all get caught! Ten Europeans get caught in Lima's airport every day!

ACHMED: And it is the French, who are on their way to France?

THE KING OF DK: It's all nations! I don't know, if there are Danes too ?! Portuguese, Brazilians - Can you understand?

ACHMED: Yes! After all, it's like a national language!

THE KING OF DK: Young Spaniels of twenty-one years! Who carries it in the stomach !!?

ACHMED: She's probably dying ?!

KING OF DK: No, she's in jail! Suburb of Lima!

ACHMED: Surely there are good conditions there ??

THE KING OF DK: No! But tolerable! Better than Colombia! Wasn't it Colombia, that she was from? Yes, they are terrible! They are not there! She has two children in Spain! A boy and a girl. Well! We need to smoke! I've seen some great documentaries! I've seen, *"The hidden side of Maret!"* The craziest neighborhood in Paris! This is where, all the gays have disco! The hidden side! And then there were "The Fools" - They basically have a strange word position! Adjectives and adjectives next to each other - *Le fu - fools - The most dangerous in France!* We don't say that!! *The fools - They are dangerous in Denmark?*? No! Because they do not have easy like comparison, just as we have good, better, best! The French don't! If they are going up at best ?? They haven't! Then they should say: *Les plus dont joure* - It's three degrees! This docu was good! It was good! There you were really allowed to see them flip! And the camera was with all kinds of schizophrenia!

Service reserved for people with schizophrenia!

Have you seen, that there is a lot with Freddie? After all, a movie is coming with him! Did I show you this last week? Where he didn't like to hide his dent? Him in jumpsuit were cute too!

ACHMED: Him? The schizophrenic??

THE KING OF DK: Yes! Goddamn! He is an artist living in Paris! His father has made it his life's struggle to serve his son in the best possible way! New CD with Mireille Mathieu tomorrow! It's a great new moment! Twelve new songs will be released with Classic! New! Sony! There are 100, who have written, that they are happy! And then someone writes:

I think, she sounds a little tired! Then he just gets attacked by 75 furious people on youtube! So I really think, they got a little lucky with her voice! I imagine, she has sung it twenty times, and then they have taken the best! For I give him justice! The man who writes it wrote:

That you could have slipped away with your 70s voice Mireille! Not with your current one! But that's not bad! I just couldn't stand hearing it on a whole record !?

ACHMED: She doesn't have the same "air" anymore !?

THE KING OF DK: No! Nor can she control the vibrato anymore, as hard as she could!

ACHMED: She has not been subject to any accidents?

THE KING OF DK: Yes! She has been in Grenoble for eighteen years, when she was in a wheelchair for fourteen days! Her vocal cords peaked in the 80's! When she was 30, her voice was at max! 40! Shut up my parents were blown away! They didn't really know, if they liked it !? Then they got tickets to hear her in Aalborg! She sang so powerfully Mireille that night, that people could hear it both directly from the stage and in the microphone of course! But it's going to annoy the French completely! It will sell in all sorts of countries other than France! But that is very nice, what they have produced! And she pays a lot for that too! It's Apelinedisk, that produces it! It's her own production company! So she has to pay the dress herself. She has to pay the orchestra herself! She even has to pay moviegoers! Audio production! It is a great orchestra then! There are many, who have to be paid! And this is Ava Maria by Shubert! In Latin!

ACHMED: Is it Latin, that she sings?

THE KING OF DK: Yes! Well, Barbra Streisand recorded it already in '67. It was not on Mireille's two Christmas records! It's one Christmas song! It was on Barbra Streisand's Christmas record! But here they make it a classic song! Now I doubt, it will be something of a hit in France !? But she has run something of a Catholic trick. She has! And made the youth mad at her! And I've heard two of the other songs, and that's ok!

In reality, I dream, that if I were to buy something, it would have to be some kind of Anne Linnet song like "Spring Day"! Where she should not stretch her voice so long, but where the French could get to know a good tune - right? Spring Day! My friend and I made four songs of it in French! And those are some incredibly nice lyrics. So she could have looked at that!

ACHMED: Mireille Mathieu?

THE KING OF DK: Yes! But now it's too late!

ACHMED: Now it's too late!? She is still alive??

KING OF DK: No, I'm not interested in her voice at this time! But I understand the man, who writes it! But they go crazy with their responds to him, just because he....??

Did you see it last time? Last Monday - Survivor?

ACHMED: Yes, I think I did - yes!

THE KING OF DK: They all cried - Twice each!

ACHMED: They're put together right?

THE KING OF DK: Yes! They cried so the tears ran down their cheeks! Joy Tear. Türker had been hospitalized with a stomach ache - for three days. And he had a really bad conscience about that. I can understand that too! And he cried, and he cried!? And I don't want men, to cry like that?! So it's too bloody! Why can't they hold it back just two times !? *"Now I have to cry today for the camera! - Then I will not mute the rest of the day! "*Can you see it? Fucking gays! Wasn't it her, who was voted out? They stabbed her in the back!

Well, tell me about the Colombian pussy!! Was it vertical or horizontal?

ACHMED: It was hairy and it was... ..?

KING OF DK: How old was she?

ACHMED: She was 25 years old! But anyway, mature of her age! She really was! And she didn't question my age!

KING OF DK: Questions?

ACHMED: Yes - I'm 45! 45 is my age?

THE KING OF DK: Yes, yes. But there you meet some, who have a completely different energy inside their heads! Now I just met Peter.

Peter is a man, who comes over from Gronnegade with his dog "Balu!" And he is fucking drunk and taxi driver! But he came with his buddy, who is also subsistent, who has experienced so much crap, that his face is broken. Peter likes older ladies. *"My girlfriend is 61,"* he told me!

ACHMED: And he is himself?

THE KING OF DK: And he himself is what? 45! He came there this summer with his two children! A twelve-year-old girl and an eight-year-old boy. And they got together with Balu, a day without Peter! And we stood up there all of us dog lovers! *Well, it's Peter's dog! It must be Peter's children, then?* And I was standing and heading into the woods, to feed the fox. I had explained to them, that it had been up on the balcony, and I had shown them pictures and so on! Then they had come home to their father, and had said, that they had met a pedophile !?

A pedophile?? Yes! Yes he tried to lure us into the forest! And we were in the woods?! I tried to look!? But the children have interpreted, and returned home and said! And the ex-wife had started calling about it, and they wanted them to call the police!? Peter said, he had to rush the kids, to find out nothing had happened?! *"At the beginning of the first fourteen days, the kids wouldn't tell, if something had happened or not! They needed to continue! And when I found out, that it was you, I told them, that they should stop immediately!!".* He found out, it was me! He was not immediately aware of, who it was, that had been the person, who had tried, to get them into the forest! *It was me, who wanted to feed the fox! Then there was nothing about us taking the pants off those kids, but they even came along!? They went out in the park and looked a little lost! And did they become a little cautious, if they had to attend a dog meeting? And I recognized the dog right away! It might come as a surprise to them!? But I do know the dog! I've walked it ten times!* But then I also said to him yesterday: *But Peter - you have put that discourse into your head, you and your ex-wife!! Or have you not made sure to keep something out!? One must hope that this does not happen again, before they become adults, and do learn to think for themselves!!*

I actually just watched youtube in the track between the programs that skipped it on *Le Police Truvil Pedopile*. That program I did not bother to watch!! But it basically consisted of a forty-minute interview, with a psychologist sitting, talking to an eight-year-old girl and a seven-year-old boy - separately! They were to tell of what, the neighbor's wife had done to them. And they wouldn't tell! In 40 minutes they said nothing, the speaker said! They had been threatened to say nothing!

The boy said, he couldn't say, what she had done!? But she had done something very ugly - *la ferm de mal*! So it consisted of that program!

ACHMED: I've been to the doctor, and had blood tests!

THE KING OF DK: For what??

ACHMED: Both because the doctor would have a test of my blood, because my metabolism was a little high last year, when I was at the doctor the last time! And hadn't followed up?! And then because frankly, I got a little nervous about the Wildcat with AIDS and all ??

THE KING OF DK: Well ?? Why did you get nervous about it?

ACHMED: Because she was like that... ??

THE KING OF DK: Do you go and consider it based on personality?

ACHMED: No, I did it for the reasons, that my dick feels different !?

THE KING OF DK: Well! It can be individual, after all: *How to feel it??* You can't feel that !?

ACHMED: But I think, I can sense something!? But there was nothing!

KING OF DK: Syphilis?

ACHMED: There was no HIV!

THE KING OF DK: The whole thing?

ACHMED: No, not all of it! What you can test in your blood!

KING OF DK: Well it's Gonorrhea and Chlamydia! No, Gonorrhea, that's piss!

ACHMED: Yes, but it doesn't hurt, when I piss. But it's just like somebody touches it !? Although there is no one, who touches it !?

THE KING OF DK: Because I wanted to say that alone being alone at Joys, and walking around with stiff cock for four hours?? It's enough to change many things around it! Then it also needs to relax afterwards!

ACHMED: And it's been stiff for many hours! Also with her!

THE KING OF DK: Well and it all gets a little more sensitive! Just wait! Now you're in your forties! Do you know, what you can risk? Spermatosa!! One in four sperms are red! Once or twice in a lifetime! Science has known about it since the Middle Ages, but nobody knows why!? Just a drop of blood to color it red! The production is strongly connected! Science has never figured out why !? But I have tried it twice! One of the times it was a hole in the urethra! And the second time I don't know?! My friend Angelo came home from touring England - All the big English cities with a dance show, in London, Manchester, Liverpool and so on last week! Then he returned home at 10 in the morning.

"Can you stand here with me at 10 o'clock?".

He then wrote from the airport bus! So I basically stand above his boyfriend! Such a world star! Then he was home for three days. Then he took the tour again! Now he is in Malta, and Cyprus. He is the star of the world. He dances. And he gives Oneman's show! He has the "perfect" body, you don't dream of it! Which can dance obviously! He doesn't know Nikolaj Hybbe! They have met each other a few times! And they don't like each other! In the same way that Bowie didn't like Freddie! And who else didn't like each other ??

ACHMED: Bowie didn't like Freddie?

KING OF DK: What was said about the two's relationship today?? Was it Trump and Obama? I just have to ask my husband! I just want to know! Mapplethorpe and Andy Warhol didn't like each other either! I saw, that Andy Warhol is actually in the Mapplethorpe book here. There is a picture of Andy! But it may have been something that happened after that ?? Did something say? Of course I can't read that now! Because we have been watching a documentary about Mapplethorpe one day! Do you remember him?

ACHMED: No!

THE KING OF DK: Yes! You have seen that picture here ?? Then the whole world has seen !?

ACHMED: Yes! It is true!

THE KING OF DK: I don't know ?? He has a few more, that are famous! No, damn it. ha ha! I'm not interested in big dicks!

ACHMED: No, that doesn't interest me either!

KING OF DK: Yes, I like them. But this is not something, that I set as a criterion! I had a weird time, when I was introduced to Mapplethorpe, when my husband bought a brick of gay art! Where Pierre and Giles are also. I am very excited about them! I am also very excited about Tom of Finland! Everyone in my generation thinks, he's the great gay artist with his drawings! There is also nothing more beautiful than a small vile picture! He is a Finn! Tom of Finland! It's only his artist name! But these are the sixties, that he starts selling to the press! Don't you know it at all??

ACHMED: Not at all!

THE KING OF DK: God! It is a chapter then !!

 In the '70s and' 80s, these were some images, that heterosexuals couldn't avoid! This is Peter Berlin, which was just a good model! And it's in his 50s, that he had that style there! He died of AIDS! Like Freddie, he spent some time in Germany! The Finns have made a feature film about their Tom of Finland! My husband and I don't think, it was good. Pierre and Giles are from Paris. They've made Mireille Mathieu! It is amazing as beautiful a picture, as they made by Mireille! They make portraits of people! There's Madonna! That's their specialty! But they make a lot of self portraits! It was the first time, I became acquainted with Pierre and Giles. But then I suddenly came to Berlin with an art school! They've made all the stars! This is Nina Hagen and her husband! There he is - Jesus! That's a lot of it centered! Boy George! Gaultier! This is a self portrait! This is what, I call supernatural. That's natural enough! But there is something more too! It's a lie about everything! They also made her, the Italian, who just died! She had the biggest breasts in the world! They have also evolved. Because in the beginning, it was portraits. Portraits with borders. Then they discovered, that their interest was great study scenes! There's Catherine Deneuve! What I wanted to show you was Rupert Everett - Do you know him? Tilda Swinton was there too! This is Khaled singing Aicha! And then they once were in Asia and swine their dicks! All the models they meet and fuck with! They are allowed to join their...??

ACHMED: Gender's book?

THE KING OF DK: I've seen this many times! It has been used for covers! The ones here are great too!

ACHMED: It must be Photoshop!

THE KING OF DK: No! It's not Photoshop! These are totally set scenes. They've had a TV team that day! And Jean Paul Gaultier, he buys them, their pictures for his commercials! They had a TV team with them, when they made a portrait of Mireille. There you could really see, how the scene was set up! I also created such a scenery around my sister as a child, but not nearly as nice! So I did not see the effect in!

There's Jeff Stryker. He lived in our rise in our building in Hollywood, when we lived there! We drove in a lift with him in between. He was such a little guy with a cannon big cock! '91. It's one of the last things to see with him. I think, he made five - seven porn movies, so ... He retired! Then you haven't heard from him since! These are the two great artists of my life, so Mapplethorpe will not be one of them! Now we move on with Survivor, and then I stand straight and roll!

ACHMED: No, she is also cheeky the Colombian and also very sensual!

KING OF DK: But she cut the cord with you?

ACHMED: No - She's coming on Wednesday - again!

KING OF DK: But you wrote, that she was flown ??

ACHMED: Flown? Yes. She had been by and spent the night, and then she had continued on the next day! So not out of my life! Like a bird?

KING OF DK: Well, it's not a question of to put quite a lot in everyone, who comes by?

ACHMED: No, but it's nice!

KING OF DK: Don't you think?

ACHMED: Like she said, she was skin hungry! She threw her clothes reasonably fast! So I was going to lie naked with her!

KING OF DK: So more and more focused sex over time?

ACHMED: In relation to the time span? There it was tuned!

THE KING OF DK: There I would say of all the guys, that I visit, there are none of them, who want me to stay! Two minutes after they came in my mouth !?

ACHMED: So is it just further in the program ??

THE KING OF DK: And know them, where I perceived it - Illusion about, that is, what turns on, it breaks, if you break it!

ACHMED: I just need to hear a little about that Builder Bob caretaker at a the school!

KING OF DK: Yes. And it was the Monk, who sent me a text last night:

Do you know someone named Peter Lamp? I say it rings a bell, but I just can't think of it?! Well but I saw otherwise, that you were friends with him on facebook?? Ohh - Builder Bob?? That's Achmed's mate! Then it was, that I asked you there and so on. *And he fuck my wife,* said the Monk then afterwards !!

ACHMED: Yeah, that's what I said: *He's Achmed's mate!!* So he has fucked Monk's wife ?? Ha ha! No!!

KING OF DK: And she's a Danish teacher at school!

ACHMED: No! No! No!

KING OF DK: Yes, yes! Then I wrote back: *Well, if that's the only thing, he does, could it be that bad?* Then he wrote: *No!* That's how you can look at it too! So if they don't start going into it!

ACHMED: He's with people to the right and on the left??

THE KING OF DK: No! I have no evidence, to say that! No, but I don't know anything about others !? You know what Angelo's husband, he's a good guy. He's thirty. He is a train conductor in uniform!!

ACHMED: From DSB or Arriva?

THE KING OF DK: He lies blindfolded, and then I come down, and ride on him! I feel so lucky Achmed! Today I was happy! You do too?

ACHMED: Feeling happy?

KING OF DK: Yes do you feel lucky or happy?

ACHMED: Yes, both!

THE KING OF DK: Is there anything that nudges?

ACHMED: I would say that my business consultant, he nudges me a bit! He wants to talk to me every two weeks! He has a lot of good suggestions, so I'm going to a job meeting at TDC in Tranbjerg !!

KING OF DK: Can't you put pressure on him to say: *Then just find the company, that wants me going! You must have some contacts then?? What can you supply? One thing is to sit down and direct my resume - Try to go out and find a company, that could build a bridge between us !!*

JOSEPH: I'm attending this job meeting at TDC on Friday at 1 pm! Where I have to listen to them for two hours about TV package service ?!

THE KING OF DK: Well, that's very good! And then you get Isa!

JOSEPH: Isa comes afterwards! I have asked Mary to fetch Isa! And then come in with her. She's there just past three!

THE KING OF DK: Well now, yes yes but uh ...

ACHMED: Well, but I'll be employed by the Colombian again on Wednesday! So it's been Friday, Saturday, Sunday, Monday and then Wednesday!

KING OF DK: Is she Danish?

ACHMED: Yes, she was raised in Hinnerup!

THE KING OF DK: By Colombian parents ??

ACHMED: Adaptive! She has Colombian parents, where her mother felt, it was a rape, and her father thought, it was voluntary! But in each case they are not together, and it was shameful! But it is out of a richer family compared to Colombian conditions! So it was not for monetary reasons. And they were young! They are two, three years younger than I am !! Her parents in Colombia!

THE KING OF DK: Yes! Terrible community! Catholicism is horrified over there. What the hell was it, that he named, the one who wrote the announced murder? The great South America writer?

ACHMED: Umberto Ecco shoes ??

THE KING OF DK: No! Bigger! These were the most common tales of an American, who went down to Colombia to marry a girl! And on the wedding night, the whole city celebrated it in the best Catholic way! But on the wedding night, he discovered, she was not a virgin! Then he threw her across the balcony!? And the whole town came to kill him, which they then assumed, had taken her maiden name!

ACHMED: Now they're all crying again, because there's a letter from home!?

JOSEPH: No, I also said to Mary, when we were together, that I would like to sign up for Survivor! But if I did, then they should not send letters or video diary or anything from home!! Because I wouldn't bother to see it! I do not believe, it is motivating for a participant to deal with it at home!?

KING OF DK: Something that I can't join! That is crying all the time. I simply can't help that!

ACHMED: No, and it gets really serious in this section where, that there is a letter from home!

KING OF DK: Well, it's always been that way! In a time when they spouted! These are all the other times, where they stand and moan! It is new! And I really liked writing for TV3! With all the recordings they must have, then they should be able to choose?? Is it necessary to cultivate, which parts are powerful, that we have to look at it every Monday?? Men standing and moaning?? Couldn't they cut it out possibly?? Isn't there something more exciting?? Shouldn't they ever fuck out there?? Can't we see that ?? In fact, I'd rather see them fucking, than I'd like to see them puke! Especially him there! I want to see, as he ties his hair up, when he takes a shit! Or whether it stands out, like such an umbrella over him?? And I want to know, who's bending their knees? And who is anal flushing? He has no one, who likes him - Türker! Uhh. I hope Jamil comes out tonight!

I could send them a condom with some sperm?? Ha ha!

ACHMED: *First time from home? Do you have a condom?*

THE KING OF DK: The craftsman I met at Birdsung at about twelve in the spring a few months ago, Shut up, he was delicious! A daddy of forty-five years! Angelo and I had just arrived, and had gone there in the morning! Then there's a white electrician's car! Then we went to the bathroom. Then he got up and followed us! Then he said:

Will you come with me to the disabled toilet? Yeah, damn, I said.

And he only speaks English Angelo, so he doesn't understand much Danish! Yes - and then we went in! Then he fucked us both standing up !! On a changing table !! Ha-ha! Naughty guy! And he wanted, what we want! A married man! There's no time to beat around the bush here! I ask: *Do you want to go to the bathroom?* - Funny! It's not like so many others, can't figure it out, and say things that way!

ACHMED: It's funny, that our first date was down at the winter bathing club. We met in the clubhouse and had lunch with dessert!

THE KING OF DK: Well - god!

ACHMED: And then we were in the sauna naked afterwards! She had never been in the little saunas for four years of membership - she says !? So we went first in the big ones, back and forth, then I suggest her the little ones. In one there are fragrances, and you can talk together, and the other is for the silent ones. But the one were you are allowed to talk, was completely stuffed. And the one in which you were supposed to be quiet, there was actually only one! So there we settled in, with the distance we are sitting here - completely naked - first date! And we sit and look at each other! It was probably a little dark! So....?

KING OF DK: So he went the other one?

ACHMED: No, though!

THE KING OF DK: Are there anyone watching all the time?

ACHMED: No! But we couldn't help but sit around trying to....? But then we were actually down for a swim the other day. After all, it was something else entirely!

KING OF DK: It's a good little game, which you then found to be able to use - finally!

ACHMED: And my parents have been preaching for a long time: *Why don't you find one in an association?* And the only association I am with is it! So it was fun, then, that there is also, someone who goes there! - So we can go together!

THE KING OF DK: One that "we" can see naked! One with short pubic lips!

ACHMED: No, she has big pubic lips, lips and strong hair! 25 years old! Nice to have!

THE KING OF DK: And she's mature, you say?

ACHMED: She is! She was involved in a traffic accident as a fourteen-year-old, where she gets hit by a van and flies twenty meters through the air and lies in a coma!

KING OF DK: Shit!

ACHMED: So for the compensation she got from that accident, she buys an apartment in Aarhus!

THE KING OF DK: Well, in Denmark ??

ACHMED: In Denmark !! Yes. She was raised in Hinnerup!

KING OF DK: Shit!

ACHMED: She comes to Denmark, as a baby of three months. So she has no recollection of Colombia! But she then traces her biological parents!

KING OF DK: Has she been in the show "Traceless"?

ACHMED: Yes, she could have had a free trip to Colombia !! No, but she has been there, and lived for a year and found both parents too. So she has actually re-established a relationship with them today!

THE KING OF DK: Well! They are fierce Catholics in the most negative way, you can imagine! They are pigging each other out! They really go into what the neighbor does, and who was present at church on Sunday?? And which of the neighbor's kids fucked with whom !? And a girl who is not a virgin?? She's not worth anything?! We have long since passed in Denmark!

ACHMED: But she's naughty!

KING OF DK: What is her name?

ACHMED: Natty Florréas Elgaard. And the day she saw the keys to her new condominium, eighteen years old: *Now I'm moving away from Dad and Mom!* Then the father of the day chooses to say: *Now I've been silent about it for almost ten years - I'd like to ask for a divorce now !!*

THE KING OF DK: Well ?? Does he say that to the mother?

ACHMED: Yes, he says that to her mother and to all those present at the festivities! That's a bad timing!

THE KING OF DK: No! There are many men, who do Achmed! Some goals are set! *I'm staying with my wife, until my daughter moves away!* You can hear that, he has said it many times! He did so! This is also, what others have done! *"I'll stay with my wife, until the boy has been confirmed!"* And then he came home after the graduation party, and told her so! Then she said: *"It won't matter - You can arrange your gay fun in peace!"* "And then you become a friend here!".

ACHMED: And then he was suppressed?

THE KING OF DK: And it's three years later!

ACHMED: But it's the women, who decide! Come on Jamil! He's Tarzan!

THE KING OF DK: Now she is hiding her madness and shooting after Jamil?? It doesn't hit? Why doesn't she shoot at Jamils? She hit the Turks. What does TV3 have to do with four wogs eventually in the program?? Why??

ACHMED: Well, it may be this year, that it is a paki, that wins ??

KING OF DK: You can hardly avoid that !! Want a piece of cake?

ACHMED: Looks good friend!

KING OF DK: So be it! Is she crying? It's a rogue version of Survivor!

ACHMED: Well, it tastes good! It's a spice cake?

KING OF DK: Don't they write letters - Wogs? Well, no they don't !!

Fuck you Zanne - You girls have to face some challenges, too! Or you can turn our entire society into a feminist hairball!

ACHMED: No, now he's rubbing!?

KING OF DK: Is he crying now too, when he should laugh ?!

ACHMED: Well then Loco wins!

THE KING OF DK: Well done anyway! I'm going to the Music House and see Shame tomorrow!

ACHMED: With Karin Salling?

THE KING OF DK: Just Mina and I! I was with Karin Salling on Tuesday to premiere on Dancer in the dark, only for the city's spikes! Mayor Thorkild Simonsen and his wife, and Karin Salling, and actors Nanna Bodker and her parents and Christian Villand and both his parents, and drank white wine! But she didn't really care! She was a little angry about it! But she said, *"Hello"!* But she was a little angry, that it lasted so long, and she had her fifty year birthday in her hands, which also has wounds all over it! She looked like a worse psoriasis patient! Then you can see! It's no use being the daughter of Jutland's richest woman ?? If you have a head wound !?

ACHMED: How old is he?

THE KING OF DK: She! Fifty and bold!

ACHMED: And have no husband?

KING OF DK: I don't know! He wasn't there! And she is cheating now too!? No, now I am going to leave! You can even see Survivor! I do not bother to see such any more!

ACHMED: Do you put more water over for coffee?

THE KING OF DK: Yes! What the hell is some tuition!? But have you seen Dancer in the dark? On film? It was Björk, who ran around as a factory woman, and had a son, whom she fought for. She was getting blind. I've been trying to see forty minutes of it without falling asleep! Because the songs didn't appeal to me, but they had been condensed.

ACHMED: I've heard the soundtrack. They are excellent the songs there.

THE KING OF DK: They were excellent the songs there. Nanna sang most of them! Christian? I think, he was fascinating to look at! He was also in the "Biedermann and Arsonist", which I was down to see last month! He is stuck at Aarhus Theater! Both Nanna and Christian's parents live in Copenhagen, but they had taken the train over here, because they played together! Christian is so beautiful! So great! And thin! When the stage light strikes him, the silhouette, thinner than....? And Nanna Bodker? There you can just see ..?

ACHMED: Now Turker is also chuckling - *"It's fucking hard!"*

THE KING OF DK: I will have to write to Ekstra Bladet then, that they have cried in all sections. It's cry princess!

ACHMED: *"You should just try it yourself!".*

KING OF DK: Well, I always cry, when it's needed! But even after sending my two grandmothers so beautifully from here, I can not cope anymore!? I only cry, when I feel powerless! I didn't even bother with my own disease course! I'm not interested in crying! That if you have a need to cry, then you will find at least one opportunity for it! Do you have something, that you haven't been crying about ??

ACHMED: No!

THE KING OF DK: Someone who has offended you in childhood or?

ACHMED: No! I wish, it had been so !!

THE KING OF DK: You would have liked some neighbor wife or pedophile?

ACHMED: Or babysitter! Something that had tricked the memory that day!

THE KING OF DK: Just like that time my babysitters had guys visiting, when they were supposed to look after me. When my father came home: *"Just breasts?!".* Yes, they were fucking on the couch, and this was the first time, I saw sex!

ACHMED: And how old were you?

KING OF DK: Yes, how old had I been? Seven / eight years!

ACHMED: Keep it up! It was early too!

KING OF DK: Yes, but I didn't associate it with any penetration! I didn't know, that sex was so extensive?? I just thought, it was kissing! And I didn't start to care about it anymore!

ACHMED: It wasn't, where it started – your interest?

THE KING OF DK: No, it didn't. First as a thirteen / fourteen year old! I remember, I just woke up one morning, and the sky was completely pink!

ACHMED: Yeah? Before or after?

THE KING OF DK: Before!

ACHMED: I promised myself, that I shouldn't have a girlfriend, while I was in high school. So all of it going crazy at high school parties, I put a lit on that myself. I said to those, who came near me, and wanted to dance or something, that I had a girlfriend!

THE KING OF DK: Well ?? Where did you get that tune into your head ??

ACHMED: I think the tune came from seeing my older brothers, who were very much intoxicated by female sex, ended up with a average grades in their high school days! So I concluded, that female acquaintances are the root of a lower grade!! It is disruptive to one's average!

THE KING OF DK: It is also right somewhere, if you really have to go into it! But women's acquaintances can also exist at an incredibly superficial level!

ACHMED: Sure, but the event didn't happen either, that I thought, here she was - *Now I'm letting go of principles and rules!!* So it ended the day, when we actually got a hat on, and had ended our trip on agricultural machinery (student wagon) Here at the last goal I was "lucky" with one of my classmates, who was the nicest in the class! One year older! Tine. Continue....!!

KING OF DK: But I also saw an interview on CNN with a rich man, billionaire in dollars! He is about to be a famous world man. He's a great guy at forty-five! He has created many companies - big companies.

And then it was an interview about, how he did it! He had married a woman as twenty-four, and he has never talked to women other than her!! He was driven straight home from the office every day except the days of overtime! Then it was, that I could see: *Ok, there really is a sacrifice in play here!* It has really been dedicated. *It's all about my businesses. It's all about my businesses!!* Just like there was a football player on TV the other day with his wife, and they sat on the evening show couch, and then the wife explained to them: *"Yes, we have some periods, when Soren couldn't ..."?* I don't know, if his name was Soren?? But *Soren couldn't ... and so on!* And Soren liked to hear himself mentioned in the third person!? *We have some days, where Soren is not cable of doing anything other than getting out and exercising at all!!* He suffers partly from depression, and then he had an OCD diagnosis, because the man could not sit still, and he could not take his children seriously! He wanted to work out! And once in a while, if the wife offered to run with*: No, no you should not come, because then I can not run as fast, as I would call it exercise!* Such a depressive man!! Absolute fat less!!

ACHMED: Sounds like the Wild Cat too - fat less!

KING OF DK: Yes? Was it lovely - hers?

ACHMED: Yes - and totally shaved! She couldn't stand hair!

THE KING OF DK: No! Neither can I! I also have to say that to people, I meet ...! Or I'm not saying anything!

ACHMED: But the Colombian girl is a bit more hairy, but she gives me a stiffer hard on than the Wild Cat.

THE KING OF DK: There you can see for yourself!! You just want to make new records all the time! You need to learn, what you really want?? You have no idea, who you are?? You've tried the three different kinds of sandwiches! But there are palettes, that you haven't tasted!!? You must be bound and polled, before you can comment on anything !! And that's how men learn all their lives! About what they prefer with their women. And there it is that Thai women and Thai culture, it suits a lot of men in the West! And then you have to ask: *What is it, that they get for their money?* It's not love! You must never think, it is love!! As soon as the wallet is empty, she is gone! But they get a fresh and fragrant pussy, that they can use! And who sits and boils rice to the very big gold medal!! There are some men, who find practicality later in life!!

There are many men, who go there, and say they want a divorce, just like the Colombian's father the day, she moved away!

ACHMED: But it's more fun, to see how they develop later on! The Wild Cat was 16, when her father moved to Greenland on the Thule base and found another one! So she didn't think, distance relationships were optimal!! But it saves some relationships ...?

KING OF DK: Yes, that saves some! I have no doubt for a moment! But it is difficult!

ACHMED: But just in this case, I know, he won't be home until three months into Christmas! And away for many months at a time! When I think of distance relationships, I think of professions, where you are on a drilling platform! Where one may be gone two to four weeks and at home equivalent or longer! It is also long distance, but it is still over the short distance, where the man is gone!! And when they are home, they have nothing to do! They do nothing!

THE KING OF DK: No! Why should they?? What do you mean??

ACHMED: They're not at work. Then they are at home with their wives, and can dedicate time to them, and make them happy. And when they are separated, they miss each other!

THE KING OF DK: Then they likely live like gays !!?

ACHMED: While sitting in a movie theater on a drilling platform?

THE KING OF DK: No! Then they fuck with the comrades! People want to have sex - about once a day! Five days a week! Then they can do something completely different, that the wife knows nothing about! It has just been investigated! What was the answer now? *One in three Danish men have sex with other men, without identifying themselves as bisexual!* That's how, it sounded. It was in the newspaper!

ACHMED: I still haven't got that picture of Putin and North Korea's leader??

THE KING OF DK: No, I'll probably - I just need my husband, to send it to me!

ACHMED: You can probably hear that piloting now !!

THE KING OF DK: Does that sound now ??

ACHMED: Yeah, I don't know, where it comes from?? No, she is naughty!

KING OF DK: Well? Now they really come to quarrel !! Now she starts to cry?? And his eyes they are shining!!

Why do you please me? I'm turning my tears into diamonds! In a good way!

ACHMED: No, I can't understand, what she says because of her tears!?

KING OF DK: I'm not crying! I am falling asleep - crying! Then she must win a symbol of feminism!!

ACHMED: They're all small babies!

KING OF DK: It's the Arabic language:

You have to bring home gold for me!

ACHMED: *I was an asshole, before I left! Now I'm still an asshole! Just in another place! I have become a more tender asshole!* Oh stop!

KING OF DK: *Mom is having a nervous breakdown now!*

ACHMED: No, I couldn't read such a letter!

THE KING OF DK: They should have had a female voice, to read what was written! With echoes on and violins!

ACHMED: I would have made up something bizarre to say instead!!

KING OF DK: *Send a couple of old dirty panties !! Ha ha!*

ACHMED: *Hi honey - What's the recipe for the good pizza? - You know??*

KING OF DK: *I've also become more sensitive over here!?* It also fits a bit in discourse with the program! *I've never cried as much in my life, as when I joined Survivor!* But is that, what is meant?? Is it an indication, that they are under pressure?

ACHMED: Is it at Tovshoj school?

KING OF DK: I don't know?!

ACHMED: Wasn't he from Aarhus?

KING OF DK: Ridiculous, what he is saying!!?

ACHMED: *Normally I don't get this angry in these situations!*

KING OF DK: *Is it so rare, that you get so angry ?? Well, then he must have really made you mad !!* But they are Arabs, and they don't like Turks! No, it's damn interesting the groups, that I have joined down at the theater! Preview! There was beer for the press and wine and everything - just for

180

the press! I also think, that tomorrow is a premiere, because she writes about it! I don't know, if it's musical or acting tomorrow??

For a long time I said no! So now I've got a little more in the mood to go along! She asks a lot! Something's up today, too! Shut up, man!

ACHMED: I notice the little things!

KING OF DK: Well, Arabs have just developed an ability to settle in the border country, between where we are in Scandinavia. Since discovering the Middle East, have we discovered, that we are villains ?? They always have some perfidious meaning in big discussions. You can always be shocked by the mindset of Arabs!

ACHMED: Yes, especially if you could understand, what they were saying!

THE KING OF DK: I remember in my class, where we had some class discussion, the Arabs just say suddenly - *I think, we need to close the borders. I don't bother having more Palestinians up here!* And I totally agreed!

I want to fuck her before the finale!

ACHMED: *I want to fuck her before a finale. Then I'm healthy! Ahh it's a death bracelet. I'll take it!*

KING OF DK: He also did that in the last paragraph, and there he lost. But he was not voted out ?! It made me furious! It makes me sad! It makes me puke! *No, I don't mean, he does either! No, you have said that several times now!*

ACHMED: But you get shocked every time? Oh, I need some water!

KING OF DK: How long will it take to drive to Randers?

ACHMED: Why will you want to drive to Randers??

KING OF DK: I was back and forth to Randers the other day, and I don't think, it took me more than 15 minutes, because I drive 150 km/h each way !!

ACHMED: 150 km/h ?? It's fast too ?!

KING OF DK: Yes. There were several, who did!

ACHMED: When I was driving to Randers, I was driving no more than 90-100km/h. But it was on the main road, and it was dark, and I was about to torpedo a trailer! Coming from a side road. And I saw it, and slowed down a bit, as I got closer to it. But I should have flashed the long light! Because he was waiting until the last second, when I got to the approaching road, then he drives right out in front of me!!?

KING OF DK: You have to calculate, that people do!! You have to anticipate, that people can make mistakes!

I see many on the highway between Skanderborg and Aarhus, driving at 130km/h and sitting on their phones – SMS?! And driving like this!? Adults!!? Just expect that!! Here the other day there was one, who drove 130km/h, and there were six, who would like to pass. As he drove into the middle, lane and I overtook, I could see, he was writing on his phone!? That is why, he did not discover, that he pulled a tail of cars after him!! Because in that moment - It's totally crazy!!? In any case, it is fifty percent of the population, that drives with the mobile on their corpus!

ACHMED: But it is only a few years more, because then the mobile becomes a contact lens! Then you just blink your eye, while you're driving, and the display is on the windshield! And self-driving cars etc.

THE KING OF DK: Then it will be legal, you mean?

ACHMED: No !!
I've seen several single profiles in the bathing club, and the club also has a singles group on facebook!

THE KING OF DK: But that's basically it: *You guys are free to search and create clubs for all kinds of perverse....?*

JOSEPH: Both Mary and her mother are in the singles group!!

THE KING OF DK: Oh for the fuck !! So can you block her? Can't you?? And then she can't see it !?

ACHMED: Could be, that it works like that?! I can't follow the Wild Cat anymore !!? She's gone !? She no longer exists for me !?

THE KING OF DK: No, it's clear! It was an experiment, which failed !! And especially with what you wrote to her !!

ACHMED: Yes, that must be said!

KING OF DK: Surely you shouldn't threaten her for life, just because they won't give you pussy !!? Ha ha.

"I have become emotionally attached to you, here the last six days of my life!! And now I want to own you!! Now don't decide anymore - Now it's me who decides !! ".

Here on Saturday I had come to bed at 9pm, and I woke up at 5am. 3.30. Then I got up, and went out for a smoke. Then came a young man with a bicycle dragging across the lawn. Nice tall guy with black pants. Light hair and dark jacket! And he dragged it through the hole there. I could hear him continuing on to the Poppels Circle! Then all of a sudden there was a bang !! Then he threw it into a car!?

Then I went in and took the bone, and called the East Jutland police! Then sounded a second - BOM. Then I started talking. Then I said:

That if you are fast, you can snag a bicycle thief, who is smashing cars at the Poppel Circle! So I don't know, how fast they were?? At least there was shouting. Then sounded number three! BOOM! Then two more minutes passed, then sounded number four! And then suddenly there was a shouting over there! But it has not been stated in the daily report, that they have caught him! But I had also jumped back and forth. It could have been, that he had disappeared among the bushes!? They probably couldn't follow him, if they got close enough!?

ACHMED: I just don't understand why, that they don't set up more cameras!?

THE KING OF DK: You must learn to ashes it there! That's because you're not used to it with your vapor. Then you can just continue to smoke! My husband is actually considering starting to 'steam'!

ACHMED: Yes, I can understand that! He will gain a better health in doing so! Then maybe he can postpone a COPD diagnosis on his last days!

KING OF DK: Yes?? I had about two difficult days of breathing last week!

ACHMED: Fuck, it's awful!

KING OF DK: Yes, but then it went away! And then I was at fitness this weekend!

ACHMED: This is how, I may feel, if I'm a little snotty, and my nostrils are stopped! Fuck man! Then it's hard to breath!

THE KING OF DK: Yes - it's awful!

ACHMED: It's been especially during the days, when I was a little overweight! Then the neck region has closed in too! So being overweight is not good! Montserrat Cabellé must also have had some breathing problems with such a corpus??

KING OF DK: Yes, what do you mean? I actually just heard Lotte Heise's pod cast, where it was about her death! And there she was, philosophizing that her husband had a tiny tap, and hers was so voluminous! But she has never hidden it, and she is a fabulous example of that! *"Une femme qui est bien dans sa peau"*. *A woman who is comfortable with her skin! I'd rather. I'd rather. I'd rather have meds!*

But he had become decadent Freddie Mercury! He was wearing big leather pants, without underpants with a big cock sticking down his leg. And always incredibly beautiful! And there for Liveaid, inside the camera - not from the front! They were filming from the side. They have been fighting a tough fight, because it was LIVE! It has already been decided in the backstage, that no one dares tell him to wear underpants. And it just hangs down here !! It hangs here! It is that long! And I might, as well look at him as gay! But this is the Freddie, he has had in those years, when he lived in New York! He has been equipped with the big cock! He would fist and take drugs! He was a coke wreck! He was a bird. He wanted to take it up the ass!

How did they agree, to send four there ??

ACHMED: I don't know ??

THE KING OF DK: There were lots of factory scenes, where Nanna Bodker played Björk's role, and she got to dance around with a lot of factory workers! And it was young dancers. And they had their gay friends with them backstage there after the show! We did not stay very long. We didn't hear the talk up there !!

Want a glass of juice? It tastes good at this time! I just discovered that! Christian and Daniel stood the other day afterwards and drank juice!

ACHMED: Ha ha - is that the secret?

KING OF DK: Yes, it gives a little upper to the blood!

ACHMED: Yeah, it tastes great!

KING OF DK: Doesn't your brother drink juice? I was absolutely convinced that he did! I think, he drinks Ribena??

ACHMED: That's why, Jamil wouldn't send Yasser. He's like Stoichkov!

KING OF DK: How much has Yasser been able to put together? None?? Ha ha !! Now take a break! Ha-ha! Oh, Yasser, goddamn it! He has proven to be totally ineffective! He's a hysteria. He knows nothing! And did you hear, what he said? That he wanted, to show his wife, that he has changed !!? Then they stood and quarreled, before he left! He is the pig, that I see in him! He shit so it smells all over the house! Shut up, man! He's four years old !?

ACHMED: *It was a fucking game! Give me something physical next time!*

THE KING OF DK: Some porn! Now he runs over in ass licking mode! I wonder, what he had the eye problem for?

ACHMED: Sand in the eyes?

KING OF DK: It could also be the remains of a battle!? They may have been up for battle, but they chose, not to show it !?

ACHMED: Yeah, if it hasn't happened in the gloom?

THE KING OF DK: It may be, that Yasser has pawned him one! He's four years inside - that man!

ACHMED: No ten!

THE KING OF DK: Yes! He has been fucked by the others in the family, cousins and uncles! *It's every time I'm mad, so I'm not myself! Then I'm another one! A fool that no one likes!*

Well, you get around the world right now!

ACHMED: Yes, I do? No, now it has happened in my apartment, and in the bathing club!

THE KING OF DK: Well!? I thought, you were buying a world map, that you could turn some crosses on !?

ACHMED: *Randers, Vejle, Silkeborg, Ikast...*

KING OF DK: *And now Colombia !! New Zealand, South Africa, Uganda?*

ACHMED: No, I've seen Kenyans!! And not a single one made my head turn! Very dramatic music!

KING OF DK: Well?

ACHMED: Then he won again? Otherwise, is it going well?

THE KING OF DK: Yes!

ACHMED: Do you get anything written?

THE KING OF DK: No!

ACHMED: Why not ??

KING OF DK: Because I'm doing everything else!

ACHMED: I can't help it at all!! I can't even agree on, what I really should!

KING OF DK: That's cool! I knuckle around the clock! And when I'm not fucking, then I sleep! And I'm going there. And I need to take action. And I'm going to Skejby. And I have to walk with dogs. And then I also have something, that I must have arranged! I know, I'm not a gentleman over time! I fool around! I have expectations for me to go along! I've made myself a new CD this week! It's simply the funniest song! It's a Frenchman, who made it. But it is in English! And it has potential. It's really good! But with a different vocal! It should have been someone else! Tom Jones? And no one cared to listen to him, and no one cared to look at him! How fun is that?

ACHMED: No, I can't help it at all!

THE KING OF DK: That's great!

ACHMED: Yes, I enjoy it! And I think something happens from time to time! And the whole process of writing. And on Thursday, there is specialist advice on starting growth. And that is, what I think, I should take advantage of, because you can get to talk to both lawyers and marketing people!

KING OF DK: On - about to start?

ACHMED: Yes, when writing a screenplay. So what? One thing is libel? And another thing is marketing? And publishing channels?

THE KING OF DK: I think ..? Do you know, what was in the newspapers last week? Never have so many authors, published so many novels. Self-paid novels like in Denmark right now!! The printing press has crowned days!

ACHMED: Yes, yes, but that's the publishing channel ...?

KING OF DK: Just take your vapor with you!

ACHMED: *"Now I want to sleep".* She calls herself Natty!

THE KING OF DK: Is she writing it now ??! What a strange life to lie and entertain other people with: *That now I go to bed!*

ACHMED: Should I write that to her ?? *What a weird thing to write. ??*

THE KING OF DK: No!! Don't write that! Don't go down that level! Then you have to live on that level there! *Now Daddy has a boner again! What can Natty, do about it ?? So that's Natty's problem!* I feel like the young guys, like to get into an SMS chain turn! I've been through something like that! Queens writing morning, noon and evening:

Good morning have you slept well ?!

ACHMED: There are also many people, who would like to meet quickly for not spending too much time on written romanticizing!

KING OF DK: *Wir alein! Es geht mir gut! Merci! Cheri! Es geht mir gut! Was machen sie?* It has been on the charts in three countries! One in Germany! One in Russia and one in France! In France it was with some Negro rappers, who sampled a number!

ACHMED: Here is her facebook profile picture! But she's not that photogenic! She is difficult to photograph, but she is beautiful!

THE KING OF DK: She is! How old is she, you say? 24-25?

ACHMED: 25!

THE KING OF DK: And she has no age complex? No, they do not have that kind of culture Achmed! They haven't! I told you so! They see you as a rescue! One who is more mature in life! And this is normal for a lot of people! But she is an adoptive child! So there shouldn't be anything with the same prejudices as the other Danish girls !?

ACHMED: But she has nothing from Colombia! Besides her hair! Well, she has always felt different here! But she actually has a big brother, who is also an adopted child from Colombia! She had someone else to mirror in! Yes, her adoptive father was there for her right through her accident, from the age of fourteen to the age of eighteen! Then he ended that relationship! That marriage!

KING OF DK: How do you come to mind telling each other such things ?? Is it important for her, to get it out or what?

ACHMED: I don't know ?? I do not remember in what context, it was said?? But she was reasonably quick to state that:

A: She fluctuated a lot in weight! B: That her voice was a little weird, because she had been in an accident ...

KING OF DK: Well? Because of the accident?

ACHMED: Yes! She's had a heavy tongue operation!

THE KING OF DK: No, no, no !!

ACHMED: And maybe her tongue hung out a little bit longer than usual!

THE KING OF DK: No, no, no !!

ACHMED: But since we're talking Colombia! Then she sounds as well, that she has a Spanish dialect! It makes her a little more authentic! But there was one, who said to her one day a few years after the accident, and where her mouth still hung a little: *So close that mouth !!*

KING OF DK: Do you like to see theater?

ACHMED: I was playing with her soft vagina!

KING OF DK: Yes, ladies like it!

ACHMED: And she came quickly! With the Wild Cat is took me two hours!! Because if I somehow broke the monotony, then I could start over!?!

THE KING OF DK: No!? Sex for two hours?? Surely no one can keep up!?

ACHMED: No! I was also breaking up eventually, because it just dragged on for ages!! I could go on and on !!

KING OF DK: She couldn't come or what ??

ACHMED: Every time I just made "a mistake", a variation - *"Don't vary!".* *"It must be monotonous !!".* Each time I made a variant - maybe the speed slowed down a quarter of a second, then she lost concentration and went all out!! Then I could start over!

Over again?? Now we have been doing this for an hour and three quarters! You don't mean that, do you?? Can't you do anything yourself?? - I won't bother anymore!! I have become paralyzed in both right and left arm now!! Ha ha!

KING OF DK: Then it was good to throw up!

ACHMED: Yes. I would say that too. Taking that into account, the Colombian is more moderate, and yet manages to be more sensual!

THE KING OF DK: It's Mireille Mathieu in Danish!

ACHMED: In Danish ??

KING OF DK: Yes. I just downloaded five songs from youtube! And it's a singer, who sings Mireille Mathieu songs in Danish! It's Svenlana! And Agnetha Fälttskog has recorded Mireille's songs! This is Ulla Pia! Shut up, she was great in every country! And in Turkey! In Germany! Everyone copied her! Yes - That's what is so magnificent about her! Because she didn't write her own songs or anything! She just sang! And yet they copied her everywhere! That's because the voice is a little better than everyone else! That's what, I wrote the other day! The frequency of Mireilles Mathieu is so high, that it benefits my exterior - My outer aura!

ACHMED: It just fixes your aura in place?

THE KING OF DK: *Now we're going to quarrel, and now we're going to pee !!* Why should it go beyond Loco?

ACHMED: Because he's Mastermind! He's gone a bit off a radar!

KING OF DK: It's incredible, that she hasn't lost any more - Flormelis? But she must be really lush in the propagation area??

ACHMED: She's probably the one, who loses the most, even though she is still thick!!

THE KING OF DK: Him who has a good side, and he has a huge coward side! He gives up as easily as nothing! He knows nothing about him - Yasser! Because he considers the others shit! Now comes revenge! *I want to take you down!* No, with Türker I think, he is right..! It's like it stands totally still !?

So it takes a lot for me to get angry! But now I'm angry! It is special, when something has made me angry, it is bad, because it is extraordinarily bad! Because "me" of the entire population of the globe? I??

ACHMED: Now they come to the Christmas decoration !!

KING OF DK: Are we there in the program, that they picked Jamil to win? Try to see! So it's a blue eye, he's had !?

ACHMED: He's on the girls' team right?

THE KING OF DK: Well, he's a girl himself too!

ACHMED: Out with Flormelis! She's not worthy of being a Survivor!

THE KING OF DK: No! In fact, I think Yasser is!

ACHMED: Yasser took a death fight!!

KING OF DK: Karina! She is Benedikte light! Ha ha! When they attack, they really attack - the boys! They are because, they dare not tell the truth! Then they come up with something like that! Now he loses courtesy! Now he becomes childish! After all, he couldn't last Yasser! Do you remember that? That's the one, he's tried before and lost! His hands are deaf!

ACHMED: He's dyslexic! It should say SURVIVOR shouldn't it ??

KING OF DK: He can't hold his fingers! That is, the program wants him lifted off!

ACHMED: Well, boys Yasser lost!

THE KING OF DK: Who will he slander now ?? He knew nothing?!

I dedicate this Survivor to my wife! She is the best on the planet!

Why doesn't he, just get up and leave ??

ACHMED: There are seven days left, he said! I don't know, if they can fill seven days in one week ?? What do you have on the program? And what happened to the show "Child molesters"!?

KING OF DK: I don't know, if it was taken by the program? But the programs are also not available !?

AMAZING PEACE OF THE Pacific!

Ext Pacific Afternoon - on a boat

THE KING OF DK:
Then there was the family at Bryggen!

ACHMED: Who was voted out of Survivor the last time?

THE KING OF DK: That was the great Dane - Jan Magnussen!

ACHMED: Well - I don't even know, who he is ?!

THE KING OF DK: Then there are midterm elections in America!

ACHMED: Is it tomorrow? How do you think, it's going to tighten up?

KING OF DK: Is a machine running or what? Well! It's the water!

ACHMED: Does it really say such a sound?

THE KING OF DK: Then it did!

ACHMED: Very nice! Very nice!

KING OF DK: What about the Evening Show. Do they have something on?

ACHMED: "Date me naked" - What language was that? Was it Denmark?

THE KING OF DK: No, it was England! But it is also available in Germany!

ACHMED: She was asked, the Colombian, if she would like to participate in "Date me naked"! But I don't think, she did. But it wasn't because, she was physically incurred!

THE KING OF DK: Well, is there anything that might indicate, that she is? It is me, who has pressed?? It can't really find the way forward! Funny, really. Yes yes.

ACHMED: Then the picture stopped there?

KING OF DK: It's coming again!

ACHMED: That's probably atmospheric disturbance ?! Willy!

THE KING OF DK: They were probably very similar to the bodies! Weren't they? There wasn't much difference between them!

ACHMED: In each case, there is one, there have been to some festivals with the bracelets - Yellow!

KING OF DK: He's been there before ?! Dull by thunder! He has been bullied as a child. You can see his face! He can't relax!

ACHMED: Uha, he's hairy. Fuck, he's great! Damn it! A tall hairy man!

THE KING OF DK: Yes, he's probably bald!

ACHMED: They seem to have a stomach!

KING OF DK: The Englishmen do! No, that was a shame! It was also the smallest cock! And he has a totally wrong self-acceptance! Damn, he's delicious the guy in the Orange booth! Sure, there are some of them, that we've seen before!

ACHMED: Awkward!

KING OF DK: Orange! Do you see, how young he is? I told you so!

ACHMED: Yeah - he's in his thirties, isn't he?

THE KING OF DK: No, the twenties! He's in his twenties! We've seen him in the Blue before! He is big! He is nice! What a little nose, and a big beast! Is it him, who is hairy? Is it him with the dark hair? So he has a comb-over!?

ACHMED: The one who didn't smile? Plumber??

KING OF DK: It was him, who was so thin!

ACHMED: Well - I thought he won !?

THE KING OF DK: No, no!

ACHMED: *Smile though !!*

KING OF DK: Wondering how to make those recordings, where they turn around?

ACHMED: Red? He is gay then? She would rather be with a plumbing man ?? *Then get that hair cut!*

KING OF DK: I don't know, what he looks like! So there I would really work with some hair, if I was him! That guy! *And then just cut a different hairstyle than the saucepan, and then get your teeth fixed !?*

ACHMED: 22 years ?! Shut up, I guessed, that he was in his thirties with that hair loss !? Thick madam!

THE KING OF DK: She's probably big, and the tummy, it has traces of birth!

ACHMED: Yeah, but she did say, she had a couple of children as well!

KING OF DK: Yes, yes! It must be fucking hardcore too, to get the body back again??

ACHMED: But that was almost, what we did last Friday - That: "Date me naked" in the winter swimming Club!

THE KING OF DK: Yes, it is then !! It's a bit of the same!

ACHMED: There we also started seeing each other naked! And we sat inside the quiet sauna! And she really looked at me!

THE KING OF DK: Did she choose him ??

ACHMED: Yes!

KING OF DK: What about those lips there? *Shouldn't you have done something about them?*

ACHMED: Fuck, he is ugly. ADDR. Only one is shown. Maybe?

KING OF DK: Who was it? I can't keep track of that !?

ACHMED: *That's nice! I think this puzzy is nice! You have got a zipper for it??*

KING OF DK: Really? No, damn it !? She's someone, who drinks too much cola !? You can see, how the body can stretch out from the inside! No!?

ACHMED: There's only Blue! Orange is completely missing the target!? No!? The shape! Puke- a- tronic!!? What is that body?! *Yes, you look amazing! You're so pretty! Uhh!*

THE KING OF DK: No, it looks like a man!

ACHMED: *Keep your clothes on for god's sake!* No, how ugly! It can only be Blue! They are all tattooed !?

KING OF DK: Yes, Blue is natural sex. I was going to make sour / sweet sauce, but then I had no vinegar!? But then I found some red wine vinegar, but it wasn't quite the same!

JOSEPH: ADDRK AAWRK

KING OF DK: How is your smoking coming along!?

JOSEPH: Well, it's gotten a little more "violent" after, it was "released!" So I smoked two or three blunts a day!

THE KING OF DK: And what about Mary? Has she discovered it?

JOSEPH: No! But it must be aired well before Friday! Ad - how creepy!

THE KING OF DK: They probably make an example out of Britta now?

ACHMED: Yes, they found her in an apartment?

THE KING OF DK: Yes, and they showed, how she was dragged away by lawyers and police in South Africa! They showed it on TV!

ACHMED: She was dragged away ??

THE KING OF DK: Yes, like a criminal with a jacket over his head!

ACHMED: No, it wasn't like Stein Bagger! But she deserved it!

THE KING OF DK: Yes, and she's going home and on the yarn stick as soon as possible!

ACHMED: Home explaining to the police about her innocence in this ?!

THE KING OF DK: Well, there are almost Mireille Mathieu songs on half of Birthe Kjær's LPs since the 60's!

ACHMED: She just stole them all ??

THE KING OF DK: No! Birthe Kjær's records, some of them! The first in 1969, was a collection of old German songs, where one of Mireille's German songs. *"In a small street in Paris, the two found paradise!"*. Because both Birthe Kjær and a singer named Lis Evers made Mireille's single in Danish! There were three Danish singers, who had it in play! It's just crazy! Birthe Kjær has ripped five or six times!

ACHMED: Fucking hell.
No, they have probably been nicer, the ones I have met!!

THE KING OF DK: Yes, than those ones ??

ACHMED: Yes!

THE KING OF DK: Oh!

ACHMED: Yes, oh! Well, now they should see her naked soon!

KING OF DK: Are these two left?

ACHMED: Yes!

KING OF DK: Well, she's cute, her on the left?

ACHMED: Yes, yes!

THE KING OF DK: She's probably big the one in the Blue box!

ACHMED: Yes, she is "grandma"! Yes, she is pretty - her there!

THE KING OF DK: Yes! And she knows it well, otherwise she wouldn't have done so much tattoo work!

ACHMED: She looks like her Wild Cat from Randers! She is just as tattooed!

KING OF DK: Well?

ACHMED: Yes! Her New Year's resolution was to get tattooed all over! So she was on it! She didn't exactly have one on her stomach, but everywhere else !!

KING OF DK: No !!?

ACHMED: It's a total favorite show then !!

KING OF DK: What ?? That??

ACHMED: I think, the tattoos dress her up! Also because she is still as good looking, as she is! Then she can wear it there!

KING OF DK: Yes, exactly. You have to take care, that it doesn't get too much!

ACHMED: I must have tattooed a spiral up my arm!

THE KING OF DK: No !?

ACHMED: And then I think up here - it should end in a circle! A grain circle with an Ace, where there are the four suits, diamonds, hearts, clubs, and spades.

KING OF DK: Mary, Cat, Natty...?

ACHMED: No !! It should only be contour lines! Then when I pull up, show my tattoo and follow the spiral. And then finally I can just make a fingerprint on the "right" color and "guess" their cards!

THE KING OF DK: I think, if I shouldn't have made such a name register, like out in the Memorial Park (Mindelunden)...?

ACHMED: With all the ones you've been with ?? Yes? Here with the date of birth and when the intercourse took place ?? Ha, ha !!

THE KING OF DK: No! Just name it! *"Peter-18cm". "John-20cm". "Niels-19cm".*

ACHMED: "Frederick - only 14cm" ..

KING OF DK: Yes, yes! Like down in Mindelunden! It could actually be a lot of fun! And then with handwriting! And then go down to the tattoo artist every month: "Jonathan". "Ibrahim".

ACHMED: *And this guy? Just call him "John Doe"! I don't know his name!? But it was 33cm long!!!*

THE KING OF DK: XXL! I think, I broke my record on Bird Song (Fuglsang)!! It was this big man, god damn it!! Tall man. Forty years! Which lured me up into the woods! Then he stood with such a mop boy! And I thought... .. ??

ACHMED: *Shit !? – How can it fit in my ass!?*

THE KING OF DK: No, I thought: *Can't it be stiff there!?* But it was! And he squirted fast !!

ACHMED: Without fainting ??

KING OF DK: Yes, yes!

ACHMED: And was it so "Massive Cum" ?? "Aahhhhh" ?!

THE KING OF DK: That was a fucking good bloke!

ACHMED: I think, they have room for more in the mold?

THE KING OF DK: It was totally unusual! I have never seen anything like that!? It was so big! So he had to take it with two hands, to keep it straight and tight !!

ACHMED: Yes, I must too !! Ha-ha!

KING OF DK: And my wife in the middle too !!

ACHMED: Ha-ha! Cough cough!

KING OF DK: Is it strong ??

ACHMED: Yes!

THE KING OF DK: Did I burn the tobacco or heat it up too much ?? But it's a little strong! There is a lot of hashish in it! Very nice - very nice!

ACHMED: No, but she's beautiful!

THE KING OF DK: Yes! You have to give it to her!

ACHMED: But I would also guess, that her parents got divorced, when she was in her teens ??

KING OF DK: Well? Yes. But sometimes you can sense some of the strongest traits!

ACHMED: Yeah, fun enough! The "Wildcat" was 16 years old, and the Colombian was 18 years old. And my twin cousin was 16, when their parents divorced! My cousin has found several men, who are at her father's age and most recently an older man in Spain!! It has made some sewer cuts in the rest of their lives, to experience their parents getting divorced at that age!!

THE KING OF DK: No! They need to stop thinking about it that way! So the last thirty years there have been sexual experiences in certain age groups like shards! And in fact, it has always been, what helped shape people! That today you try to adjust the culture to something else !! Obviously, there is a transitional period with some victims! One should not feel like a victim! Life is about something, that must happen to you without being a victim! So the one who has self-pity, it is nobody, who benefits! It only leads down !! The only thing life does not have pity for - is self-pity! Is not that right?

ACHMED: Yes it is! It is such a shame for us !!

KING OF DK: Because all those who you feel sorry for ...? For example, I think, it was a damn shame for those guys, who were in prison in Peru. So I can't help, but think! Also for their mothers who have no idea, what to do! I think, it is a shame! Ha - It remembers where we were last !!

ACHMED: But it's nice, that you've muted the sound! It wasn't going to stop listening!

THE KING OF DK: It's the mother of one of the guys, who is imprisoned in Peru! She says, she can do nothing. Other than keeping up with him on the phone! Lima!

ACHMED: But why do they speak French ??

THE KING OF DK: It's French !! It's the mother. She's from Marseille! She is from France, and lives down by the Mediterranean!

ACHMED: Well! "Specialite" !?

KING OF DK: Yes. He is in a special team, that hunts with dog patrols! They invest $ 150 million in the fight against "drugs"!

ACHMED: But the worst thing is, that they make cocaine out in the jungle. And then they do this, when they're done! Then they let the gasoline, they have used into the wild - the jungle! Instead of legalizing it and setting up laboratories, where they could deal with that pollution !? And make it for those, who could benefit from it ??

KING OF DK: Are they coke fields? You must have a permit! But then you can!

ACHMED: But they use coca leaves for other purposes! After all, it's not just cocaine! It is also for tea, and flour and everything!

THE KING OF DK: It's the grandmother! She chews coke!

No. There are guinea pigs!

ACHMED: It's there, that they come from, don't they?

THE KING OF DK: Yes!

ACHMED: And they eat them or what?

THE KING OF DK: Yes! They've had an action the same day!

ACHMED: You should not sit next to them while driving around in a patrol car, if the rifle was to go off ??

THE KING OF DK: Well! It's a whole country chasing itself! The two road users.

ACHMED: What does he say?

KING OF DK: He says, he has nothing. And he has a wife and children!

ACHMED: *Now you soon get it in the ass by a lot of men with tattoos !! And you will love, to get it in the ass! You will develop teats with your comfort eating disorder!*

THE KING OF DK: *Avol direct pour Amsterdam* - They fly direct to Amsterdam! Lima is the most watched airport in the world!

ACHMED: It's probably something of a body scanner! There you just get irradiated at the airport!

KING OF DK: When I think of five of the last six times, that I was in Israel, I had 10 grams up my ass!

ACHMED: That was before body scanners?

THE KING OF DK: Yes!

ACHMED: Seven kilos?? In the stomach!? Then she gets a cocaine trip in a little while, if she is not allowed, to take a shit?! Then they should pick it up!?

KING OF DK: There she is! She looks old by a twenty-two year old ??

ACHMED: They all have kids and prams ?!

THE KING OF DK: No, imagine getting kids in jail !? Well, they are cute!

ACHMED: They enjoy themselves!

KING OF DK: What are you saying?

ACHMED: They enjoy themselves!

KING OF DK: Yes, yes! There is no doubt, that there is no need for "failure"! Kids have fun with other kids!

ACHMED: Yes, and there are plenty of other kids too! And at the same age.

KING OF DK: But growing up in a prison, must be a strange woman's land? She was nineteen years old, when she was taken, and she is twenty-two now. She had a child, but she sent it to her mother!

ACHMED: It was probably very good! It was very exciting then!

KING OF DK: That clip from Live-Aid with the drag and Queen. That's the highlight of Queen's career! 104 men live in each!

ACHMED: No, how crazy! One in the Green Room. They have a good grip on his neck ?? Then he got the heat !?

KING OF DK: He was bitten! Well, he's a nice guy! *When I turned my back, they shot me!* But he's not mad ?! It is remarkable! He's not mad at the boy at all !? *I still feel aggressive!*

ACHMED: He is completely exhausted in bed! It doesn't sound like, it's in sync - Huh??

KING OF DK: What do you mean?

ACHMED: He speaks French !?

THE KING OF DK: He's French - and it's in France !!

ACHMED: Well ok!

THE KING OF DK: He sounds like, he's from Marseille? Shut up, he'll be mad at him now huh? *"Did you sleep well?"*.

ACHMED: Domir means sleeping - in Spanish!?

THE KING OF DK: Yes! He will increasingly beat people! That's why, he spent the night clinging to the bed! He is a fucking maniac!

ACHMED: It was such a place, to just impose the death penalty! After all, it costs millions to have such institutions running forever!

"Do you have a little willy" ?!

THE KING OF DK: They ask, what he did last night! They tease him a bit! He's lying down! *I made fools! - mischief! Je fais des ennuis - I am doing, and I have done some mischief!* I just got it! Can you hear the difference? It is a difference between the present and the past tenses! Future. Ha-ha: *J'ai futuro des ennuis! You're the future!* Before future!? Ha-ha!

ACHMED: It's Loco!

KING OF DK: Yes the locomotive boy! He does this! And then he gets, the new nurse removed. For him who can't stand other people! *I feel aggressive,* he says again! It was him, who struck out in the beginning! He must be cut! He could make a helmet out of it! He was only fifteen, when he got there !?

ACHMED: It's a hospital or what?

THE KING OF DK: Yes, it is a closed institution for the most dangerous criminals in the world !! Most of them have murdered or raped!

ACHMED: Keep it up!

KING OF DK: He looks scary huh?

ACHMED: Yeah, he looks very creepy! Oh no! He just turned off the frontal labs. *Oviento!*

KING OF DK: I wondered, why they didn't have sexuality at such an institution?

ACHMED: Isn't it because, they get some pills that just ... ?! Blur them !! Shut up, it looks like Gerald Depardieu as a youngster!

THE KING OF DK: No !! Not at all! Gerald were just beautiful!

ACHMED: But he is not anymore!

THE KING OF DK: No! "G-e-r-a-l-d D-e-pa-r-d-i-e-u". That one! I think, he's twenty years old. He's just arrived!

ACHMED: As a singer??

KING OF DK: He doesn't sing!

ACHMED: He just sits there and smoke??

THE KING OF DK: Yes! Diana Dufresne is from Canada, and he is from France!

ACHMED: Was he a model or what?

THE KING OF DK: The French had something to put people in music videos, who don't sing a song!! He just has to sit on the ground. He has been told so!

ACHMED: But he was an actor back then?

THE KING OF DK: Yes!

ACHMED: He's a little Javier Bardem-like!

KING OF DK: Yes. He has played the same role internationally, hasn't he? And they have also backed his career so much in France, that he has had an international breakthrough! But it was a way for him to conquer Canada, by playing with Dufresne, who is the one most singing over there!

ACHMED: She wasn't pretty then ?! No, she looks creepy!

THE KING OF DK: She's never married before now!

ACHMED: And it was with a childhood friend ??

KING OF DK: No, but it was like Barbra Streisand, that she met someone from inside the circle!

ACHMED: What role does he play Gerald Depardieu ?! How long can he keep smoking on it ?? Shut up what a video! She is a real red stocking, and he's got great makeup on! He was great already then! But she must be big, because he is big !?

I think, I want to go home to see my "duvets". Good night! Shut up man.

KING OF DK: Yes. A new one has just arrived with Diana Dufresne. It will be the last! Depardieu.

IT IS DIFFICULT TO MAKE OTHELLO COOKIES!

Ext. On a boat in the Pacific somewhere. Day

THE KING OF DK:
Shut up - it's heavy!

ACHMED: Yes, I stood and had to wait twenty minutes! Then suddenly there were three or four others as well. And there were only two Othello cakes!? But there was just one, who jumped off, because I stated that, I wanted one too! And I had been waiting for twenty minutes!!

THE KING OF DK: Well, were there no other than Othellos?

ACHMED: Not of the whipped cream pies!

KING OF DK: Not of Wales bars?

ACHMED: No! Now god damn it. Then all the tricks apply!

THE KING OF DK: Then these are some stupid cousins! There aren't any of them, who haven't flipped twice! I had completely forgotten about Survivor!

ACHMED: Did you?

THE KING OF DK: Yes! Didn't you?

ACHMED: Yes. No, I hadn't forgotten! I've been looking forward to it all week! I'm really looking forward to it! Walk the Plank!

KING OF DK: Have you ever followed in the Britta mystery?

ACHMED: Yes, those daughters with competition horses for 50 million, and their mother has paid their bills, no questions asked ??

KING OF DK: Did you see it on channel 5? No? Give me a break!

ACHMED: Yeah, it looks so good! Have you eaten dinner?

THE KING OF DK: I'm so low in sugar, that half could be a lie!

ACHMED: Are you?? Are you so exhausted?

THE KING OF DK: Yes! I've been to Joys! From 1pm to 6pm! At 5.30 pm there I realized, I was just leaving! There were only five. I'm not bothering about this!

ACHMED: No, to have seminal emission with five men ?!

THE KING OF DK: No, It don't make me sick.! There was just him, the trans, a tall guy, but with total doll face! Like her Sasja, who has been on the television changing gender? Well, yes, it was her, who joined Survivor! Her who was born as a boy! She was in the evening show last night and told that, she gets so many hate emails from Danish men!

ACHMED: Because she was a boy and now a pretty girl!? That's a shame!

THE KING OF DK: Then they went crazy on her! So exactly they don't like them !!?

ACHMED: Well, that's weird enough !? Because I couldn't tell, that she had been a boy!?

KING OF DK: So says my husband! It is exactly there, that it lies !! If it was just something, that you could see, that she has been a boy ??

ACHMED: Well, that's ridiculous!? That she is so beautiful a woman, and then she is more hateful !?

KING OF DK: But that's because, she activates the smaller guys. And it's just the youngest guys, who can't control themselves! After all, it's not something like 35-year-olds is writing to her !? But 22. year-olds:

What the hell !? Don't give me hard-ons sow !?

ACHMED: Yes, but "she" is a sow!

THE KING OF DK: She is! Because she has nothing in her head but sex! After all, that's what, it's all about for her!! She also said this in the evening show: *That all Danes are allowed to be sexy!* There they are on the plank! High up!

ACHMED: We haven't seen that before – that high! Eight meters ?!

KING OF DK: So - these are the biggest chickens, they have in Survivor at all !! Ha ha.

ACHMED: How can he win an altitude competition, when he has altitude fright!? Well my vapor should have some power soon! You have a charger somewhere?

KING OF DK: You just have to keep an eye on it! It's there. No or what?

ACHMED: Well, but I had a really nice visit this weekend!

THE KING OF DK: Well from which country?

ACHMED: Colombia!

KING OF DK: Again?

ACHMED: Yes .. 25 years!

THE KING OF DK: Well. Is that something daddy related?

ACHMED: No, it really isn't !?

THE KING OF DK: Shut up, there was a man of 52 years, my age, who came down to Joey's....

ACHMED: Did he look good ??

THE KING OF DK: No! But he was really commanding:

Now you come here!

Yes, it does not fit into a civilized society! No! Well! And then it wasn't even the first. There weren't that many out there! But there were four or five women, that I just didn't get a look at, and they had great men! 32 year old at this size...!! And Joys just rebuilt. Where we could go round and round some booths in the past - Now they are shut off! Now they have built two rooms in one direction, and then they have built a large room in the middle with a round bed. There I was with one from Randers and a daddy from Aarhus V. And the TV screen was not switched on! But the next time I looked in there, there were two of the fat giant girls licking pussy on each other while their slender, handsome men took them from behind. Oh they were screaming. One screamed as if... ?? I was in the other room at one point, it sounded like someone being murdered !? They yell at each other and then all of a sudden, they just lie and scream about the hood?! *AAAAAHHHRRRr.*

No, I do not like to hear such sounds?! Then I took a bath and drove home! I didn't care anymore. Otherwise it was just then, that some of the great guys came! They probably came straight from work! A small, tall thin guy and he was tattooed up and down his leg.

ACHMED: Filthy rich?

THE KING OF DK: No! Yesterday I stood down at Birdsong, and talked for an hour with one of the biggest butplugs from North Jutland, and he told, how he got so mega much cock up on the coastal road at Aalborg. A swinger place where many couples come. But I know the "coastal road", because there is someone in my chat in the morning, who writes a presentation after a presentation. He is 157 tall and weighs 108 kilos! He writes one side after another, about how stupid people are, and why they didn't get out of the cars, when he came walking !? Ha-ha!

Then I wrote to him this morning: *I went to Bird Song. I saw you Friday afternoon walking down the parking lot and down through the woods.* Then there were eleven men behind the trees! Nobody jumps out of their cars to such a man there!? But many who go like this!? Ha-ha and showing their ass at a distance! A Somalian came and asked me, if he could borrow a smoke. Then he took the cigarette. Then he went to an old man and fucked him, and then he smoked the cigarette! I don't know what to illustrate?? I would like to ask him: *Tell me what happens right there ??* But that is not an opportunity for Bird Song. There also came an Arab man at Joy's twenty-five years. Him we did not see much?? He settled into the new rooms. Then he lay down and close to the gloryholes, and then he sucked cock for an hour. And then he slipped!

ACHMED: Then he was filled up ??

KING OF DK: Do you need a cup of coffee anymore?

ACHMED: Yeah god damn.

KING OF DK: We have eaten cake every day. Mireille Mathieu is here LIVE at 8:40 PM. Mega drama about her all week! Her record is obviously that good. Her Classic Collection. It started at number six on Amazon, and number ten in France. And now it's number four! Then there will be trouble. So today, a week ago, one of the French newspapers wrote about Mireille's conflict with Jajari Home, which is the one. He's the one, who has a show called Quotidienne. The Daily Talk Show! And the second is, what I follow: Una Parque Che! She's not in that either!? She has said to the two shows: *No thanks!* After all, all shows want someone, who is number four on Amazon's list! And why? She does not want to be in it, because he wore Mireille Mathieu wig - Four times! He simply makes the funniest imitations. And he dumps her in the way, he does it!! He's a really nice guy! So I can understand, that she's mad at him! The other is, that he calls her the soccer head!! Repeatedly! And he has such a ridiculous mood! So I'm used to seeing him. So I haven't notice, he's that bad! But there are many, who get angry with him, and get up and leave the show! In the "We can't sleep" program! Then she chose the show tonight called: Don't Touch My Duck! And it's a Moroccan. Seril Haroum, who is going to interview her tonight! And then she should probably stop appearing on French TV. With that many records, she doesn't sell in France! She should be on CNN now, too. And Russian TV and German TV! Because it is them, who buy it and makes a sell record like that !! I hadn't expected that!?

That she should have such a big hit!? It may be her biggest record since Ennio Morricone record in 1974!! Pretty big! No. This pie is so delicious! There are many, who respond! That is why, they have reduced sales! That is the reason why, they first started selling just now!

And there were only Othello tarts or what?

ACHMED: There were three. No, there were probably four! But there were some in the queue, who wanted two tarts! And we were four queuing up! But it is also naughty to order two Othello tarts, when there are only four ?? And we all stand in line for whipped cream cakes!?

THE KING OF DK: Why are they doing this ?? Should they use them or ?? Or were they opportunists?? They said in the Evening Show, that she was going to attend tonight! He's a parody!? So you know what? She is the coolest of them all! Karina, she's been exposed to some things! But again? What is she cool about ?? But her Zanne is pretty cool too! Yeah. He just said too much shit. He's just about to get kicked out! But it must be enough to make it a winner! Who is the finalist? It's not Zanne? Yes? No, it's good! Well, they are bland ?! Does it get narrower and narrower? Well! It was then a lousy balance ??!

ACHMED: Yes, yes, but boys have some difficulties with balance. They tried to count the seconds, that the Italian national team players could stand on one leg!! Seconds!!? And not many of them even could do that !?

THE KING OF DK: I do that in my bodypump workout!! I can do that anytime!! I am so well-balanced! And in those days when I can't, I'm clearly influenced by something !?

ACHMED: That high-ranking man has a no-body ?! He doesn't have much to offer !?

KING OF DK: Have you heard that, they shot a Paki here in town this afternoon?

ACHMED: Yes. They have said out in Brabrand, nothing about the Gellerup park!? *No, it's in Brabrand on Karen Blixen's road!* That's it in Gellerup!

THE KING OF DK: Yes, why do they render like that?? I'm going to see Carmen on Saturday with Mina! And then backstage afterwards! Yes. There should be some fagots in between!

ACHMED: *I love you long time!*

THE KING OF DK: *I give you honor!* That was good enough... Even in the mirror, I think, I looked fat, when I was young! But it was fun enough as the guys out at Joys, they ran after me! And I thought, it was him from Randers, that they ran after, because him and I were together! But it was not! But several times they would touch mine! And he was ten years younger, and slender than me! I don't know, if it's because, I'm a little more tanned, than he is? Is the time at 20.40? Nah .. Well it must taste good! Now have break! Ha-ha! Her I like! Such a behavior I like! I think, she's acting out Zanne! She's like the girls, I know from university, Karina! So she's not addicted, to what the boys are thinking, she's sexy!

ACHMED: No - she is a dike !!

THE KING OF DK: And she's reasonably sexy without makeup! Zanne is sitting there with artificial eyebrows and... ?!

ACHMED: But she's easy at smiling!

THE KING OF DK: So she's a boy girl! She looks weak! No, it's a mistake to start talking one of the others up! But she looks strong Zanne! He looks skinny! But that's because, they modify it! They modify it from section to section! *But then you don't mind winning man!!* Shut up, he is stupid! No, damn it. She's lost her footing, because she looks so bad! She's bad! Frances Lai just died!

ACHMED: Who is it?

KING OF DK: It's a young Parisian composer, who got an Oscar in 1965 and in 1970! He has created a great career. There are two French composers, who have Oscars. Maurice Jarre. Jean-Michel Jarre's father! He ordered a single for Los Angeles, when he was to receive an Oscar! Then he never came home!? Jean-Michel Jarre has sat, and poured water out of his ears on TV many times. He never saw his father again! When he died, Maurice Jarre of Beverly Hills, he had a young blonde! All the money Maurice Jarre has earned from his soundtracks to Doctor Zivago, and such great movies! There was none of the money, that came to Paris, as a legacy to Jean-Michel?? American law does not recognize at all the existence of a country called France!? They just wrote France out of the US Constitution, because they were angry with France, then in 1779!?

ACHMED: So descendants get nothing??

THE KING OF DK: Not a penny!! Maurice Jarre had children with his American wife. And they got it all. And Jean-Michel got none! You could have imagined, they shared the money?!

ACHMED: He couldn't have written a will?

THE KING OF DK: Yes - if he had! But he hadn't!

ACHMED: Well, it's nice, that he didn't think about it!

KING OF DK: Well, I don't think, there has ever been peace in the family, where they have been seeking each other!? Because then you could! And Francis Lai who just died. He was one meter and twenty-two tall! And wrote two themes, that were recorded by five hundred people over three years. And he lived his whole career of *cola and vanilla* with the two songs!? Don't you know the one, I just whistled? *Phhyy — phii –phi-phi-phi-phi-phi-phhyy-phii-phi-phi-phi-phi-phi?* He plays the harmonica! *Doo-doo-doo-do-do-do-do-do?* Among other things, it is from such soundtracks, like those who have written music for "Clown"! Which has been inspired by something Parisian-sounds! Oh. We need to smoke!

ACHMED: Yeah, hell!

THE KING OF DK: Now Francis Lai has also tried to do the art himself - many, many years after!

ACHMED: I've been trying to squeeze some poetry into the "Silence Scrolls"?

THE KING OF DK: Into what ??

ACHMED: Into the "Silence Scrolls of Hell"!

KING OF DK: What do you mean?

ACHMED: Now I started with your poetry, and a studio in Serge Gainsbourg and his lyrics!

KING OF DK: Well? - It is fun!

ACHMED: And then I compose some lyric myself!

KING OF DK: Yes? So some songs like Serge Gainsbourg sits in his home in the 70s and writes - "Pamela Popo - Pamela Popo"! That's what, you say about a French woman! Pamela Popo! Then he makes a whole song, which will be a huge hit for him! Pamela Popo and Lolita. I don't know how many songs, he has with some Lolita??

He must be damn glad, he didn't survive the "Times Up" campaign!! Ha-ha! But the women almost always threw themselves at him! All the women: Brigitte Bardot... ?!

ACHMED: *I want to fuck you !! What did you just say?!* Whitney Houston!!

THE KING OF DK: It was her first trip in Europe! She was so sweet! She wasn't the next time, she came! There she would have slammed him one! Then she was furious! He is crazy! But he went into his daily life, and he gathered up words, he heard about the hypersexual! He also made cartoon songs with women, that he asked to say *POP* - the ones who speech bubbles! *POP!* Behind Brigitte Bardot, she has such a completely logo-shaped song, that sings all the sounds! *BRATZH* and ..? And then she was mega sexy in the footage! She was! I can see that - Immediately! Like her the German model? Ursula? What is her name?

ACHMED: Bündchen ?? - Gisele? She is from Brazil!

THE KING OF DK: Yes! She's pretty good too! And have kept it for 30 years!!!

ACHMED: And Helena Christensen?

THE KING OF DK: Yes, she is also... ..?

ACHMED: 70 years ??

THE KING OF DK: 170 years !! Ha-ha! She must stop soon !! Ha-ha! The forces are enslaved! So now it begins!

FINAL OF THE YEAR

Ext. In a boat in the Pacific somewhere.

ACHMED:
So should the computer run at the same time as Survivor??

THE KING OF DK: Yes, we have to! Because it will not be retransmitted!

ACHMED: Why don't they just draw straws?!

KING OF DK: It's the new Johnny Hallyday! There comes a program, and it is now a year ago, that he died! A new CD has just arrived with him, after he died! But the money goes to Latifa in the US, and not to his children in France! So there are many French people, who oppose, and will not buy it! Is it incredible, that he gets so angry!?

ACHMED: Pull straws!!

THE KING OF DK: Not only does he not want to fight himself. But he will also decide, who to fight?? He's a cunt! *I think, you need Michael!* No!? Such! Then there is power! We just need a piece of cake!

ACHMED: Yes! It's also a long time ago!

THE KING OF DK: He has increased the prices! The baker in Kvickly. I think! The other day, a honey bomb cost three dollars!? Then I said to the lady out there: *I buy them in Fotex – They have four for five dollars!!*

ACHMED: Did you say that to the baker in Kvickly ??

THE KING OF DK: The Fotex baker had four honey bombs for five dollars, and one cost three out in Kvickly! And I said that out loud to the Kvickly baker! And then she pulled her arms. She couldn't do anything about it! But I still expect her, to tell it to the boss! I can taste, that his quality is really good. Now you get one with kiwi again?!

ACHMED: Oh, damn it! I'm allergic to kiwi!

KING OF DK: Are you?

ACHMED: No!!

KING OF DK: It's hard to make Othello tarts!

ACHMED: Yes, you say that! It's good, that we shouldn't make them!

THE KING OF DK: Well?? But how did they convince him, that he should??

ACHMED: I don't know !? Loco wanted to take it again, but he has taken death bracelet almost every time! So Michael thought, he would man up!

THE KING OF DK: This is also the first time, that Michael is in something! No, it's good! It is much better than Fotex! Well! They simply run against each other?? She's in bad shape huh? At her age, I could swim at max speed - back and forth!! There has never been anyone in Survivor, who has been as strong as me in life! Until I was sick! And I was definitely not the highest profile sportsman in my area! But a combination of medium strength and great will! It was enough on several occasions. I became the second runner at the Marselis race, last time I joined! In my group! In the group of 35-40 year olds! Obviously, there are many, who run faster than that group! And it was also only four miles! Pooh, it's hard huh? It's just taking a deep, deep breath! Weep, weep, weep. Now is he crying too!? Well, then let the older generation come forward god damn it! There are so many rich elders. I can sense that! Yes - He can take twenty years more in the labor market! Now the two should be in a 69 tonight! *Now I'm the only girl!!* What's his name?? Yasser! He is furious at them! He doesn't want Jamil to win! If he went in, and believed in him self now - Loco, he would win !

ACHMED: So does he! He is just playing his part !!

THE KING OF DK: Then he would appear in a way, so that the others would like it too! No, the face that shouldn't win!

ACHMED: He's pretending, he shat himself!?

KING OF DK: Yes. So if he wins?? Then I write to TV3: *That you and I will punish them all next year by choosing to watch another program!! Then we will see "Drama Queens in the Jungle" instead!*

ACHMED: Yes, and Cover Wives !!

THE KING OF DK: Yes! The family at Bryggen!! Then the ones who lost Survivor are in a hotel in Bangkok waiting, and then they are allowed to eat and ..?

ACHMED: Bangkok ?? Isn't it far away ??

THE KING OF DK: Yasser - uhh ?? He is probably also unsympathetic !? *Why did you vote me out ?? Why do you treat me like an idiot??*

ACHMED: It looks like Borat in a new movie!!? *You have fluttered like a slut! I opened a restaurant down here. I call it Survivor Restaurant!*

THE KING OF DK: *Please be quiet – you swizzle spine!!* He has too many ears around him! He's a human eater?! He has eaten people in his last life?? God damn it, his tattoos are ugly, Turks ??

ACHMED: Do you think?

KING OF DK: Yes, he looks like a dirty boy! Huh? It just went wrong?? What she said?? *"And I'd like to be boned"* ?! Well, now Jamil gets furious at them! David Hallyday is coming to TV next week! For the first time since his father died! I'm looking forward to it! The whole of France has been waiting to hear it from his own mouth, if he could get near Johnny, when he was dead?? For he was in Marnes-la-Coquette, the same town as his father the day he died last November! But now he says:

"No, the medical staff kept us out of the hospital!"

ACHMED: So not even his own son could be there??

THE KING OF DK: No !! Isn't it strange ??

ACHMED: Yeah, that sounds weird !?

KING OF DK: He is moaning, that there was nothing really new with Hallyday's son!? They have a very active evening program!! Well, that's like showing the Evening Show for two hours on all channels! They have it in France! Permanent commentators, they all have opinions!

Do we need more coffee?

ACHMED: Yeah, shouldn't we? I'm about to fall all the way through the couch! You lie damn well!

KING OF DK: Hopefully I have an extra cup? BURP. Oops! Where are you going to be at Christmas? And who is going to have Isa at Christmas?

JOSEPH: It's me, who has Isa at Christmas!

THE KING OF DK: That's nice!

JOSEPH: Officially, I have her from the 21st to the 28th. But Mary wants to spend some Christmas with her. Mary even holds Christmas with Ignatius at the Healing Center on the 24th and the first Christmas day, on a silence retreat!

THE KING OF DK: Where do you say ??

JOSEPH: At Ignatius Healings Center!

KING OF DK: What is it ??

ACHMED: It's a healing center for the sick !!

KING OF DK: Is she associated with that??

JOSEPH: Yes, she is in an "internship" there - again!

THE KING OF DK: I would say, that if she was going to the women's center in "Bethlehem", then I think, you should put your foot down !!

JOSEPH: No, no! No, Isa is with me for Christmas itself! So the question is, whether Mary should have her some more days at one end or the other? So Isa also gets to celebrate Christmas with that part of the family, when they are gathered! And then I have some extra days with her at another time! But we should have just switched week, so it is the reverse next year. Because it would be a bit of a shame for Mary, if both fall holidays and Christmas are with me every year!? But you have to see that in a calendar! So we might switch during the summer holidays, where we started sharing!

THE KING OF DK: Yes!

ACHMED: Thank you! It is hot!

THE KING OF DK: What a fool! What do they need now?

ACHMED: Contest! But I hadn't guessed, that Loco would be in the final!?

THE KING OF DK: No! He has been hiding and anonymous!? I don't think, he had been filmed in the first five episodes at all!!?

ACHMED: No, no! There, then, do I think Türker was more justified ??

KING OF DK: Yes? No, he just has to leave! You can't win such a joker?! There are many of the celebrities, who wish they were unknown!! It's damn hard to be known too!! It's not the same, as it was twenty years ago! There people had respect for the known. They thought they were famous, because they had done some extraordinary! Today there is a billion ways to become known!? And in our society just suddenly here where the equality and everything possible, it becomes more and more central to be anonymous! Greed will be cursed in the future!

To drive around in big cars and expensive clothes and so on. The generations are going to move towards something more communist! Otherwise the globe can't deal with it either!?

ACHMED: So you mean, we're all going to be wearing uniforms??

THE KING OF DK: Well, that will end! So the uniform has the material for financial correctness! And it ends, as Ballard's short stories describe, that we all live on one square meter.! And the rich, if you can save together, get 1.6m2! Because why would people live like this!? It's pointless then. Just take most of my neighbors....?!

ACHMED: Just take my parents' childhood living quarters.

KING OF DK: What number do they live in?

ACHMED: 88 - The other day I was able to overtake two city buses – ten minutes apart by foot on a 500 meter stretch on Ring Road between Stadion Allé and Harald Jensen's square - That many cars were queuing and driving in a snail's pace!? If you took a still picture, of how many people actually stayed on that stretch, maybe it was about a hundred people!? Which fill so much in each their vehicle! And the hundred people could have been gathered in two buses!?

THE KING OF DK: Yes! Shut up, they are miserable people too! And all those who text on the phone while driving!? After all, it's almost a common disease now !!?

ACHMED: I also text from time to time, when I ride the motorcycle!!

THE KING OF DK: Well, that's unbelievable, that you can't do without!?

ACHMED: It could be something important??

KING OF DK: No, stop! Not while you're driving!? Stop it! How the hell did they get Mireille Mathieu into that program - I don't understand!!?

ACHMED: So are you going to start winter bathing?

THE KING OF DK: No !! There is nothing wrong with me! *Cough, cough.*

ACHMED: *Cough, cough* !! Ha ha!

THE KING OF DK: It is only this evening that ...... ?? Well, yes, but we're moving on with Survivor!

ACHMED: Yes! After all, I had my blood tested for both STDs and the metabolism, which I had not followed up on last year, when she said it was alarmingly high! Didn't I tell you that the last time? That it was pretty normal the whole thing, and that there was nothing?? Then it might be worthwhile to switch to a more vegan diet!

THE KING OF DK: No! Well that is good!

ACHMED: Yeah, hell!

SURVIVOR PARTICIPANT: My vote goes to...?

THE KING OF DK: Loco! Idiot in fact! So is Michael looking for that?

ACHMED: No! Him and Jamil have to fight to get to the finals! But it is also something of a competitor!

THE KING OF DK: Yes, because it will not be so strong! It is very well controlled by Jamil and Michael after this conflict, that they had at the start of the program! Who the hell is that, who has a hammock? Well! Yes, I like to hear that!

ACHMED: He doesn't beat Jamil!

KING OF DK: How long has it been, since they last met? It was last night. Then they slept last night, and ...? Don't you think?

ACHMED: *Yes! You should swim around that island on the horizon!*

THE KING OF DK: Well - Then it's because, they want Jamil to win, that they set them up on such a track like that – Miles long!?

ACHMED: Yes! He also pauses. He's a lane behind! *Will you help me??* Yes. It was Jamil, who would win it! He still has to swim a course! He will take it at his own pace!

THE KING OF DK: Well! Well he can do that for half a year! Well. But then it should probably fit him, to win that guy Michael! Now Michael is drowning! Ha ha! Try to see here! There is a fool, who writes four paragraphs about, how terrible it is to cruise up the coastal road in Aalborg! And people just sit in their cars, and don't come out and follow him into the woods! Then he asks a question here in the middle of it all:

Are lighted lamps a way to signal something?? Then I write above: *Yes!*

Ha ha! Arithmetic. No, how interesting!

ACHMED: They're tough too!

THE KING OF DK: No!

ACHMED: There are also four numbers, that they need to remember!

KING OF DK: And Michael is probably better at that! But he wasn't! There he smashed Michael!

ACHMED: Yeah, it was too physical! It was too hard!

THE KING OF DK: He has said that all the time! That tune he played the second time too!

ACHMED: Jamil, Loco and Zanne in the final! An immigrant change is planned!

KING OF DK: Yes. Women Against Wogs !!

ACHMED: When will the award be raised to one million?

THE KING OF DK: Jamil can't remember everything ??

ACHMED: And do you think Loco can?? I think, I would stop halfway through the trials and say: *And what was it, that we were supposed to do?? Should I pick it up first, or should I smash it in? Or back? Do you have to go that way? And step on??* I would have so many questions!?

THE KING OF DK: Then there is lemonade!

HOST: Are you ready.

CONTESTENTS: Yes!

HOST: Are you ready.

CONTESTENTS: YES!

ACHMED: He has a bad hearing - The host ??

KING OF DK: So is it Zanne the grandmother, who is going to win??

ACHMED: Yes, she has come a long way! Cool Zanne. That's it! It's not just physical! Loco?? What did Loco do??

KING OF DK: Aren't they on the same track or what?

LOCO*: I get Ambien shits, just being two feet above the ground. That's my fear of heights*

THE KING OF DK: No. My system is disturbed by the fact, that I simply cannot eat much, of what they served! But I was really thirsty! I don't know, what water cost?? But there was free coffee. I was just so busy. I just don't bother coming out with a bill of 20-30 dollars!

Neither could you afford my friend?

ACHMED: No! But if I was thirsty, then I had bought something to drink!

THE KING OF DK: There was Odin the other day, who told me, what he had bought....?? Odin who is a cash beneficiary. Every day he buys sandwiches!? That is sure a financial abuse!! And he has a bill of 100,000 dollars, which he has to pay! I bought twelve chickens in Foetex. I think, there were deals?

ACHMED: Fresh?

KING OF DK: What does she do - Miss Colombia?

ACHMED: She's teaching at a private school!

KING OF DK: Does she speak Danish?

ACHMED: Yes. She's adopted! Born and raised!

No, it will be Jamil, who wins!

THE KING OF DK: Why should it be Jamil, who wins ?? I do not understand?? Well. Did Loco overtake her??

ACHMED: Yes, but she has collected items, Loco does not have that!!

KING OF DK: It was good, that you came!

DOG BARKING

There's one in the yard.

ACHMED: Where??

THE KING OF DK: There's a dog in the yard! Because they only walk around the yard in the evening.

DOG BARKING AGAIN

ACHMED: But you taught it well??

THE KING OF DK: Now there are more! Yes, we have no hare at the moment. The fox has taken them all. Although I have seen five dead foxes in Aarhus, road kill! So there are many foxes obviously!

ACHMED: Yeah it's totally crazy!

DOG BARKING

THE KING OF DK: *Yes, you've got!* (Dog biscuits) *Hi. He's got two! But he doesn't really want anyone! You may want to get one more Max. Her Max! It was the third one! Hi hey hi. Yes you are welcome!*

ACHMED: They don't enjoy it!

THE KING OF DK: Nah! But they would like their dog to have a treat. A dog owner thinks, it is so much fun to get a treat or something! There aren't any of them, even those with the new Scots, coming!

ACHMED: If I was a dog owner, and was out for a walk, and there were a neighbor luring it every time with a treat?? Then I would be forced to go there, because the dog wanted to!?

KING OF DK: This is also why, you should not have a dog for the time being!! Because you will find that, when you have a dog, that has a lower intelligence, it is the one, who decides!!

ACHMED: Yes. There is no choice! It's just like with the ladies !!

THE KING OF DK: She's getting prettier and prettier?! They put filters on the camera now!? Lighting her at the right way and... ?? What is he talking about ??

ACHMED: *So count right the first time! That's what lazy people do!*

THE KING OF DK: It is so slavish!

ACHMED: Then she wins!

SHE: I had counted 19 millipedes, but there were only eighteen!?

THE KING OF DK: May she go up, and replace it or what?

ACHMED: I don't know !?

KING OF DK: What does she need to know, when she knows, what the answer is ?? Then the Paki won goddamn!! What was that mistake she made!?

HOST OF SURVIVOR: Now it's over, and we found a deserved winner of Survivor. Should you join? Then go in and sign up for Survivor!

ACHMED: Shouldn't you join? Then you don't have to sit here and eat Othello cake, and laugh at it instead??

THE KING OF DK: You have to wear a muzzle! We have to stitch your mouth together!

ACHMED: Yes! Up in the asshole on someone else! No! That's it! End of story! Then another year goes by! Is it the chat?

KING OF DK: Do you include anything on Facebook about Survivor, so you can see, what's being written?

ACHMED: No !!

KING OF DK: I'm speechless!

ACHMED: Over?

KING OF DK: That he became the Survivor winner!? Jamil! Such a fagot!

ACHMED: I think, he was better suited than Loco!

THE KING OF DK: And he had to stay silent to his class students until tomorrow! When he gets back to his classes! Because it's been a long time, since it's been recorded! He has taught four months afterwards! Because it is not like in the old days, where it is only in the studio somewhere!?

ACHMED: I think, it was, because the winner was revealed four months earlier, they had to change it!

THE KING OF DK: Well. It was a big disappointment - Survivor! I must say!

ACHMED: It wasn't the winner, that you had expected ??

KING OF DK: Do you bother to take the remote?

ACHMED: Yes! Can you see, what the result are in the soccer game Denmark against Ireland?

JUSTICE MINISTER: Then you should call the police, if you have had a burglary. Then they should be notified again!

THE KING OF DK: Yes, then it comes out! It is too bad too! One of the recordings, was from Menu in the city of Tilst!

ACHMED: Well! There I was just past today, when I had to drive my brother to the mechanic on Viborgvej!

THE KING OF DK: Well! Were you then in Menu?

ACHMED: No!

THE KING OF DK: Well! That's what he apologizes for! One in two?? Do they really intend to ramble on about it all day?? They get criticized for this - the police! No. They look at you well enough! Well, isn't there anything called shop alarms, for everything she steals?? I do not understand!? One should really, with the equality and so on, then create a remake of an Olsen gang, where there are three women instead!!

ACHMED: Yes, that was a good idea!

THE KING OF DK: And then Yvonne must be a man! And of course it must be a fat man!

ACHMED: Because Yvonne was thick ??

THE KING OF DK: No! But that's the average man today! I think, that the figure is 51 or 52 percent of the Danish population, who are overweight!

The Menu business, it's hit hard! They go in without a shopping cart??

Yes! Well? Aarhus! City of Smiles!?

ACHMED: Well? It is nice!

THE KING OF DK: Ha. For fuck sake!! The police are losing this case. It's great! Because the police came here after one minute recently, when a stupid bitch called one morning and said, *that there are four dog owners without a leash on their dogs!* There the police came, and listed our names!? But they don't have time to move on to a theft like that?! And it was 7 o'clock in the morning! No! 8.30!

ACHMED: But that's the highest alert! Dogs without a leash?!

KING OF DK: Now I could just post on Facebook, that we had been notified to go with the poodle dogs without a leash!! At that time...? We came up arguing with a lady standing with two pitbulls! Our loose dogs were running towards them, and then she started to yell!? And then I cried out to her: *Now you behave properly! Then you must take your medicine, before you come over!* Or something? Then she called the police!? And three minutes later where we were at the Poppels Circle, we met the police!

ACHMED: And then you were listed ??

KING OF DK: Then we were listed by name!

ACHMED: How annoying! And you don't even own a dog!?

THE KING OF DK: There are some groups of people, who are not at all...??! Why not shoot them with a power gun or something !?

ACHMED: Yes, or splat guns! They can just shoot! I had!

KING OF DK: The police came and told me, not to interfere with her medicine!!

ACHMED: What?? Did they really say that ??

KING OF DK: Yes, the cop said!

ACHMED: Yes! It is also on the border!

KING OF DK: I turned around and said to the cop:

No, it's not something, I know anything about either! It's just something, I guess when two-thirds of the population is on sedative medicine?! Then I thought her, the fat pig, she's probably one of them!?

ACHMED: That was a good reasoning then! Ha - Yes!

THE KING OF DK: And they haven't responded or anything the police – about this theft!? Now we are in Brabrand!! No. I am glad, that I do not have a store, and put up with something like this!! *No!? But you can, after all, count it as waste against it.* Goddamn it!!

ACHMED: Then have a guard employed in the door for crying out loud!! They have been robbed for more than a million a year!? They could have saved DKK800,000, by having a guard worth DKK200,000 standing in the door!

THE KING OF DK: They just steel it that obviously?!

ACHMED: Yes!

THE KING OF DK: No, she can't go that way, to get things in the bag !? It must be some recordings, that they have constructed !?

ACHMED: Yeah, damn it! The cameraman reveals her !! Ha-ha!

THE KING OF DK: Well, but it was the Minister of Justice, who thinks, that something should be done about it! Fun! How he wants to solve it? After all, we have already put max capacity in!? But Lone, who was also noted, she probably writes tonight!

ACHMED: Yes, it is so dangerous to be a dog owner nowadays! Did you get a ticket?

THE KING OF DK: I'll go to the police Facebook pages and see, if anyone has commented on this program!

JOURNALIST: *When three young men stole more than a hundred kilos of candy in the Menu in Valby, Brian Rosendal posted pictures of all three thief's on Facebook!*

ACHMED: He mustn't!

JOURNALIST: *But it was against the law!*

KING OF DK: How should I express it, if I just had to write it quickly?

Three weeks ago, the police quickly made their way to the Botanical Gardens, to note the names of three public pensioners!!

ACHMED: Sclerosis affliction?!

THE KING OF DK: *Who walked their dogs!* Is it bait, that they have set up?

ACHMED: Yes it is! They tempt weak souls!

KING OF DK: But I ask: *What are 3-4-5 delivery trucks with Polish license plates doing there??*

ACHMED: Working??

THE KING OF DK: No!! Workers come in the Volkswagen Kombi with five or six people! These are some, that you can't see!? I wonder, what they are doing?! And I wonder, if I should call the police!? After all, I never do that!! No such thing! They are really naughty!! Well! They deal with alarms! Ha ha. Shut up, man! There was one, who wrote:

Just remember this, the next time you go to elections!

ACHMED: I've seen motorcycle officers fixing bicycles with pliers for a pensioner, who were punctured!?

KING OF DK: Three weeks ago there I popped a thief, who took a bike and smashed windows on cars! But I do not know yet?? So the day report has no arrests described!? So I don't know, if they got hold of him?? Because I heard shouting over there from five minutes after! I don't know, if he got kicked out of them?? Or if they forgot to write a day report?? After all, I try to keep good friends with the police! But it might not be cool, that I write it with the dogs?? I can only write:

That is not the case with the police! They will come and get you, if you are walking your dog without a leash on!!

ACHMED: Yeah, you didn't say anything !!

THE KING OF DK: They have been advertising the program here for three days, and it is Lone, who has said that: *Now you must remember to watch that program tomorrow night!* It's a good little world, that I have with the regular features, and then Lotte Heise and the stars that enter! And now I met Isabel Christensen the other day. She is cute! Clever girl! Very fucking noble and a good girl! She created that name: Isabel Christensen! She's fucking rich! She was on the morning TV with her new collection in Paris! There is a lot of money in there! But just as I am right now, I wouldn't give it up!? What should I make money from? What do I need it for?

ACHMED: You can give them to me !!

KING OF DK: Yes, but that's not much! That's not much motivation! I'd rather have a gang bang....! I'd rather "enjoy" myself from 10-11 o'clock than go to work!

ACHMED: Yes, I think, I will too!

KING OF DK: Yes, I think everyone will! I just talked to a couple of leopard guys out at Joys today. I think, it was at 1 o'clock in the basement! Who was very relieved to be there - *Relax*, I said then. *I've been here for twenty-five years.* And then we figured out, that Joys was made in about '95. Five, ten, fifteen. *Yes, it's about seventeen years ago. I've been there, since the beginning! I had no trouble banging! I fucked with both a boy and a girl in the same month! But I've never been able to do anything, that might seem gay! And I could never think of marrying a woman,* I told him! He was totally happy, when I said it! *Well? Are you then married to a man? Yes! I'm not gay!*

ACHMED: *Yes! I'm not gay!? It is only to stand by my principle!*

THE KING OF DK: Yes! So my principle was: *You can't build as close, safe life with a woman, as you can with a man! Same degree of loyalty!*

ACHMED: No, plus every month you have the premenstrual!! Like her the Colombian girl was almost breaking the relationship over a text message last month?! And then a few days went by, and then she was completely happy again, and wanted to meet! So it just goes up and down, when we are dealing with a woman !!

KING OF DK: Well? And therefore also the PHD, who said that, Danish women turn on their husbands on average for three years. Three years - on average!

ACHMED: But this theme with: The Separate Divide? I am considering taking the whole action with us talking, and then moving out on the Pacific Ocean! It is still a retreat just on a boat!

KING OF DK: On a boat out in the Pacific??

ACHMED: Then we continue there and discuss ...? I think, it will be good for the plot! Is the protagonist schizophrenic? Is he also multi-disabled?? ALS hit and has a lot of helpers! And so are the voices inside his head!?

But now we're on a boat!

THE KING OF DK: Well !? Yes that sounds exciting !!

THE KING OF DENMARK FARTS

SEXUAL DESIRE IS MORE RELIABLE THAN TRAIN SERVICE!! Ext. On a boat Pacific - Day

ACHMED:
Yes, it was with that coffee track, that they found out, that it ended up in an Arab kiosk.

THE KING OF DK: Well ??

ACHMED: Yes, and he pretended nothing! He had just been asked, if he had a considerable loss himself! *Yes - for hundreds of thousands! Well, we tracked down this coffee from Menu, and it has ended here !!*

KING OF DK: Yes? What did he say then?

ACHMED: *Yeah? I do not know, how it happened !?*

THE KING OF DK: That's also the thing about mixing the two culture together! They are fundamentally different, when it comes to being honest. There they do not feel the same obligation to be honest, or not to lie! They almost don't know, what you mean, when you approach them:

"Don't you know the sixth commandment, that says you must not lie"?!

"Lie? I've learned to lie from my mom and dad, since I was two! There I was told, that I should just say nonsense really! ".

ACHMED: *I was beaten every time, I said something like that!*

THE KING OF DK: Yes! Well, then there are five days until Friday! Are you going to Colombia? Or doesn't she come down here? So is she home in Randers?

ACHMED: No, she lives in Aarhus!! She has her own apartment on Trojborg, which she bought for her compensation! But she is practicing as a school educator at Aarhus Free School.

KING OF DK: Is it a wogs school or what ??

ACHMED: No, it's a free school!

KING OF DK: What does it mean?

ACHMED: A school of music that all the musical heads have probably attended: Michael Falck, Lis Sorensen, Anne Linnet ..!?

THE KING OF DK: No, Lis Sorensen attended the School in Engdal!

ACHMED: Well ?? Didn't she attend the free school?

KING OF DK: No, but I don't know it at all ?! But this is something, that is not subject to the Ministry of Education's programs! But maybe it's just as good? Is she happy about that?

ACHMED: Yes, She is! But she still thinks, the school system is a little bit Laissez Faire!

THE KING OF DK: Well - Laissez Faire! Well, I liked that! I think, they were tiring the ones who….?

ACHMED: Followed all the rules?

THE KING OF DK: No, we all should! No. Yes. The ones who said too much at the meetings! And the young people who come in and, who are idealistic about everything! It is a requirement to have an assistant teacher by your side for an entire hour. If the young people could not relax around everything, they are entitled to !? What she could possibly invite was…? What is her name?

ACHMED: Natty!

KING OF DK: *Natty? Just try listening here Natty! You come as new and fresh teacher! But we are some, who has actually made us a life here.*

And there you have to help her too, so she doesn't put them on overtime every day, if she thinks, it's Laissez Faire!! You can help by saying that to her. There is nothing more difficult than fighting with idealism!

Now I just heard that two hundred teachers from university, just learned that they have not finished their degree??

ACHMED: And they are working as high school teachers already!?

THE KING OF DK: Yes! So it slows down my pedagogy!

No, it is nice out on Joys! My immune system is up and running, and I have mixed viruses with seven, eight different men this evening! So it makes everything good!

ACHMED: Does it benefit your immune??

THE KING OF DK: No! It's tearing down my immune system! I am strong as an ox! All the battles that go on inside me, I win them! Odin had just watched a TV show with a girl in Germany, who had been with 15,000 men! It was a Hamburg girl! And she was only 24!!

ACHMED: How can she keep track of it??

KING OF DK: Well, she had worked as a prostitute, since she was seventeen! In one of the street windows in Hamburg, she has had eight to ten customers a day!

ACHMED: So she just broke your record ??

KING OF DK: She hit me far!! Three times! But I also don't quite believe it!?

ACHMED: But whether there were fifty or seventy-five, is it also difficult in any case to keep track of, when the game is underway !?

THE KING OF DK: Yes! There is also an intention in mine! So there are some, who are recurrent!

ACHMED: So it only counts for one, if you've been with a guy five times?!

KING OF DK: Yes. I can hardly keep track of, whether I have been with five thousand, when I have been with the same several times!? But that's also a reason to say: *That I don't bother seeing you anymore !!*

ACHMED: *I've tried you my friend !!*

KING OF DK: What is it? A kidney belt!

ACHMED: A back shield!

KING OF DK: Have you become a turtle ?? Is it, if you overturn then ?? Is the back much better protected ??

ACHMED: Yes, I would say, it does!

KING OF DK: Well, but now drive cautiously, because people drive like crazy! So stay away, so they can respond! See you!

ACHMED: See you!

***

IT WAS JUST BEFORE CHRISTMAS, AND ALL THROUGH THE HOUSE...

EXT On a boat in the Pacific DAY

ACHMED:
Yaksemash?

KING OF DK: Have you come to work ??

ACHMED: Yes - yes - complete!

KING OF DK: Are you in internship?

ACHMED: No, I'm not! I'll meet with a business consultant on Friday! Then he will need a CVR number! I told him, *I have somewhere after Christmas, but before Christmas? It's hopeless!? Well yes, but see you next Friday! So I have to come up with a CVR number!*

KING OF DK: I just use you to warm up my voice. I'm going to call the headmaster at Randers State School! It was her, who I had to write an application for on Monday! I'm having a hard time establishing the energy to sit down to get those applications written!? I simply cannot concentrate! I'd rather have cock!

ACHMED: Yeah?

THE KING OF DK: Yes!

ACHMED: Amen! I don't feel the same way, but still a little!

KING OF DK: You have the opposite sign?

ACHMED: Yes! But Aarhus Stift is also looking for a building consultant, to help with inspections and to determine the value of clerical housing! What does it cost for the clergy to rent such a 350m2 mansion of a masonry villa! 4-500 dollars a month maybe ??

KING OF DK: Yes - it's just you!

ACHMED: And the hourly wage is about a 150 dollars!

THE KING OF DK: Well. Yes it is lovely!

ACHMED: And then it's called $200, if you have to sign some declarations! And it's bi-employment! So I should have just called her too, and had asked, how many hours are in it??

JOSEPH: But I have to work a few hours!

KING OF DK: Do you have Isa?

JOSEPH: Yes, I have her until Friday, and then there is such a handover! Then Mary usually has her for a week until Friday. But because of Christmas, she wants to keep her for a few more days! In fact, on both ends, she would like to have Isa more! And I can understand her, when it is Christmas! But I do not quite know, where to compromise her??

KING OF DK: I think you have to compromise at one end! So you can almost hear it yourself ??

JOSEPH: But then I've considered, that she'll keep her until the 23rd. Then she'll come here on the 23rd of the evening! And then we celebrate a little Christmas Eve here, and then her mother goes! Then I have Isa for the rest of the week!

THE KING OF DK: Yes! That is very fine! It must fit your needs!

JOSEPH: Yes - of course! Now we had Christmas dinner at Uncle's. It was then Isa and I stepped up, and cousins, uncles and aunts were there. And aunt's son and his new girlfriend! But there was no attention on Isa. Not very much! So she's actually allowed to just sit on the couch with an Ipad! We arrived at one o'clock, and we did not go, until it was over seven! It's a lot of hours for her, not to be included! And that's with my own family !? So I have doubts, if I bother to expose my young to it again this Christmas??

THE KING OF DK: It is then your own fault Joseph!! It is then you, who have been so curling about Isa, that she has not made any connection between her family members?! More can not be said about that! So one of the great things I am witnessing at the moment is, that both my niece and her little boy are very communicating to their grandmother and great grandfather !! Her boy goes to his great-grandfather all the time!

ACHMED: And great-grandfather also looks at him and says: *Hello??*

KING OF DK: Yes, he picks him up, and does all sorts of fun stuff with him! But he probably didn't make himself as crazy about him, as he did to his other great-grandchild. There he was more playful then! But still, here when he has been a bit ill, he could barely sit down, my father! He is better now! But he's been getting stronger from training for the past six months! Now he is more and more busy with his great-grandchild! It's amazing to see, also, that my nieces are aware, that it is my dad, who sits on the money!! Ha ha! But they are damn good the little kids, to be with all of us! They dart away from their parents!!

ACHMED: Sure, but now both your nieces have had children at the same age, so they also have each other and the option to play together! So it's almost also more fun for me, to have Christmas somewhere where other children are present too ?? Out to meet some single moms!!

THE KING OF DK: It helps a little at that! It does! I have to show enough...? I think probably tomorrow, I'll go to Randers tomorrow afternoon! But then Wednesday, I just think, I should bite into the sour apple and bake gingerbread! Because I added the gingerbread dough to ferment a month and a half ago! And they should be baked like rabbits! So please feel free to come by - Wednesday afternoon - and see me bake rabbit honey cakes!

JOSEPH: Yes, but she goes to school every day, but I usually pick her up between 1 or 2 o'clock! So we can sit in the bus, and take it a few stops longer?

KING OF DK: Yes. You could! And just get into the gingerbread kitchen, and then I could drive you home?

JOSEPH: Oh. That would be good!

KING OF DK: Good. Because then comes Thursday! And into all that I have, I must sent an application today and tomorrow! And then I have to call someone, when I hang up!

ACHMED: Well, you're pretty diligent about that job search?? I respect that!

THE KING OF DK: I get nothing now! I've signed out of the A-funds!

ACHMED: Have you? Why??

THE KING OF DK: Because I didn't have any cash benefits left!

ACHMED: No more sickness benefit?? You can't be sick anymore? It is over?

KING OF DK: I was notified on the seventeenth of November! It's almost a month ago !! I thought that you knew ??

ACHMED: No - not at all !?

THE KING OF DK: No. From the seventeenth of November I was aware, that I only had two weeks' daily allowance!

ACHMED: And then it just stops ?? So it's called cash assistance? But "Kings" are not entitled?

THE KING OF DK: No, I'm not entitled to that! So now I'm income-less, and living like begging around! My dad and my husband! Then I hope the old man, gives me a hundred thousand DKK!

ACHMED: Well, it's good, that it's Christmas soon!

THE KING OF DK: Yes! But I'm not nervous. And I'm glad these days, that I can rest in choosing the right diva. Mireille's record "Classic" lies...?

ACHMED: Number one?

KING OF DK: Number one in the whole world! Have you seen it?

ACHMED: No!

THE KING OF DK: It was number six last week, and this week after all that hustle in Germany and Russia. Then the Russians and the Chinese have bought so many copies, that it is number one! Ha-ha. That's hilarious!

ACHMED: Yeah, that's impressive.

KING OF DK: The impressive thing is, that it will be Mireille Mathieu's biggest hit, fucking-ever?! And that's not her best record?! I can't quite go into that !! It's a bit unkind! But I said to Kai, a guy I was with down at Salling Rooftop the other day. He said, *"I'm going to Paris!"* Then I said: *Please bring Mireille Mathieu's new CD home to me!* So now I've ordered it! But that's fucking weird !? Number one on Amazon I'll tell you??

ACHMED: It could only be, because someone thinks, they owe her a gift with her long career, and she seems to be near death!

We better hurry and buy before her record... !?

THE KING OF DK: So the audiences of different countries have different reactions to the record. I can see that week after week! Now she traveled to Germany last week, participating in a Saturday show, and another Monday night show. Both are Germany's two biggest fucking shows!! And in the first show, they had even filmed the dress, which was transported by train from Paris in a huge box! And then this week Sony released a video called: *The Making of the Classic!* And it got a lot of attention! Then she brought the German audience along! So I don't know, what happened to the Russians, that they bought so many, that it went all the way up on Amazon!? Both on the classic list and on the pop list!? It is hilarious!! And in Germany it says, she is dying?! And in France, there are writings every day in the newspapers. What was said about her big quarrel with France Gall?? She's never fucking quarreled with France Gall?! It was a journalist, who went crazy, and thought that Mireille Mathieu had overshadowed France Gall?? And France Gall just died! So it is just to put all her fans up against !? But you can see with the yellow vests in Paris, the culture of France at the moment, it is actually about this Rome's decaying phenomenon, called old money and new influences!! So it is all the elderly, who have the resources in France! And the young people have a mega unemployment, and that's, what it expresses! And she can't help, but become a symbol of old money somewhere !? There is so much hate directed at it!

ACHMED: But it's almost a whole culture match after all?

THE KING OF DK: Yes, it's a culture match! There was one on Sunday called Wolfgang, who wrote in German: *It's damn good, when you're 90!* So I wrote down below: *90??* Then he wrote: *Yes, she will be 100 soon and she will be on her last tour!* Then I wrote below: Blöd! I woke up at the wrong side! Fuck, did he flip out!? He wrote two A4 sheets of German swine?! I think, it was a little too flat! So, when she has such a success, there is no reason to change things! She's 72!

ACHMED: The fact that he writes, that she is 90, is equivalent to saying that Helene Christensen is 70 !! Ha-ha!

THE KING OF DK: Yes, it does! And I'm also into his humor, but what I didn't agree with, was his answer !? It was too soft! Because half an hour later, a woman down from Frankfurt wrote:

Mireille Mathiue is not ninety years old yet. She is twenty-two. And I don't need google, she wrote! She didn't need to google to know, how old she is! And then he wrote: *Oh sorry, she is only seventy two??* And that was just the thing, that I wanted to pull out of him, but eh !?

ACHMED: There was also news broadcast about some elderly people, who had started soccer training after having prostate cancer. But this one hadn't been in such good shape, since he was 70 years!?

KING OF DK: Yes, I think, I saw that broadcast, because I heard one say exactly the same! You said it was from a week ago, didn't you? After all, it only shows Achmed, how good and important it is to train. Exercise! And I work out a little legally, because I drive to the body pump every

Saturday at 12, and then I spend all Sunday on being smashed and totally unloved ?! And so today I'm damn healthy! But it would probably be more appropriate for me to workout twice a week, but he is absolutely right! Even for a 70 year old to start exercising, does wonders!!

ACHMED: That's it. Once you start to lie in bed, and lie there for too long, then the bedsores come !!

THE KING OF DK: Well, I don't know, what kind of musculature you get, if you don't workout all the muscles through once in a while !? After all, we sometimes have some new ones on the body pump team. Sometimes there come some new thick ladies. Is there such a thing, of course, that they have been excused for not having contact with their stomach for 30 years ?? *Tense your abdominal muscles! Well, how to do it ??*

ACHMED: *Yes - Where are you behind all that fat??*

THE KING OF DK: No! And what I was even more pressured about on Monday, when I wrote the draft, I was to write an application. I got to meet him from Randers at Joy's at 1pm !! But I didn't talk to you at all ?? It was Odin, who I told, I got spunk from 28 men?

ACHMED: In a glass??

THE KING OF DK: 28! That's my new record!! On an afternoon !!

ACHMED: Well, you probably going to reach those 15,000! You're fighting a brave fight, to reach the 24-year-old prostitute in Hamburg !?

THE KING OF DK: Yes, I do !! And I am very envious of her record !!

ACHMED: Well, that's something to strive for too!! I think, I'll post for number fifteen the next time !! Ha-ha!

KING OF DK: No, how nice !!

ACHMED: I'm a little slow on the cover!! But yeah, I've got new covers on!! The color Black!

THE KING OF DK: I would say that with lovers, it's like going into a new house!! So there is room to see again!

ACHMED: Well, yes and then sometimes you have to use a little caution!

THE KING OF DK: Well, it is special about girls, they have a greater aroused sexuality, that they either want very specific things, maybe only sexually? So all the fucking trunks all around, who are used to using garters, candles and alcohol in all sorts of ways to get horny!? That in itself seems like an outdated tradition!? You still hear about that! At Joys there you still see someone coming in with their men. And right away trying to draw attention from seventy people - by being loud - yelling?? And then they don't like the presence of other women! You can notice that! And there are also men, they come with their wives out there, who do not like the presence of other men?? After all, it is also crazy about Joys !?

ACHMED: But that's it: *The Separate Divide!!* But there are still many women, who have the best in company with other men, and have problems with other women!

THE KING OF DK: You seek a balance in that! For life, after all, is a wide range of meetings between people! It also creates some problems, where fluctuations between frequencies of equal sex occur! Just look at Joys! No, now I just have to save myself and have a job. And I should just focus on that. That's the only thing, that can save me!

ACHMED: When you have one, you just get me hired!

THE KING OF DK: So you can become a teacher of architecture, or a caretaker ?! And then you can drag the teachers into the basement just like Builder Bob!

ACHMED: Yes, just having my own office, where I can close the door!

KING OF DK: The Monk from Broken Beats has been in the studio all last week. They released a Christmas song yesterday! And it is very good! The text is as usual some worse gossip!! Understandable gossip!! But it is good and Christmas-like. However, I would say, that it does not come close to his latest Christmas song. *"So Christmas!"* And that is the only Christmas song, that I have, where you meet God in person! All the songs revolve around it a little. By some of those who meet Jesus and the disciples and so on. But in the Monk's Christmas song, he opens the door, and there God stands and sells rice toppings! Ha-ha!

ACHMED: Did you help him with the lyrics?

THE KING OF DK: No its himself! Typical Monk! And I went there two years ago, when I saw "So Christmas", when it was on the P3 play list. There I went and hoped, it would be a hit in a Catholic country though! For they will be very offended at meeting God! It's almost blasphemous?? So the Monk made a really blasphemous song, that would not go in a Catholic country !? But no one was praying ..! No!

ACHMED: And now he's a carpenter??

THE KING OF DK: No, now he's in the studio with The Broken Beats! But that's probably, what one can criticize about his Christmas song, that's probably his voice! Because he doesn't sing that well anymore!

ACHMED: No, not like Mireille Mathieu ??

KING OF DK: No, I don't know, what to say about her?? It must be a synthesizer, that Sony made her sing the sounds like her?? Its probably some new technique?? Otherwise, I can't understand, that they can improve her voice so tremendously?!

ACHMED: No, it's a "good" microphone, that you use today!

KING OF DK: Yes, but it's not just the microphone! So are her breaths. Is it also able to hit some higher nodes, than she has been able to hit in the last ten years ?! So I think, that's scam ?? I think, it's a scam ??

ACHMED: Yes, of course! You buy that! I have also improved the voice of the Moronican significantly, for our meditative-empathy-booth project! Because he is also tryyy tooo drraaag aaalll wooooords!! There you can just "help" a little, so that you do not fall asleep along the way!

KING OF DK: Set it up in speed or what?

ACHMED: No, not just speeding it up a bit, but also cutting out some spaces, where the dramatic pause is four seconds instead of thirteen!

THE KING OF DK: Yes, exactly! Fuck, I could fix myself, when doing French interviews, I could correct the grammar in it, if I had made a mistake! Then it's just to say the same thing again in the right one, and then splice the two together! That way I've fixed some errors! Ha! But I have to focus, on what I need now! And I intend to do that!

ACHMED: Yeah, that's cool! Because there are not many job listings for teachers !?

THE KING OF DK: No, there is none of it, like there was five years ago!! But VUC in Randers has just put one in, today! They lack a substitute! And Langkjær is desperate for English teachers, but I do not intend to apply! I won't bother such a negative environment again! It's too bad! It is not the student composition, that I think of. It's the teachers! It is possible, that the new principal has been able to create a different atmosphere in the teacher's room, but I do not bother with them! There wasn't anyone, that I connected with! No, simply no! And then it is an IB teacher, that they are looking for. It is not so completely free to teach IB! There you have to teach for some specific documents!! Whether the students find it exciting or not, they have to go through it!? And I know! So. No! I drop it! But then I am looking for a shipping company, a forwarding position that needs a French speech! And I had decided not to apply! But now I've decided to look for it anyway! Then I write an application, which is very much on my terms!

So, if you can use it here, turn it on! Otherwise don't!

ACHMED: *And you can only reach me in between 1-4 today! Otherwise please don't contact me!!*

THE KING OF DK: Ha-ha. Well. But, I'm going to move !!

ACHMED: Well, it was a happy Christmas! So will we see you tomorrow?

KING OF DK: Yes? I'm almost sure, that it is there, that I have to bake ??

ACHMED: We are coming by bus at around 2.30!

KING OF DK: That's okay! That's good my friend .. Hi!

ACHMED: Hello!

THE KINGS OF THE DESPOTERS

EXT - PACIFIC PEACE IN A BOAT - EVENING

ACHMED:

All tyrants / men's first ladies turn out to be greedy, possessive souls behind the veil of foundations and contributions, for charitable purposes! The program revealed striking similarities between all wives of people in power. Now try watching the program, and then have Mary, Alexandra and Marie in mind! The Princesses of Denmark! There is a clear pattern that all these ladies behind "power men", who often stand as banner bearers of women's rights, etc. Who are economic aristocratic big consumers, who shovel contributions from different sides each month on private accounts to their charitable efforts! Is there any documentation for this? Could be great to produce a similar program as the French documentary, where we describe, how the Princesses in Denmark similarly crusade for "human rights", and gain almost immunity afterwards, and might run for parliament! Is there not enough material available on the web to draw a clear parallel to Mary, Marie and Alexandra - the princesses and x princesses ?? A two to three minute video that could go viral as an advertisement for the King of Denmark? The speaker, of course, speaks with French accent!

THE KING OF DK: It sounds exciting, and a little depressing... But true... Who are we to film ??

ACHMED: Maybe we should film ourselves, as investigative journalists? Maybe with "The Special Divide" as the official theme? Establish some appointments with Mary, Marie and Alexandra and ask them, if they would like to do a Walk and Talk interview? And if not? We could just use some of the many clips and stories, that are publicly available!

KING OF DK: Did not see more than the last five minutes. Have recorded them, but "Yes"! That is a good idea. They usually want to get rid of their adapted versions of the drama ... Alexandra has a lot to tell about her former gay marriage!

THE END

ACHMED'S LETTER OR REVELATION - a cry in the desert.

Ext - Sahara Desert, Morocco - DAY

ACHMED:

No, this is a Gospel (the Gospels) and that means good news. A good and happy news for the community. The Four Gospels; they are also anonymous!! But are they traditionally attributed to Matthew, Mark, Luke and John respectively?! In church art, the gospels are symbolized by four cherubs described by the prophet Ezekiel by four winged figures: a human being (Me) (not an angel!), A lion (My father), an ox (My element) and an eagle (The one I have on each shoulder). The rationale was, that just as there are only four corners of the world, four wind directions, and four pillars to hold the sky up, there can only be four gospels?? Matthew was one of Jesus' disciples. He was also called Levit (Maththaios/Matta'i, Mattiya', or Mattiyah/Mattith-yahu). Markus (full name: Johannes Markus/Ioannes-Markos). Loukás - He was just called Lukas!! And then there's "The Baptist in the Desert" Ioannes, whose displays I saw in Damascus. Four anonymous people in the desert!! Like us! No, I will never forget the study tour inside the big mosque in Damascus, Syria, where there was a very tall bearded man, crying like a whip in front of a big booth!? Apparently, Ioannes or John ('s head) was stored inside!? I don't know, what was most scary, the crying man, vs. the head?? Or the massive Arabic chat that sounded in the high carpeted room, where children played among the kneeling masses?! A great Who-is-who game! *Have yours got a beard,* he asked, and everyone bowed! John the Baptist's head lay in large glass displays in the mosque in Damascus!? It was impossible to see, but the older gentleman, who stood at one end crying like a whip, looked like Bin Laden?! He cried like it had been his best friend, and that he had just died in a violent accident! It probably didn't help the mood with the massive masculine chanting that filled the high halls with deep tones. The ceiling was as beautifully ornamented as the huge large wall to wall carpet. Well, but we could all be baptized, when we were there!!

Most of the above were fishermen and writers in their spare time!! The King also loves to fish. I've only caught one fish in my time! A flatfish! Small one. My little dog got it, it loved fish! And I couldn't eat it! It had been out in the sea, that Jesus walked on!!? Newspapers designates the "Newest Testament" four new gospels as "canonical" simultaneously, as they described - the rest as "full of blasphemy!"!

The real word you should look for, is forgiveness. And self forgiveness!

Schizophrenic: I'm just saying, we're more, than you think! But we have all been baptized by John - each with our name now!

So we know, who he is talking to between his sermons!!

Ali
Alx
Alim
Ajax
Axel
Albert
Achmed
Achwel
Alexander
Felix
Joseph
Joe and The King of Denmark.

***

But what did you actually do in Syria?? Are you an IS warrior?? No, damn it! It wasn't my idea either! Or my fault that the dissatisfaction arose! For there was peace, while I was there! And painted glasses on all Bashar Al-Assad's posters!! Damascus, the 6,000 year old city that was just built in layers on top of each other in time! No, good that I reached out on time! It was an architecture study trip, combined with a jump to UA and Dubai! Total contradictions! Continue!

Ali, Alim, Achwel, Achmed, Ajax, Axel, Albert, Alexander, Felix & the King of Denmark?? It wasn't much "we" heard from Ali, Alx and Alexander?? No, they should just be quiet!! All that rainforest wasted on these paper pages!! If we had to "listen" to them too, then the scroll would have been twice as long ... !? They get their speaking time at "The Prince of Pride"! It's scroll number four, which is buried fifteen kilometers away - in that direction towards Algeria! Where they speak French - Like the King! Do you see, where I'm pointing? Just follow the sound! Schhh...

It would be more sustainable, if everyone just kept their mouths shut. Thanks!

THE END

WHAT ?? Does it end the way you think!? The book's number must be divisible by four, according to the INFORMATION PRINTING?! So it MUST NOT END ON PAGE 238!!? So what? Who the hell has OCD here?!

The story is over! But what if there was a little more?? Can it go on? Are there more scrolls buried in the sand?! What happened then, when the forty days had passed in the desert, or was on the Pacific?? Behind which sand hill is the next scroll buried? Did you come home to Denmark? Don't you say anything to someone? Or are you just sitting still? Don't you like your voice? Are you really a monk huh? Who then is up for further victimization? You!? What's your name? What? Higher! I can't hear, what you're saying?! Are you unteachable or just completely demented?! Well, why do you keep reading then?? The story is over for fuck sake. It was Crown Prince Frederik! Prince Whiny baby!! After all, he "works" only 16 days every three months, and keeps a lot of secrets for the public!?! And now he lives in Switzerland in his cabin!?

Where did you meet him?! Here in the desert?? Together with me! Are you going? If you have a good fable up your sleeve, write to me at: 40daysvolunter@inter-fear.com. I'll be your guide for our next trip together in the desert. In silence. I go twice a year with a whole team of people and nomads. Spring and fall, so you just call me in between, yes or write! Silence and contemplation. Where are you from? I'm from the port. Where are you going? Where do you end up? You end up in the grave! Together with me! Now shut up. Shh!! Silence.

Listen to your tinnitus. Can you try to set the frequency? Can you change it? Have you tried holding your hands up to your ears, and the skull a little behind the ears, and with your index fingers on top of your ring finger? As you flick a finger, you now "knock" your fingers into the skull. Try with ten times first. Do you want to lose weight too?? Then take ten deep breaths a day, breathing out the air, just as slowly. All the fatty pounds are rattling off. Fuck Survivor. The new KING RULLS - And keep quiet .. Schhh and don't tell anyone. Many illegitimate children of the "royal" band are also found in Aarhus. But if I was a bachelor upstairs at Royal Hotel for more than two decades – with all those ladies and fuckrooms, then there were also many, who were balding around in the streets with beards. Well, yes – there are!!

Word list

Alternative stories * A formulation of quantum theory in which the probability of a given observation is calculated from all possible stories, that could have led to this observation.

ACHMED:

There, I can't remember my head anymore, for now. The memory that opens in deep silence with the mind. Enjoy the silence out there with yourself. When you can for a quiet moment. Only by yourself. Then I come, and disturb your mind. With my spin, and the two of us. Yes, who is us? Us two - you and me? I dance and I stop. My hair in a strong position. Yes you. Why did you go your way though? Come on, come on? No more, no more, I don't bother anymore. Damn it That must be enough. Okay?? STOP READING. SIT STILL. THE HANDS ABOVE THE DOUBLE, I SAID.

Was it really buried in the desert?? Yes .. But you can't believe an Arab!! You heard the "King" yourself!

BANG! Did I trick your infantile brain? Or should you also be stabbed in the arm?? Will we be finished anytime soon? After all, it costs a whole rainforest... Still, it's better to be an unemployed architect, than to be unemployed!? Okay. Monk. So now we reached page 240 - It's divisible by four !! FORWARD WITH THE Pocket calculator. So it's over now?! JUHU! Why did you suddenly write in big letters?? Is it because "you" are good at counting?? Thank you for not letting the book's page count end at the world's top prime! Thank you is only a poor word, but thank you anyway. Thank you for downloading or spending your precious time and really saving money on buying these scrolls! Now you are also in my prayers, because you reached all the way. By the way, you're pretty good at reading! Pat yourself on the shoulder. But OK the words here in this international scroll weren't that hard either! You probably understood most of it at first reading, I suppose? Also the little things and details? What was the name of the singer, who got a doctorate in Moscow? Well - I hope you find the other paper scrolls - there are some chapters missing in this one, I can see! But it lies over there behind that tree in that direction, somewhere. And the first ones are buried in the other direction! There! Make a good day out there (on the couch!) you lazy people ;-)

Alx S Architect and now evangelist / Monk & the 12 disciples.